TRUST IN ADVERTISING

A NOVEL BY
VICTORIA MICHAELS

OMNIFIC PUBLISHING
DALLAS

Omnific Publishing
P.O. Box 793871, Dallas, TX 75379
www.omnificpublishing.com

First Omnific eBook edition, July 2010
First Omnific trade paperback edition, July 2010

The characters and events in this book are fictitious.
Any similarity to real persons, living or dead,
is coincidental and not intended by the author.

Library of Congress Cataloguing-in-Publication Data

Michaels, Victoria.
    Trust in Advertising/ Victoria Michaels – 1st ed.
    ISBN: 978-1-936305-29-2
    1. Romance—Fiction. 2. San Francisco—Fiction. 3. Advertising—Fiction.
    4. Corporate Espionage—Fiction. I. Title

10 9 8 7 6 5 4 3 2 1

Book Design and Cover by Barbara Hallworth

Printed in the United States of America

TO BOBBY...

· PROLOGUE ·

L exi sat quietly in the second row of metal folding chairs, looking out from the stage at the audience before her. The auditorium was filled with the smiling, happy faces of parents, grandparents, aunts, uncles, and siblings. Today was not only about endings but also about new beginnings. Flashbulbs went off constantly, hands waved in the crowd, and tears of pride were shed.

She peered out and saw her dad, Harry, sitting proudly down in front, his eyes glancing up at Lexi, full of respect and a touch of sadness at realizing that his little girl was growing up. Uncomfortably dressed in a shirt and tie, Harry fidgeted with his collar, then fanned himself with his program to provide some relief from the increasing temperature in the small room. He winked at her when she looked his way, and Lexi couldn't help but smile.

Life hadn't been easy for Lexi and her father since her mother, Marie, suddenly died six years ago. They held on tightly to each other and together made it through the darkest moments, coming out on the other side, a piece of them missing, but able to embrace life again. Two years ago, with no other family left, Harry moved them from Tampa to Riverdale, a town a few hours outside San Francisco where he had lived when he was a boy. Many of his old friends had moved from the area, but for Harry, it was still a comfort to get away from the memories of Tampa and go back to his hometown.

The voice of Michelle Fulton, the class valedictorian, rang loudly from the podium, breaking Lexi from her thoughts. "And so, my fellow classmates, I encourage you to leave this place and find yourselves. Become the person you are destined to be. Find that which truly makes you happy and have the courage to go after it, fight for it, and attain it. Let nothing stop you, because each one of us is special, and we have something unique to offer the world. Never forget to be true to yourself and go after your dreams, for dreams really do come true. Congratulations to the class of '98!"

Thunderous applause rose from the crowd and filled the auditorium. Mr. Barnes, the principal, came up onto the stage and stood next to the tall stack of diplomas on the table near the podium. He slipped the top one from the pile as the vice-principal took her place behind the microphone and began calling names.

On cue, the front row of students stood up from their chairs and began heading toward the podium, lining up for their big walk across the stage. Their movement allowed Lexi an unobstructed view of her classmates.

"Martin Alexander." A tall boy with red hair sprang across the stage, gave a triumphant bow to the crowd, and held his diploma high over his head before returning to his seat.

Lexi tried her best to focus on the audience and keep her promise to herself to let it go, but she couldn't. Her eyes briefly darted to her left, and she caught a glimpse of messy dark brown hair. She forced herself to immediately look away.

"Denise Banks." The six-foot tall basketball star lumbered across the stage and shook the principal's hand before walking past Lexi to return to her seat.

Lexi took a deep breath and lowered her head, knowing it would be over soon.

"Benton Claymore." Lexi glanced a few seats over at Michelle, who clapped furiously as her boyfriend, Ben, strode across the stage and accepted his diploma. Michelle and Ben had been dating for two years and were voted cutest couple by the senior class.

"Anna Drake."

Lexi smiled and stole a peek at Anna, the one girl who had always been kind to her and even attempted to get her to come out of her shell a little. The two had been in various classes and clubs together, but a real friendship never quite took root because of how awkward Lexi was with people. And then there was the issue of Anna's twin brother...

"Vincent Drake."

Lexi's heart pounded in her chest, but she refused to look up. Laughter erupted from the crowd seconds later, and she knew he'd probably done something funny or dashing because that's just the kind of guy he was. Most popular, most likely to succeed, best body, nicest eyes, you name it, Vincent had been voted it by the graduating class. She could even hear his girlfriend, Jennifer Stanton, clapping loudly for him. Lexi's eyes stayed firmly planted on her hands, which she had clutched together in her lap. Her long nails dug into her skin as she fought the urge to look up at him. She smelled his cologne as he walked past her to return to his seat in the front row.

"Michael Fitch."

From her first day at Riverdale High two years ago, she'd had a crush on Vincent Drake. In a school this size, it was easy to get lost in the crowd, and that was exactly what Lexi had done. Vincent probably didn't even know her name. The closest interaction they ever had was when he would cheat off of her in Government during their senior year. Unless it was test day, he probably wouldn't have noticed if the ground had opened up and swallowed her whole.

Vincent and Jennifer had been dating for almost a year, and they were the face of Riverdale High. They were invited to every party, and for every event at school, one of them was on the planning committee. He was the star football player, she the head cheerleader. They lived up to every high school stereotype of the perfect couple.

Lexi tried her best to ignore Vincent, tried to date other guys, but the only time her heart did that crazy flip-flop thing was when she saw him. Every day, when Lexi went to her locker, he'd be standing there, leaning against the locker right next to hers, waiting for Jennifer. He never uttered a single word to Lexi except the occasional "sorry" if he was in her way.

As Tommy Jameson strutted across the stage, it was time for the students in her row to rise from their seats and make their way over to the front of the stage to receive their diplomas. Lexi stood up and smoothed her graduation gown, taking careful steps, not wanting to trip on her big day. A few deep breaths later, Jennifer Stanton stepped forward and eagerly took her diploma, hugging the principal and creating a spectacle, as usual. Lexi saw her dad with his camera poised and ready to catch her big moment on film, and a small smile crept across her face.

"Alexandra White."

Her name hung in the air as she forced her numb feet to move across the stage. Out of the corner of her eye, she saw the flash from Harry's camera and heard his loud cheers of encouragement. Before long, she was settling herself back into her metal chair, clutching the large, leather-bound folder that held her diploma, or her parole document as she liked to think of it, from the prison of Riverdale High.

Her fingers ran over the cool leather surface as she heard the vice-principal say, "I present you with the graduating class!"

Hats flew into the air as the graduates cheered, their high school days officially completed. Lexi looked around to see friends hugging, hands shaking, and kisses being exchanged all around her. She quickly grabbed her cap and diploma and stepped off the stage into Harry's awaiting arms.

"Congratulations, Lexi! I am so proud of you, honey ... and you know Mom is too." He swept her into his arms and squeezed her tightly against his chest.

"Thanks, Dad." Lexi smiled and held back the tears that threatened to spill from her eyes for a multitude of reasons. "Can we go?" she asked Harry, anxious to close this pathetic chapter of her life as soon as humanly possible.

"Did you get a chance to say goodbye to all your friends? Some of these people you might never see again, Lex." Harry scanned the crowd and saw a friend of his. "I'm going to go say hello to Mr. Marpay. Say your goodbyes and meet me by the car, okay?" He gave her a quick peck on the head, and then made his way through the crowd.

Lexi stood alone in the sea of people, glancing at all the familiar and unfamiliar faces around her. Students posed for pictures with teachers and the principal. Parents handed gifts to the graduates, and groups of friends huddled together for even more farewell pictures. Distracted by the things going on around her, Lexi's graduation cap slipped from her hand and fell onto the floor. She scooped it up and spun toward the door to make a swift exit from all the reverie, when someone crashed into her shoulder, nearly knocking her down.

A strong arm stretched out from nowhere and saved her from a nasty fall. "I'm so sorry. I wasn't looking," a deep voice apologized in her ear.

Lexi didn't need to open her eyes or look up to know who it was. She'd know that voice anywhere. Vincent Drake.

"Are you all right?" He leaned his head even closer to her, making sure she could hear his question over all the noise around them.

Lexi's heart fluttered when she realized he was still holding her arm. She could smell the spice of his cologne and feel the heat coming off his body. The crowd around them shifted, so he pulled her against his chest so she wouldn't be swept away. Her head started to swim when he gave her arm a gentle squeeze because she wasn't answering his question. Determined to leave the place with one iota of her dignity intact, she opened her eyes, raised her chin confidently, and said, "Yes, I'm fine. Thank you, Vincent." As his name passed through her lips, Lexi's stomach flipped one last time. "Congratulations."

Before he could say anything, before she saw him try and remember who she was, before he pretended to know her name, she simply collected herself and walked away from him without another word. Her heart, however, thundered in her chest.

Lexi made her way through the slowly dispersing crowd and mentally wished her classmates well. Then she walked out of the auditorium, her head held high, and never once looked back at any of them. "Goodbye," she whispered as she stepped out of the doors of the school and into the bright June sunshine.

· 1 ·

Lexi opened the door to her apartment. In her arms she carried two overflowing grocery bags. She balanced the precarious load, and then set it all down on the counter, kicking the door shut behind her. As Lexi emptied the groceries into their proper places, she turned on the radio, filling the apartment with flowery pop music as she went about the job at hand.

Dancing her way around the kitchen, she made quick work of the bags. When everything was finally put away, she grabbed a large frying pan from underneath the cook top and started browning the ground beef for her dinner. As the taco seasoning hit the meat, the savory smell of chili powder filled the apartment. Next to the frying pan on the stovetop, Lexi warmed a can of refried beans and began the messy job of chopping the lettuce, tomatoes, and onions. Just as the last bit of onion was diced and scooped into a bowl, there was a sharp knock on the door.

Lexi put down the knife and with a knowing smile on her face, opened the door wide. "Hi, Hope. Hungry?" She smirked at the curvaceous brunette standing in the hallway wearing baggy, grease-smeared, navy blue coveralls.

"Tacos? You know they're my favorite. I could smell them across the hall. Don't worry, I didn't come empty handed." From behind her back Hope pulled out a bottle of tequila and margarita mix. "I brought the drinks." She grinned and strode into the apartment, setting the bottles down on the counter. "You have no idea how glad I am you moved in across the hall. You're a great friend, don't get me wrong, but you're an even more amazing cook." Hope laughed as she unzipped her blue jumper and stepped out of the greasy mess, revealing her shapely form in basic jeans and a white T-shirt. She made herself comfortable on one of the stools at the counter and watched Lexi put the finishing touches on dinner.

Lexi had moved to San Francisco five months ago, just after her father died. She left Riverdale following her graduation from high school to attend NYU on a full scholarship. Opening her acceptance letter had been the proudest moment of her life. She may not have finished first in her graduating class, but second apparently wasn't too shabby in the eyes of NYU. Unfortunately, mid-way through her sophomore year, she received the phone call that changed everything and put her life on hold for the next eight years.

Lexi remembered every word of the conversation that day when one of her father's friends had called and told her that over the previous two months, her father had become more and more confused. He couldn't remember phone numbers or codes he had used for years. Someone had even found him standing next to his car one day, unsure of how to open the door. Her father's friend had rattled on about other incidents, but Lexi stopped listening. She hung up the phone and booked the next flight back to Riverdale. Two weeks after she arrived home, Harry was diagnosed with the early stages of Alzheimer's disease. She still remembered the look on his face when she told him she was dropping out of school so she could stay in Riverdale and help him. Her father was devastated and begged her to go back to school, but Lexi refused. They had no other family; it was just the two of them, as it had been since Marie died all those years earlier.

So, instead of living the life of a college student and spreading her wings, Lexi was pulled back to Riverdale to take care of her father. Instead of nights spent out with friends at clubs or parties or pulling all nighters studying for an exam, her nights were spent making her father dinner, bathing him, and calling the doctor. The only books she cracked were in leisure. She read books on everything from molecular biology to American literature, trying to emulate courses she would have taken at NYU. She even bought herself a boxed set of language courses on tape and acquired a decent understanding of both Spanish and Italian in the many months she spent at Harry's bedside.

When she wasn't at Harry's side, she was working at a local diner, trying to make enough money to cover whatever Harry's disability insurance couldn't. It wasn't the inspiring college experience she'd been expecting in her early twenties, but it was the right thing to do, and Lexi never regretted her decision to leave NYU and care for Harry.

"Lexi?" Hope's voice broke her from her gloomy trip down memory lane. The knowing look on her friend's face told Lexi that she understood completely. Hope's parents had passed away a couple years earlier, and it was one of the things that bonded them together. They really understood each other in a way most people couldn't. "Today's your dad's birthday, isn't it?" Hope's hand reached out to meet Lexi's and gave a comforting squeeze.

A single tear rolled down Lexi's cheek. "Yep, he would have been sixty-three years old today." She brushed the tear from her face. "But he's spending this birthday with my mom, so that makes me feel better. He missed her so much after she died." Lexi took a deep breath and raised the margarita that Hope had poured her. "Happy birthday, Dad."

"Happy birthday, Harry!" With a sad smile, Hope raised her glass as well, tapping it against the side of Lexi's.

Hungry, Lexi heaped jalapeños onto her taco, making Hope's eyes nearly bulge out of her head.

"You aren't going to eat those, are you?" She shook her head in disbelief. "You'll burn the tonsils right out of your mouth!"

Lexi laughed out loud. "One of these days I'm going to get you to come to that Thai restaurant on High Street with me, Hope. Then you'll have a whole new appreciation for spicy foods." Lexi crammed two more peppers onto the taco before taking a huge bite out of it. "So, how was work?" she mumbled, her mouth full of food.

Hope owned one of the busiest custom body shops in the bay area, Crowbar. The shop was known in all the car circles, and did everything from restorations to custom paint jobs, interiors, and body work. Hope had eight male employees, and every single one of the burly guys that worked at Crowbar was scared to death of her. Hope's dad, Big Al, had taught his only daughter at a very early age not to take crap from anyone, and Hope learned that lesson to a T. She had inherited the shop from him when he passed away.

"It wasn't too bad. This guy came in and wanted this custom, two-tone paint job with these intricate freehand flames painted down the length of the car. The jerk had the nerve to get pissed when I told him how much it would cost. He actually accused me of ripping him off and made some rude comment about women having no business working on cars, so I had Max show him the door." Hope shook her head in disgust. "I mean, come on. Just because I'm a woman they think they can push me around so I'll change my mind or back down? Please. And I'm sorry, I don't mean to be cocky, but no one in town but me can do what he's asking. Mark my words; he'll be back, and soon."

"How can you be so sure?" Lexi asked as she wiped the sour cream from the corner of her mouth.

"Because he's one of those street racers, and he wants that car to be all badass for his next race. Of course when he comes back," Hope confidently flipped her dark hair over her shoulder and leaned back in her chair, "I'm jacking the price up another five hundred dollars, and I think I'll make him beg me to do it in front of all the guys. That should teach the little prick some manners."

"Will these guys ever learn to not mess with you, Hope?" Lexi shook her head, laughing.

"If they're smart, they will." Hope followed Lexi into the kitchen with her empty plate and began rinsing it off in the sink. "So, how was your day? Any luck on the job hunt?" She bent over and placed her plate in the dishwasher, then she began gathering up the bowls and putting the leftovers into Tupperware.

For the last couple of months, Lexi had been working as a cashier in a vintage record store. She was able to chat with customers and listen to all kinds of music during the day, but it was hardly a career. She was twenty-eight years old, and it was time to start thinking about what she wanted to do with the rest of her life, a life that was now hers to lead without anything holding her back.

"I went and interviewed at this law firm for the secretarial position they were advertising, but it wasn't for me. All those years of just Harry and me, it's hard to get used to having people barking orders all the time. I'm used to doing things on my schedule, not theirs." Lexi snapped the lid back onto the sour cream. "Maybe moving to San Francisco wasn't the smartest move. But I had to get out of Riverdale before I was smothered to death."

Hope wiped down the counter, tossed the towel into the sink, and lead Lexi by the hand into the family room. She snatched the newspaper off the coffee table and sat on the couch, patting the soft leather until Lexi reluctantly sat down beside her.

"You did the right thing coming here. Don't let yourself get overwhelmed by everything. Let's take baby steps and work on the new job thing. I want to start at the beginning. Before you left school, wasn't your major marketing?" Hope flipped through the paper looking for the classified section and handed it to Lexi, then scooped up Lexi's laptop and waited for it to startup.

"Technically, I was studying business. I wanted to go into advertising, and probably would have minored in graphic art. My dream job would have been to work for an ad firm and work on print ads and presentations, but that was a lifetime ago. Now I'd probably be best at a job in home health care, nursing, or housekeeping since that's what I've been doing for the last eight years. Look and see if there's a job for adult babysitter; I'd be good at that," Lexi said with a defeated sigh.

Hope looked up from the computer where she was searching the web for job listings in the area. "Lexi, you have to move on now, decide what *you* want to do. What do you want to be when you grow up?" she asked with a cheeky smile, trying to lighten the mood.

"Fine, my dream job would be in advertising. However, I don't think my year and a half of college credits will be enough to even get my foot in the door these days. Nor will my resume with 'home healthcare provider' listed as my primary job for the last eight years. I have nothing to offer them—no experience, no portfolio stuffed with projects I've worked on. Chances are they'd just laugh in my face and send me on my merry way." Lexi's shoulders sagged as she tossed her head back onto the leather cushion of her couch. "Just find me a waitressing job or something."

"Who cares if you don't have a fancy degree or a thick portfolio? You have ideas, tons and tons of creative ideas, Lexi. Look at how much business I've gotten since I started advertising in the local car trades and automotive magazines. You basically designed that ad. You even took the picture. It was all you. So don't tell me you don't know what you're doing. You're a natural. I can see that, and if these people have half a brain, they'll see your potential, too. Now, let me look and see what I can find on-line. You dig through the paper, and between the two of us, we'll find something good."

They spent the next two hours scouring the paper and the internet for something in advertising. There were plenty of jobs that Lexi was totally unqualified for—marketing director, project manager, client relations—which required post-graduate degrees and at least five to seven years of prior work experience. They discovered that if Lexi wanted to go into the world of exotic dancing, there were opportunities a-plenty, but in the hard-nosed world of advertising, there was nothing she was remotely qualified for. She found two leads: one was a personal assistant job, and one was a secretarial position. Neither of them was her dream job, but both would be a way to get back into the swing of things and see what was new in the world of advertising.

"This one looks good, Lexi. It's with an ad company downtown. They need a personal assistant to the human resources manager. I know it's not exactly what you were looking for, but I checked them out and they're notorious for hiring from within. It might be a good place to get your foot in the door, watch, learn, and keep an eye out for a chance to jump on something opening up. Human resources will know about any job openings in that company first. What do you think?" Hope wore an encouraging smile. "It's worth a shot. Just three interviews and you'll be done. Who knows, you might be surprised." Hope gave a nod toward the paper in Lexi's hand. "If not, you could always try your hand at dancing."

Lexi mulled it over, and unable to come up with a real reason to say no, she grabbed a pen and paper and jotted down the companies she needed to contact in the morning. "I think I'll go with Option A, please. I don't think my boobs are big enough for me to make a decent living in the world of exotic dancing," Lexi laughed lightheartedly.

Her decision made, Lexi was finally ready to get back out there and be a part of the real world once again. Reid Inc., Parketti Associates, and Hunter Advertising wouldn't know what hit them once Lexi White walked through their doors.

✦

Three days later, Lexi paced around her room, trying to calm her nerves. She took a deep breath, then stepped out of her bedroom to find Hope's smiling face waiting for her on the couch.

"Today's the day! You're going to knock them dead, Lexi," Hope said proudly. "I love those shoes, by the way. They really pull the outfit together nicely."

Lexi shrugged uncomfortably. "I just hope I don't break my neck. Do you have any idea how long it's been since I've been in heels? I think it was probably on a date back in college, and before that, prom. Are you sure I can't wear my flip flops?" She strode across the room to the couch, her heels softly clicking on the wood floor as she concentrated on each tiny step.

"Oh, stop it. You'll be fine." Hope glanced at her watch. "I have to go, but are we still on for tonight?" They had plans to meet at Olive, a new Italian place downtown.

"Sure, I'll meet you at a little after six; does that sound good?" Lexi stood up and straightened out her gray pencil skirt.

"Perfect! And the drinks are on me." Hope grabbed her purse and keys and headed for the door. "Good luck, Lexi. If one of these firms doesn't hire you, they're idiots." She gave a quick wave. "Love ya."

"Thanks, Hope. Keep your fingers crossed." Lexi watched her door close as Hope left for work.

Lexi went back into the bathroom, flipped on the light, and took one last look at herself in the mirror. The sides of her hair were pulled back into a clip behind her head, leaving the rest of her light brown waves flowing freely over her shoulders. With her hair out of her face, Lexi's big green eyes sparkled. For good luck, she wore a beautiful pair of delicate, pearl earrings that had been Marie's. The black, cashmere V-neck sweater hugged her body, and while it wasn't her first choice, Hope assured her it looked very professional when paired with her pencil skirt. The outfit was topped off with a brand spanking new pair of black, peep-toe heels that she and Hope had bought the day before.

"Here goes nothing," she told her reflection just before she turned off the light and walked out the door.

As she walked down the hallway, a line from Michelle Fulton's graduation speech flitted into her head. *Never forget to be true to yourself and go after your dreams, for dreams really do come true.*

Lexi stepped onto the sidewalk and whispered to herself, "Let's see if she knew what she was talking about."

Lexi's feet were throbbing by the time she dragged herself up the short flight of stairs toward the ornate, wrought iron doors of Olive. The delicious smells of garlic and basil from the quaint Italian restaurant filled the air, and a small crowd of people sat inside the entrance, patiently waiting to be seated.

With a quick smile at the hostess, Lexi made her way over to the bar where she found Hope sipping a glass of wine and chatting with an incredibly good-looking man, as usual.

Hope looked stunning in her black, V-neck, banded dress. The snug fit of the hem across her thighs accentuated her insanely long legs. The outfit was topped off with a pair of strappy silver heels and a chunky silver bracelet that sparkled even in the dim lighting of the bar. The guy perched on the stool next to her had long black hair, broad shoulders, and wore a dark suit. He leaned toward her and laughed. Slipping his arm around Hope's shoulders, he began slowly running it along the exposed skin of her back.

As if she somehow sensed Lexi's presence, Hope swung around in her seat the moment she stepped through the threshold. "Lexi!" Hope's face lit up. "Come here." She jumped off her barstool and grabbed Lexi's arm. "I want to hear how it went today."

Lexi slid into her seat and quickly glanced over at the guy Hope had been talking to. His chiseled features were handsome, but in more of a boyish kind of way, not at all Hope's type. He seemed slightly annoyed with Lexi's sudden presence, probably upset he wouldn't have Hope's undivided attention any longer.

Hope caught him looking at Lexi and made introductions. "How rude of me. Lexi this is Scott."

"Stan," the guy quickly corrected her.

"Sorry. Lexi, this is Stan. Stan, this is my best friend, Lexi." Hope leaned out of the way so Lexi could shake his extended hand.

"Hi," Lexi said shyly.

"Hello, Lexi. It's very nice to meet you." In an effort to appear suave, he brought her hand to his lips and placed a gentle kiss on her knuckles, causing Lexi to blush.

Hope turned her back to Stan and rolled her eyes so only Lexi could see. "So, tell me about your day."

Lexi tried not to laugh at Hope's reaction to Stan, then sighed. "My feet hurt, I have a headache, one of the partners tried to hit on me, I met the biggest bitch alive, and," she said with an embarrassed grin, "I'm really hoping you saved those help wanted ads for exotic dancers, because I think that's my best bet for getting a job now."

"So, you're a dancer?" Stan's head popped over Hope's shoulder, his interest now piqued. He definitely looked like the type of guy who would have a wad of singles and a favorite table at the local gentlemen's club.

"Listen, thanks for the drink, but my friend and I have a date, so I'll see you around," Hope said curtly, flashing him a fake but brilliant smile.

Stan stood up and flipped a twenty onto the bar to cover the drinks. "Can I get your number?" he asked as he leaned in to kiss Hope on the cheek, not picking up on the major brush-off.

"No, you most definitely can't. But have a nice evening." Hope didn't even wait to watch him slink away. Instead, she turned in her seat and gave Lexi her full attention. "Okay, it couldn't have been that terrible. I want to hear everything."

Lexi caught the eye of the bartender. "Chardonnay, please." She gave him a weak smile then launched into the story of her interviews. "Where should I start?"

"I want to hear about the bitch first, then we'll work our way to the creepy guy hitting on you."

"The bitch it is. Well, I went to that place, Parketti Associates, to interview for the secretarial position we found. It was a beautiful office, extravagantly decorated down to the ornate, polished doorknobs, but the company was on the small side, I think twenty-five people, all women. Adria was the person who interviewed me, and she was the nastiest person I'd ever met, male or female. It felt more like an FBI interrogation than an interview. All that was missing was the bright light shining in my face."

Hope scowled. "What in the world did she ask you about?"

"What didn't she ask me? Why did I drop out of college; why didn't I ever go back; why didn't I at least take night classes at a community college? Did I have any self-respect? She even had the nerve to ask if Harry left me a big inheritance when he died. Can you believe it?" Lexi shook her head and took another sip of her rapidly emptying glass.

"What kind of question is that? She needs a smack upside the head, I think. That's terrible." Hope gave Lexi's hand a reassuring squeeze. "Are you all right?"

Forcing a smile, Lexi laughed. "I'm fine, thanks. She's certainly a piece of work. She's probably one of those insecure people that come at you like a bull in a china shop to keep you from picking up on it. That, or she's a total bitch, one of the two. Oh, and did I mention she threw me behind the receptionist's desk and made me man the phones for an hour with absolutely no explanation or orientation? Just 'here, sit down, and get to work,' and then she walked away."

"Get out."

"I think I hung up on three people, and somehow, when I was trying to get an outside line to return a call, I'm pretty sure I called Germany." Lexi started giggling. "I didn't know if I should hit zero, one, or nine to get an outside line, so I hit them all, and then dialed. All I know is I heard 'Guten Tag,' and then the guy on the line said a bunch of other stuff in German that I didn't understand."

Hope laughed out loud. "Let me get this straight—you accidentally called Germany on her dime? I hope you left the phone off the hook."

"I should have, but I hung up as soon as I realized what I did," Lexi snickered. "But really, that place was a nuthouse. Then Adria started screaming at one of her employees right in front of me. When I walked away to give them some privacy, she glared at me like I had committed some major sin by exercising some free thought and leaving her side. She wants a lackey, not someone with a brain. So, needless to say, I don't think Parketti will be calling to offer me a job, and I'm fine with that. I'd sooner work at Hooters."

Hope got her laughter under control and began tapping her nails on the smooth bar top. "Now, tell me about this guy that hit on you." The corners of her mouth twitched in amusement.

"Stop laughing. It was creepy, not funny." Lexi shuddered. "It was the first interview this morning—at Reid Inc., the one in the Transamerica Building? The office was bigger than Parketti. They probably had closer to a hundred employees, and the office was decorated in that ultra-chic minimalist style."

"Ugh, I hate that. Everything is pale and white. No thanks. So, tell me about the guy."

"I'm getting to it. So, the whole office was stark, bare walls and everything, except right when you step off of the elevator there is this *huge* portrait of a guy standing beside a chair with one hand resting on the back of it, and the other firmly planted on his hip. He looked like Henry the Eighth or something in one of those regal poses." Lexi snickered at the memory.

Hope's brow wrinkled. "Define huge."

Lexi chuckled. "Floor to ceiling portrait … larger than life."

"Someone's in love with themselves." Hope rolled her eyes and drank the last sip of wine from her glass. "So, did the guy in the portrait hit on you?" she asked sarcastically as she gave the bartender the high sign for another drink and waved at Lexi's nearly empty glass too.

Lexi's cheeks turned red. "Yes," she answered so softly Hope almost missed it.

"What?" Hope gasped and started coughing as she choked on her wine.

"While I was interviewing with the woman in human resources, there was a knock on the door and in walks the guy from the giant portrait. I almost started laughing when he stood behind the poor woman's chair and assumed almost the identical pose from the painting."

"You've got to be kidding me."

"I swear to God, Hope, he sauntered into the room and was trying to be subtle, but Mrs. Bartlett, the lady running the meeting, gave him a really dirty look. I get the feeling he may interrupt all her interviews to check out the new candidates for himself. He seemed like a real control freak." Lexi softly thanked the bartender as he set a full glass of wine beside her. "Then, before Mrs. Bartlett could ask me anything of substance, he offered to give me a tour of the whole office. I thought she was going to deck him."

"So, your interview consisted of a tour around the office?" Hope's mouth fell open in disbelief.

"Yeah, he gave me a quick tour, which ended in his office." Lexi looked down and began nervously twisting her hands in her lap.

"Lexi, did anything happen? Because if it did, I'll send Marco, Jimmy, and a tire iron over there." Hope reached for her cell phone and was about to start dialing when Lexi finally looked up.

"No, nothing happened. He just made me feel uncomfortable, that's all. He kept complimenting my sweater and staring. Well, I guess staring at the V in my sweater is more accurate."

Hope growled, "Lexi…"

"It's fine, really. He was creepy, but harmless. He did offer to take me out to dinner tonight and discuss the details of the job, but I let him know I already had plans with a mechanic friend of mine."

"And being a dick-headed pea brain, he assumed your mechanic friend was guy, right?" The blush on Lexi's face answered the question for her. "What a jerk," Hope snarled.

Lexi peeked over the rim of her wine glass. "Want to hear about the last interview?"

The twinkle in her eye told Hope this interview went a little better than the previous two. "Hunter Advertising, right? I get the impression this is the one you really want?"

Lexi's face came alive as she started talking. "This would be such a great company to work for. They were huge, around a hundred and fifty employees, three floors of offices right downtown. This is the one that mentioned how they liked to promote people from within."

"Wasn't this the place with the really low level entry position though, in human resources?" Hope asked as she motioned toward an available table in the corner and the two of them sat down. The waitress handed both women a menu and excused herself.

"Yeah, the job is terrible. I'd basically be a gopher, but if I could get my foot in the door there…" Lexi's voice trailed off, but then she shook her head and sighed. "Unfortunately, I saw the resume of the person who interviewed right before me. He was a recent graduate of Princeton with a double degree in marketing and advertising. There's no way I can compete with that." The twinkle in her eye was quickly extinguished, replaced by a darker shadow of insecurity.

"Screw Princeton boy. He can go fly a kite. You want this job. Let's practice some positive thinking here, Lexi. You're smart and witty. You're so talented and really have an eye for advertising. Trust in that, and trust in the person who interviewed you today to see that about you." Hope set her menu on the table and gave Lexi a pep talk. "It's all going to work out. You have to go after your dreams, make them happen. Maybe this is the beginning of something wonderful."

Lexi sighed and finished Hope's thought in her head ... *Or the beginning of yet another gigantic disappointment. Your dreams have a way for falling apart right before your eyes. Don't forget that, Lexi.*

The two women spent the next hour chatting about random events from their day and savoring the delicious pasta. As the waiter set a piece of warm apple pie with a large scoop of vanilla ice cream in front of Lexi and a healthy slice of chocolate cake with raspberry sauce in front of Hope, a phone started ringing.

"I'm so sorry. I thought I turned the silly thing off," Lexi apologized as she reached into her purse and silenced the small, silver phone, glancing at the number of the caller. Her eyes grew wide, and then she dropped it back into her purse like it was on fire.

Hope caught the flicker of recognition and leaned forward in her chair. "Who called?" She watched as Lexi shifted nervously in her chair, embarrassed by the question.

"I ... I think it was from Reid Inc."

"Well, for goodness sake, why didn't you answer it?" Hope grabbed Lexi's purse and quickly dug through until she found the phone and began clapping her hands. "There's a voicemail. Let's see what they said!"

Lexi rolled her eyes. "Can't I finish my dessert before we ruin my appetite?"

"If you're too chicken, then I'll check." Before Lexi could stop her, Hope had called Lexi's voicemail. "There are two messages." Hope sat there tapping her long nails on the table as she waited for the first message to begin.

"You have a dentist appointment at seven thirty a.m. on Thursday. Why you make your appointments so early is beyond me." Her voice trailed off as she held up one finger and listened intently. "This is it," she whispered then turned her attention back to the phone. When her lips spread into a huge grin, Lexi let out the breath she had been unknowingly holding deep within her chest.

"You have a job at Reid if you want it." Hope beamed as she slid the phone across the table. "Of course it was the slime ball who 'personally wanted to offer you a position at Reid Inc. and hopes you will accept not only the job offer but let him take you out to dinner to celebrate.'" Hope made a small gagging gesture at the end of her imitation of Mr. Reid.

Lexi put on a brave face. "Well, at least I know I have a new job if I want it, right?"

"Yeah, but do you *want* to work there?"

She shook her head. "Not really, but if it gets my foot back in the door, it might not be a bad idea to take whatever I can get for now."

"Promise me you won't make any decisions until you hear from the other two, though, Lexi. No matter how poorly you think the interview went, got it?" Lexi nodded her head obediently in agreement.

"The others said I was the last interview so I should hear from them in the next day or two."

"Good, now give me a bite of that apple pie."

It was almost nine o'clock when they finally arrived home from *Olive* and found themselves in the hallway between their apartments. With her painfully uncomfortable shoes clutched in one hand, Lexi unlocked the door to her apartment and ushered Hope inside. The two women flopped onto the couch and sat together in a comfortable silence.

A few minutes later, Lexi dragged her weary body into the kitchen. "Those shoes are evil; I think I should burn them." She stuck her head into the refrigerator, yelling to Hope, "Do you want a bottle of water?"

"Yes, please." Hope stretched out on the couch and flipped on the news.

As Lexi was about to leave the kitchen, she noticed a red light blinking on her answering machine. "A message." Lexi pressed the play button beside the light.

"You have four new messages," the machine chirped, making Hope pop up off the couch and rush over to the counter to listen with Lexi.

The first message was from the dentist's office again. "Boy, they take their oral health seriously, don't they?" Hope laughed as she fast-forwarded to the next one.

The second message was from Parketti. "We're sorry, but we offered the job to someone who was actually qualified for the position."

"Bitches," Hope snarled.

"It's fine. I would've been miserable working for them." Lexi smiled, appreciating her friend's display of loyalty. "My confidence in my people skills is shaky at best these days. Make me work for them, and it would be non-existent. Plus, I'm not a doormat. Isn't that what you keep telling me?"

Hope grinned proudly at her friend until a deep, phlegmy voice began spurting from the answering machine. Collectively the girls rolled their eyes when the third message was from the infamous Mr. Reid.

"God, this guy needs to get a life," Hope griped while they listened to a repeat of the message he left on her cell phone. The pair began laughing at the absurdity of it all.

Finally, they heard an unfamiliar voice coming from the answering machine. The girls were still laughing about the last message from Reid and almost missed the message.

"…we would like to offer you a position…" The female voice said softly as Lexi's head whipped toward the machine, her eyes wide in disbelief. Her finger slammed onto the replay button, and she held her breath and waited.

"Good evening, Lexi, this is Mrs. Dee from Hunter Advertising. I'm sorry for the lateness of this call, but you were the final person we interviewed, and I didn't want to wait until morning; I know you also had other interviews today. I'm happy to tell you that we would like to offer you a position with us at Hunter."

Lexi missed the end of the message because she launched herself at Hope and the two of them jumped up and down, squealing over the good news. The smile on Lexi's face gave away just how badly she had wanted this offer. She had tried to play it cool, expecting the worst, never daring to even hope, but when the good news came, she couldn't contain her joy.

"I'm so happy for you! I take it from your reaction that Hunter is the winner?" Hope asked as she clutched her friend's hands in hers.

"I can't believe they offered me the job," she murmured as tears welled in her eyes.

"You must have made quite an impression on this Mrs. Dee person." Hope laughed as she pulled two stemmed glasses out of the cabinet, filling them with wine.

"Actually, my interview was with Mr. James. I have no idea who this Mrs. Dee woman is. I never met her. Maybe she called the wrong person." A twinge of panic laced Lexi's voice.

"No being negative. She said 'Lexi' in the message, so the offer is most definitely for you. Now stop being a downer and celebrate!" She thrust a glass into Lexi's hand. "To new beginnings!" Hope cheered as she raised her glass proudly into the air.

"To new beginnings!" Lexi sighed, still overwhelmed by the events of the day.

She took a moment to let it all sink in and smiled. *Maybe, just maybe, this time my dreams could come true,* Lexi wished silently.

· 3 ·

Bang, bang, bang!
Lexi groaned as she put the final coat of mascara on her left eye, nearly blinding herself in her haste to answer the door.

"Good morning, Hope." Lexi laughed as she slipped her still-bare foot into one of her black pumps. "What brings you here at this, what do you call it? Oh yeah, this ungodly hour of the morning?"

A bleary-eyed Hope in pink pajamas waved a huge cup of coffee under Lexi's nose. "I wanted to make sure that you were fully caffeinated for your first day, my little working girl." She brushed past Lexi and took up a perch on one of the stools at the kitchen counter, pouring a ton of sugar into her coffee. "Did that loser call again last night trying to get you to come to work for him?"

"Yes. Then he finally came out and asked point blank who I accepted a job with, and I wanted to get him off the phone, so I told him I was extremely happy to be employed by Hunter Advertising." Lexi quickly ran lipstick over her lips and gently pressed them together. "He wasn't too pleased to hear that's where I'd be working, so I told him there was someone at the door and hung up on him."

"Good girl!" Hope raised her cup in the air in praise, and then took a big sip.

Lexi did a little spin for her friend. "So, how do I look? Do I pass inspection?"

"You look fantastic—professional, but womanly. I like it." Hope drank her coffee as she continued to appraise Lexi's outfit.

It had taken Lexi two hours last night to decide what to wear, and her room officially qualified as a disaster area by the time she was done making her selection. After an endless array of outfit combinations, Lexi chose a simple, black skirt and an emerald green sweater with lace detailing on the cuff of the three quarter sleeves. She kept her jewelry simple—a small gold chain that held Marie's wedding ring on it, and a gold watch Harry had given her when she graduated high school. Neither piece was particularly expensive or showy; they were mainly good luck charms for Lexi, sentimental mementos from her parents to give her strength on this big day. Her only real splurge was the shiny new pair of strappy pumps on her feet, a gift to herself for landing the job she wanted.

Hope stood up from her stool and plucked out the clip that held Lexi's hair in a tight twist. Her long, caramel-colored locks cascaded over her shoulders, softly framing her face. "There, now you look perfect."

All of a sudden, the nerves hit. "I feel like I'm going to throw up." Lexi paled as her hands twitched with anxiety.

"You're going to be great, Lexi. Just go and get yourself oriented. No one is expecting you to revamp the world of advertising today, for goodness sake. Maybe just learn where your desk and the bathrooms are and when you get paid. That should be your main focus for your first day." Hope draped Lexi's purse over her arm and tucked the coffee into one of her hands and her car keys in the other.

"I can do this," Lexi whispered to herself.

"Of course you can. Now go get them, tiger!" Hope grinned proudly at her friend as she headed for the door. "Oh, and I want you to bring the car into the shop sometime soon. I need to check the oil and make sure the repair on the hose is holding." She kissed Lexi's cheek and shoved her out into the hallway.

"Will do." Lexi pushed the elevator button, then glanced back at Hope as she waved goodbye.

"I want details tonight," Hope shouted down the hall, "and text me if anything really good happens." Her voice trailed off as the elevator doors slid shut.

◆

Lexi took three deep breaths as she stood inside the elevator of the Barrington Building and waited for it to reach the twenty-first floor. Her palms were sweaty, and she was nervously grinding her teeth on a piece of peppermint flavored gum.

When the elevator doors opened, she stepped out and paused, watching the flurry of people that moved through the offices of Hunter Advertising.

The receptionist smiled at Lexi. "Can I help you?"

Lexi swallowed nervously, her gum scraping down the back of her throat. Her voice was just above a whisper when she finally spoke. "I'm Lexi White, and this is my first day of work."

"What department, honey?" the receptionist asked as she picked up the phone, holding it to her ear.

"Human resources. I'm working with Mr. Wells."

The receptionist smiled and began dialing. "Tim, your new employee is here, so why don't you be a gentleman and come get her settled? I'll let her know." She winked at Lexi. "He's on his way. A nice guy, but sometimes he needs to be reminded of his manners. I'm Sue, by the way. I've been working here for almost twenty years. I think you'll find that this company is more like a family than some big corporation."

The warm smile on her face put Lexi at ease. "Thank you, Sue. I appreciate it. I'm very excited to start, but I know there's so much for me to learn."

"Alexandra," a short man with light brown hair called as he walked in with his hand outstretched. "Welcome to Hunter Advertising. I'm Tim Wells, and we are going to be working together."

"Very nice to meet you," Lexi said softly as a faint blush swept over her cheeks. "Please call me Lexi."

"Okay, Lexi, let me show you to your workspace." Tim began walking briskly down the hall without even waiting for Lexi to follow.

"That man can be such a boob sometimes." Sue rolled her eyes and pointed down the hall. "Bathrooms are on the left, and there's a lounge on the twenty-second floor where you can eat lunch or take a break. The coffee in there stinks, and people steal red pens in this office like they're made of gold, so hide them."

Lexi mouthed a quick thank you, then took off down the hall to catch up to Tim, who probably could have qualified for the Olympic speed walking team. As she got closer, she heard him rambling on to no one in particular.

"...and here are the bathrooms, down this hall on the left."

They weaved their way through a mass of cubicles, past a large room that looked like an art studio, and finally ended the mad dash in a long hallway lined with office doors. Tim led her to a small alcove at the end of the hall. A desk and a chair were tucked into the space.

"Here you go. This is your desk." He patted the short section of Formica countertop and smiled. "Phone, trashcan, plant, and computer. I'll show you where you can get office supplies. To get an outside line, dial nine. Someone from tech support will come by later and help you set up an E-mail address. I'll give you a minute to get situated, and then I'll start the grand tour." He turned on his heel and ducked into the nearest office door.

"Home, sweet home." Lexi dropped her purse down on the floor. She opened the top drawer and found a pile of menus to every restaurant within a ten block radius and a notepad. "Looks like I'm in charge of lunch," she laughed softly.

After spending a few minutes playing with the phone and computer, Lexi began flipping through the notepad that had been tucked in with the menus. It seemed as if she would be responsible for getting around fifteen lunches a day, and some of these people seemed rather picky: *dressing on the side, no onions, only fat-free skim milk, and no cheese (lactose intolerant)* were just a few of the messages scribbled alongside the orders.

Tim appeared in the hallway. "Ready to get started?"

Lexi smiled. "Absolutely."

✦

It was after six that evening by the time Lexi finally knocked on Hope's door.

"Get in here and tell me everything!" Hope grabbed her arm and dragged her over to the black leather couch in the middle of her apartment. "Spill!"

Lexi smiled at her friend's exuberance. "Well, the guy I'm working with, Tim, is a goofball. A nice guy, but I can see why he needs an assistant. He's one of the most hyper people I've ever met, a real HR kinda team-building/motivational-speaker guy. He had me running all over the building today."

Hope snickered. "No, he didn't."

"Oh, yes, he did—all three floors! I hiked the stairs more times that I care to count. The little adventure took up most of my morning." Lexi laughed as she slipped her shoes off and tucked her legs under herself.

"As goofy as it felt to be wandering around the office like that with a little checklist, at the end of the day, I met a number of the people who I'd be working with, and they all seemed really nice and welcoming." Lexi grabbed a potato chip out of the bag on the coffee table. "Oh, and my desk is tucked in an alcove at the end of a hallway, the bathrooms are down the hall on the left, and I get paid every other Friday starting on the ninth. So, all in all, I'd say I had a very successful first day."

Hope went to the kitchen and brought Lexi back a glass of iced tea. "So, do you have any idea what you're actually going to be doing at Hunter? Did he go over your responsibilities?"

"Well, the best I can tell, I do a little of everything." Lexi focused all her attention on the ice cubes floating in her glass.

"And what does that mean?" Hope asked suspiciously.

"Okay, my main responsibility each day is to get the lunch orders and not poison anyone." Lexi buried her face into her hands at the admission.

"You're 'lunch lady' Lexi?'" Hope asked incredulously. "There has to be more to this job than that. They're paying you way too much to be the lunch delivery girl."

Blushing, Lexi raised her head and shrugged. "I know. I need to get them lunch, and I get to make all their copies, so I better become intimately acquainted with the copy machine. I think basically if they need something, they're going to call me, and I get to run off and do it. I'm not exactly sure what I got myself into with this job."

"Look on the bright side—at least you won't get bored. Every day should be a new adventure," Hope said, trying to sound optimistic.

Lexi sighed. "I suppose you're right. I never looked at it that way. But you know what? I'm just going to do my job and keep an eye open for any new job openings within Hunter." Lexi smiled as she stood up and stretched. "I better go back to my place and eat a real dinner, and I want to do some laundry before bed."

"I'll talk to you tomorrow." Hope waved goodbye from her spot on the couch as Lexi let herself out.

"Later!" Lexi called over her shoulder.

✦

The rest of the week went by smoothly for Lexi, but she was still relieved when Friday finally arrived. She was getting into a routine at work. Her day started bright and early—she was usually there by seven-thirty to find a pile of papers that seemed to magically appear on her desk each morning. The papers were always covered in fluorescent sticky notes asking for copies or edits to certain aspects of the documents. There were also luncheons to be scheduled and phone calls to be made.

After Lexi finished up with the things that popped up overnight, she went from office to office and took lunch orders. Usually, people would place their lunch requests and in the next breath hand her a new file or paper to work on. By taking the lunch orders in the morning, she left herself plenty of time to get the additional work done by the end of the day.

As Lexi sat at her computer, placing the lunch orders with the café courier, a green file folder landed on her desk with a smack. She looked up to see Tim standing in the doorway. "Hey, I need a favor."

"Sure, what do you need?" Her fingers flew across the keyboard of her computer as she scanned the lunch orders before hitting send.

"I need a little inventory done." The apologetic tone in his voice made her wary.

"Okay, what kind of inventory?"

Tim led Lexi into a massive workroom. Her entire apartment probably could have fit into it. Every inch of wall was covered in either dark cherry wall cabinets or floor-to-ceiling shelving. In the center of the room were two huge work surfaces, also with drawers and shelving underneath. Tucked in the corner was a large, white copy machine that Lexi had nicknamed "Bertha" and a refrigerator.

Over the next fifteen minutes, Tim explained that he needed the inventory done for the quarterly supply order. It became Lexi's job to go through each cabinet and document all of the unopened packages—every pack of pencils, pens, paper clips, and pair of scissors needed to be accounted for by Monday evening.

Lexi glanced around the room feeling completely overwhelmed with the task Tim had just tossed into her lap. She wandered down the hall back to her desk and flopped into her chair. *Shit, Shit, Shit.* Lexi cursed in her head, wondering how the hell she was going to get this done. Resigned to her fate, she picked up the phone and called Hope to let her know that she'd be late meeting her that night. This new assignment would keep her there well past five o'clock.

She spent the rest of the day on a step ladder, numbering all the cabinets, and then she made her way around the room, starting with the upper cabinets, and recorded the supplies. When she finished a cabinet, she taped it shut with a piece of green tape to help her remember which ones had already been counted.

Around 5:30, Lexi finished the last upper cabinet and would have jumped up and down if her back hadn't been killing her. She still had all the lower cabinets, which were jam packed full of supplies, to go through. She ran up to the vending machine in the lounge to buy a candy bar and a soda.

Very nutritious dinner there, Lexi, she chastised herself.

Without wasting time, she went back into the supply room and found that in the three minutes she had been gone, someone had come into the workroom and rummaged through cabinet number eighteen.

"Oh, come on, people!" Lexi slammed her soda on the counter, sending bubbles cascading out of the can and onto the work surface. "Damn it," Lexi muttered as she found some paper towels under the sink and soaked up the sticky mess.

She blew a stray clump of hair out of her face, rolled up her sleeves, and bent over the counter to search her papers for the sheet where she'd listed the contents of cabinet eighteen. When she found the correct sheet of paper, she climbed up the ladder and re-counted the stock.

"Red pens? What's wrong with everyone around here?" she grumbled when she found out what the thief had stolen from her sealed cabinet. "There's a whole drawer of them." She flung open a nearby drawer and waved her hand over the pile.

A while later, Lexi found herself in the back of the room sprawled out on the floor, her papers scattered on the carpet as she counted boxes of legal envelopes that were so dusty they had probably been there since the early nineties. As she emptied the next drawer in the stack, she heard a loud banging noise, followed by some colorful cursing.

"Stupid, worthless copy machine! I have a deadline, you know. The least you could do is cooperate, you little bastard," a female voice snarled.

Lexi peeked her head over the counter and found an older woman with long brown hair slightly streaked with gray shaking the copy machine violently. After she gave Bertha a swift kick and then winced in pain, Lexi cleared her throat.

"Can I help you with something?" Lexi walked over and leaned against the refrigerator, smiling. "I might have a hammer you can use on it. Your foot, however, seems to be taking a real beating."

The woman grinned sheepishly. "Sorry, dear. I didn't know anyone else was in here to witness my brutal assault on the office equipment. Why in the world are you still here at this hour on a Friday night?"

Lexi shrugged. "The joys of inventory." She pointed to the flash drive in the woman's hand. "What were you trying to do before you decided to annihilate the copier?"

"My assistant brought me this PowerPoint presentation for a late dinner meeting I have this evening, and I need to print out the pages to make the final presentation packet, but the copier won't recognize the flash drive, and then the paper jammed when I pulled the tray out while it was making copies…" her voice trailed off in shame. "Okay, I admit some of that was probably my fault, but… well, the copier started it." She laughed at the absurdity of her own behavior, and then threw up her hands in resignation. "Help me, please, before I do something I'll regret to this no good hunk of junk."

"Let me mess around with this for a second." Lexi pressed different buttons on the keypad, and then started opening drawers and doors on the copier until she pulled a snarled piece of paper from between the rollers of the copier. "Okay, that was the easy part." She laughed, tossing the blackened paper into the trashcan.

"I don't mean to dump this on you, dear," the woman sat down on a nearby chair and ran her fingers through her hair in frustration, "but I'm on deadline."

"Trust me, it's fine. If I count one more box of pens or package of tape, I'll scream. This is actually a welcome distraction." Lexi slipped the flash drive into the slot and again went to work on the touch screen of the copier, trying to retrieve the PowerPoint. "This might take me a few minutes." Lexi scrolled through the help screens and reached for the instruction manual.

"That's fine. Would you mind if I ran back upstairs? I have my presentation materials spread out in the lounge, and all I need is for someone to set a coffee mug on my storyboards."

"I'll be fine," Lexi said with a smile. "How many copies do you need me to make of everything?"

"Lexi, you're a lifesaver," the woman mumbled as she scribbled out a long list.

"I'm sorry, I've met so many people this week—I forgot your name." Lexi looked down at the floor as her cheeks blazed crimson with embarrassment.

"It's fine, dear. It has been a while. I'm Mrs. Dee, nice to see you again." She held out her hand, and Lexi quickly shook it and smiled, happy to finally have a face to go with the voice on her answering machine.

"Nice to meet you, too. Give me a few minutes to get this figured out, and I'll bring up the copies when I'm done."

"I can't thank you enough, dear. I'll be upstairs organizing the rest of the presentation so I don't make a fool of myself tonight. Thank you." Mrs. Dee dashed out the door. A hint of her perfume lingered in the air as Lexi began the intricate task of outsmarting the copy machine.

Soon, Lexi was victorious in her battle with the large piece of office equipment, and pages began flying into the printing rack. When the whirl of the gears slowed, Lexi grabbed the first crisp stack of papers and began looking through the presentation out of curiosity. It was an ad campaign for a new shoe line that had a great deal of buzz on the west coast because of the famous celebrity who designed the sneakers. When Lexi hit the third page, she found a spelling error.

"What the heck?" She went back and began pouring over each page of the presentation, thoroughly examining each word of the text, and found not only spelling errors, but switched slides that gave the presentation an awkward flow.

Lexi glared down at the papers, biting her lower lip as she struggled with what to do next. *Should I go fix it myself or tell her first? She's pressed for time...* Without another thought, Lexi jogged down to her desk, slid the flash drive into her computer, and began editing the misspelled words in the presentation. As she typed, she cradled the phone on her shoulder and dialed the extension for the lounge.

"Yes?" A stressed tone cut through Mrs. Dee's voice.

"Sorry to bother you. It's Lexi."

"Oh God, the copier isn't working." Her rising voice reflected her panic.

"No, I got that to work, but there's another problem."

"Kill me now. What is it?"

Lexi heard papers shuffling on the other end of the phone. "Well, there are spelling errors, one in the brand name that's particularly obvious." Mrs. Dee cursed softly. "And then some of these slides are jumbled." Lexi immediately froze. She'd never asked who actually made up the presentation. If it was Mrs. Dee, then she'd basically just told her that she thought her presentation was terrible. Lexi tried damage control. "But then again, I have no idea what I'm talking about. I'll just fix the errors and leave the prese—"

"That idiot!" Mrs. Dee snarled. "Lexi, dear, please fix the presentation however you think it flows best. I have a phone call I need to make to the person that dumped this pile of crap in my lap." The line went dead.

Get to work, big mouth, Lexi told herself as she quickly spell checked the remaining slides, and then shifted some others around to what she thought would make the presentation flow better from the client's perspective. With only minutes to spare, she ran back to the supply room, printed out copies of the slides, and collated them into presentation bundles. She also printed out a condensed version of the entire slideshow before her revisions and one after so

Mrs. Dee could quickly look between the two versions and decide which she wanted to go with.

As Lexi stuck her head through the door to the lounge, Mrs. Dee ran over and hugged her fiercely. "I cannot thank you enough for catching the mistakes and getting everything done so quickly." Mrs. Dee beamed as Lexi handed her two different papers.

"The first one is the original, which I left on the flash drive as-is, after fixing the typos, of course. The second one is just what I thought might help make things flow better, but if you don—"

"This is fabulous! I love how you moved the history and other ads in the market to the beginning. And did you change the background, too?" Mrs. Dee's eyes quickly scanned the sheets of papers as she took in all of the new images.

"Well, as I was reading it on my computer, the background was distracting so I thought simpler was better in this case, especially when the proposal is so flashy to begin with. Let the product stand out, not the background of the slide." Lexi tried to explain the reasons for the changes without casting a negative shadow on the other person's work.

"Well, I'm sold. I'm going to use your slides. Give me one of these presentation packs for Mark. I want to leave it on his desk with a note so he can see what a high-quality presentation should look like. Well done, dear." She shoved the last of the papers in her briefcase, slid the shoulder strap of her laptop case on her arm, and headed for the door. "Welcome to Hunter. I knew it would be a good idea to hire you." With a wink, she disappeared out the door.

"Good luck!" Lexi called out after her. "I saved the new version as plan B."

"Got it." Mrs. Dee's faint voice drifted down the hall.

With a proud smile, Lexi went back to the supply room, turned out the lights, and then headed back to her desk to leave for the night and meet up with Hope at Moon for a well deserved drink...or ten.

Lexi and Hope had spent the weekend shopping in an effort to beef up Lexi's less than impressive wardrobe. When she stepped off the elevators onto the twenty-first floor of the Barrington Building in her brand new designer wrap dress, she looked and felt like a million bucks.

"Good morning, Sue." Lexi gave a small wave to the receptionist as she passed by her desk.

"Good morning, Lexi. My, you look beautiful today." Sue winked her approval.

"Thanks." Lexi smiled. "Have a great day!"

Finally starting to feel comfortable at her new place of employment, Lexi made her way through the maze of desks and hallways until she reached her tiny alcove. Papers and files were already scattered haphazardly on the pale Formica surface of her desk. On top of that, she still had half of the workroom to inventory by that afternoon.

"I hate Mondays," Lexi sighed as she sat down in her chair, the good mood she had been in moments ago faltering.

As she rummaged around her desk in search of a highlighter, Tim's head popped out of his office. "Lexi, my office, ASAP." His tone was extremely clipped, which seemed unusual for him

"Sure thing, let me just gr—"

"Now, Lexi," Tim snapped, then he disappeared into his office.

Oh, hell, what did I do now? Oh my God, that presentation from Friday! I messed it up. I'm fired. Well, crap, it was fun while it lasted. I'm so stupid. Lexi continued chastising herself as she sulked into Tim's office.

"Tim, I'm so sor—"

His hand flew up to stop her from talking. "I hate to say this, but you've been promoted."

Lexi's mouth fell open in complete and utter shock, then quickly snapped shut as her mind reeled from the news. "Ex-excuse me? I think I must have had a small seizure. What did you say?" She leaned closer to make sure she caught every word that came out of his mouth.

Tim leaned back in his chair and let out a frustrated sigh. "You got a promotion."

"Me?"

"Yes, you are Lexi White, aren't you?" Tim said dryly.

Breathe, and just find out how many more lunches you have to get per day.

"Sorry, Tim. This was just unexpected."

"You can say that again."

"What I mean is, how many more lunches do I have to get per day?" Lexi blurted out as she clutched her notebook, ready to jot down the names of the people she was now responsible for helping.

"One," Tim said flatly.

Her head snapped up from her paper. "Only one more?"

Piece of cake. Wow, one extra person. That's some promotion, Lexi. Way to freak out over nothing.

Amused by the look of total confusion on Lexi's face, Tim chuckled. "You've been promoted to executive assistant, Lexi. You need to report to the twenty-third floor, now."

The pen slipped out from between her fingers as Lexi stood there in a daze. "Executive assistant? There has to be a mistake." She shook her head from side to side.

"No mistake, Lexi. I got the call this morning. I'd be lying if I said I was happy about this. We're really going to miss you down here. And lucky me, I get to start the hiring process all over again and train another person." Tim came out from behind his desk and placed the fallen pen back into Lexi's hand. "Good luck up there. That's the big time."

"I … wow … thank you, Tim, for everything. I feel like I'm leaving you in a lurch with the workroom," Lexi sputtered.

"We'll manage. Now go. Leigh is waiting upstairs to get you settled. She's the executive secretary for the floor. If you need anything while you're up there, she's the person to ask."

Lexi was still in a daze as she made her way back to her desk and gathered up the few personal belongings she'd managed to bring to work over the last week. Her hand grazed her cell phone, and she immediately snatched it out of her purse and called Hope.

"*Hola*, Chica!" Hope sang into the phone. "*Que pasa?*"

"Hope, I – I …"

"What's wrong? Are you all right?"

"No, yes, I'm fine. I got … a promotion." Lexi sank into her chair to steady herself as she uttered the still unbelievable words out loud.

"Lexi, that's amazing! We're going out and celebrating tonight. Did you get a raise too?" She clapped with excitement on the other end of the phone.

"Not sure about the raise. I don't even have any idea why I got this promotion. What do I know about being an executive assistant? I think I'm going to throw up." Lexi clutched her stomach and leaned toward her trashcan.

"Don't you dare throw up, Alexandra White. Suck it up and get your butt to those executive offices. What better place to see what's new in advertising than with the movers and shakers in the biz?"

"I know you're right, but what do I know about dealing with executives? Last week I worked in a record store, and before that, I was a waitress at an all-night diner." Lexi's head began to spin.

"You're not running the company, just getting some lunches, making phone calls, scheduling meetings, and maybe picking up some dry cleaning. Breathe, Lexi." As always, Hope had a way of cutting to the chase and putting things back into perspective.

Lexi took a deep breath, and brushed the hair out of her face. "You're right. I can do this. It's not rocket science. Thanks for the pep talk, Hope. I have to go upstairs and figure out what I'm supposed to do now, and I'll ask about that raise."

"Good girl! Let's meet after work."

"Will do." Lexi snapped her phone shut and headed for the elevators.

"Congratulations, Lexi." Sue looked up from behind her desk as Lexi nervously paced in front of the elevators.

"Thanks. They weren't kidding about promoting from within, were they?" Lexi laughed, trying to make light of it, but the look on Sue's face told a much different story.

"Um, no one has worked down here for a week then gone straight upstairs, dear. This is a first."

When the elevator arrived, the bell rang, startling Lexi. She stumbled in, glancing back at Sue, who gave her a big smile and a wave. "Good luck, Lexi!" she shouted as the doors closed.

When the elevator opened on the twenty-third floor, Lexi was once again in awe. Tim's little tour on her first day had included a brief walk-through of the executive suites, but they had come up through one of the stairwells, not the main elevators. Seeing the office from the same perspective as a new client was truly impressive.

The walls were a deep, rich maroon color with beautiful crown molding throughout. The classically styled chairs were upholstered with a light pinstriped fabric that complimented the décor perfectly. Behind a huge mahogany desk sat a smiling woman with long, blond hair and hazel eyes. She appeared to be only a few years older than Lexi.

"Good morning. Welcome to Hunter Advertising. Can I help you?" She folded her hands on her desk and smiled politely.

"Good morning, I'm Lexi—er—Alexandra White from downstairs? I was told to come up—"

"Miss White, yes, good morning." The woman jumped to her feet and came around the desk to shake Lexi's hand. "I heard you were going to be working up here now. My name's Leigh. It's so nice to meet you. Can I get you something to drink? A cup of coffee or a bottle of water?"

"No, no, thank you." Lexi blushed at the offer, feeling like she should be the one asking Leigh if she wanted coffee. "And please, call me Lexi."

"Okay, Lexi, let me show you where you'll be working." Leigh took her by the elbow and gently directed her down the main hallway. After two quick rights, Leigh held her arm out indicating that they had reached their destination. "Here we are."

Lexi found herself at a modest desk with two arm chairs that matched the ones in the lobby sitting in front of it. On top of the desk sat a sleek, black flat-screen monitor with the Hunter Advertising screen saver swirling. Beside the monitor was a phone that looked like it could possibly launch the space shuttle with all the buttons on the thing. To the right of the desk was a huge wall of framed ads that Lexi presumed were Hunter designs and an ornate office door with a dark brown knob. Taking her purse off her arm, Lexi sat down in one of the armchairs and patiently waited.

Leigh chuckled behind her. "Lexi, what in the world are you doing?"

Blood flooded Lexi's cheeks. "I was just waiting for someone to come out of that office and tell me what I'm supposed to do up here. Why? Oh gosh, am I not supposed to sit in these chairs?" Lexi flew to her feet and ran away from the chair like it had been covered in tacks.

As Lexi fidgeted nervously beside her, Leigh laughed. "No, I just meant you were sitting on the wrong side of the desk." Lexi gave her an even more confused look. "It's your desk." Leigh spoke very slowly to make sure Lexi understood.

"Get out." Lexi sighed as she ran her fingers gently over the shiny desktop. She turned to Leigh. "Seriously?"

"Yep. Now, put your bag down so I can finish the tour. The bottom drawer locks; key's in the top one." Leigh sat down in one of the armchairs as Lexi tentatively lowered herself into the plush, black leather chair behind the desk.

Lexi locked her purse away and slipped the key deep into the pocket of her dress before following Leigh down the hall to resume the tour. The break room, copy room, and supply room were all pointed out to her in detail, since she would be spending a great deal of time in those areas. There were also a few introductions to the other assistants as she passed them in the hall, but many were gone since there was a big meeting that had all the executives out of the office for the day. After about half an hour, Leigh returned Lexi to her desk, and again took her place in one of the armchairs as Lexi sat timidly behind her new desk.

"So, what do you think?" Leigh's eyes twinkled.

"This is all so amazing and overwhelming." Lexi fidgeted with a pen that was sitting on the desk.

"You'll do fine. Basically, all you have to do is follow directions, and you seem like a very sharp person, so you should be fine. I hope." Leigh mumbled the last part under her breath.

"When do I meet my new boss?" Lexi asked, glancing at the office door and wondering who was sitting on the other side.

"Not for about a week. He's on vacation right now, but he usually checks in daily. I'm sure you'll have some contact with him tomorrow." She leaned forward in her seat and spoke in a lower voice. "I should let you in on a few things about him. His family owns the company, and he's a bit … difficult."

"Difficult?" Lexi's heart raced in her chest. *Maybe this was a bad idea. They couldn't have filled my position downstairs already, could they?* "How difficult? Define difficult."

"You're the fifth assistant in as many months. How's that for an explanation?"

Lexi searched Leigh's eyes for some indication that she was kidding, but found none. Her shoulders hunched over in disappointment and fear. "That's pretty clear. Thanks."

I knew it was too good to be true, Lexi chastised herself for getting her hopes up.

Leigh smiled. "I think you'll be fine. Just don't let him get to you. The yelling and grousing is a defense mechanism I think."

"Yelling?" Lexi squeaked.

"She's gonna kill me. Never mind, Lexi. Just take some time and get yourself settled. I'll be back in a few minutes with all the paperwork that I need you to fill out."

"Okay," Lexi said as she gnawed on her fingernail, nervously eyeing the office door.

When Leigh left, Lexi threw her back against her chair and let out a huge sigh. *What have you gotten yourself into, Lexi? You could have worked downstairs for years. Instead, you get moved to a job that you are destined to be fired from in a month or less.*

By the time Leigh returned, Lexi's head was resting face down on the desktop. "Chin up, you'll be fine!" She gently swatted Lexi with the stack of papers in her hand. "Grab that pen. I need you to fill these out so I can get you your BlackBerry, corporate credit card, laptop, and flash drives."

At the word BlackBerry, Lexi's head snapped up. She found Leigh grinning at her, a shiny onyx colored PDA in her hand. "Get out!"

Laughing, Leigh set it on the desk in front of her with Lexi's new phone number on a small sticky note. "This is your lifeline. This must be on you twenty-four seven from this day forward, and I encourage you to find a ringtone you like, because that damn thing can ring nonstop on days when we're getting ready for a big presentation around here." She slid a stack of forms toward Lexi. The places she needed to sign or fill out were clearly marked with a red X.

"I'll give you some time to work on these. I'll be back."

Once Leigh was out of sight, Lexi picked up her new phone and began flipping it over, examining every button. She was so engrossed that she didn't even notice that Leigh had returned until a large black case landed on her desk with a thud.

"Whoa, what's in there?" Lexi set the BlackBerry down.

"This," Leigh tapped the object, "is your laptop. The flash drives are in the pocket. The rule of thumb around here is to back up everything in triplicate. Leave one copy in the office, one copy at home, and have one on you at all times. Trust me on this."

"I feel like a kid at Christmas." Lexi laughed as she stared openly at the growing pile of goodies on her desk. "Not to appear ungrateful, but what's wrong with the computer on my desk?"

"Nothing's wrong with it, but you need something to work on when you're on the go. That's where this will come in handy." She pushed the laptop toward Lexi and sat back down in the chair across the desk. Leigh held in a laugh as she watched Lexi gingerly slide the laptop case to the side of her desk and start playing with her BlackBerry again.

"I almost forgot—you'll get your corporate credit card in a few days." Leigh laughed when Lexi's mouth dropped open. "Don't worry, it has a fairly low limit, and the statements are gone over with a fine tooth comb, so just make sure you save the receipts for anything you're asked to purchase and submit them every month. And this," she slid a slip of paper to Lexi across the desk, "is your new salary."

With a shaking hand, Lexi took the small folded paper and cautiously opened it. Her head was still reeling from the cash and prizes that were currently sitting on her desk, and she wasn't sure she could handle any more surprises.

"Holy cow! Are you sure this is correct?" Lexi pointed at the number, her eyes wide in shock.

Leigh humored her and leaned forward, checked it, then nodded her head. "It's correct. Do you have any questions?"

A loud laugh escaped Lexi's lips. "Only about a million."

"Well, let's hear some. I have a few minutes."

Lexi folded the piece of paper and tucked it in her pocket. Then she laid the BlackBerry down and turned her attention to Leigh. "I'll start simple. What's Mr. Hunter's first name? I should probably have a clue when he calls."

"Drake."

"Drake Hunter," Lexi murmured to herself as she scooped up the phone and programmed the information into her contact list.

Leigh's laughter danced through the air. "No, Drake is his last name. Vincent is his first name. Vincent Drake, that's your boss."

Lexi's BlackBerry tumbled from her hand and landed with a loud crack on her desk. "Say that again?" Lexi couldn't catch her breath.

No, no, no. Impossible, no way, nope, never.

Images of a smiling teenager filled her memory. His dark brown hair falling over his eye, the wicked smirk he would give girls, buckling their knees instantly, and the deep tenor of his laughter. All the memories of high school that Lexi had fought so desperately to bury deep in her subconscious suddenly sprang forward at just the mention of his name, and she was seventeen again. Her pulse raced with both panic and excitement at the possibility. But there was no way it could be him; it had to be a different Vincent Drake.

The man Leigh had described—the angry, furious individual—was not the Vincent Drake Lexi remembered. Back then, he was all smiles and charm, and he used it to get whatever he wanted from teachers, parents, coaches, and girls. She couldn't imagine him ranting and raving at someone he worked with. There was no way it was him.

Lexi could feel Leigh watching her closely, probably trying to figure out what exactly was going on in her head as she fumbled nervously with her phone. "His name is Vincent Drake. Lexi, what's wrong?"

Lexi began chewing on her fingernail again. "How old is he? Sixtyish?" *What was his father's name? Maybe it's his dad, Vincent Drake Sr. It has to be.*

"I'm not sure, but he's probably close to your age. What are you, like twenty-eight?"

Lexi's stomach flipped as she tried to imagine a more mature Vincent Drake. The words "sexy" and "charming" immediately popped into her head as her body temperature rose a few degrees. *Act normal, Lexi. She thinks you're insane. Pull it together. There's no way it's the same Vincent Drake. No way. And this isn't high school, anyway.* "Oh, I…I just assumed he would be older. No big deal. I was just surprised." *Nice cover, Lex.*

The rest of the afternoon progressed with Leigh flooding Lexi with so much information that she didn't have time to freak out over Vincent Drake. She showed Lexi the computer system, giving her a quick rundown of Vincent's typical day when he was in the office. Then she printed out his upcoming schedule so Lexi would know it backward and forward before he even walked through the door. Leigh kindly advised her about his pet peeves: tardiness, lack of productivity, and the word "no" were all unacceptable to Vincent Drake. According to Leigh, if she remembered those things, she would fare much better than her last four counterparts.

Leigh came by Lexi's desk at quarter to five and opened the door to Vincent's office. "I need to grab the Keller file off his desk. Do you want to come in and have a look around? You probably should know where everything is in here before he gets back." She paused at the door. "I warn you, the place is a bit of a disaster. Mr. Drake isn't known for his organizational skills."

Lexi's stomach flipped and her pulse quickened. *I'm going inside Vincent Drake's office!* She kept up the calm façade, hiding her inner schoolgirl who threatened to escape, then mentally gave herself a hard slap. *Knock it off Lexi, you aren't seventeen anymore. Grow up.* She shook her head, then stepped through the doorway and took in her new surroundings.

Vincent's ornate desk sat in the middle of the room, buried somewhere underneath a massive pile of papers that covered every inch of the flat surface, piles leaning upon other piles. Pens and pencils were strewn everywhere. How Leigh was supposed to find anything in the chaos was beyond Lexi.

As Leigh searched for the needle in the haystack, Lexi became distracted by a picture that hung on the wall. It was a framed article from San Francisco Magazine featuring Vincent Drake, an up and coming star in the advertising world. Lexi's heart leaped as she gazed at the photograph, because she would have recognized that incredibly handsome face anywhere.

Completely enthralled, she couldn't tear her eyes away from the image of Vincent. He had the same dark wavy hair, intentionally messy, and the years had changed his features from boyish good looks into mature sex appeal. He exuded confidence and a masculine swagger even in the photograph. He wore a black suit with an emerald tie that made his green eyes stand out. Lexi caught herself staring at the curve of his full lips when Leigh came and stood beside her.

"He's even more handsome in person, just so you know."

"That's what I'm afraid of," Lexi said so low that Leigh thankfully missed it. She shook her head and gathered herself. "Well, it's good to have a face to go with the name." Lexi glanced over her shoulder at the disarray that was his desk. *I'll have to get on that tomorrow. There's no way he can find anything in there.*

With her hand on the light switch, Leigh asked, "You ready to go?"

Lexi stole one last look at Vincent's picture and without warning felt her pulse race through her body as she joined Leigh at the door. "Yeah, it's been a long day. And I for one definitely need a drink."

✦

Hope sat at the bar, watching a baseball game on the large screen plasma TV that hung on the wall. She was swirling an olive around at the bottom of her martini glass when Lexi claimed her spot on the stool beside her, slamming her purse onto the bar and barking at the bartender.

"Vodka, neat. Make it a double."

"You okay?" Hope looked over at Lexi, stunned to hear her drink order, but was even more shocked when the bartender handed her the drink and Lexi downed it in a single gulp, then ordered another.

"Long day," Lexi hissed as the alcohol burned down the back of her throat.

"What happened?"

She threw her head back and laughed. "What happened? I'll tell you what happened." Lexi slammed the second drink, then stared Hope dead in the eyes. "Two words: Vincent Drake."

Hope's mouth curved into a perfect O as her eyes almost bugged out of her head. "*The* Vincent Drake? From high school? No way." But Lexi nodded her head in confirmation. "Where did you bump into him?"

"On the twenty-third floor."

"He's a client of Hunter? I bet that was weird. How's he look? Does he still have all his hair?" Hope winked as she popped the tiny, green olive into her mouth.

"He's not a client, Hope. He's... he's my new boss." Lexi nodded at the bartender for another drink.

Hope began choking on the remaining bit of olive in her mouth. "You're working for the guy you were hopelessly in love with in high school? This is unreal." She studied Lexi and saw her with the drink at her lips. "Oh my God, what are you going to do?"

Lexi slammed her empty glass back onto the bar top and grinned. "Quit!"

· 5 ·

Lexi's alarm started blaring at six a.m. sharp. With her mouth feeling like it was full of sawdust, she cracked open one eye just wide enough to see the irritating contraption and hit it with her fist, sending it crashing to the floor. The body beside her moaned.

"Shh, sleeping," a raspy voice growled into the pillow.

"Shh, head hurts," Lexi whispered in response.

"Maybe you should lay off the vodka next time." A hand patted Lexi roughly on the head. "It makes you do crazy things, darlin'."

Lexi groaned and rolled over, coming face to face with her bedmate. "You snore."

"I do not!"

"Hope, trust me—you snore like a hairy wildebeest. I think that's half the reason why my head hurts so much this morning." Lexi pressed on her temple in an effort to relieve the throbbing.

A feather pillow smacked Lexi square in the face. "Your head hurts because you drank half a bottle of vodka in less than an hour, just because your new boss happens to be a hunky guy who you had a huge crush on in high school."

"Bite me, Hope." Lexi rolled herself out of bed and fell onto the floor. "It's not too late for me to quit."

"Don't you dare!" Hope sat straight up in bed and glared at her friend crumpled up beside the bed. "I stayed up past three this morning convincing you to stay at Hunter Advertising, and you *promised* you'd give it a try."

"Hope," Lexi whined as she stood up on her still wobbly legs and brushed her hair out of her face.

A yawn escaped Hope's lips, then she laughed. "You promised me. And you, my friend, are a good person. You wouldn't break your word to me or leave Hunter high and dry. So, get your little butt in the shower and quit your whining."

Lexi's feet thumped angrily against the hardwood floor as she stormed off into the bathroom to shower and get ready for work. When the door slammed shut, Hope slowly rolled over with a satisfied grin on her face and went back to sleep.

✦

Still annoyed at Hope for making her act like a grown up and return to work, Lexi began texting her every five minutes after leaving the apartment. When Hope shot off a message with every curse word known to man, Lexi felt victorious.

"Look who's here bright and early." Leigh beamed as Lexi stepped of the elevator.

"Good morning, Leigh." Lexi laughed, pausing to tuck the BlackBerry into her purse.

"Go get yourself settled. I have a feeling today will be a busy one." Leigh seemed to be trying a little too hard to sound nonchalant.

With a suspicious look on her face, Lexi sighed. "Okay, I'll get a few dozen cups of coffee in me, twenty or so ibuprofen, and then I should be good to go. I'm going to mess around on the computer today and try and look through some current projects and proposals so I have an idea what everyone is talking about in meetings."

A huge grin broke across Leigh's face. "That sounds like a great idea, Lexi. Don't let me keep you." She waved her hands dismissively, and then busied herself behind her desk.

Lexi said good morning to a few of the other assistants on her way to her desk. Each of them wished her luck, which Lexi found odd, but she had so much she wanted to get accomplished that she shrugged it off and headed for her desk.

She no sooner sat down than the sound of her chirping bird ringtone filled the room, making her head throb. Suddenly, her heart nearly leapt out of her chest, when she wondered if it could be Vincent calling to check in for the day.

"Lexi White," she said nervously into her phone.

Hope's laughter rang out. "Lexi White? That's how you answer the phone now, not 'Hey, Hope'?"

Lexi let out the breath she had been holding. "Hope, I'm hung over, exhausted, and about ten minutes away from a nervous breakdown, and you called to give me grief?"

"Absolutely," Hope chuckled. "You need to lighten up and breathe, Lexi."

Drumming her fingernails on her desktop, Lexi waited. "Are you done?"

"Has the hunk called you yet?"

"Hope!" Lexi looked over her shoulder to make sure no one heard the little outburst. "His name is Vincent, and no, he hasn't called yet."

"So, what are you doing?"

Lexi shuffled the papers on her desk. "I'm looking over one of the files from his desk to find out what projects we're working on."

"Sounds exciting," Hope said sarcastically. "So, are you still nervous to talk to him?"

"No, I figure I'll keep my head down and my mouth shut."

Lexi heard Hope snort over the phone. "Whatever you say, Lexi. I'll let you get back to work. Text me later if anything exciting happens. I'll be at work with the meatheads."

"Give them my love. Bye." Lexi ended the call and flipped the phone around in her hand as she continued reading through the papers on her desk.

For a solid hour or two, Lexi poured over file after file, learning every detail of the projects Vincent was currently working on and the accounts he was in the process of acquiring. She was taking a pile of files back into his office when her phone chirped. Lexi rolled her eyes, wondering what Hope could possibly want now. When she saw "Vincent Drake" in bold letters on the display, she nearly dropped everything she was carrying onto the floor.

Lexi's hand started trembling, her mouth going completely dry at the thought of having a conversation with Vincent. She breathed a much needed sigh of relief when she saw it was only a message.

Alexandra,
Welcome to Hunter Advertising. I hope that you are more competent than your predecessor. You have three minutes to reply to this message.
Vincent Drake

Lexi rolled her eyes at the obnoxious message. His clipped introduction, laced with a haughty arrogance, helped her push aside any leftover fantasies she had of him from high school, and her already throbbing head lowered the chances of a tactful response. "Leigh wasn't kidding. You are a prick now." Lexi typed out a quick reply and hit send.

Vincent,
Thank you for the warm welcome. I'm sure you'll find me more than
competent.
Lexi

She set the phone down and had just gathered up the files when her phone chirped again.

Alexandra,
Prove it. What is my middle name?
V. D.

"Jackass sounds about right." Lexi pecked out "Giovanni" without blinking and hit send. She sat at her desk for a moment, waiting to see what insane hoop he threw at her next, but her phone remained silent.

"Round one goes to Lexi," she snickered as she picked up the files and put them back on top of the massive mess on Vincent's desk. She wrestled with the mountain of papers in an effort to keep them from plummeting to the floor in a document disaster of epic proportions and grumbled, "Question my competency."

Twenty minutes passed and still no response. No warm welcome, no "Alexandra White? From Riverdale? Didn't we go to high school together?" Lexi realized the all too depressing truth: Vincent didn't remember her at all.

Her plan to go through high school unnoticed had worked perfectly, much to her dismay. Still, she held out a slim hope that maybe seeing her in person might jog his memory, but until then, Lexi was just another assistant sent to infuriate him.

The tone of the messages he had sent weren't the most welcoming, but Lexi could sympathize. To him, she was a complete stranger, and he was testing her. That was understandable if his previous employees hadn't done their jobs effectively. He wasn't going to give her the time of day until she proved herself worthy of his time. Never one to back down from a challenge, Lexi got back work.

Vincent Drake clearly wasn't the same person he had been all those years ago, but neither was Lexi. She had been through too much in her short life, lost too much, to ever be that girl again. She was still struggling to find herself after all these years, and if part of that process required her to go toe-to-toe with this man to earn some much needed respect, she would do it. She would not be a doormat; she would prove him wrong and be the most competent hire in history. By the time he stepped off that elevator, Lexi would know Hunter Advertising inside and out. Then she'd make sure he stood up and noticed her this time.

Lexi was still deep in thought when Leigh came flying in through the office door. "Lexi!" she shrieked. The papers in Lexi's hand flew up into the air and rained down from the ceiling like confetti at a ticker tape parade.

"What?" Lexi gasped as she started gathering the scattered sheets into a disorganized pile on the floor. "You just about gave me a heart attack, Leigh."

"Giovanni." Leigh snatched the Blackberry off the desktop and scrolled through the contact list. "His middle name is Giovanni."

"I know. I replied already." Lexi shrugged as she placed the last of the loose papers back into the folder.

Leigh just stared at her, dumbfounded. "You … you answered his question … without help?" She couldn't have looked more shocked if Lexi had sprouted a second head.

"Yeah, it really wasn't that difficult. I take it he tests all his new employees this way?"

"No one has ever," Leigh continued muttering incoherently to herself as she wandered back to her desk, leaving Lexi to her work. "… not without my help."

Just when Lexi started to relax, her phone chirped.

Alexandra,
Congratulations on mastering Google. Now let's see if you can use your brain. I need the advertising budget breakdown for the Fox Jewelers account. I want the advertising expenditures for the local Chicago affiliates and the greater Boston area. I needed them ten minutes ago or you're fired.
V. D.

"Google this." Lexi flipped her phone the bird before popping another ibuprophen. "God, he's even more arrogant now than he was in high school." Lexi made her way into his office and blew out an exasperated breath as she looked at the mountain of papers on his utterly messy desk. "What have I gotten myself into?"

She began searching through each pile, trying not to move anything for fear of messing up his organizational system, whatever that might be. But after ten minutes it became clear—Vincent had no system other than total and absolute chaos. She was more and more discouraged with each hour that passed, knowing she would probably see the words "You're fired" in Vincent's next text message, but Lexi was nothing if not stubborn. Before she let him fire her, she would find that damned file if it killed her.

She eventually came across the tattered Fox Jewelers file tucked inside a massive file for an inactive account from a couple years ago. "I found it!" She danced around the office, waving the manila file wildly over her head until she was pulled out of her celebration by loud clapping from the doorway.

"Congratulations," a deep voice snickered from behind her.

Lexi froze, her face turning bright red at the sound of the man's voice. Mortified, she spun around to see an incredibly handsome gentleman standing in the doorway and grinning down at her. His shaved head gave him a dangerous air, but his striking features and dimples made her heart beat a little faster, and his warm smile put her at ease.

"Oh, thank you. I'm so sorry; was I really that loud?" Lexi nervously tucked the file under her arm and played with a piece of lint on her skirt.

"No, I was on my way in here to drop something off when I heard you … celebrating?" He took a few steps towards her and extended his hand. "I'm Sean, by the way. Sean Adler."

"Hello, Mr. Adler. I'm Lexi White. I'm Vincent—I mean, Mr. Drake's— new assistant."

"Lexi, nice to meet you, and don't ever call me Mr. Adler; it's Sean. A word of advice, if I may? When working for Vincent, don't let him push you around. The guy can smell fear. I know he's a real prick sometimes, but underneath it all, he's a softie."

Lexi chuckled. "I'll try and remember that. Thanks."

"So, what did he have you searching for?" He pulled the folder from under her arm and laughed when he saw the name on it. "Holy shit, you found it!" Sean's hand flew to his mouth then slid away as he grinned sheepishly. "Sorry about the language. I'm working on it. But wow, Vincent was tearing his hair out looking for this file all last week before he left for vacation. He's gonna sh—I mean, he's gonna *die* when he sees you found it. Well done." He winked and handed the folder back to her.

Lost it? He had me searching for a lost file? Lexi did her best to hide her annoyance at this bit of information.

"Quite frankly, I don't know how he finds anything in this disaster." Lexi waved her hand at Vincent's desk.

"He claims to know where everything is, even in the mess."

"Yeah, well, I have proof that isn't true now, don't I?" Lexi tapped the folder with her fingers, earning a wide smile from Sean.

"Please don't quit. I like you." Sean tossed his arm over Lexi's shoulders and smiled. "And if you do quit, come work for me."

"I'll remember that." Wearing a grin, she shuffled out of Vincent's office and held out her hand, offering to take whatever it was that Sean wanted to leave for him and keep it safe on her desk so it wouldn't get lost.

Sean tossed the manila file folder to her, and said a quick goodbye.

Lexi plopped down in her chair and began thumbing through the missing file, learning as much as she could about Fox Jewelers, the campaign, the target demographic, and budget expenditures for different markets. When she found the information Vincent had asked for, she picked up her BlackBerry and grinned as she sent off her message.

> *Vincent,*
> *I have the file in my hand. The Boston expenditure was $235,000 and the Chicago expenditure was $452,000, but there is a note about charges that aren't listed, so I assume it's higher than that.*
> *Who do you want that information sent to? That is, assuming I'm not fired.*
> *Lexi*

Lexi wished she could see his face when he realized she had found the missing file. But then she began second guessing herself, wondering what on Earth had made her be so flippant in her reply. He was her boss, after all.

When the phone chirped, Lexi cringed but didn't pick it up, afraid to see his response. When the noise continued, she went into a full-fledged panic—this wasn't a text message. The phone was actually ringing, and she had to answer it and speak coherently to him.

Shit, shit, shit. Lexi's heart pounded like a jackhammer in her chest, and she felt like she might throw up. *Calm blue ocean, Lexi,* she repeated over and over in her head to try and settle her nerves.

"Hello?" Lexi's voice quivered as she spoke.

"You have the file in your hand?" Vincent's deep, sultry voice took her back ten years, making her stomach flip and her palms sweat.

Hello to you too, Vincent. Long time no see. How have you been? I'm fine, thanks for asking.

"Yes, Vincent, I'm looking at it now."

After a long, uncomfortable pause, he spoke. "There should be papers in there about the early pitches. What were the two layouts they rejected before finally accepting our campaign?"

Another test? He thinks I'm lying about finding the file. Can you say "major trust issues"? What the hell happened to him?

"Um, hang on ... Well, from what I can find, it looks like they rejected the 'Once in a lifetime' pitch and 'Say it with diamonds' last October before finally accepting the 'Eternal love' concept in mid-June of this year."

Silence on the line.

"Fax those numbers to Mrs. Kimber at B and B Associates. Their number is in my Rolodex. They're the Hunter accountants, and they needed that information last week," he said gruffly without a single word of thanks.

"Anything else?" Lexi tried to hide the annoyance in her voice.

"You're not fired, *yet*. Goodbye, Alexandra." And without even waiting for her response, he hung up.

"The name's Lexi, but thanks, Vincent. Your appreciation is really over-whelming." She wanted to scream, but instead marched into Vincent's office and found the Rolodex buried under a pile of magazines marked with a colorful array of Post-it notes.

As she lounged in his large leather chair behind a wall of clutter, Lexi decided that her project for the next day was to organize Vincent's desk. That way, she wouldn't waste hours the next time he called with a ludicrous scavenger hunt.

✦

The following morning, Lexi walked into work in a comfortable pair of slacks and a sweater, the perfect outfit for crawling around on the floor of Vincent's office, separating mountains of papers by category, project, and date.

"You have a message, Lexi." Leigh held a tiny pink paper out to her.

"Do I even want to know?" Lexi asked as she hesitantly turned the paper over and read it. Thankfully, it was from Sean.

Thought you'd like to know Vincent called me last night and said he was impressed with you yesterday. I know he'd never tell you himself. If he tries to fire you again today, my offer still stands.
Sean

Lexi grinned and tucked the paper into her pocket while she headed to her desk.

"Have a nice day," Leigh called after her.

"Thanks!"

Lexi's morning reorganization project got off to a slow start, thanks to none other than Vincent Drake himself. He had her running all over the building picking up designs from the art department, faxing copies down to his hotel in Grand Cayman, and searching his desk for yet another missing file or microscopic piece of paper. She even had to go pick up his suit at the tailor's. By lunchtime, she was ready to throw her phone out the window just for the sheer joy of seeing it smash onto the concrete and shatter into a million tiny pieces.

"Who works this much while they're on vacation?" Lexi wondered out loud as she stopped a stack of folders from toppling off Vincent's desk. "Honestly, go sit in the sun, drink a fruity drink with one of those cute little paper umbrellas and a piece of pineapple in it, and leave me alone so I can get some work done." She was sorting papers into the piles she had scattered across the office carpet when her phone chirped.

Alexandra,
I am still waiting on the phone number for the photographer we used on the Wilson shoot. If it's more than you can handle, I can always hire someone who doesn't find the job as challenging as you do.
V. D.

"You're not going to fire me, pal, after I've run my fanny off for the past two days. I'm lasting long enough for you to get back into town so I can tell you I quit to your face." She gripped the edge of Vincent's desk and pulled herself to her feet. "And my name is Lexi!"

Vincent,
If I don't have that phone number for you in ten minutes, I'll grant your
wish.
Lexi

She pressed send and stormed down the hallway, a woman on a mission. She rounded the corner, breezed past the chairs outside the office, and without knocking, threw open an office door to find Sean leaning back in his black leather chair, his feet propped up on top of his desk as he chatted on the phone.

"Come on, babe, I can't help that. Now you're being ridiculous. Well, what do you want me to say?" He rolled his eyes and motioned for Lexi to have a seat. "Hey ... Wha- ... No, listen, someone's here. I have to go. Can't we just talk about it later? Hello? Hello?" He slammed the phone down on the desk. "Sorry, domestic situation. So, what can I do for you? Or better yet, what has Vincent done now?

"I need a phone number."

"Hired assassins don't come cheap, Lexi. Do you have enough cash on hand?" Sean leaned forward and began flipping through his Rolodex. "Guido the Squid is good and works on credit, but he's kinda messy. How about Jimmy? You get a discount if you use him, cuz he only has one hand."

"I'll keep that in mind, but not what I'm here for ... yet. I need a phone number, and I can't find it in any of Vincent's files. And believe me, I've searched every scrap of wrinkled paper in his office. I'm looking for the number for the photographer from the Wilson shoot last month."

"Well, of course *that* isn't in his office." Sean went to one of his file cabinets. "What a jerk. He could have just called me about it." He flipped through a few folders, and then tossed a small business card into her lap.

Lexi read it and sighed in relief. "Thanks, Sean. You're a lifesaver!"

"What are you supposed to do with the phone number?"

"I need to text it to him in—," Lexi glanced down at her watch, "—less than four minutes, or I told him I'd resign." She jumped up from the chair she had been sitting in and headed for the door so she could get back to her phone in time.

Sean chuckled. "I have a better idea. Tell him to just hit three on his speed dial. That photographer, Erik Caldwell, is his brother-in-law."

I swear I'm going to kill this man.

Lexi didn't even remember storming down the hall, but the next thing she knew, she was sitting behind her desk, clutching her BlackBerry so tightly that it was seconds away from crumbling into dust in her grip. Calmly, she sent Vincent the phone number.

Vincent,
Here's the phone number you so desperately needed. I hope your brother-in-law and Anna are doing well.
Lexi

✦

That was the last communication she had with Vincent that day. Over the next three hours, she finished organizing his office and was amazed at how much bigger his desk looked minus all the files. Everything was coded, dated, and filed. She even downloaded many of the active account files onto her BlackBerry so she would have everything at her fingertips no matter where she was.

Let him try and confuse me again tomorrow. Lexi snickered as she stood in Vincent's office admiring her handiwork.

"Sweet merciful crap! What the hell happened in here?"

Lexi smiled over her shoulder at a gaping Leigh. "Looks pretty nice, doesn't it?"

"He's gonna die," Leigh answered as her hands covered her mouth.

"Did you even realize he had such a beautiful desk underneath that giant pile of papers?"

"There you are, Leigh. I've been trying to call you…oh my God. Wait, did I turn down the wrong hallway? Whose office is this?" Sean stood in the doorway and glanced at the shiny silver nameplate on the desk. Then he stared at the girls with a look of horror on his face.

"It's still Vincent's office. I just cleaned it. Doesn't it look nice? Now I won't have to bug you so much, Sean. I know where every single paper is in this office."

Sean and Leigh exchanged a knowing glance.

"Okay, why the silent treatment?"

"Vincent's going to have a heart attack." Sean rubbed the back of his neck and looked around the room.

"A good heart attack or a bad heart attack?" Lexi asked, suddenly questioning her decision to reorganize the office of the executive vice president without his permission.

Sean let out a sigh. "I guess we'll just have to wait and see." He winked at Leigh. "You better call me the *second* he steps off that elevator."

✦

Still feeling dejected by the potential disaster brewing at work, Lexi dragged her weary feet all the way up to her apartment. Instead of crawling into bed like she should have, she walked across the hall and began banging her head against Hope's door. The bronze-skinned beauty opened the door, still dressed in her overalls from the shop, and froze.

"What's wrong? And why are you knocking on my door with your forehead?"

"Well, do you want the good news or the bad news?"

"Give me the good news first." Hope ushered Lexi into her apartment and sat her down at the kitchen table.

"Okay, the good news. I managed to successfully complete all of Vincent's mental Olympics for the day."

"Good for you! Does the idiot remember who you are yet?"

"No, he's still clueless and that might not be a bad thing once you hear the bad news."

"Lay it on me."

"I cleaned his office." Lexi rested her head on the table, her cheek pressing against the cool, polished wood surface.

"And that's bad news, why?"

"Apparently, he doesn't like people touching his things, which I didn't know. I mean, he's had me rooting around in his office for the last few days. But according to Sean, Vincent lives his life in an 'organized state of chaos,' and I just messed with that elaborately screwed up system. I'm in so much trouble."

Hope rubbed her hand over her friend's back, trying to console her. "You don't know that for sure, Lexi. Maybe he'll be impressed with the fact that you took the initiative."

"I'll be fired before my butt hits the seat of my fine Italian leather chair first thing Monday morning. I can kiss my onyx BlackBerry, laptop, and corporate credit card goodbye. I knew this would be a disaster. Honestly, only Vincent

Drake could drive me absolutely insane like this, and I haven't even spoken to the man yet. I feel like I'm in high school all over again, driving myself crazy over someone who doesn't even see me standing right in front of him."

"Oh, honey, I'm sorry. But maybe it won't be as bad as you think." Lexi raised her head slightly and rolled her eyes. "Okay fine, your world is about to explode—so, you wanna get drunk?" Hope's big blue eyes twinkled as she waited for an answer.

Lexi sighed loudly against the table top. "I thought you'd never ask."

· 6 ·

The next day, Lexi's BlackBerry remained eerily silent the entire morning, allowing the paranoia plenty of time to settle in. She was so fearful the phone was malfunctioning that she had Leigh call her three different times from her desk just to make sure it still worked and she hadn't accidentally set it to silent.

As Lexi sat at her desk, she wondered if Sean had called Vincent and told him what she'd done to his office. Had she already been fired, but no one had told her yet? As the day passed with no communication, Lexi thought she was going to explode from the crushing silence. She stared at her phone and waited and waited.

After pushing her lunch around on her plate for an hour, she returned to her desk and found new files stacked in a pile. The first one was for Maximillian's, the most well-known car dealership in the entire bay area. They sold only the finest European imports. If it was outrageously expensive and fast, Maximillian's was the place to find it. Apparently, Hunter was handling their new ad campaign after a vicious battle with Reid Inc. for the account. The first photo shoot was scheduled for early next week.

Lexi was completely engrossed in the brochure that she had found in the file. She flipped through the pages, admiring the sleek, colorful vehicles. Her father had instilled in her a love for fast cars and a deep appreciation for horsepower and all things muscle when it came to automobiles. She let out a wistful sigh over one of the new Ferraris, and then suddenly the hairs on her arm stood on end. Her head shot up when she realized someone was silently standing on the other side of her desk, looming over her.

"Can I help yo—" Lexi started, but all the air rushed out for her lungs mid-sentence. Her mouth went dry and fell open in absolute shock. Standing in front of her was the picture of perfection, Vincent Drake, in the very masculine flesh.

It may have been ten long years since she had last laid eyes on him, but she would have known him anywhere. And her foggy memory simply hadn't done him justice. His face was even more handsome than she remembered. Time had not only made him look more mature and distinguished, but if possible, even more attractive. His olive skin was still flawless. The strong line of his jaw, the light stubble on his face, and his spectacular green eyes sent her heart sputtering into overdrive. His hair was more tamed than it had been back then, but it still made Lexi want to run her hands through it to feel the delicate strands tangle between her fingers.

With her mouth still gaping open, Vincent silently stood before her, his arms folded across his broad chest. His pristine Hugo Boss charcoal black suit hung off his defined shoulders. The crisp, dark gray shirt he wore underneath was accented by a solid, ebony tie. He looked like he just stepped off the runway in Milan with that model-look about him, complete with an expression of arrogant annoyance frozen on his face.

Lexi sucked in air slowly and began stammering. "Wh-what are y-you doing here?"

"This is the door to my office. I'm Vincent Drake. You must be Alexandra." He stiffly extended his hand and frowned when he noticed the Maximillian file wide open, the papers spread out everywhere.

"I know it's your office, Vincent. Sorry, I—I wasn't expecting you until Monday." Lexi stood up and began nervously scooping the things off her desk, gathering them neatly back into a pile, unable to look him in the eye.

"I wasn't aware I needed to clear my travel plans with you." Vincent brusquely reached down and grabbed his messages off the desk. "Is there a particular reason you were thumbing through the Max file?"

"I—I just wanted to be prepared."

"Well, that really isn't your concern, Ms. White. I need a cup of coffee, black," he snapped, flipping through his messages.

The quick dismissal and "Ms. White" confirmed that even after seeing her in person, he had no recollection of her from high school. To him, she was just another unqualified person taking up space behind that desk, somehow destined to screw up his day just like all those who had come before her had done. The callous way he spoke to her proved that he expected her to fail, and to fail miserably.

Even with his boorish treatment, Lexi still thought he was the most handsome man she had ever laid eyes on, much to her dismay. No matter how hard she tried, she couldn't stop the thundering of her heart or the blush that flooded her cheeks in his presence. Shyly, she glanced up and watched him read the messages. Everything about him was attractive—from the way his lush red lips moved ever so slightly as he followed the words across the paper to the exotic, spicy scent of his cologne. He had the dark and brooding thing down to an art form.

Years ago, when she was a swooning teen, Lexi had innocently wished Vincent would ask her to go with him to the local pizza joint after a football game. But now, as an adult with very real womanly desires, she watched him stand before her, exuding confidence and power, and Lexi wished he'd ask her for something very different than pizza. And she knew she'd enjoy every minute of it. Her cheeks flushed with embarrassment as the naughty thoughts flashed through her mind, but she was pulled from her daydream when she heard the deep rumbling of his voice.

Vincent scanned his messages, and then began barking orders without even bothering to make eye contact with her. "I also need you to go down to the production office and tell that asshole Tony I want the mockups for the Maximillian photo shoot—now. If they aren't ready the moment you ask for them, you can also inform him that he's fired. Hold my calls for the next hour. I need to get settled and look a few things over." He turned on his heel and walked toward his office door. That was when everything began happening in slow motion.

Vincent was about to walk into his office.

Lexi had been so overwhelmed with seeing him again that she forgot about his possible reaction to his newly cleaned office. Each step he took brought him closer to the big reveal, and that knowledge made Lexi's head spin. She once again leapt to her feet, her mind now in overdrive trying to figure out exactly what to say to prepare him for what was waiting on the other side of the door.

Out of nowhere, Sean came screaming down the hallway. His booming voice thundered. "Wait!"

Vincent froze mid-step and turned back to his friend, annoyed and confused. Sean jogged toward him, and then collapsed into the nearest chair.

"Damn, that's a long run." Sean's chest heaved up and down as he tried to catch his breath. He glanced over at Lexi and winked. With a grin, he held his fingers up to his ear like he was talking on a telephone. "Leigh."

Oh, sure, she calls him about Vincent's arrival, but not me? Great. Lexi rolled her eyes at Sean, then looked straight at the floor, nervously wringing her hands together.

"Sean. To what do I owe this warm welcome?" Vincent seemed unamused by the lively entrance.

"Can't I just come welcome my dear friend and business associate back from his vacation without raising suspicion?" Sean put on his most innocent face while Lexi silently peeked up from under her eyelashes and watched Vincent's glare become even more critical, his crappy mood definitely still on the downslide.

"Lexi, tell Vincent here that I come in peace."

Caught completely off guard, Lexi's mouth stopped functioning, and she began sputtering, "I—I—I d-don't..."

"Sean, do you *need* something?" Vincent's patience was obviously evaporating quickly. A pissed off Vincent was not who she wanted walking through that office door.

Sean picked up on Lexi's tension and ended his cryptic jokes. "Nope, just saying hello. Glad you're back, Vince. Looks like you got a little sun while you were gone."

"Yes, there was sun. Now, if you'll excuse me, I do have paperwork to get to. Alexandra, I'm still waiting on that coffee and the mockups." His hands grasped the doorknob and gave it a turn as a panicked Lexi remained frozen in place. "Can you handle those two simple tasks?" Without waiting for her answer, he turned to his friend. "Sean, I'll talk to you later."

Lexi covered her face when the door swung open. Sean, however, sat back in his chair with a grin and waited patiently for the fireworks.

"What the hell happened to my office?" Vincent's furious voice roared.

Without a word, Lexi's head fell, and she went to her desk and began packing up her things. She cringed as she heard drawers opening and slamming shut and Vincent's furious cursing. The leather desk chair rolled across his office and crashed into the bookcase as he continued his rampage. Lexi laid her BlackBerry on top of her desk next to her computer. As she started getting her purse out, Sean put his hand on her arm.

"What are you doing?" he managed to get out between his chuckles. Every time Vincent slammed a drawer and yelled "Goddamn it!" he started laughing again.

"Please just let me get out of here."

"I've got your back," he whispered just as the heavy door swung open to reveal an irate Vincent.

"Who did *that* to my office?" Immediately his eyes fixed on Sean, who threw up his hands defensively.

"Not me, man. I'm innocent."

Vincent's stunned gaze fell on Lexi. The hostility rolled off him in waves, and she couldn't bring herself to look him in the eye. "Ms. White?"

"I'm sorry, Vincent. I was just packing my things. I'll be gone in five minutes."

"Vince, wait. The girl was just trying to help." Sean stepped in front of Lexi. "They've been telling you for months to clean up that shit hole. Lexi here just saved you the trouble. You should be thanking her."

"Thanking her? Are you insane? I have no idea where anything is. Her incompetence will cost us not only clients but time as well. Do you have any idea how long it will take me to find anything now?"

"It's fine. I'll go," Lexi barely whispered. Mortified beyond words, with her eyes still fixed on the floor, she made her way out from behind her desk and took her coat off the elegant rack in the corner. "Sorry about the office, Vincent. Sean, thanks for all your help this week. It was great meeting you." She raised her chin slightly, tucked her jacket over her arm and started to walk down the hall.

Lexi tipped her head back, desperately trying to keep the tears that had welled up in her eyes from falling until after she was safely hidden inside the elevator. She wouldn't give him the satisfaction. With each step down the hall, the sounds of Sean's and Vincent's arguing voices became softer. Guilt riddled her body as she made her hasty retreat, and the elevator doors gleamed like a beacon a few feet ahead of her. Once behind those thick, steel panels, she would be free to release the sobs that threatened to spill from her mouth. Just a few more steps and a push of a button and it would all be over.

"Cutting out early?" Leigh smiled warmly as Lexi repeatedly pressed the small button, silently willing the elevator to move faster.

"Something like that," Lexi offered with a sad smile. Luckily for her, Leigh was distracted by the ringing phone and looked away. Lexi immediately turned her attention back to the elevator doors, begging them to open so she could dive inside. As the elevator chimed, she felt a hand on her shoulder.

"Lexi, wait."

"Leigh, I just need to get out of here. Let me leave with a little dignity, please? I made a mess of everything."

"That was Mr. Drake on the phone. He told me to stop you." Her apologetic smile made Lexi's blood run cold. "He wants to see you in his office."

Her plan for a quick escape clearly thwarted, Lexi took a deep, cleansing breath, gathered the remnants of her dignity and started the long walk back to her desk. On the way, she assured herself everything would be all right; the worst he could do was yell for a while, and then it would be over, no big whoop. She already knew she was fired, so if he got out of line, she wouldn't have to hold her tongue and could tell him what a horse's ass he was. She was unsure if she would ever have the nerve to do that, but telling herself these little lies gave her more confidence. She approached Vincent's office just in time to hear Sean spit out a few closing words.

"Try not to be a total ass," Sean snarled before looking up and meeting Lexi's gaze.

"Alexandra, in my office." Vincent leaned against the edge of her desk as she walked past, his eyebrows pulled tightly together.

"Fine." She stepped into the disheveled room and gently rolled the large leather chair back to its place behind the massive desk; then she righted the toppled armchairs at the foot of the desk and sat down, fidgeting with the strap of her purse the entire time she waited.

Vincent strode through the door, shutting it tightly behind him. He stopped short when he saw his chair back behind the desk. He quickly recovered, unbuttoned his suit jacket, and sat down, straightening the small, pink message squares he had thrown down onto his desk in his haste earlier.

Lexi watched him meticulously stack the pieces of paper into a pile, each corner perfectly lined up until the last square was placed on top. He slid the neat little pile toward his computer monitor, and then folded his hands on the desk. Only then did he look up at Lexi, his darkened eyes not nearly as harsh as they had been a few moments earlier, but still nowhere near pleased.

"Alexandra—"

Lexi cringed at his sharp tone as he said her name. Certain he was about to launch into a lengthy verbal reprimand, she was suddenly overcome with a horrible case of diarrhea of the mouth and began rambling.

"Vincent, it's fine. I quit. I left my laptop and BlackBerry on the desk, and you can search my purse for stolen office supplies if you want, but I don't know what else there is left to say. I made a mistake and am very sorry. I spent the last few days digging through every slip of paper on that desk trying to figure out where the files you wanted were, but your system made absolutely no sense, so I...I just...organized it. It wasn't until Sean, I—I mean Mr. Adler, told me how particular you were about your things that I realized what I had done and that I had overstepped my bounds. I apologize."

Vincent sat silently behind his desk, clenching and unclenching his jaw as he seemed to be making up his mind about what to do. The silence in the room became deafening while Lexi waited for the yelling and screaming to begin. Instead, she was shocked when Vincent slumped back into his chair and sighed.

"First of all, Alexandra, I don't accept your resignation right now." He bent over and yanked open one of the file drawers at the bottom of his desk, and then glanced back at her. "Second, you aren't going anywhere until you explain this meaningless filing system to me so I can get some work done." Vincent's eyes softened ever so slightly as he leaned forward in his chair. "And third, I'm still waiting for that cup of coffee."

Lexi stood up from her chair and remained frozen in place for a minute, debating what the hell she should do next. Part of her wanted to bring him that coffee and then dump it square into his lap for the way he had treated her the last few days and for his tantrum a short while ago. But as she stared into his eyes, she felt herself getting lost in them. He was peeking up at her. The scowl had been replaced by a much softer expression as he waited for her to make up her mind.

As she tried to decipher the look on his face, it finally dawned on her—this was her chance. For some reason he was giving her an opportunity to redeem herself, to prove her worth and show him exactly why he should keep her at Hunter. Lexi mulled it over in her head, and her stubborn streak set in, causing her to dig in her heels and fight for what she wanted. And for now, she wanted this job, with him. God help her. Before she could stop herself, the words fell out of her mouth.

"Black, right?"

Vincent slowly nodded his head.

Lexi stumbled out of Vincent's office, still in a daze. *What just happened?* Vincent was obviously still upset about what she'd done, but for some reason he was giving her another chance, and from what Leigh and Sean had hinted at all week, that never happened. Lexi picked up a coffee mug off the shelf in her office and tried to figure out the reason for Vincent's uncommon charity towards her.

Could he have suddenly remembered her and that was the reason for this last minute reprieve? The fact that he continued to refer to her as Ms. White or Alexandra, however, told her he still had no clue who she was. The only other thing that made sense was that she owed Sean big time. Whatever he'd said to Vincent had made him back off and treat her like human being rather than a malfunctioning robot.

Lexi brought the steaming cup of coffee to the door of the office and gently knocked, figuring it was better to be overly formal at this point rather than assume she could just walk back in there.

"Yeah." Vincent responded. He had stripped out of his suit jacket and loosened his tie. Distracted, he stared at the files in his drawers, deep in thought.

Lexi carefully placed the mug on his desk and waited for Vincent to say something. She watched him stubbornly stare at those files for a good five minutes before he sat back and shook his head in frustration.

"What the hell do the dots mean?" He spat out the question like it was the most awful thing that had ever crossed his lips.

"It's a color-coding system. I thought it would make it easier to distinguish different kinds of files."

"I get that it's a system; I'm not a complete moron. What I am asking is—what do the colors represent?"

Lexi stood up, her legs shaky from her nerves as she slowly approached him and knelt beside the opened drawer. She could smell the rich spice of his cologne when he bent over her shoulder to watch intently as she began her explanation. He was so close that she could actually feel the heat coming off his body. Her heart raced, and she desperately tried to keep her voice even as she spoke.

"Files with a black dot are accounts we went after, but never got. Red dots are closed accounts. Yellow dots are files that are for campaigns that are over, but there is still some part that is active, or we are in talks with them about the next season's ad. Green dots are active campaigns, or companies we are currently trying to acquire as clients." Lexi pulled a few examples for Vincent to flip through.

He handed back the folders, then reached around her to pull a file of his own, his larger body crowding hers. Lexi shivered as his tie brushed against her arm and prayed he hadn't noticed her reaction.

"What do two dots mean?"

Over the next half hour, Lexi explained every detail to Vincent. The system wasn't elaborate or complex. It was actually very straightforward once the reasons for grouping certain items together were clear. During that time, Lexi also began to understand Vincent a little better. She watched him pause and try to figure things out himself before asking a question. Most people would have sat back and let her explain every detail, but not Vincent. He would stubbornly study things and get frustrated with himself when he couldn't understand. Then he'd finally ask the question that he couldn't answer. After the fourth time this happened, it was obvious to Lexi that Vincent Drake did not like to ask for help.

That was probably what bothered him the most about Lexi's reorganization—the fact that he couldn't figure it out and was forced into the uncomfortable position of needing to rely on someone other than himself. Lexi saw him visibly relax as he felt more confident with his understanding of things.

She was replacing some files into the tall file cabinet in the corner when the sound of his voice caught her off guard. What shocked her even more was what he said.

"Thank you."

Lexi's mouth hung open slightly as a pained look crossed his face when he said the words. Not wanting to irritate him further, she tried to be nonchalant. "Any time. It's what I'm here for." She closed the cabinet drawer and went back over to the other side of his desk.

Before she could say anything else, he cut her off. "You can go now."

"I really am sorry, Vincent. I feel like we got off on the wrong the foot here."

Vincent didn't say another word. Instead, he just nodded his head in agreement, his intense eyes locked on hers.

"Well, I think that's it." Lexi slipped her arms back into her coat, then picked up her purse from the floor and slung it over her shoulder. When he didn't say anything to stop her departure, she began rambling. "If you can't find something, they have all my phone numbers downstairs. Just call and I'll come back in and try to figure out what I did with it." A nervous smile crossed her lips as Vincent sat in his chair like a statue, still allowing her to blather on. "Well, it was nice seeing you again, Vincent. Take care."

Lexi gave him a curt wave, and then scrambled out of the office, desperate to get away from his intense stare. A goodbye would have been nice, or at the very least some indication that she had actually done a decent job, but that was probably asking too much after what she did to his office. Lexi leaned against her desk and took one quick look around the little area that she had spent the last week getting to know every inch of. She turned off the monitor on her computer and was about to walk away when she heard the chirp of her BlackBerry. Puzzled, she picked up the phone.

Alexandra,
The work day doesn't end for a few more hours and there is still plenty for
you to do. I expect you to get those mockups from Tony and bring them
to me immediately. And don't forget, if they aren't ready or he gives you
any trouble, fire him.
V.D.

At that moment, Leigh snuck around the corner and saw Lexi standing next to her desk with a look of complete shock on her face. She ran over with a box of Kleenex clutched in her hand as she wrapped her arms around her and rocked her from side to side. "Lexi, what did he say this time? I swear, if he was rude, I'll pummel him. The last girl, he demanded to see her elementary school report card because there was no way she could have possibly been promoted past the sixth grade in his opinion. The poor woman was hysterical by the time she hit my desk."

Lexi pulled herself away from Leigh and stared at the tiny display. After the third time she read the message, she bit her lower lip to suppress the grin that was about to explode across her face. She had done the impossible. She somehow earned herself a second chance with Vincent Drake. When she showed the message to Leigh, her jaw fell open, and she flopped into one of the chairs beside Lexi's desk.

"Now I've seen everything." She looked up at Lexi and grinned. "I swear, if I were you, I'd stop and buy a lottery ticket on my way home from work, because this is probably the luckiest day of your whole life."

Lexi shrugged out of her coat and quickly tossed it onto the rack beside her desk, ready to get back to work. She slipped the BlackBerry back into her pocket and linked her arm with Leigh's. "Okay, now tell me where on Earth I'm supposed to find this guy, Tony."

Leigh groaned. "Tony's a pig, so be prepared. If he gives you any attitude, tell him to cram it." As Lexi pushed the down button on the elevator, Leigh gave one final word of advice. "And just to be safe, don't let him within arm's length of you. The guy is one more grope away from a sexual harassment lawsuit."

"Good to know," Lexi called back nervously as the doors closed behind her. Of course, if she survived her run-in with Vincent Drake, how bad could this Tony guy be?

Lexi had been down to the twenty-second floor a couple times before, but was still a little unsure about where she was going. As she tried to get her bearings, she turned a corner and ran into someone.

"I'm so sorry!" Lexi quickly bent down and grabbed the papers that had fallen to the ground. When she lifted her head, she was met with a bright smile.

"We meet again, Lexi." Lexi sighed in relief when she saw Mrs. Dee grinning above her. "What brings you to this floor?"

"Um, sorry about crashing into you." She handed her the papers. "I'm actually looking for Tony. I need to get some mockups for Vincent."

"He's down at the end of the hall, last door on the left. Sorry I can't stay and chat." Mrs. Dee tapped the folder in her hands. "I have another presentation to get busy on. Have a nice day, Lexi."

"Thank you!" Lexi called after her, wishing she had been able to ask her a few questions about dealing with Tony.

She crept down the hall, and found the door to the production room open. A small group of people were gathered around a table. Not feeling comfortable disturbing them, Lexi stood silently in the doorway until someone noticed her there.

"Can I help you?" one of the women asked as she looked over her shoulder.

"Sorry to interrupt. I'm looking for Tony?" A dark haired man stood up, his eyes blatantly roaming over Lexi's body. Her stomach began to lurch as he stepped closer with a sneer on his face.

"To what do I owe this pleasure?"

"Vincent sent me down to get the Max ad mockups," Lexi said, backing away from Tony as subtly as possible.

"Vincent sent you down?" He barked out a laugh. "Did you hear that, guys? *Vincent* sent her down here." The group stopped what they were doing and began chuckling while Tony folded his arms across his chest and leaned closer. "How is my dear friend, *Vincent*? Does he still have that large pole jammed up his ass?"

Lexi did her best to keep her composure, but everything about Tony gave her the creeps. Vincent was right—he was an asshole, and for some reason Tony seemed to have a major beef with Vincent too.

Tony crept closer and dipped his head toward her neck unexpectedly, drawing in a deep breath. "Mmmmm. I'd love to get a taste of you, honey."

Creep.

After the day she'd had, Lexi was done playing Tony's game. "First, my name is Lexi, not 'honey.' Second, I need those mockups now. Vincent's waiting." How she managed to say that with such authority and conviction, Lexi had no idea, but she thanked her lucky stars that it worked. Her sharp response knocked Tony off guard and, more importantly, shut him up for a second.

When he heard the snickers behind him, he snapped out of it and went on the offensive again. "Let him wait. What do I care? I think we still have a few things to touch up on them, anyway. I'll get it to him tomorrow, maybe." Tony snarled. "Now where were we?" A sinister grin slid across his face as he stepped closer to Lexi, practically backing her up against a wall.

She stuck out her hand and planted it firmly on the center of his chest, allowing her nails to dig into his flesh as he tried to press in closer. *I am not a doormat,* she reminded herself.

"*We* weren't anywhere. You were bringing me those mockups in the next thirty seconds, or I'll happily pass on the second part of the message from Vincent, which has to do with you being fired if you make me wait for them any longer than that." She dropped her hand so Tony wouldn't feel how badly she was trembling as she faked her bravado.

The humor and slimy charm were wiped off Tony's face by Lexi's biting words. They were soon replaced by simmering rage. He turned on his heel and stalked across the room, snatching up two large presentation boards and thrusting them at Lexi.

"Anything else you need, honey?" he sneered, trying to save a little face.

Lexi paused to appraise the boards, even though she had absolutely no idea what they were supposed to look like. She wanted to make him squirm, arrogant jerk that he was. She felt Tony's beady eyes lock on her as she kept him waiting. The room heaved a collective sigh of relief when Lexi smiled sweetly.

"This should do it. If Vincent has a problem with them, I'm sure you'll hear from him yourself." She gave a polite wave to the rest of the group. "Thank you for your help. Have a great day."

When the door was safely closed behind her, Lexi slouched back against the wall and heaved a sigh of relief, her heart nearly pounding out of her chest. She had no idea where the brazen, ballsy side of her had come from, but she was sure glad she had found it; otherwise he probably would continue to pull the same crap whenever he saw her. If nothing else, he would probably think twice about how he spoke to her in the future.

With a new sense of confidence, Lexi took the elevator back to the twenty-third floor. She flashed Leigh a big smile and a thumbs up as she walked past her desk carrying the large presentation boards under her arm. She was hopeful that Vincent might be slightly impressed that she had marched into the snake pit with Tony and come back with the prize.

Another test passed, Lexi thought as she set the boards on her desk.

She was about to buzz Vincent when a gorgeous brunette glided past her desk, making a bee line for Vincent's office. The woman reeked of perfume. Not wanting to face the wrath of Vincent if someone walked into his office unannounced, Lexi jumped up and positioned herself between the woman and the door.

"Can I help you?"

"Excuse me? Are you serious? Get the hell out of my way." The woman glared down her nose at Lexi, her attitude almost as offensive as her scent.

Lexi stood her ground. "Do you have an appointment?"

"With Vince?" The woman's fury grew as Lexi raised an eyebrow and waited for an answer. "Yes, I had an appointment with him this morning in the shower. I also had a rather long one last night in the back seat of the limo on the way home from the airport. Should I go on?"

So this is the girlfriend. She's even more unpleasant than Leigh described.

"No, thanks, I get the picture. But he's on the phone, so would you mind waiting until he's done before you go inside?"

The woman's lips pulled back in a sneer. "I don't believe we've been formally introduced."

"I'm Lexi, Lexi White. Vincent's new assistant."

Lexi politely extended her hand to the ill-mannered woman, who regarded it like it was covered in toxic waste. "Lexi, how lovely. I'm Jade, as in the international supermodel Jade, and for your information, I wait for no one. So why don't you go scurry back to your desk and make me a cup of coffee, non-fat creamer and two Splendas?"

As Jade was about to muscle her way inside the office, the door flew open. Vincent filled the doorway, glaring at them. "Do you two mind? I'm on the phone with a client, and all I can hear is your incessant bickering."

Jade pointed her lengthy acrylic claw at Lexi. "Sorry, Vince. But she wouldn't let me in to see you." Her brightly painted lips turned out in a ridiculously childish pout as she played with his tie.

Lexi bit back a grin as Vincent swatted Jade's hand away. When he looked over at her, Lexi's eyes went down to the floor, embarrassed at making yet another mistake where Vincent was concerned. "I'm sorry. I didn't know who she was."

"Jade, have a seat. I'll be with you when I'm off the phone," he said coolly before slamming the door shut in both their faces.

"This is bullshit!" Jade snarled before flopping down into one of the chairs by Lexi's desk and glaring at her. "Great, now he's all pissy. Thanks a lot."

Lexi bit her tongue and sat back down behind her desk, setting the mockups safely against the wall when Jade rudely propped her spikey heeled pumps on her desktop without regard for what she might be ruining. Out of the corner of her eye, she watched her dig through her gaudy designer handbag and pull out a nail file. She completely ignored Lexi, which was just fine with her.

The phone broke the awkward silence. "Vincent Drake's office, Lexi speaking. How may I help you?"

"Lexi, it's Leigh. Is the wicked witch of the west still there?"

"Why, yes, as a matter of fact that's correct." Jade's head popped up. Her ears must have been burning.

"Did she get into his office?" Leigh asked nervously. "I should have warned you she was pushy."

"That would have been helpful, but don't worry, no harm no foul." Lexi began scribbling random notes on a scrap of paper to keep from laughing.

"You kept her from barging in? Oh God, I bet she was pissed."

"Absolutely," Lexi said sweetly, not missing a beat. Jade's eyes narrowed and fixed on her as she leaned forward and tried to see what Lexi was writing. "Is there a message I can pass on for you?"

"Yeah, tell the scrawny lightweight to go eat a cookie. Some decent food might put her skinny butt in a better mood."

"I agree completely. Thanks for the call." Lexi quickly hung up the phone and grinned, forgetting that Jade was scrutinizing her every move.

"Something funny? Was that a personal call? I bet Vince would be very interested to know that you were taking personal calls at work."

Still amused, Lexi couldn't help but smile back at Jade. Her good mood only annoyed the supermodel further. "Actually, that was Leigh giving me a message."

Jade rolled her eyes at the mention of Leigh's name. "Figures you two would be friends." She muttered something about them being two peas in a pod, and then turned her attention back to her nails. "And where the hell is my coffee?"

Lexi grudgingly got Jade her coffee. However, the job became much more entertaining when she realized there was no Splenda to be found. Not wanting to come back empty-handed, Lexi improvised and used real sugar, tucking the empty packets deep into her pocket to hide the evidence, and then tossed in a splash of half-and-half for good measure. She placed the steaming mug in front of Jade without a word and went back to work while the viper sucked down every last drop of her calorie-enhanced coffee.

Lexi noticed the small red light that indicated Vincent was on the phone go dark, and she waited for him to come get Jade out of her hair, but that never happened. For fifteen minutes Lexi watched Jade alternately check her watch, look over at Vincent's door, and let out a loud huff. By the end of the fifteen minutes, the vein on the side of her head looked like it was going to burst.

Finally the door opened. Vincent's face was buried in a pile of papers. "Alexandra, did you get those mockups yet?"

"Alexandra? What the hell? How about 'Jade, darling, thank you so much for waiting'?"

Vincent's head whipped up at the sound of her voice. It was obvious he had forgotten that she was even there. "Jade, yes, what are you doing here, exactly? I thought you had a meeting with your agent."

"I did, but it ended early, so I came to see you." She glanced over her shoulder and gave Lexi a dirty look. "Can we take this conversation into the office where we can have some privacy?" Without even waiting for his answer, she brushed past him and wormed her way inside.

He rolled his eyes in irritation, then glanced back at Lexi and saw the mockups leaning against the wall. "Is Tony still employed?"

"Unfortunately, yes." Lexi sighed.

The corner of Vincent's mouth turned up slightly into the closest thing to a smile that Lexi had seen on his face yet. "Damn."

"Vince!" the impatient banshee wailed from behind him. "Come here, baby."

His tiny grin vanished as he turned and ducked back inside his office. Before he closed the door she heard him groan, "Jade, please get off my desk."

Lexi spent the rest of the afternoon running errands for Jade. Jade needed bottled water; Jade needed a salad from the deli with fat-free dressing because her blood sugar was low. Vincent needed a reservation at Umami because Jade had a taste for Sushi tonight. And apparently her world was going to end without a new tube of red lipstick.

A few minutes before four, Lexi went up front and sat down on the floor behind the large receptionist desk with Leigh.

"Is that miserable woman still here?" Leigh sympathetically patted Lexi's shoulder. "Or was I lucky enough to be away from my desk when she made her grand exit on her broomstick?"

"Nope, she's still here." Lexi stuck her hand on the desk and fished around for a piece of paper. "Does Vincent have any messages?"

"Sorry, not right now. Only Mr. Adler."

Lexi climbed to her feet. "Well, give me those. I'll go walk them back to him. I have nothing to do. Jade's holding Vincent hostage, and he can't get any work done, so I'm free until she makes her next low-calorie or fat-free demand."

Sean wasn't in his office when she got there, so Lexi slipped the papers on his desk and was about to make a hasty retreat when his booming voice greeted her.

"What, you organized Vincent's desk, now you're going after mine? Doesn't he have anything to keep you busy?"

"I'm just dropping off messages. I've learned my lesson, I swear!" Lexi threw up her hands in surrender to his dimpled grin.

"Have a seat." Sean motioned to the chair beside his desk as he scooped up the messages. He quickly glanced through them and then set them to the side and leaned back in his chair with his hands tucked behind his head.

"So, a little birdie told me you were down in productions today."

Lexi knew he must have heard about her run in with Tony somehow, but she shrugged it off, hoping he would drop the subject. "Yeah, Vincent needed the Max mockups."

"M-hmm. So, how was Tony?" Sean's knowing grin made Lexi's cheeks turn pink.

"Fine. He gave me the boards and I left."

"Really? Because the way I heard it, you stiff-armed him in the chest and gave him forty-five seconds to put the boards in your hands or he was fired."

Lexi looked down at her hands folded in her lap and shrugged. "Well, that's not entirely accurate." She peeked up at Sean and smiled. "I only gave him thirty seconds."

Sean doubled over in laughter, his hands slapping down onto the desk top. "I bet the guy blew a nut over that! Next time you need to go down there, you have to come get me."

"Sure, Sean, next time I'll bring an audience."

"Why are you wandering the halls, Lexi? What's Vincent up to this afternoon?"

"Jade." She had to stifle a giggle when Sean moaned.

"I knew I smelled sulfur in the hallway earlier." Sean shook his head as he grumbled a few other choice things under his breath. "Well, feel free to hide out in here for as long as you need to, but I'm actually leaving for the day. I get to go check out this sweet Ferrari that we're using for a photo shoot next week."

"Sounds like fun. I better get back to my desk. I have a few things I want to get finished before I leave." Sean led her to his office door. "I also wanted to thank you for whatever you said to Vincent today. I thought for sure he was going to fire me, so thanks."

Sean leaned against the door and smiled. "Sorry, Lexi, I wish I could take the credit, but the reason you're still at Hunter is all you. Vincent was dead set on firing you when I left his office. I just told him not to be a jerk when he did it."

Lexi was still trying to sort out what Sean had told her when she sat down behind her desk. Knowing that she had managed to save her job on her own gave her quite a sense of accomplishment. She only wished she knew what it was she had done to impress Vincent.

Lexi's good mood was instantly quashed when she saw Jade slink out of Vincent's office. "See you at eight, Vince." Jade made a show of straightening out her clothes and hair as if they'd just had some illicit tryst in his office.

Ew.

Ignoring the childish posturing, Lexi turned her attention to her computer screen until she heard the repeated tapping of Jade's talons on her desk. "Yes?" Lexi asked.

"I just want to get something straight with you. If you ever make me wait to see Vincent again, I'll have you fired within minutes. I kno—"

Lexi's phone rang, so she held up a single finger to Jade, stopping her venomous tirade in its tracks. "Yes, Vincent?"

"I need those mockups now."

"I'll bring them in as soon as Jade leaves." The hateful woman crossed her arms and tapped her foot impatiently while she waited for Lexi to get off the phone.

Vincent sighed. "I thought she left."

"No, she's just... explaining something to me. This shouldn't take much longer." Lexi casually spun her pen on the desk, not letting Jade know how badly she was getting to her.

"Let her know I can't leave the office until I see those boards, so if she wants dinner... Never mind. Just bring them in when she leaves." The line went dead.

"No problem," Lexi said sweetly to the dial tone. Jade's eyes bugged out of her head a little more. "Sorry, Jade. Where were we?"

"We were nowhere, you little snot. Just know Jade's watching you, and you really don't want her as an enemy."

"Lexi will try and remember that." Lexi got up from her desk, picked up the presentation boards, and headed for Vincent's door. "Have a wonderful dinner tonight." Lexi grinned as she heard a loud huff escape from Jade before she stomped toward the elevators.

Lexi tapped on Vincent's door and waited to be invited in.

"Yes?"

She found Vincent hunched over a file on his desk, furiously skimming over presentation notes. He had a pen tucked behind his ear, and his lips moved as he read. Lexi took a deep breath and stepped inside.

"Here are the mockups. Where do you want them?"

"On the desk." He quickly closed the file, and Lexi bit back a smile when she saw him neatly slide it back into his bottom drawer where it belonged. At least he was trying.

She laid the boards side by side and watched Vincent take a step back to appraise the work. He said nothing for quite a while, and Lexi debated whether she should stay in his office or go back to her desk. Before she could take a step, his deep voice startled her.

"That didn't take long." Vincent didn't look away from the boards.

"I'm sorry? What didn't take long?"

"Jade's grand exit speech. Usually she keeps my new assistant tied up for a good twenty minutes."

"Well, maybe she could sense that I'm a quick learner, so she didn't have to go into as much detail." Lexi shrugged, not daring to look at Vincent. Instead, she turned her attention to the mockup and gasped. "The date is wrong."

"What?" Vincent's head snapped up.

"Right here." Lexi stepped closer and pointed to the logo that incorrectly said Maximillian's opened in 1970. "It should say 1971, right?" she offered quietly, but when Vincent's face turned into a scowl she immediately backtracked. "I could be wrong, though. I just thought I saw in the file that—"

Vincent cut her off. "No, you're right." He grabbed the phone and furiously punched in the four-digit extension. "Tony, you idiot, what date did Maximillian's open their doors? Correct. Then can you tell me why the mock up says 1970? I expect this corrected by nine a.m., and I don't care how long you need to be here tonight to fix it." He slammed the receiver down and began scrutinizing every inch of the board.

Lexi leaned forward and quickly scanned the background information while Vincent examined the campaign philosophy. "Do you see anything else?" he asked quietly while he continued checking his side of the board. "I am so sick of Tony and his games."

"He did this on purpose?" Lexi's brows knit together in confusion.

Vincent never answered her question. Instead, he continued scouring the layout. "Find anything?"

"No, this part is fine. I think it was only that date. Everything else looks good." She took a few steps toward the door to allow Vincent time to get his work done.

Vincent must have seen her out of the corner of his eye and looked up. "Thank you again, Alexandra." His eyes were dark but appreciative.

"Just doing my job. See you tomorrow?" The last part came out as a question, because Lexi still didn't feel like she was on the best footing with Vincent yet. Part of her wanted to make sure she still had a job.

"Yes. I get in at seven a.m. sharp every day." He turned his attention back to his desk. "Don't be late."

"I wouldn't dream of it." She closed the door behind her and let out a huge sigh of relief before going home to celebrate.

Good morning, Lexi. How was your weekend?" Leigh smiled broadly as Lexi stepped out of the elevator early Monday morning.

"Not bad," she sighed as she gathered up Vincent's messages off the counter. "Oh, but I did get into a rather colorful argument with the stuffed shirt at that fancy steakhouse Rio when I was trying to get a lunch reservation. He got a little testy because it was only two day's notice."

"Rio? Isn't that place booked…"

"Three months in advance? Yeah."

"So, what did you do?"

Lexi grinned. "It cost me a hundred dollars cash, a half hour of sweet-talking, and I think I might somehow now have a date, but Vincent and the gentlemen from Max will be stuffing their faces with overpriced cuts of red meat tomorrow at noon." She bowed her head in victory as Leigh clapped her hands and laughed.

"You, my friend, are good."

"And out a hundred bucks," Lexi yelled over her shoulder as she headed down the hall.

She set her laptop on her desk and quickly began brewing a large pot of coffee. It was a few minutes before seven, which meant Vincent would be walking past her desk in less than ten minutes, and she still needed to double-check his schedule for the day.

With the precision of a fine Swiss watch, at exactly seven, a perfectly put together Vincent breezed past her desk, wordlessly grabbing his schedule and his coffee, both of which Lexi had placed on the edge of her desk, and then disappeared into his office. Lexi looked at the closed door and smile. She was quickly learning that the man was nothing if not a creature of habit. Over the last week, she had watched him and learned a great deal about the way he operated. She discovered that if she was able to anticipate his moves, she could always be one step ahead of him, thus avoiding disasters and keeping everything running smoothly.

Anticipation was a valuable skill that Lexi had learned when dealing with her father. He too was a proud man who hated asking anyone for help, especially when his Alzheimer's started getting worse and he became more forgetful. Lexi could see that Harry was struggling, and she'd had to get creative in the way she helped him so he wouldn't realize she was doing it. The lessons she learned in dealing with him helped her understand her boss much better.

Vincent arrived at the same time every day without fail. His suit, shirt, and tie were always a dark shade and perfectly put together. He would spend half an hour in his office, come out to bark a few orders at Lexi, then either stay holed up in his office until it was time to leave for a lunch appointment or storm down to the production department and get into it with Tony and company. Wednesdays, however, he blocked out for meetings with clients either at Hunter or at their offices, and for whatever reason, on his busiest day of the week Jade routinely stopped by to visit, causing him to fall behind schedule.

Whenever Jade called, Lexi tried to explain how busy his day was, but that meant absolutely nothing to her. If she wanted to see him, she showed up regardless of whether it was a convenient time or not. Leigh told Lexi that it wasn't unheard of for Jade to stroll into board meetings and simply plop herself into a chair like she owned the place. Some people were so star struck by seeing her in person that she often got away with murder. Lexi, however, remained thoroughly unimpressed by the self-centered woman, who broadcast to everyone within hearing distance that she was Vincent's girlfriend every chance she got.

As she learned more about Vincent, Lexi found that his lunch order was as predictable as his behavior. Some days however, it also depended on whether or not he had company. Whenever his rabbit-food-loving girlfriend was staked out beside his desk, he would get a small Calypso salad, minus the bacon, with fat-free dressing and bottled water—just like Jade's lunch.

A few days later when Lexi went out to pick up their lunch at the deli, she swung by Frank's Diner to grab herself a bacon cheeseburger and made an interesting discovery in Jade's absence: Vincent Drake was a burger junkie.

She chuckled as she remembered how God had smiled upon her that day. Jade's agent had called with a last minute "go see" for her, so she had to leave her perpetual post at Vincent's side earlier than expected and decided to take her lunch to go. She grabbed the food from Lexi's hand as soon as she stepped off the elevator, bitched her out for taking too long, and then disappeared in a swirl of smoke and evil.

When Lexi made it back to her desk, she noticed that Vincent was on the phone, so she set his salad at the corner of her desk and began eating her burger and fries and returning E-mails that had unexpectedly piled up. She found something that needed to go down to Sean's office, so she ran it over to him before he stepped out for the day. When she returned, she found Vincent leaning over her desk and greedily swiping French fries.

"What? The extra sprouts on that mini salad didn't fill you up?" Lexi snickered as Vincent jumped away from her desk like he had been electrocuted. His cheeks turned pink with embarrassment over being caught red handed. "Have *you* been the one stealing my fries? I thought I was going crazy or that maybe I had a tapeworm."

"Guilty." He smirked like a boy caught with his hand in the cookie jar, giving her a glimpse, even if it was just for a second, of the person she had known back in high school.

"You know I can always get you your own burger and fries if you like. All you have to do is ask."

Vincent shrugged. "The salad really is the healthier choice." He glanced longingly at the burger and fries, and then retreated into his office, clutching the tiny plastic container of tasteless roughage.

The next day that Jade made an appearance at the office, Lexi took pity on a weary-looking Vincent and brought him his usual salad, but as soon as Jade left, she went into his office to give him the Barrington file and dropped the extra bag from Frank's on his desk. He didn't say a word about it until later in the day when he called her into his office. He handed her a stack of papers with a small note scribbled on the corner.

Alexandra,
Next time, extra tomato, please.
V.D.

Progress... Lexi smiled to herself, finally feeling like maybe she was beginning to win her war against the closed off man that Vincent Drake had become.

It was hard for her to understand this dramatic change in Vincent's personality. Ten years ago, he had been the big man on campus, the football star, the guy every girl wanted to date, the boy who was always surrounded by a pack of friends. She remembered watching him walk down the hall, saying hello to every person who looked his direction. Lexi wished that just once she had been brave enough to talk to him.

He had been somewhat arrogant back then, but it was hard not to have an inflated ego when girls threw themselves at him and guys lined up to be his friend. At eighteen, it was difficult to understand the complexities of popularity—the doors it opened weren't without costs.

Even so, the boy he was did not match the man he had become, and Lexi wondered what made him close out the world and be so mistrusting of everyone around him. He didn't have any friends in the office other than Sean as far as she could tell. As a matter of fact, Lexi often walked in on people gossiping about Vincent, talking about his temper, rumors about his wild sex life—which Jade probably started herself—or wild theories on why he'd been promoted to vice president at such a young age.

It seemed there was a lot of animosity directed at him, and Lexi found herself questioning what came first—his bad attitude or the hurtful gossip. And it seemed that the hostility was only directed at him; everyone else at Hunter seemed to get along very well. They were the happy family everyone portrayed them as. For Vincent, however, it seemed to be no better than the rumor mill of high school all over again.

Lexi eventually became used to walking into the lounge only to have conversations stop or drop to a hush. She assumed that no one wanted Vincent's assistant to hear what they were saying about him, and this day was no different. She had her head ducked into the refrigerator, looking for her cherry yogurt, when she heard them talking.

"Oh, please. Why is it always my fault that the guy can't check his facts? I mean really, he's the big shot VP. Shouldn't he know that the owner, Richard

Trumbell, wouldn't find it funny to be referred to as Dick in the ads? I heard the guy chewed him out for a half hour on the phone and told him he would never even answer a call from Hunter again."

Lexi recognized Tony's voice the moment he began spewing his hate.

"And what about that new assistant of his? You know, I hear they're already sleeping together." Tony's female companion giggled at his blatant lies. "I mean, who did she think she was, talking to me that way? She probably spent most of the morning on her knees under Vincent's desk."

Angry tears began to well up in Lexi's eyes as she slammed the refrigerator shut and spun around to face the pair, ready to set the record straight. She opened her mouth to tell them how wrong they were when the cavalry arrived, led by the most unexpected person.

"Tony!" Vincent's deep voice snarled as he filled the doorway and loomed over the couple. "Apologize to her immediately."

"Oops. Did I let the cat out of the bag, Mr. Drake?" he sneered.

"If you have a problem with me, then take it up with me, but Alexandra never did anything to you other than pass on a message." Vincent held his hand out to Lexi, ushering her toward him. She tentatively stepped to his side, praying the tears in her eyes would stay put a minute longer and not give away how hurt she was by Tony's vicious insinuations. Vincent turned his back on Tony, ignoring him as he tried to guide Lexi safely out of the room. "Come on, I need your help with something."

"I'll bet you do." Tony and his companion snickered until Vincent spun around and backed him up against the wall.

"You give her any more trouble and it won't matter anymore who your parents are. You'll be fired on the spot, and I'll let *her* be the one to do it!" He placed his hand on the small of Lexi's back and led her out the door. "Watch your step, cousin." He gave Tony one more murderous glare and then disappeared down the hall with Lexi.

She stumbled back toward her desk, trying to put as much distance between herself and Tony as possible before she lost it completely. Vincent kept pace with her, but said nothing except "I'm sorry."

For some reason, that infuriated Lexi. "Why on Earth are *you* apologizing to me? Tony was the asshole, not you. All you did was defend me." She stopped and sagged against the wall, catching her breath. "Thank you for that, by the way."

"His problem is with me, not with you, so try not to take it personally."

"Oh, I take it very personally when someone accuses me of…" Lexi waved her hand in the air suddenly at a loss for words. "Well, you know exactly what he was accusing me of." She blew a stray hair out of her face and crossed her arms. "This sucks."

Vincent leaned his shoulder against the wall beside her and nodded his head. "Welcome to my world."

"Promise me one thing."

Vincent raised his eyebrow as Lexi watched him expectantly. "Name it."

"That you'll keep your word, and if he crosses the line like that again, I get to fire him."

Vincent winked at Lexi, pushed off the wall, and started walking to his office. "Hell, I'll even let Sean videotape it."

◆

Lexi buried herself in her work for the rest of the day after the unfortunate run-in with Tony. When she arrived at work on Tuesday, it was back to business as usual. Vincent stayed in his office preparing for an important meeting the next day, and Lexi ran back and forth to the copy room, collating presentation packets and adjusting the graphics.

When she finally sat down at her desk, the phone rang right on cue. Lexi rolled her eyes and answered it. "Good morning, Vincent Drake's office. This is Lexi White speaking. May I help you?"

"Good morning. This is Anna Caldwell, Vincent's sister. I wanted to check his schedule for the day… wait, Lexi White? I went to school with an Alexandra White. Odd question, but you didn't go to Riverdale High by any chance did you?"

Lexi's eyes grew huge with surprise, and then she smiled. "Hi, Anna. I'm shocked you remember me after all these years. How are you?"

Anna laughed. "How could I not remember you? We worked on the yearbook together junior and senior year." Lexi found herself grinning at Anna's excellent memory. "I'm great. How are you? I can't believe you're Vincent's new assistant. How weird is that? What a small world." Unlike her brother, Anna sounded like she hadn't changed a bit since high school. Her kind nature drew people to her. "I bet Vincent freaked out when he saw you."

Well, he freaked...just not in the way you're thinking, Lexi laughed to herself. She answered as honestly as she could. "Actually, Anna, I don't think he remembers me."

"Wait...what? Are you serious?"

"Yeah, but it's fine. It's not like we were friends back then or anything, and it has been ten years."

"That man is the most unobservant moron. Oh, the reason I called is that my daughter Madison and I were going to stop by today. How does his schedule look?"

"Actually, he's free around noon, and he doesn't have any lunch meetings today so that's probably the best time. I'll let him know you're coming."

"No, I think we'll surprise him. Madison and I showing up unannounced won't be nearly as surprising as finding out he went to high school with you. You must have just started there not too long ago. I bet he's been a complete jerk, too. I can't wait to see his face! See you in an hour, Lexi." Before Lexi could protest, Anna hung up the phone, her infectious laughter still ringing in Lexi's ears when she placed the receiver back into the cradle.

Well, hell...

Lexi spent the next hour making sure there was a fresh pot of coffee, all calls were returned, and Vincent had everything he needed before Anna arrived. She wanted him in the best possible mood before he found out who she was. Part of her was afraid he would see it as a betrayal or the last straw and fire her on the spot, but the other part of her wanted to see what would happen. Would he remember her at all, or was she actually as invisible in high school as she had tried to be?

Anna and Madison arrived at Hunter just before noon. "Lexi!" Anna wrapped her arms around Lexi. "You look gorgeous, exactly the same."

Lexi blushed at Anna's kind words and was stunned by the show of affection from someone she hadn't known very well or seen in years. "And look at you. I love the short hair."

Anna ran her fingers through her curled tresses, which were the same rich color as her brother's hair. "Thanks!"

A smaller version of Anna with long hair and the same big brown eyes stepped forward and extended her hand to Lexi. "I'm Madison Caldwell, and I'm five years old. Nice to meet you, Miss White."

Lexi bent down to Madison's level and smiled. "It's very nice to meet you too, Madison. Please call me Lexi."

"So, Lexi, tell me what you've been up to. I remember you went out east for school, right?" Anna sat down in a chair, and Lexi slipped into the one beside her. Madison hopped up into the leather chair behind Lexi's desk and began pecking away on the computer.

"Maddie, stop."

"It's fine." Lexi stood up and stepped behind the desk. "Do you want to type a letter for Uncle Vincent?" Madison grinned and eagerly nodded her head as Lexi opened up a word processing program so she could type freely.

"Thanks." Anna smiled as Lexi returned to her seat. "So, what have you been doing the last ten years, and how did you end up working at Hunter?"

Lexi shifted uncomfortably in her chair, not sure if she was up for spilling her long and painful history to someone she barely knew, but Anna's warm smile and welcoming personality made Lexi feel like it would be all right, so she opened up about everything. She told her about dropping out of school to take care of Harry, about how she'd basically spent the last eight years as his nurse until he died a few months ago. A stray tear fell down Anna's face as she listened to Lexi's story, and by the end, they were both clutching tissues and wiping their eyes.

"Lexi, I'm so sorry about your dad."

"Thanks."

"Mommy, look what I made!" Madison's brilliant smile lifted their spirits.

"That's fantastic, honey."

"Here, let me print it out for you. Push this button, and then the paper will come out right here." Lexi pointed under her desk.

Madison jumped off the chair and intently watched as the paper crept out of the printer inch by inch. "I got it!" she cheered and waved it over her head. "Wanna hear what I said?" she asked Lexi.

"Absolutely." Lexi smiled as Madison crawled into her lap and began reading the random letters and numbers.

"Dear Uncle Vince." Lexi bit her lip to keep from laughing, assuming Madison must be the one person on Earth who could get away with calling him Vince without him minding. Lexi had noticed the way Vincent cringed when Jade used the nickname. "I want you to come to my house and play Barbies tomorrow. Mom said it was okay, and this time you can pick the wedding dress, I promise. Love, Madison Caldwell."

"That is the greatest letter ever. I'm sure he will love it." Lexi stood up with Madison in her arms. "You know what we need? An envelope. Do you want to come with me to find one, and maybe on our way back, we'll stop by the lounge? I know where Leigh hides the chocolate chip cookies."

"Mommy, can I please go with Lexi?" Madison's big brown eyes pleaded with her mom.

"Sure, honey. I'll go talk to Uncle Vincent about boring grown up stuff until you get back." She gave her daughter a quick kiss and patted Lexi on the arm. "Thanks."

"No problem."

"Good afternoon, dearest brother of mine!" Anna sang as she strolled into Vincent's office unannounced.

"Would it kill you to knock for once, Anna?" Lexi heard Vincent's deep voice chuckle as she walked away.

Lexi carried Madison down to the supply room in search of the perfect envelope for her precious letter. As soon as Lexi set her down, Madison pushed a chair over to the counter and climbed up, watching Lexi open the cabinets and pull out a box of white envelopes.

"Do you have any pink envelopes? This one is yucky."

"No, sorry, only boring old white ones. But I do have some markers you could use to decorate it. Would you like to do that?"

"Yes!" Madison squealed.

Lexi gave her a small pile of highlighters and colored pens. Madison bent over and drew an adorable picture of two blobs. She explained the one with a bow in its hair was her and the one with a tie was Vincent and they were having a tea party.

"Do you like having tea parties?" Lexi asked as she watched Madison continue her art project.

"Oh, yes. Uncle Vincent is my best guest. He drinks all the tea!" She giggled and swung her feet over the side of the counter, recounting all the details from her last party, including the purple hat that Uncle Vincent looked very pretty in.

"That sounds like fun." Lexi smiled, imagining Vincent on the floor drinking tea, sporting a glorious, purple brimmed hat on his head. When Madison declared her masterpiece done, Lexi helped her tuck the letter into the decorated envelope.

The little girl stuck out her tongue, and Lexi gently ran the flap across it, then let her press it down, sealing the envelope.

"You have to come to my next party, Lexi. It would be so much fun." Madison grinned, then jumped off the counter and put her hands on her hips. "Now, let's go find those cookies!"

Lexi held Madison's hand as the pair made their way back to the lounge. She hoped they wouldn't run into Tony or his accomplice this time. If he was there, Lexi decided she would take Madison downstairs to the deli and buy her one of their giant cookies rather than risk Tony saying something inappropriate about Vincent around his niece. She was relieved to find the room empty as she crouched down beside Madison near the corner cabinet.

"Leigh puts cookies in here for me. She said I can share them with all my friends, so would you like one?"

"Please." Madison's smile grew exponentially when Lexi gave her two cookies instead of just one. "Lexi, I like you."

"I like you too, Madison. I'm glad you came in to visit your uncle today."

"Next time, I'm coming to visit you too." She threw her arms around Lexi's neck and hugged her tightly.

"I would love that." Lexi smiled, enjoying the feel of the tiny girl in her arms. "Come on, you have a letter to deliver."

"Can we take a cookie to Uncle Vincent? He eats cookies with me all the time."

"I think he would love that."

✦

When they arrived back at Lexi's desk, Vincent's door was still shut. He and Anna were obviously still in the middle of their conversation.

"Let's go give this cookie to Uncle Vincent."

"I don' think we should interrupt your mommy and uncle when they're talking. That would be rude." Lexi directed Madison back to her desk and sat her back in the leather desk chair. Lexi hopped up and sat on the desk.

"Okay." Madison munched on her cookie, crumbs falling onto her navy blue dress. "Can I call him?" She eyed the telephone with a big smile.

"I think that would be a wonderful idea." Lexi leaned over and rang Vincent on their private line, putting him on speakerphone so Madison could hear him as he answered.

"Yes, Alexandra?" Vincent's voice over the speaker made Madison giggle.

"Who's Alexandra?" she whispered loudly to Lexi who smiled and pointed at herself. "Oh, no, it's not her. It's *me*, Uncle Vincent!"

Vincent suddenly sounded alarmed. "Madison, are you alone out there? Where did Alexandra go?"

Lexi rolled her eyes and shook her head. "I'm right here. Relax. Madison has something for you, but we didn't want to interrupt you and Anna."

"It's a present!" Madison held the cookie toward the phone like he could see it.

Vincent chuckled. "A present, for me? Sure, come on in."

Madison jumped off the chair, holding her remaining cookie in one hand and the cookie for Vincent in the other. Lexi followed after her, carrying Madison's letter and smiling.

"I got cookies!" Madison flew through the door, laughing.

"Wow, you sure do." Vincent smiled as the small girl crawled into his lap. "Wherever did you find something so delicious?"

Madison handed him the smaller cookie, then began eating her second one. "She," Madison pointed her finger at Lexi, "showed me the hiding spot, but I can't tell you, Uncle Vincent, cuz it's a secret."

Anna grinned when she noticed the crumbs all over her daughter. "And just how many cookies have you had, sweetheart?"

Madison smiled sheepishly. "Two?" Anna just nodded her head, winking at Lexi, who had sat down in the chair beside her.

"Lexi said it was okay, Mommy. Don't worry." Madison noticed Vincent hadn't taken a bite of his cookie yet and frowned. "You gonna eat it or what?"

Vincent took a bite, putting a smile back on his niece's angelic face. "Delicious."

"He likes it. I told you he would," Madison said smugly.

"You're a very smart girl." Lexi laughed, watching the pair enjoy their treats.

"Lexi, can we—"

"Alexandra," Vincent corrected his niece. "Her name is Alexandra, honey."

Anna rolled her eyes and shook her head. Madison just giggled at him. "No, it's not, Uncle Vincent. You're so silly. Her name is Lexi." She quickly turned to Lexi for confirmation.

"Yes it is, Madison. Thank you. I've been trying to tell your uncle that for days. Now maybe he'll remember." She winked at the little girl bouncing in Vincent's lap.

Vincent smirked at her. "Sorry, *Lexi*."

"No problem, *Vincent*."

Anna threw her hands up. "Oh my gosh, Vincent, are you really this stupid? I obviously got all the brains when we were in utero." Vincent looked at his sister, startled by her outburst.

Madison chanted, "Stupid, stupid."

Lexi stood up to slink out of the room. "I'm just going to go back to my desk," she said softly, trying to excuse herself from the impending altercation.

"Freeze, Lexi White." Anna grabbed her arm and pulled her back down into the chair beside her.

"Anna!" Vincent snapped. "What has gotten into you?"

"Lexi White." Anna said each word slowly. "Doesn't that name sound familiar to you?"

Vincent's brows furrowed together. "Yes, you're sitting right beside her. Are you on something, Anna? A new medication perhaps?"

"What is it about the Y-chromosome that makes men so dense?" Anna muttered softly to Lexi who had to stifle a laugh. "Think, Vincent. Lexi White..."

Lexi, feeling the intense scrutiny of his gaze, blushed and began examining her shoes, unwilling to look up at his hypnotic eyes at that moment. Even partially hidden behind the veil of her hair, her pulse raced under the microscope of Vincent's stare. Vincent let out a frustrated sigh before she finally lifted her gaze to find him running his hand up and down his cheek as he continued thinking, his dark hair falling into his eyes.

"Madison, has Mommy been acting strange all day?" he asked. Madison giggled and crammed a piece of cookie into his mouth.

"We went to high school with her, Vincent, you moron," Anna blurted out of nowhere.

Vincent snapped his head back to Lexi and began choking on the cookie in his mouth while Madison happily sang, "Uncle Vince is a moron. Uncle Vince is a moron!" He grabbed his bottle of water and took a sip, trying to calm his cough.

"*You* went to Riverdale?"

A beet red Lexi nodded her head. "Go Spartans," she feebly cheered, pumping an unenthusiastic fist into the air.

"What year did you graduate?"

"She was in our class!" Anna rubbed her temples, her brother's idiocy wearing on her patience. "Yes, *our* graduating class. I worked with her on the yearbook for two years. She was in every one of your classes, I'm sure. She was almost valedictorian, but that girl Michelle somebody beat her by the smallest margin in Riverdale history or something. Don't you remember any of this? How can we be twins?"

"Did we have any classes together?" Vincent ignored his sister, his attention focused solely on Lexi.

"A few." Lexi's heart thundered in her chest. She would never admit it, but she knew for a fact they had four classes together senior year and could name each one and where he sat in the classroom. If she tried hard enough, she could probably remember his entire schedule from senior year, including his locker number.

Stalker.

"Don't you remember, the middle of junior year, a new girl moved to town and people went goofy over it?" Anna's attempts to jog his memory didn't appear to be working.

"You used to cheat off of me in Government senior year, if that helps."

He paused, then shook his head in disbelief. "No, I cheated off this new junior who was taking government a year early for some reason."

"No, that was me." Lexi smiled at the memory. "You sat one row over to the left and when you didn't know the answer you would drop your pencil into the aisle between us and peek at my paper as you picked it up."

Now it was Vincent's turn to blush.

"My brother cheated? Ha! I knew you didn't pull an A in Mrs. Blackstone's class on your own! And you teased me about my B." Anna mocked her brother, who just kept staring at Lexi.

"It was you … but I don't remember you." He looked away and his brows furrowed. He remained quiet for a very long time, his face scrunched in concentration. "I'm sorry, Lexi. If I would have known."

"Nothing to be sorry for, Vincent. We weren't friends back then, and I was horribly shy, so it's not your fault. I probably should have mentioned it the day you came back, but when you didn't say anything, I figured there was no point in bringing it up."

"Uncle Vincent!" Madison clamored for his attention, oblivious to the awkward tension that filled the room. "Wanna play? Oh, Lexi, where's my letter?"

Lexi handed the little girl her fluorescent envelope and stood to leave, wanting to put some distance between her and Vincent. "I have some work to finish up. If you need anything, let me know."

"Wait." Anna was on her feet following behind Lexi. "Madison, you can play with Uncle Vincent for a few minutes. I'm going to give Lexi the guest list for the gala and go over a few things with her, if that's okay with you."

"Sure that's fine." Vincent turned to his niece and smiled. "You have been so patient while we talked. What do you want to play?

Anna left the office and laid a paper in her hands. "So, that went well."

Lexi's eyebrows rose in disbelief. "Yeah, that was only mildly awkward." She had no desire to talk about Vincent's reaction, or lack thereof, to finding out the truth about who she was. Instead, she began examining the list of names in front of her.

"What's this?" Lexi scanned the paper that included some of the most prominent people in San Francisco.

"The guest list for the gala. The people who have RSVP'd have a star next to their name." Anna scribbled a few more stars on the paper, confirming it was accurate.

"Sorry if this is a dumb question, but what gala are you talking about?"

"The Hunter Advertising Charity Gala. We host it every year and raise money for different organizations in the Bay Area. This year we are focusing on the new leukemia wing at Children's Hospital. It's in two weeks, and not only does it raise a great deal of money, but it's a work event where contacts are made and deals are brokered. Basically, it's the biggest night of the year for Hunter Advertising, personally and professionally." Anna slid out a beautiful black and white invitation with elegant raised script lettering and handed it to Lexi.

"Sounds like a wonderful event. So, what do you need from me?" Lexi punched the date and time into her calendar before she forgot.

"Vincent will go into more detail about this, but briefly, he is going to get you a hit list of people."

"A hit list?"

"Sounds much more sinister than it actually is." Anna winked. "It's a list of people he wants to make contact with at the event. Advertising is all about who you know, and this is one way to expand that list."

"Hit list. Got it. So, he needs me to do some background on them personally, wives' names, kids, girlfriends, beloved pets, favorite sport. Then find out current campaigns, what worked, what didn't. Pull marketing statistics and demographics information for them? That kind of thing?"

Anna's face broke out in a brilliant smile. "In a nutshell, yep." Anna glanced down at her watch. "Crap, Erik gave me something to take down to Sean. I'll be right back. I'm going to leave you this list, and I'll E-mail you as I get more RSVPs." Anna rummaged through her bag for a book and took off down the hall, but before she was out of earshot she yelled, "Men wear black, the women all wear white, so make sure you have something to wear."

Lexi's head came crashing down onto the top of the desk at the thought of attending a black tie affair with the elite of San Francisco. How was she going to blend in with this crowd? She frantically scanned the invitation again to see if it mentioned anything about being a masquerade ball so she could cover her face and make an anonymous fool of herself.

Out of nowhere, the most beautiful sound came from Vincent's office—laughter. A deep belly laugh harmonized with high pitched giggles.

Intrigued, Lexi crept over to Vincent's door and peeked inside. What she saw took her breath away. Vincent's suit jacket was draped neatly over his chair, and his black dress shirt was now untucked and completely wrinkled. He was on all fours, without shoes, crawling around on the floor with Madison perched high on his back, screeching in delight. She had taken his designer silk tie and pulled the knot to the back of his neck, using the long end as the reigns.

"Do it again, Uncle Vince!" Madison laughed, kicking her "pony" in the ribs with her tiny heels. Vincent reared up on his back legs and neighed as Madison grabbed him around the neck to keep from sliding off.

He was a completely different man. This man was playful and acting silly without hesitation. The smile that lit up his face transformed his features from serious and sullen to youthful and carefree, something that up until now Lexi didn't think he was even capable of anymore. And yet with Madison, he wasn't Vincent Drake the VP of Hunter, he was just Uncle Vince, and from the looks of it, he was loving every minute of it.

"He really is amazing with her," Anna whispered in Lexi's ear, back from her trip to Sean's office. With a smile, the women continued their spying. "Whenever he gets in a really bad mood, all I have to do is bring her around and he glows. She thinks he hung the moon just for her."

Lexi watched as Anna walked in and announced it was time for the pony ride to end and helped Madison get her shoes on to leave. Vincent's laughter stopped, and he shot up when he noticed Lexi standing in the doorway watching him.

"What are you smiling about?" Vincent asked in a clipped tone.

"Nothing, it was just ... nice. That's all."

"What was nice?" Vincent asked as he slipped his shoes back on his feet, brushing the lint off his slacks.

"Seeing you smile again. I thought maybe you had forgotten how to after all these years."

Vincent shot her a sarcastic smirk.

"You really should do it more often," Lexi said softly and smiled before going back to her desk to answer the phone.

"Bye bye, Uncle Vince. I gotta go home. Don't forget to come play Barbies soon."

Vincent scooped her into his arms and gave her a big hug. "I will. I promise."

"Bye, Vincent." Anna stood on her tiptoes and kissed his cheek. "And please be nice to Lexi. She's a very sweet girl and smart. You need to keep her around."

"Bye, ladies."

Just as Vincent began wiping the cookie crumbs off his desk, Lexi came crashing through his door.

"Vincent!" She grabbed his suit jacket from the back of his chair and began shoving his arms into it. "Drop the crumbs and get this jacket on. Now."

"Would you please tell me what the hell is going on?" Vincent wiggled out of her grasp and fixed the jacket himself, tucking in his shirt at the same time.

Lexi took a deep breath. "Sean just called. He's stuck on the bridge with a flat tire, and he's supposed to meet—" She didn't even need to finish.

Vincent's eyes nearly bugged out of his head. "He was going to meet with Mr. Walden, from the bookstore chain and get the contract signed. Christ. How long do I have?" He immediately ran his fingers through his hair, trying to tame the messy mane.

"Twenty minutes, but traffic should be light at this time of day, so I think you'll make it."

Lexi stepped closer to him and without thinking, wrapped her tiny arms around his neck, fumbling with the collar of his shirt. Vincent shivered as her warm fingers brushed against his neck and her soft body pressed into his while she adjusted his collar. In her hurry to get him ready, Lexi didn't notice how overwhelmed Vincent suddenly seemed by her closeness.

"Aha!" She wrenched his neck to the side, pulling his tie back to the front of his shirt. When Vincent stared at her in confusion, she snickered. "You need this up front now, unless you were planning on playing pony with Mr. Walden too."

Her green eyes sparkled playfully as she smoothed the silk down his chest, quickly adjusting the knot so it was once again neat and perfect. She reached up and wiped Anna's lipstick off his face with her thumb.

"I'm never going to live this down, am I?" His self-deprecating words broke her focus.

"Which one? Not remembering me from high school or being caught playing pony?"

"Both," Vincent answered as she stepped back and buttoned up his jacket. He was once again the picture of dark, masculine perfection.

"Probably not." Lexi laughed as she handed him the address of the restaurant and a copy of the papers that needed to be signed. Just before Vincent rushed out the door, she said, "And just wait until Sean hears about this."

He groaned and cursed slightly under his breath, then disappeared out of the office to save the day for Hunter Advertising once again.

· 8 ·

Lexi, you know I love you, right? But this is just creepy," Hope mumbled with a spoonful of Captain Crunch in her mouth. "I mean, who the hell are these people?"

"They're on the hit list for the gala."

Hope's eyebrows shot up at the words "hit list." "So, who gets whacked first, Mrs. Soprano?"

"You're hilarious, Hope. Seriously, I need to know these people on sight by the end of the week, so it seemed like a good idea to . . . live with them for a while?"

"Well, your apartment looks like a police station, not that I've ever personally been inside one. I'm a law-abiding citizen, I swear. But you've got the big suspect board of possible axe murderers, and a bunch of well-dressed murderers at that. Is that an original Valentino she's wearing?" Hope let out a low whistle, then shoveled more cereal into her mouth.

"Francesca Marradesi? Yep, she comes from the one of the wealthiest families in Italy. They own a cosmetics company. She and her husband Paolo and his brother Dante run the corporation, and they—"

Hope put her hand firmly over Lexi's mouth, silencing her. "It's six o'clock in the morning Lexi, and honestly, I don't care who the hell they are. I just like her dress. Now pass me those Rice Krispies. All of a sudden I feel like some puffed rice."

✦

Lexi arrived at work at 6:45 just like she had every day. Leigh, of course, had been there for half an hour already and handed her a small pile of messages for Vincent. Continuing with the morning routine, Lexi printed out his schedule, made the changes, and got the coffee ready.

The more time Lexi spent with Vincent, the easier it was to be around him. He still made her heart race when he smiled or glanced in her direction, but instead of seeing him as the unattainable god he'd been to her in high school, she saw him for the man he was, flaws and all.

To Vincent, there was nothing more important than his work. Everything he did was for the benefit of Hunter Advertising. He put in ridiculously long days, and Lexi received text messages and E-mails from him at all hours of the night, so she knew that even when he went home, work continued to be his priority.

But as dedicated as he was, his people skills sucked.

The day after Anna's big reveal about them all going to high school together had been awkward. But over the next few days, they both became so immersed in planning for the gala that there simply wasn't any time to be worried. They had too many things to get done.

In spite of the heavy workload, there was still plenty of time during the day for Lexi to watch Vincent. Even though their relationship was boss and employee, Lexi's body couldn't have cared less. Every time she caught him looking at her, she blushed. Every time he brushed against her, her knees buckled. And if he came up behind her when she wasn't looking and leaned over her shoulder, her tongue stopped functioning, and she couldn't speak coherently. And, in Lexi's opinion, the suits he wore were just plain unfair. No woman alive could resist Vincent Drake in Prada menswear.

As he stalked past her desk that morning and grabbed his pile from the corner, he noticed Lexi studying stacks of colored index cards.

"What are those?" He cocked his head to the right to get a better look.

Lexi blushed. "They're my flashcards. See?" She held up a yellow one with a picture of a beautiful blond woman in her mid-forties. "This is Maria Fontaine, wife of?" She waved the card in front of Vincent's eyes to see if he could name her spouse correctly.

He thought about it for a second, and then sat down on the edge of her desk and shrugged. "Mr. Fontaine?"

"No, David Thoms of the restaurant chain. She kept her maiden name because her mother was huge part of the feminist movement, and you better remember that when talking to her or you're going to get yourself into big trouble. Call her by her first name, not Mrs. Thoms, or she'll have your head on a platter." Lexi flipped to the next yellow card and showed it to him.

"Easy one. That's Rebecca Shay, heiress to the Shay diamond fortune. She designs jewelry for the A-list celebrities, and she's recently divorced. It was a messy one because of a bedroom video that made it onto the internet. She plays tennis every Monday and Wednesday at the Gables Country Club."

"Very good. Someone has been doing his homework."

"Give me another one from the blue stack." Vincent smiled and took a deep, dramatic breath. Lexi rolled her eyes at him and flashed a new card. Without blinking, Vincent recited, "Julian Stone, clothing designer. Elusive and dramatic, and if we can land him it would make my day, because I know that weasel Reid is kissing his ass at lunch as we speak." Vincent's lips curled up in a mischievous grin. "Reid would be furious if Hunter got that account. Naturally, I want to know everything about Stone."

"I'll make you a more detailed fact sheet and have it to you by noon." Lexi jotted a note to herself on a piece of paper before putting the cards away. Vincent sat there with an amused expression on his face.

"Yes?"

"So, let me get this straight, you made one of those for every person on the hit list?"

"Don't knock it till you've tried it. If you'd used this technique to study in high school, you might not have needed to cheat off that *junior* in your Government class."

Vincent ignored her jab and leaned closer. "What do the colors mean this time?" He raised his eyebrows expectantly and waited. "Come on, Miss Organized, I know they mean something."

Lexi was surprised. This was the most relaxed she had seen him in the two-and-a-half weeks she'd worked at Hunter, and it was nice.

She sighed in resignation when he folded his arms across his chest and refused to let the subject drop. "Hair color. I figured it would be the most logical way to do it. Then if I get stuck and I see a blonde, I know to grab the yellow pack out of my purse."

"You're bringing them with you?" he asked incredulously.

"Are you going to remember all fifty people on sight?"

"No."

"And when you can't remember, who are you going to come ask?"

His lips slowly turned up in a sheepish grin. "You, probably."

"Exactly. Hence the reason I'll have the cards on me at all times. This is the stuff I get paid the big bucks for, you know." Lexi laughed.

Vincent opened his mouth to say something, but decided against it. Instead, he hopped off her desk and snatched the flashcards out of her hand. "I'm going to borrow these for a while if that's okay."

"Sure, whatever," she said, trying to sound nonchalant. She focused on the computer, but watched him walk to his office out the corner of her eye, sifting through the cards as he disappeared behind his door.

✦

Lexi spent the rest of the early morning hours researching the elusive Julian Stone. Not much was known about him. He had just graduated from the New York School of Design two years ago and happened to be in the right place at the right time. He won a New Designer contest and was able to do a small show at Fashion Week. The right people saw his work, and he immediately became the hot, new face of fashion. His clothing line was hip and edgy, mainly for the eighteen- to twenty-six-year-old demographic. Lexi gathered up every detail she could find and printed out a copy for Vincent.

"Nice job," he told her as he quickly scanned it before running out to a meeting.

A couple hours later, the phone gave an evil sounding ring. "Put Vincent on," Jade's shrill voice barked.

"He's not in his office right now."

"Well, find him."

"Nope, he's not in my drawer." Lexi slammed her desk drawer shut as hard as she could so Jade would pick up the sound on the phone.

"Listen, you little—"

"He's not in the building, Jade."

"He's not picking up his cell, either. I tried already. Where the hell is he?"

Lexi bit back the response she really wanted to give and glanced over at Vincent's schedule. "It's Wednesday, Jade. He has meetings all morning, just like he does every Wednesday."

"Don't give me attitude. Just tell me when he'll be back."

"After lunch."

"I need a time. What *time* is he going to be back?"

"Around one thirty, I think, but this afternoon they have the Max—" At that point, Jade hung up and Lexi was left listening to the dial tone. "Always a pleasure, Jade." Lexi slammed the receiver down and was startled by a deep voice chuckling beside her.

"What does she want now?" Vincent was leaning against the wall with his hands tucked into his pockets, one eyebrow raised in question.

"To know the precise moment you step foot in the building. Should I call her?" Lexi mentally slapped herself. "I'm sorry, that was out of line. I mean, she wanted to know when you were coming back from your meeting."

Vincent mumbled something that sounded like "great" as he walked past her desk. Before he went in his office, he looked back at Lexi. "So, how long to I have?"

Lexi's face broke out into a wide grin. "I told her one-thirty, which means she'll be here at one. Want me to go get you a burger for lunch early so you have time to hide the evidence?"

He winked at Lexi, making her heart race and a delicious warmth spread throughout her body. "Can you add a chocolate milkshake to that order? I had a long morning."

Lexi stood up and grabbed her purse. "Consider it done." She ran down the street to Frank's and got him the usual, plus a milkshake. When she returned to the office, she walked in on a very heated conversation between Sean and Vincent. Sean was frantic, waving his hands wildly in front of Vincent's very pissed off face.

"I swear to God, Sean, I'm going to kill you if you blow this for us." Vincent shook his head from side to side.

"They said I could take it for a spin. I was just—"

"You were just driving a high-performance automobile that you had no business sneezing on, let alone doing a hundred miles per hour in—while talking on your cell phone!"

"But—"

"No buts, Sean. What are we supposed to do? The shoot is in three hours, and the star of that shoot is currently sitting on the curb with a giant dent in the fender." Vincent began pacing back and forth as Lexi silently slipped behind her desk and pretended to be working.

"I wouldn't say giant. I hit a card table, not a stone wall." Sean flopped into one of the chairs at Lexi's desk. "Hey, Lexi."

"You hit a card table?" Lexi asked, completely confused about how he might have managed that one.

"Go ahead, tell her what an idiot you are while I try and figure out how to fix this," Vincent snarled.

"We're using one of the cars from Max in the photo shoot. As a thank you for all that we've done for them," Sean shot Vincent a dirty look, "they said I could go pick it up and drive it over here, and then take it to the shoot. So, I showed up and they handed me the keys to an extremely hot Ferrari Scuderia Spider, a yellow one. It's amazing, Lexi. The purr of the engine as I went down the highway was … orgasmic."

Lexi cocked her eyebrow at Vincent while Sean closed his eyes, grinning while he described the car in great detail, down to the yellow stitching on the black leather seats.

"When I got off the highway, where I might have been exceeding the posted speed limit for a very short period of time, I turned onto Ninth. The gas pedal is very sensitive, and I might have given it a bit too much gas as I dialed my cell phone, and I *might* have clipped a street vendor."

"You hit someone?" Lexi's hand flew to her mouth in horror.

"No, the guy's fine. He dove behind a newsstand. But the fake Prada bags and sunglasses went flying when I took out the table. Why couldn't I have hit the guy selling silk scarves?"

"How badly is the car damaged?" Lexi cringed.

"It's got a dent about the size of a softball in it."

"Oh," Lexi said, "that's not too bad."

"Not too bad? It's a Ferrari worth more that Sean's life." Vincent rubbed his hands up and down his face.

"Did you find someone who could fix it?" Lexi looked over at Sean, who shook his head.

"I've called everyone I know. No one's willing to touch a car like this on short notice. What the hell are we going to do?"

"We? *We* aren't going to do anything, Sean. *You* are the one up Shit Creek. I'm simply standing on the shore watching your corpse float past."

"I might be able to help you," Lexi said. The two men continued arguing, and as their voices grew louder, so did Lexi's. "I said I might be able to help you!"

"How?" Vincent asked suspiciously. "Happen to have another Ferrari in your purse?"

Lexi shot him a dirty look as she picked up the phone and called the one person she knew who might be able to pull this off.

"Hey, it's me. I need a favor—a huge favor. I have a Ferrari Scuderia with a card table-induced dent that I need fixed. No...yeah...I have no idea. Someone I work with did it. I assure you it was an accident. No, he isn't. Listen, if I bring it by, can you fix it? We have a photo shoot in three hours." Sean leaned over Lexi's desk, holding his breath as he waited for the answer. When Lexi flashed him a thumbs up, he began dancing around the room. "Fantastic. We'll be right there."

Sean scooped Lexi into his arms and swung her around the room. "Vincent doesn't deserve someone as awesome as you. Run away with me and be my assistant, please?"

"Put me down. We have to get that car to the garage now or we're screwed. And make sure you bring your checkbook. This one's gonna cost you." Lexi whacked Sean on the chest, and he gently placed her on the floor.

"Let's get out of here. Where are you and I speeding off to?"

"Oh no you don't." Vincent grabbed Sean's keys from his hand and waited for Lexi to get her purse before the three of them headed for the elevator. "Don't tell him anything," he said to Lexi. Then he turned to Sean. "She's coming with me, and you can follow us. I don't need you doing a hundred-and-twenty-five miles an hour to get there faster and hitting something else."

"Come on, man," Sean whined, but Vincent just gave him a droll stare as he leaned against the wall of the elevator. "Fine," Sean pouted. "Take my truck. It's just up the street from the Ferrari, around the west entrance."

When they made it downstairs, Lexi's mouth fell open at the sight of the gorgeous car parked in front of the building. The yellow paint glistened in the sunlight. A crowd of people had gathered around and were taking pictures of each other beside the vehicle.

"Move it, people. Everyone step away from the car." Sean pushed his way through the crowd to the driver's side door.

Lexi went to the front of the car and took out her BlackBerry to snap a picture of the damage.

"What are you doing?" Vincent asked, suddenly right beside her.

"They wanted a picture so they could start getting things ready since we need this done fast."

"Let's get this show on the road!" Sean yelled from the convertible, tapping his hands on the steering wheel impatiently.

"This way." Vincent slipped his hand onto the small of Lexi's back as he led her to Sean's enormous black Escalade that was parked down the street. He opened the passenger's side door for her and offered her his hand as she climbed up into the truck.

Lexi sent the picture over to Hope at the garage with a note that they were leaving. Hope was excited to get her hands on the Ferrari, and of course was one hundred percent certain she could fix it.

"Where am I going?" Vincent asked as he started the SUV.

"The garage is called Crowbar. Do you know where it is?"

"No, but I see ads for that place all the time."

Lexi bit her lip to hide her grin. "Get on the highway and get off at Jefferson."

Vincent sped down the street with Sean hot on his heels. He was very quiet as he drove, the only sound being the occasional tapping of his fingers on the steering wheel. The awkward silence lasted until Lexi finally broke it with a few more directions, then they safely arrived at Crowbar.

"Lexi, baby, what's shakin'?" a large burly man with colorful tattoos down both arms greeted her as she stepped out of the truck with Vincent.

"Not much. I brought you a little present, Marco." She waved her hand toward the Ferrari. "Do you like it?"

"Except for the giant dent in it, hell yeah. You're too good to me."

Lexi rolled her eyes and jerked her thumb in Sean's direction. "Get the keys from him."

Sean reluctantly handed them over after reminding Marco to be careful. Then he stalked through the door of the shop with Lexi and Vincent right behind him. For some reason, Sean had a sudden surge of testosterone and went all macho man. Lexi knew exactly why.

"Let me handle it from here," Sean said as he held up a silencing hand to Lexi and Vincent.

Inside the modest showroom, Hope stood behind the desk, studying a driver's manual and looking as gorgeous as ever. Her long black hair draped over her shoulders, and stray pieces fell around her face. The white tank top she wore peeked out from under her unzipped overalls, contrasting with her deeply tanned skin. She tapped her painted nails on the desk while she concentrated on the book. Lexi's mouth hung open as Sean strutted up to the desk like a proud peacock and leaned onto it with one elbow.

"Hello, gorgeous," he purred. "I'm Sean. Sean Adler."

Lexi stopped dead in her tracks when Hope's head snapped up. Vincent noticed and paused beside her. "What's wrong?"

When Hope's eyes narrowed into slits, Lexi shook her head and laughed. She knew what was coming next, so she leaned over to Vincent and whispered, "Just watch this, Sean's about to make a complete ass of himself."

"That's nothing new." Vincent was not amused.

Instead of introducing herself, Hope tucked a piece of paper into the book she was reading and with a bored expression said, "Can I help you?" She looked Sean up and down, taking in every feature from his striking yet sexy shaved head, to his dimples, to his lean, muscular build. No detail escaped her notice. There was a slight twinkle in her eyes as she glanced over at Lexi, but it immediately vanished when Sean spoke again.

"Yeah, I need to see the owner. He in?"

Dead man walking, Lexi thought to herself.

"No, *he's* not in."

Sean frowned. "Look, I need to talk to the guy in charge then. I just brought in that Ferrari and I need it fixed ASAP."

"There is no *guy* in charge here today."

"Okay, sweetie, listen. Can you just get me one of the guys who are going to work on the car? I need to ask him a few questions."

The patronizing tone of his voice set off every warning alarm in Lexi's head. "Oh, crap."

Vincent's gaze went from Lexi to the woman behind the counter, then back to Lexi. In that moment, he figured out who Hope was and chuckled. "He deserves it."

"You did not just call me sweetie," Hope snarled, glaring at Sean.

Sean glanced down at his watch. "Honey, I'm behind the eight ball here and running out of time. Is that guy Marco in charge, the one who met us out front? If I could just ask him—"

"My name is Hope, Hope Greyson, and if you call me 'sweetie,' 'honey,' 'baby,' or any other condescending term, you won't be behind that eight ball anymore, pal, because it will be shoved directly up your ass!" She spun on her heel and opened the door to the garage. "Marco, get in here, someone wants to talk to you."

Sean glanced over his shoulder at Lexi and Vincent and mouthed "What the hell?" at them. Lexi covered her mouth to hide her laugh, and Vincent simply shrugged.

"What you need?" Marco stuck his head in through the door.

"Ask Captain Dipshit." Hope threw Sean a deadly glare.

"Listen man, I just had a question for someone who knew what the hell they were talking about, and this chick decided to go all psycho on me." Sean held up his hands in surrender.

Hope's nostrils flared when Sean referred to her as "this chick."

Marco glanced at Lexi, who giggled uncontrollably. "Dude, you must have a death wish." Hope had both hands clenched into fists.

"No, I have a Ferrari out there with a dent that I need fixed fast. If not, my balls are gonna be roasted on a spit. No other shop in town would even touch it, so I just need to know that you can pull this off." Sean nervously rubbed the back of his neck.

"Me? Hell no, I can't do that repair. I'm the leather guy. I do interiors. You need the best body person in the business for that."

"Well, is he here?"

"No, *he* isn't." Hope stepped within punching distance of Sean.

"Lexi, you better save your boy before he's hanging on the wall over Hope's head. Right next to that big buck she helped Al shoot a few years back."

Lexi decided it was time to put Sean out of his misery. "Sean, I would like you to meet Hope Greyson, my best friend, owner of the Crowbar, and best body person on the West Coast."

A string of profanities fell out of Sean's mouth as Hope grinned spitefully at him.

Right on cue, Vincent sprang into action, just to rub salt in Sean's gaping wound. "Good afternoon, Miss Greyson, I'm Vincent Drake, and I'm grateful that you're willing to help us out with this. I have every confidence that you'll be able to fix the car. My friend here will pay whatever you charge without complaint. Again, thank you for your time." His smooth voice caught Hope's attention, and her eyes became as wide as saucers when he'd said his name.

Hope glanced over Vincent's shoulder at Lexi, who barely nodded in acknowledgement that he was, in fact, *the* Vincent Drake. "It's so nice to meet a man who isn't a chauvinist pig and knows how to speak to a woman." Sean started to sputter an apology, but she cut him off. "Let me guess, you're the dufus who crashed it in the first place?" Sean's mouth snapped shut. "Give me an hour, and I'll have that Ferrari as good as new." Hope turned to Lexi. "Are you going to wait for the car?"

"No, I think we have to get back to the office," Lexi answered, and Vincent nodded his head in agreement. "Sean will wait, but please don't hurt him."

Hope rolled her eyes, zipped up her overalls and whipped her hair up into a high ponytail as she started to walk out the door and into the garage. "Make sure the jackass has his checkbook on him, because this is going to cost him big time."

When the door was safely shut, Sean fell into a chair and grinned like a fool. "I think I'm in love."

"I think you're lucky to be alive. No one has ever talked to Hope like that and lived to tell about it," Lexi said with a laugh as she patted him on the shoulder.

9

So, is everyone from Hunter going to be at this swanky party?" Hope asked from her perch on the bed.

"Yep. Why?" Lexi answered from the bathroom.

"Oh, no reason, I was just—" When the door swung open, Hope let out a slow whistle and forgot her question completely. "Girl, you're a knockout!"

Standing in front of her full-length mirror, Lexi gave a quick spin like she used to do when she was a little girl. She loved to see her dress flare out and move. Hope had spent the entire afternoon helping her get ready for the gala and at the same time preventing Lexi from having a panic attack. As Hope had curled and pinned her hair up, Lexi studied her flashcards, adding last minute guests to the hit list whenever Anna E-mailed more names.

Fifteen minutes before Leigh was due to pick her up, Lexi stood, staring at her reflection in the mirror, hardly recognizing herself. Her white, tea length dress had small, braided spaghetti straps, a fitted bodice and a flared skirt adorned with iridescent white ribbons that hung down from the waist. The ribbons gave a hint of shimmer as the light reflected off them. Lexi's porcelain skin glowed against the pearly white fabric while a few of her caramel locks hung down around her face in soft curls. The pale color of the dress also brought out the tiny flecks of blue in her green eyes.

"You really do look like a princess. This was really Marie's dress?"

Lexi gave Hope a sad smile. "Yep. Harry saved it for me after she died. I found it when I was emptying the attic before I put the house on the market and just couldn't bear to part with it." She smoothed the ribbons down the front of the dress. Her nerves had been kept in check for most of the day, but now, as she stuffed her color-coded note cards into her tiny purse, the enormity of what she was about to do became too real. "You sure I look all right?"

Hope nodded her head vehemently. "You look like one of the San Francisco elite. Really, Lexi, you need to breathe and just try to have a little fun. It *is* a party, for God's sake."

"Breathing is a good thing to remember." Lexi fanned her face with her hand, suddenly feeling extremely warm. "I think I need more deodorant."

"Why are you so nervous?" Hope watched her friend pace back and forth in front of the window.

"You know me. How often does my mouth get me into trouble? I always speak my mind, even when I shouldn't. I'm used to taking care of myself, doing things on my own. I don't ask permission or think things through, and I'm fairly certain that I'll manage to do something stupid tonight. Vincent said this was the most important night of the year for Hunter. I don't want to embarrass him or the company in any way. I have to meet all these people, most of whom will probably mistake me for one of the servers."

"Not in that dress they won't," Hope said confidently.

"I'm not sure what scares me more—the potential for disaster, having to make small talk with these big-name potential clients, or…"

"Or?" Hope prodded.

"Or seeing Vincent all dressed up and fabulous." Lexi threw her hands up in frustration. "What is wrong with me? The guy is my boss."

A sly smile spread across Hope's face. "Well, of all the things you just listed, which one makes your heart beat the fastest?"

Blushing, Lexi gave Hope a pointed glare. "Don't make me say it out loud."

"Seeing Vincent?" When she didn't answer, Hope chuckled. "You've got it bad."

"Stop it. No I don't. Vincent's my boss and nothing more. He has a super-model girlfriend and a wonderful family. He doesn't need anything from me other than his messages and coffee at seven a.m. sharp every morning. All of these feelings are simply the resurrection of a long dead high school crush. Except now it's not cute; it's just plain pathetic. So, it doesn't matter how unbelievably attractive I find him, or the way my insides melt when he walks into a room even after all these years. It doesn't change anything. He's my boss, nothing more." Lexi took a deep breath and shrugged it off as if a nonchalant movement of her shoulders would turn the lies she just spewed into the truth.

Hope saw through her charade. "Still slipping him burgers for lunch when his weed-eating girlfriend isn't looking?" She raised a single eyebrow in question.

"Shut it." Lexi grabbed her purse and wrapped a shawl over her shoulders when Leigh's car stopped in front of the building and the horn honked.

"Please, God in heaven, don't let me make a fool of myself," Lexi prayed as she tucked her keys into her purse, took one last look in the mirror, and headed for the door.

"Be sure to snap a picture of that rat bastard if he looks hot," Hope yelled from the kitchen.

Lexi leaned back inside the door and chuckled. "I'll tell Sean you said he was hot!"

"I said he was a rat bastard with the potential to be hot!" Hope screamed as the door shut.

Lexi laughed all the way to the elevator. When she had called Hope to work on the Ferrari, Lexi knew her friend was the only one who could pull it off, and as expected, even the guys from the dealership couldn't tell where Sean had damaged the car. Hope was that good. The photo shoot went off without a hitch, and in the end, Sean got a really great price on a yellow Ferrari.

From the moment Sean had sauntered into the Crowbar and laid eyes on Hope, Lexi could tell that he was shamelessly smitten with her friend. Marco had informed Lexi when she called the shop later that day that Hope had been so beyond pissed off by Sean's chauvinistic assumptions that she hadn't even spoken to him for the entire hour hour he sat at the garage. Not a single word passed her lips in his direction. And when she was done with the bodywork, Marco said she'd grabbed Sean by the ear, led him into the garage and pointed at the car, then shoved a bill for over two grand in his face and held out her hand, waiting for payment. When the check hit her hand, she'd reached down into her bra and pulled the keys from their hiding place deep between her breasts and tossed them at Sean's head. Then she'd locked herself in her office for the next half hour.

The next day at work, Sean had peppered Lexi with questions about her friend. He'd wanted to know if she was seeing anyone, what her favorite flower was, her favorite restaurant, what kind of guys she dated, had she said anything about him? He'd tried to call again and thank her personally, but for some reason, every time he called, Marco told him Hope was busy with a customer. After two days of phone calls, he gave up his attempts to woo her and sulked.

Lexi grinned as she stepped outside and saw Leigh waving from inside the car. For the first time in a long while, life was exciting, and instead of stressing, Lexi took a deep breath and prepared to live a little.

Leigh put her at ease and had her laughing before they even made it to the highway. Through the laughter, Leigh helped her see that her job at the event was to be an observer and a reference for Vincent. He needed her assistance, but she didn't need to have the weight of the world on her shoulders. Feeling more at relaxed, Lexi planned on quietly fading into the background until she was needed.

◆

The ballroom was gorgeous. Elegant maroon and gold fabrics were draped everywhere, and the huge glass windows gave a spectacular view of the Golden Gate Bridge off in the distance. The grand staircase allowed the guests to make their entrance in style and be seen by everyone in the room. Spectacular floral arrangements adorned the center of each table; the scent from the roses filled the room, welcoming the guests as they arrived.

Lexi took a deep breath, and with Leigh at her side, she began the long journey down the staircase. Once safely at the bottom, she stopped and watched the flurry of activity before her. Well-dressed servers glided across the room in elaborate crisscrossing patterns, carrying large silver platters covered with succulent finger foods. How they maneuvered around the guests and each other without colliding was nothing short of miraculous.

Leigh tugged on Lexi's arm and pointed across the ballroom. One of the tall bar tables was already filled with a small group of people laughing and drinking. From the bar, Leigh grabbed a glass of wine for both of them, and then they joined the group.

"Leigh!" A girl with short black hair popped out of her seat and hugged Leigh then stuck out her hand to Lexi and smiled. "Hello, I'm Erica. I work at Reid. Have we met before? You look familiar and I never forget a face." She stared at Lexi quizzically.

"I actually interviewed with Reid about a month ago. I'm Lexi White." Lexi shyly waved to the others at the table as she slid into her seat and took a sip of her wine, hoping it would help calm her nerves.

"That's right! Now I remember *you*. I'm Mr. Reid's secretary. Sorry about all the annoying phone calls. The guy took quite the liking to you, and he has a problem taking no for an answer."

Lexi blushed, not quite sure what to say. "It was a very tough decision between Reid and Hunter, but I had to follow my gut." She tried her best to be diplomatic and avoided mentioning how the thought of working with David Reid made her skin crawl.

Erica rolled her eyes and turned to Leigh. "You didn't tell her she could speak freely about my freaky boss yet, did you?"

Leigh laughed. "No, sorry. I forgot. Lexi, Erica's cool. Her Christmas card last year was a picture of Reid practicing his smile as he recited his daily affirmations to himself in the mirror. I still want to know how you got that picture of him."

"God bless cameras on cell phones." Erica grinned and winked at Lexi. "Come on, we're all friends here—tell me the truth; what grossed you out the most, meeting David in the flesh, or the freakishly large homage to his narcissism that greets you when you get off the elevator?"

"Actually, I think it was the way he talked to my boobs rather than my face." Everyone at the table burst out laughing.

"Word to the wise," Erica warned with a laugh, "avoid David like the plague tonight. I'm sure he'll remember you, and the man has an irrational love of the tango. If the music starts, he grabs someone and then writhes around them on the dance floor. It's quite awful, trust me. I speak from experience." She shuddered at the memory.

"Thanks for the heads up." Lexi laughed as she scanned the growing crowd for any faces she might recognize.

The conversation flowed easily between the small group of women. Erica worked at Reid, another woman, Kim, the most laid back person Lexi had ever met, worked for Erik, Anna's husband. Kim kept them all entertained with stories of Madison on set with her dad. The last person to join them at the table was Claire, who had recently been hired by Parketti. Her heavily painted-on makeup made her look like the perfect porcelain doll. Lexi wondered what ugliness Claire might be hiding underneath all that fake perfection. When Claire sat down at the table, she remained very quiet, but listened intently to every word. Leigh gave Lexi a small kick under the table, but Lexi had already figured out that Claire was doing recon for her bosses and was not there to socialize. The conversation immediately veered away from work and onto their personal lives.

"So, Lexi, are you seeing anyone?" Erica asked. The other women leaned forward, anxiously awaiting her answer.

"No, not right now."

"Too bad that gorgeous boss of yours is such an arrogant ass." Claire finally opened her mouth and offered her spiteful two cents to the conversation.

"Excuse me?" Lexi immediately became defensive.

Claire chewed on the olive from her dirty martini, the corner of her painted lips curving up. "Oh, sorry, I had no idea that you and Mr. Drake were..." she trailed off suggestively.

Lexi took a deep breath and tried to think before she let the words fly from her mouth in anger. "Vincent and I aren't... whatever you were implying. He's my boss, and I enjoy working for him. Personally, I don't know why everyone feels the need to attack him. I don't think he's an ass at all. If anything, he treats people the way they treat him. So, if someone you work for told you he's an ass, then maybe you're work—"

Leigh jumped up and interrupted Lexi before she started a war. "Let's go tackle one of those cute servers and grab something to eat. I'm starving!" Without even waiting for an answer, she helped Lexi out of her chair and escorted her away from the table.

"Sorry." Lexi shoved a giant prawn from a passing platter into her mouth.

"Are you kidding? Don't be sorry. That was fantastic! Up until the part where you were about to tell her she was working for a bunch of assholes." Leigh giggled. "That probably would've got us all in trouble."

"Lexi would never get herself into trouble. She doesn't know the meaning of the word," a deep voice rumbled from behind the women.

Lexi jumped a mile and let out a squeak of surprise. "Sean! Give me a heart attack, why don't you?"

Sean looked amazing in his black tuxedo and vest. Rather than a traditional bowtie, he had opted for a long black one, which suited his personality much better. He gracefully moved around, flashing his million dollar smile at the people who passed by. He turned his attention back to Lexi and flashed his dimples mischievously at her. "So, what trouble did you get yourself into already?"

"I resent that."

Leigh nodded her head toward the table where Claire was sitting. Claire appeared to be contemplating several different ways to kill Lexi. "She almost told this witch from Parketti that she was working for a bunch of assholes." Leigh shrugged innocently in response to Lexi's scowl and took a bite of food. "He asked."

"I'm completely innocent," Lexi said indignantly.

"Of course you are," Sean chuckled.

Wanting the attention off her, Lexi tried a diversionary tactic. "Where's your date, Romeo?" Lexi looked around for a woman gorgeous enough to be on his arm, but came up empty. "Is she in the bathroom?"

Sean blushed a little before he answered. "I'm going stag tonight. I've recently come back on the market, but the lady I wanted to ask... Well, let's just say she wouldn't return any of my calls." His sheepish grin gave it away.

So, he really doesn't have a girlfriend anymore? He was going to ask Hope to be his date. She's going to die! Lexi thought to herself as she watched Sean smile and wave at people, occasionally reaching out to shake a hand or two. She stood back and observed how he smoothly kissed the wives' hands while impressing the men with his knowledgeable banter. His confidence and charisma were incredibly attractive. Throw in the dimples along with the bad-boy allure of his shaved head and she wasn't quite sure anyone could resist him, not even the obstinate Hope Greyson.

"So, Sean." Lexi casually reached out and stole a stuffed mushroom from him. "Hope asked about you."

The smooth operator quickly turned into a pubescent high school boy right before her eyes. The hors d'oeuvre in his hand never made it to his mouth, but rather hung in mid-air as he interrogated Lexi. "Really? She asked about me? In a good way or a bad way? What *exactly* did she say?"

Leigh excused herself and went to talk to some other people.

"Well, she asked if 'everyone' from Hunter would be here tonight, which is Hope-speak for 'Is Sean going to be there?' She's incredibly stubborn, if you hadn't figured that out yet." Sean stood beside her, hanging on her every word and nodding his head. "Then she asked..."

"What? She asked what? For my phone number?"

"Sorry, champ, no. She asked me to, and I quote, 'take a picture of that rat bastard if he looks hot.'"

Only Sean would find a way to take that comment as a compliment.

"She asked you to take a picture of me? She thinks I'm hot? Really?" His face lit up like a kid in a candy store. "Well, get that phone out and let's send the woman a little something to think about." Sean popped the last mushroom into his mouth and thought about it for a second. He finally tucked his hands deeply into his pockets, hunched his shoulders forward, dropped his chin and lifted his eyes to the camera from underneath his long thick lashes. His dimples accentuated the sexy smirk on his face as Lexi snapped the picture.

"She's gonna love that. You know, maybe Jade can get you a modeling gig. That was very GQ of you." Lexi quickly sent the picture to Hope with a note that said, "What do you think?" She elbowed Sean in the stomach when she caught him peeking over her shoulder trying to get Hope's phone number.

"Modeling isn't my thing. Too many uptight, skinny bitches in modeling. Oh, speaking of which, are Vincent and Jade here yet?" They both took a quick inventory of the room and came up empty. "They're always late."

Lexi's phone suddenly chirped. Sean ripped it out of her hand and laughed as he pumped his fist in the air. He proudly handed the phone to Lexi, showing her Hope's message.

That man is totally lickable.

"If you ever tell her you saw that message, I swear I'll glue your office door shut."

"Scout's honor." He strutted away with a shit-eating grin on his face and a newfound bounce in his step.

Lexi wandered around the ballroom, trying to take stock of the guests who had arrived already. More famous faces slowly trickled in, and Lexi was happy to see a few couples she recognized from the hit list. She watched to see who they talked to, and more importantly, who approached them. She was about to get a glass of water when she heard someone squeal her name.

"Lexi! Is that really you?"

She turned and found a petite, gorgeous woman with beautiful, long bronze hair standing behind her with a huge smile on her face. "Christina?"

Christina launched at Lexi and wrapped her arms tightly around her. "You look gorgeous! What are you doing here? I was so bummed when I heard you quit the record store."

Every Monday like clockwork, Christina would come into the vintage record store looking for rare albums, hoping to find a hidden treasure. Lexi helped her find quite a few Beatles albums for her boss, who apparently was a huge collector. Just before Lexi quit, she had found the last one in a small antique shop to complete his collection. Christina had literally jumped up and down in the store when Lexi put it in her hands.

"Thank you. You look amazing too, Tina. I'm sorry I didn't get to say goodbye to you, but you hadn't been to the store for a few weeks," Lexi explained. "I decided to try out a new job, see if I could get back into the career I was working on before I got sidetracked."

Christina nodded her head in understanding. Lexi had shared a surprising amount of information about herself with Christina during her frequent visits to the store.

"So, give me details. Who are you working for?"

"Actually, I'm working for a company called Hunter Advertising. I'm the executive assistant to—"

"Vincent Drake?" Christina interrupted, laughing.

"Yeah, do you know him?"

"I know of him. Remember when I told you that I worked in fashion? Well, I work for a fashion designer. You might have heard of him, Julian Stone. Vincent has called a few times to try and set up appointments."

Lexi's jaw fell open, and then snapped shut. He was one of the people Vincent was most desperate to make contact with, and Lexi had known his assistant all along. "You work for Julian Stone? He's the one collecting the Beatles albums?"

"Yep, that's him. Sorry I didn't mention it before, but it's not something I walk around broadcasting—that I work for one of the hottest fashion designers—ya know? People tend to act all weird when they find out."

"I can imagine. So, how long have you worked for him?"

"A little over a year. He's a great guy, lots of fun."

"Aw, Christina, you talking about me again?" A platinum blond gentleman who looked more like a surfer than a fashion designer wrapped his arm around Christina's shoulders and placed a playful kiss on her temple. Lexi noticed the slight blush that rushed into her friend's cheeks at the gesture.

"Isn't there someone who wants to schmooze you somewhere in this room, Julian?" Christina halfheartedly tried to shrug away from him, but Julian wouldn't have it. He held her beside him and continued smiling.

"You know you love me, Tina. Hi there, I'm Julian Stone." He leaned forward and extended his hand to Lexi.

"Lexi White. It's very nice to meet you, Mr. Stone."

Julian barked in laughter. "Please call me Julian, only Christina here has to refer to me as Mr. Stone." She rolled her eyes and elbowed him in the side.

"Lexi works for Vincent Drake over at Hunter Advertising, and she's the one that found that autographed White Album for you, you big idiot."

"You're my album goddess? I love you!" Julian released Christina and threw his arms around Lexi's neck, pulling her into a hug. "Any chance you know where I can find a Japanese-produced Stones box set?" He released her from his grasp and returned to Christina's side.

"Off the top of my head, no. Sorry. But I'll keep my eyes open for you if I hit up any auctions over the next few weeks."

"That would rock. Thanks, Lexi. So, you work for Drake, huh?"

"Yes, I've been there a few weeks now. Do you know Vincent?" Lexi knew very well the two men had never met. Julian Stone was a difficult man to get an appointment with. He had a reputation for being quite elusive, letting very few people into his inner circle.

"Never met the guy, but he's been asking to meet with me about the new line. What's he like? He seems kind of like a stiff." Julian waved over one of the champagne servers and handed a glass to each of the women before taking one for himself.

"Honestly, he *is* a little stiff, until you get to know him. But he's very good at what he does, that I can assure you. The campaigns he's constructed over the last few years have been very successful for his clients." Lexi tried not to sound like a Hunter Advertising cheerleader, but she also wanted to be honest with Julian and make sure he had all the facts about Vincent. "He'll be here soon. Maybe I can introduce him to you." Lexi held her breath and waited for his answer.

Julian stood there and stared at her for a minute as if he was trying to see into her soul and gauge if she was lying to him about her boss or had been working Christina.

"Oh, quit with the stare-down thing. It's so annoying. Lexi, find me later when Vincent gets here, and I'll drag his stubborn ass over to meet him." She turned to Julian and scowled. "And *you* will be polite, Mister Famous Fashion Designer, and talk to him. If I had to chat with that wretched woman from Parketti, the one with the claws, you can talk to Vincent. Stiff sounds better than trashy to me."

"Yes, boss," Julian said sarcastically as he mockingly saluted Christina, then excused himself to go back to making the rounds. "Lexi, awesome meeting you. I was just being a jerk before. Bring Vince by to say hello. I'll try and get a few drinks in him and see if we can loosen him up that way."

As he walked away, Christina's eyes remained glued on Julian until he disappeared into the crowd. When she turned back to Lexi, she realized she was caught and blushed. "Sorry about him. He has this whole macho thing he does, but really he's a big softie."

"So are you two dating?" Lexi asked, trying to hide her smile.

"No, yes... oh, hell, I have no idea. All I know is the man makes my knees weak, and when he walks past me, I just want to grab him and kiss him. That is, when I don't want to slap him across the face because he's driving me crazy."

"Is it really okay to bring Vincent by, or will it annoy him? I have to admit he really wants to meet Julian, but if it's not the right time, then I'll explain it to him."

"No, bring him by. If Julian goes with Hunter, then we can see more of each other. And if you say Vincent's a good guy, that's all the recommendation I need. Anyone has to be better than that strange guy—Reid? Something's off about him, and I really don't feel like talking to him all hours of the night on campaign things. I'll work my magic on the big guy, don't worry. It'll be fine." Christina glanced over her shoulder and saw Claire heading in Julian's direction. Suddenly feeing territorial, Christina excused herself and ran off in pursuit.

Left on her own, Lexi's head began to swim with excitement. *Oh my God, I think I just got Vincent a meeting with Julian Stone.* It took every bit of self-control she had to not do a happy dance in the middle of the ballroom.

The party finally began to pick up, and the elite of San Francisco poured into the ballroom at an alarming rate. Donation checks were being written left and right, and the champagne flowed. Lexi stood off to the side and took inventory of the guests, noting that about half of the people on the hit list were already in the room. Celebrities that Lexi had only seen on television stood ten feet away from her, and she had to fight the urge to gawk at them or ask for an autograph. When Cameron Lett, the star of the biggest action film of the year, said hello to her and complimented her on her dress, Lexi was completely star struck. Fortunately, Leigh found her and led her back to the table before she could make a fool of herself.

"I can't believe all the people who I recognize from the newspaper and magazines," Lexi told Leigh as she watched Anna, Erik, and Madison make their entrance down the staircase. Madison was dressed to the nines, complete with long gloves and a sparkly tiara tucked neatly into her hair. Anna's husband, Erik, was a well-known photographer in the business, and as soon as they made it off the last step, people crowded around the couple, greeting them and admiring their daughter, who instantly became the center of attention.

"I saw you talking to Julian Stone earlier." Leigh leaned in closer to get the skinny. "Is he nice?"

"Yeah, he was a normal person. I think I might have gotten Vincent a meeting or at least lunch with him. Word is he wasn't too thrilled by Reid when they had their meeting last week, so hopefully Vincent can dazzle him a little."

"That's awesome, Lexi! What a snag he would be for Hunter."

Lexi continued watching the people come in and out of the room, marking them present and accounted for on her mental tally. Out of the corner of her eye, she spied a very distinguished-looking taller man with long, whitened hair standing off to the side, talking with someone. She knew the man to be Paolo Marradesi, one of the heads of Marradesi Cosmetics. Curious, she sprung to her feet and decided to do a little snooping and perhaps grab a snack from the flock of servers hovering around the man.

"I'll be back. I'm going to grab something to eat."

Just as she got close to the spot where he had been standing, the sound of Paolo's fluent Italian faded. She looked around and saw him being led across the room by his wife Francesca where he was greeted by a large group of people, one of whom was David Reid. Any chance she had of eavesdropping was gone unless she wanted to risk contact with Reid. Dejected, she grabbed a crab cake and continued her people watching from a secluded corner of the room.

"Lexi?"

She spun around to see Mrs. Dee standing right beside her with two glasses of wine in her hand. She offered one to Lexi.

"You look spectacular, dear." Mrs. Dee smiled warmly.

"Thank you." Lexi blushed. "What are you doing lurking in the corner?"

Mrs. Dee sighed. "I need a few minutes to myself. There are quite a few people here, and a person can only make small talk for so long before they want to scream. Besides, I saw you standing here by yourself and figured I'd come keep you company."

"You weren't kidding about there being a lot of people here."

"What do you think of the gala so far?"

"I've never seen anything like it. We didn't have parties like this where I lived before I moved to San Francisco." Lexi chuckled as Mrs. Dee shook a few hands of people passing by.

"I have to ask, how are you enjoying your job?"

"It's great."

Mrs. Dee didn't even try to hide her surprise. "Really? You enjoy working for Vincent?"

"Sure. He can be short tempered, impatient, and stubborn, but I pay attention to the way he does things and make sure that everything is in order for him. That seems to help make him less irritable. He actually chatted with me today, so I think maybe I'm making progress," Lexi said hopefully. "But underneath all the hostility, he's a nice guy. I can tell."

"That's wonderful. I'm glad you don't regret your decision to come to Hunter. Of course, I hear Mr. Reid is still hoping to change your mind this evening and get you to work for him. He said something about a dance?"

Lexi paled considerably, her jaw dropping in shock. Mrs. Dee quickly laughed and let her off the hook. "I'm sorry, dear. I was just kidding. The Reid tango is infamous. I assumed Leigh warned you."

Lexi let out a huge sigh of relief and watched Mrs. Dee greet more guests. She introduced Lexi to the Warners, who owned a large investment firm based in Seattle, as Lexi knew from her cards. They were considering moving their base of operations to San Francisco, so Vincent wanted to make sure he took a moment to introduce himself.

"What do you do at Hunter, Lexi?" Mrs. Warner asked.

"I'm Mr. Drake's assistant."

"How is he to work with?"

"He's wonderful. Everyone at Hunter is. It's like a big family, very supportive and welcoming. I'm very happy there."

"I've heard wonderful things about them, so I told Arnold we needed to come say hello. He can be so stubborn sometimes, but when I get a feeling about things, I make him listen to me. For some reason, I have this feeling that

Hunter is a company we could work with." Her husband gave her a little nod, indicating he saw someone else he needed to talk to. "Duty calls. I must go be a social butterfly. It was lovely meeting you, Lexi."

"You too, Mrs. Warner. Good luck in the marathon." Lexi remembered this detail from her research at the last second.

"Thank you so much!" Mrs. Warner turned to Mrs. Dee and beamed. "I like this girl. We'll talk more later. Tell Vincent to save me a dance."

"Brava, Lexi!" Mrs. Dee clapped happily. "Mary Warner is one tough nut to crack, and you just impressed her."

"Oh, thank God. This is so nerve-racking trying to keep everyone straight. She was either training for a marathon or had recently taken up painting, but I couldn't see her wearing a stained art smock, so I went with my gut. I don't know how Vincent does this." Lexi glanced around and saw Anna and Erik slowly inching their way across the room.

Mrs. Dee smiled and watched the crowd move around them. Lexi saw her nod her head and make eye contact with certain guests, giving them that extra welcome to make them feel more comfortable. Her floor length dress sparkled as the light from the candles on the table flickered, casting rainbows on the curtains behind her. Lexi's eye was drawn to a spectacular piece of jewelry around her neck.

"I love that necklace."

The gorgeous emerald solitaire was framed by diamonds on either side. The way it caught the low light in the room and sparkled was magnificent. The matching pair of emerald earrings brought out the deep color in her eyes.

She touched her neck gently. "It was a gift from my son." The pride in her voice told Lexi the piece of jewelry was very special to her.

"Well, he has great taste."

Mrs. Dee was clearly distracted by something and said, "In some things, yes. But not everything."

Lexi turned and followed her gaze up toward the entrance, and that's when she saw them. Vincent and Jade were perched at the top of the staircase, looking like a perfect wedding cake topper, except for the fact that the bride was dressed more like a streetwalker than a virgin. Jade, of course, was striking a pose and waiting until everyone in the room whispered and pointed at them. Her dress was a reflective silver rather than white, the hemline barely hitting mid-thigh.

She stood on her tiptoes and gave Vincent a peck on the cheek, revealing the deep V in the back of her dress that went lower than good taste should allow. Lexi was certain most of the attention Jade was garnering wasn't positive, but Jade didn't seem to mind in the least as she continued preening for all to see. As Vincent offered his elbow to her, she snaked her arm around it, and the pair began their descent.

They were such opposites. Lexi couldn't understand what Vincent saw in her. Other than the fact that she was beautiful, she was nothing like him. He was focused and determined. She was flighty and all over the place. Vincent worked his tail off day in and day out, but Jade's biggest concern seemed to be choosing the correct nail polish, yelling at her agent, and deciding where to make Vincent take her to dinner. They continued their approach, Jade basking in the attention, while Vincent was all business, completely focused on work and scanning the room for the people he needed to make contact with.

While Sean looked debonair in a just-one-of-the-guys way, Vincent looked sophisticated, aristocratic even. He walked into the room, and people whispered and pointed at him, intimidated, but captivated. Women blushed when he smiled in their direction, and men nodded their heads respectfully. His crisp, black tuxedo was a perfect contrast to the casual disarray of his hair, which Lexi could tell he tried very hard to tame. But in the end, it had a mind of its own, and once he ran his hand through it nervously, as he so often did, the sexy, untamed waves returned.

Lexi had no idea how long she had stood there, heart fluttering wildly in her chest, but she was vaguely aware that she had begun mumbling. "Heavens. It should be illegal to look so good. I mean just look at him."

Mrs. Dee overheard her quiet ramblings and smiled. "He is a handsome young man. However, his choice of dates makes my skin crawl."

Lexi stifled a laugh.

"Oh, my goodness, did I say that out loud? How embarrassing."

"You think that's embarrassing?" Lexi chuckled, sipping the wine in her glass. "What if I told you I had a crush on him in high school and never had the guts to say a single word to him? I was so shy that he didn't even remember me when I started working for Hunter. Now *that's* embarrassing. Oh, and I've been giving Jade regular sugar and whole milk in her coffee instead of Splenda and non-fat milk for the past two weeks because I hate the way she barks 'Lexi, coffee' every time she steps foot in the office."

As soon as the words had left her mouth, Lexi wanted to suck them back in, but something about Mrs. Dee's kind disposition put Lexi at ease and made her say things she wouldn't normally share with anyone but Hope.

Mrs. Dee arched an eyebrow at Lexi's confession. "Really?"

"Unfortunately, yes, to all of it. I was hoping the extra calories would put Jade in a better mood, but sadly, my plan failed. And the thing with Vincent... never mind. " Lexi sighed and wistfully stared at Vincent leading Jade in their direction. She watched the seductive way his shoulders rolled with each graceful step and the tempting way the corners of his mouth twitched as he smiled at the guests around him. As he scanned the room, he finally caught Lexi's eye, and her stomach flipped when his eyes locked on her. Rather than look away, his intense gaze raked over her body, as if taking in every detail from her hair to her shoes, making her cheeks warm with blush.

"Well, he was an unobservant boob in high school," Mrs. Dee whispered in her ear as Vincent and Jade came to stand beside them, Vincent's eyes still fixed on Lexi. "However, that may be changing."

Jade appeared to be utterly bored until she saw Lexi. Then she cast a murderous glare, looking her up and down, appraising her gown and trying her best to make Lexi feel inferior. "Well, isn't this cozy?" Jade sneered.

Vincent shot Jade a reproachful look, and then turned his attention back to the women. "Ladies, you both look beautiful this evening." He briefly met Lexi's eye again and smiled, then he kissed Mrs. Dee on the cheek. "Mother, they're almost ready for you to give your speech."

10

Lexi froze, looking repeatedly from Vincent to Mrs. Dee as her face turned a bright shade of red. "D for Drake... Mrs. Drake?" Lexi squeaked out, stumbling slightly from the shock of it all.

"Please, call me Elizabeth."

Everything began moving in slow motion for Lexi as she watched Vincent and Jade exchange a confused look while Elizabeth simply grinned. The conversation she had been having with Mrs. Drake moments ago came roaring through her head, and her embarrassment grew exponentially with each passing second.

Lexi pointed a shaky finger at Mrs. Dee. "You—you're Mrs. D-Drake?" Her throat constricted uncomfortably.

"Yes, dear. I'm Mrs. Drake," Elizabeth said with a smirk, the same smirk she had seen on...

Lexi spun to face Vincent, and then she glanced back over her shoulder. "You're his mother?" Mrs. Dee nodded her head while Vincent stared at Lexi like she was a lunatic. "Oh, my God, now I remember." Lexi clasped her hand over her mouth as a vague memory of Elizabeth in the kitchen of her house making sandwiches for the yearbook committee hit her like a ton of bricks. She had probably only crossed paths with Elizabeth Drake a handful of times, but now each and every one of the encounters became crystal clear in her memory. Lexi kicked herself for not recognizing her sooner. "And I just told you..." Lexi's voice trailed off as the room began to spin.

She felt so stupid. Leigh had told her Vincent's family owned the company, but she had been so flustered over seeing him again, that she hadn't put it all together...until now. Not only had Lexi said these things to Vincent's mother, she's said them to the *owner* of the company.

"What's wrong with you, Lexi? Are you drunk?" Jade snapped. "Who the hell did you think you were talking to?"

Lexi didn't know if she should laugh or cry. She opened her mouth and random sputtering came out, so she tried to cover the verbal breakdown with coughing. "Sorry, crab cake down the wrong pipe." She sank down into a chair, covered her face, and tried to catch her breath.

Someone, please kill me, Lexi thought over and over in her head.

Vincent took a step closer to check on Lexi, but Jade wrenched his arm and held him at her side. Instead, he asked stiffly from a distance, "Are you okay?"

Jade rolled her eyes and did nothing to hide her displeasure. "She's fine, Vincent. Come on, let's get a drink. I see some *interesting* people over by the bar. Sober up, Lexi, before you make a complete ass of yourself. Elizabeth," Jade said with a curt nod, then steered Vincent away from the women.

Mrs. Drake shrugged her son and his girlfriend away with a wave of her hand. "Always a pleasure, Jade," she said through gritted teeth as she sat down and turned her attention to Lexi. "Are you feeling better, dear? Ignore Jade. I do."

"Jade is the least of my worries right now. Can we please erase the last ten minutes from the record? That, or just kill me now and put me out of my misery." Lexi's cheeks flamed red with embarrassment as the realization sank in that she had just confessed her deepest, darkest, secret crush to none other than Vincent's mother. She was absolutely mortified and afraid to look Mrs. Drake in the face.

Elizabeth's warm hand settled on Lexi's shoulder. "I only have a few minutes, but I need to make a confession, Lexi. I remembered you." Her voice was as soft as a whisper. "As soon as I saw your name on the job application, I knew who you were. I may be the president of this company, but before we hire someone from the outside, I'm personally involved in the selection of candidates. And when I saw your resume, I knew you were exactly what we needed."

"Mrs. Drake," Lexi started, only to be interrupted.

"It's Elizabeth, dear."

"Elizabeth," Lexi said slowly, "why exactly am I here? I don't want to be a charity case." Lexi's pride kicked in, and her insecurities roared to the surface as she began convincing herself that Elizabeth only hired her because she felt sorry for her.

"It most definitely was not charity, Lexi. You're here because I needed you, because my son needed you. Whether he understands that yet or not. It's a long story, but he needed someone to be on his side." She laughed. "Someone to be brutally honest with him, but most importantly, someone he can trust."

"And that's me?" Lexi asked incredulously.

"I think so," Elizabeth said softly. "He's been having a hard time the last few years, trusting the wrong people and making more enemies than friends. In case you hadn't noticed, he's not the same boy he was back in high school. I hoped I could trust you to keep an eye on him, if that makes sense, and you've come through in spades."

"You do know we weren't friends in high school."

Elizabeth smiled sweetly at her and patted Lexi's hand. "True, but Anna spoke highly of you back then, and I volunteered in the school office once a week. You'd be amazed the gossip you hear in there."

"Oh, gosh," Lexi cringed imagining the rumors that had probably been spread about the weirdo new girl during her two years at Riverdale High.

"Don't worry, dear. It was all good about you. Your teachers always spoke of how hard working you were. Vincent on the other hand ..."

Lexi couldn't stifle her laughter. She had overheard plenty of stories about Vincent's antics senior year, mainly pranks he pulled not only on the students, but faculty as well. "Remember the time the football team dared him to put the principal's house up for sale in the newspaper? The poor man came home one day and saw the 'for sale' sign and thought his wife had thrown him out."

Elizabeth rolled her eyes and joined Lexi in her laughter. When Vincent appeared out of nowhere, the two women could barely breathe. He watched the pair wipe their eyes on tiny cocktail napkins.

"Mother, they're ready for your speech. Dad has been looking everywhere for you."

Elizabeth stood up and wrapped her arms around Lexi. "I'm glad you're with us, dear. And I hope you can forgive my tiny deception. We'll talk more about it later, okay? And if my son does anything to upset you, let me know." On her way to find her husband, she patted Vincent's cheek, and then she disappeared into the crowd.

"Do I even want to know what that was about?" Vincent asked Lexi.

Lexi tried to hide her grin, but the attempt was futile. "Probably not." She watched his brow pucker in confusion and laughed. "Where's Jade?"

Vincent shook his head. "She's in the restroom, something about her dress being tight. I have no idea."

Their conversation was interrupted when the music paused and the lights dimmed in preparation for the program to begin. Everyone in the room quieted down, many taking their seats at the dinner tables. A portly man with white hair took the stage to say a few words of welcome to the many guests that filled the ballroom. Vincent remained beside Lexi, his attention focused on the gentleman speaking.

Next, a representative from the children's hospital launched into a speech about the generosity of Hunter Advertising over the years. Through Hunter's charitable giving, many programs and buildings at the hospital had been improved, allowing for a higher quality of healthcare for children at the San Francisco hospital.

Vincent casually reached for something off a passing server's platter and stepped closer to Lexi. His earthy cologne filled the air, making Lexi's head swim. She tried not to react as his shoulder brushed against hers, but her heart fluttered like a hummingbird's wings when she felt his head dip towards hers, his deep voice whispering in her ear.

"So, who's here?" He kept his head tilted toward hers so he could hear her response without disturbing the people around them with their discussion.

"Most of the people on our list," Lexi said in a low voice, sipping her wine to hide their conversation. She listed who she had seen in attendance as they compared notes.

"Paolo Marradesi?"

Lexi nodded and made the mistake of looking up at him. The proximity of his face, the curve of his luscious lips, and the heat of his body sent her senses into overdrive. She found herself staring at his lips longer than she should have, wondering if they were as soft as they looked and imagining, for just a second, what they would feel like skimming down her neck or along her collarbone.

She cleared her throat and answered his question. "Yep. He's here. I tried to spy on him, but he got away." Lexi took a long swig of her wine and looked anywhere but at Vincent's face. Even so, out of the corner of her eye she saw him looking at her and doing something completely out of character—smiling.

"Explain that one, please."

"Oh, don't panic, I wasn't hiding under the table, wearing a fake mustache or lurking behind a large fern. I just tried to get close and eavesdrop on his conversation to see if I could pick up anything we could—I mean anything that *you* could use when you spoke with him later."

Vincent came even closer, his lips right next to her ear. "And how did that go?" he asked with a chuckle in his voice.

"He was on to me and ran away with his wife."

"Stalk anyone else before I arrived?"

"Stalk is such a harsh word. I prefer corporate reconnaissance or intentional overhearing."

Vincent's shoulders shook as he silently laughed. Lexi gave him a quick elbow to the side, and then joined him in hushed laughter.

"Wow, I made Vincent Drake laugh. Do I get a plaque or something?" Lexi was happy to see Vincent let his guard down with her even for just a few moments.

"You're absolutely ridiculous sometimes, do you know that?" He quickly composed himself and put back on the usual Vincent façade before anyone noticed.

"Be nice or I won't tell you about my conversation with Julian Stone."

Vincent snapped to attention at the mention of Stone's name, moving even closer to her, not wanting to miss a word she was about to say. All hint of playfulness was gone. He was again focused on business as his large body crowded hers, waiting for an explanation.

"You spoke to Julian Stone?"

"Technically, *he* came over and spoke to *me*."

Vincent's mouth fell open and he was about to ask for every detail, but then a loud round of applause echoed through the room when Elizabeth took the stage, halting their conversation.

Lexi glanced up at Vincent and saw him smiling proudly at his mother as she made her way to the podium. She listened as Elizabeth spoke lovingly of her father who had founded Hunter Advertising when she was a young girl. She shared a few anecdotes from her childhood and explained how philanthropy was ingrained in her at a very young age by her parents and that she was proud to be continuing the Hunter tradition of giving back. She thanked everyone for their astounding generosity, then invited them to take to the dance floor and enjoy the rest of their evening.

The music started again. Some guests sauntered out to the dance floor while others began milling around the room, getting a drink or grabbing a bite to eat. A loud trio of men came over to Vincent with hands extended.

Lexi immediately recognized them from the hit list as the Lewis brothers from the successful line of board games. The word on the street was that they were going to modernize some of their classic games and wanted to do a huge national and international ad campaign. Vincent smoothly greeted each man by name. He even cast a quick glance in Lexi's direction to see if she noticed he'd done his homework. Lexi smiled and gave him a quick nod of praise. With him buried deep in conversation, she tried to slip away, giving the men some privacy to discuss the business matters at hand. She wasn't able to take two steps before she felt Vincent's strong hand clamp down on her wrist and hold her in place.

"And who is this beautiful young lady that's tryin' to sneak away from us?" James Lewis, the oldest of the three sons asked in a deep southern twang.

Vincent released her wrist and slid his warm hand to her lower back, gently ushering her toward the gentlemen who were so interested in meeting her. She was acutely aware of the physical contact, her body warming in response to his light touch. She tried to steady her breathing but nearly turned to jelly when he gave her back a reassuring pat.

"Good evening, Mr. Lewis. I'm Lexi White, Mr. Hunter's assistant. How are you all doing this evening?"

"We're great, little lady. Thank you for askin'. So what's it like to work for old Vince here?"

"Vince," Lexi smirked, knowing he probably wanted to strangle her for calling him that, "is wonderful to work for, but probably not as much fun as you gentlemen are. I hear you three are quite the pranksters." Stories of them having one another's cars towed from fancy restaurants under the guise of being repossessed or of them having thousands of pumpkins delivered to each other's lawns on Halloween made the tabloids constantly. So many rumors swirled around these three that no one could tell the fact from the fiction anymore.

"Ha! You're right darlin', we do know how to have fun. Did you hear my latest?" Lexi smiled and shook her head as James Lewis laughed loudly. "I convinced Joey there that he was invited to have dinner with the president. I made fake invitations and everythin', had my girl call his girl, made it sound all official. He strolled up to the White House like he owned the place and told them he was invited personally by the president himself. The Secret Service had him flat on his stomach in the bushes in less than twenty seconds flat. He cried like a baby as they threw him in the pokey."

"It was a holding cell, not the pokey, Jimmy, you fool. And I hit my head on the sidewalk. That's why I was cryin'." Joey scowled at his brother for a second before a grin snuck out. "I did nearly soil myself in them bushes, though, when the feds talked about prison. I'm too pretty to go to jail."

Everyone laughed as the brothers continued to banter back and forth with one another. When the laughter finally died down, James agreed to an appointment with Vincent early the next week. Lexi pulled out her BlackBerry and confirmed the date, added it to Vincent's schedule, and sent an E-mail to Mr. Lewis's assistant to make sure everything was in place before the men left. The men walked away still chuckling amongst themselves.

"You were amazing with them."

"Just doing my job," Lexi said nonchalantly, even though inside she was jumping up and down at his praise.

Vincent visibly relaxed at that point. A smile crept onto his face, and the tightness in his body vanished, replaced by a hint of the smooth, carefree demeanor that Lexi remembered all too well from years ago. He ran his hand through his hair, then slipped his arm around Lexi's waist. He held her tightly against his side as he led her through the room. "Now, tell me about the miracle you pulled off with Stone."

Lexi's heart pounded so loudly in her chest that she almost missed the question. All she could think about were his fingers pressing firmly into her hip and the delicious warmth that rushed to all parts of her body from the contact.

"It...it wasn't a miracle. Just a lucky coincidence. Turns out I know his assistant, Christina, and while we were talking, he came over and introduced himself, asked a few questions, and after a few minutes of me singing your praises, he asked me to introduce you to him."

"What did he ask about me? And what did you say exactly?"

Lexi shook her head. "What are you, thirteen years old? You sound just like Sean. What is it with you two? I had no idea you were so girlie." When Vincent raised his eyebrow, stubbornly waiting for an answer, Lexi rolled her eyes. "Relax, *Vince*. I told him you were very good at what you did. Oh, and I agreed with him when he said you were stiff, so if he offers you a drink, I think you should take it and loosen up around him if at all humanly possible."

"You said I was stiff?" His voice sounded confused. "And stop calling me Vince. I despise that name."

Lexi was about to explain her comment when she saw David Reid waving at her from the dance floor. As subtle as an elephant, David then began shouting her name and heading in their direction. His annoying overzealous behavior caught Vincent's attention. "Looks like someone wants to put his name on your dance card, Lexi."

11

A grinning David Reid snaked his way through the crowd, his eyes devouring Lexi with each step he took.

"Crap, Vincent. Please, I swear to God, I'll never call you Vince or say you're stiff again if you get me away from him. I'm going to make a break for it to the ladies' room. Just tell him I ate a bad scallop or something. That should keep him away from me for the rest of the night." Lexi turned to find the restroom, but it was too late. David was on them lightning fast.

"Lexi, small world! How wonderful to see you again. Please, you must do me the honor of sharing a dance with me. Perhaps I can get the band to play a nice tango for us?" His eyebrows waggled flirtatiously. When she felt Vincent poke her playfully in the back, urging her toward David, she nearly laughed in his face.

"Mr. Reid, I . . . I . . ."

"Please, call me David. Now about that dance."

"David, I—"

Vincent stepped between Lexi and David. "Sorry, Reid. I made Alexandra sign a 'no tango clause' in her contract when I hired her. She's only allowed to dance with a member of Hunter Advertising while in our employment or she risks losing her job." Vincent's deadpan expression stunned David into silence. "Of course, truth be told, I'd never fire her. She's the best hire we've made in years."

David's jaw clenched as Vincent smiled smugly beside Lexi. "Well, then. I'll let you two go. I'll just have to find another dance partner." He gave a small nod to Lexi. "It was wonderful to see you again, and when you wise up and quit working for Drake, give me a call." David slipped a business card into Lexi's hand, but not before he kissed her knuckles, leaving a moist reminder of their short encounter before disappearing into the crowd.

Lexi looked down at her hand, and her lip curled in repulsion. "Ew."

"I wonder how many asses those lips have kissed tonight." Vincent, always the gentleman, handed her a handkerchief from his pocket. Lexi grabbed it and gratefully wiped her knuckles clean. She pulled some hand sanitizer from her purse and used a generous amount to disinfect the area.

"'No tango clause.' Nice save, boss." Lexi grinned at Vincent as they headed toward the bar.

"He believed me for a good thirty seconds too." Vincent waved to the bartender, and two glasses of wine appeared. He handed one to Lexi and kept the other for himself. A few awkward seconds passed in which Vincent didn't say anything. He simply sipped his wine and watched Lexi. His eyes slowly roamed over her face, taking in every detail before settling on her lips. "There was no way in hell I was letting that slime ball get his hands on you," Vincent admitted as he raised his glass to his lips.

Lexi watched the way his green eyes twinkled and then darkened as he moved closer. Her heart raced. She tried to look away, but she was mesmerized by the way the corner of his mouth turned up into a dark, seductive smile. Just looking at him made her feel sinful. She took in every detail of his features, even the small scar on his chin, and longed to run her fingers over his plump lower lip, but she knew it would never happen. It was all just a fantasy, one that at the moment was way too real for her heart to stand.

"Vincent, I—" Her breathless plea was interrupted by the shriek of a banshee.

"Vincent, darling. Sorry I left you all alone. Jon Luce from *Vogue* just wouldn't let me go. He tried to talk me into flying to Paris with him for a photo shoot. He's such a horrible flirt, and you know he'd do *anything* to work with me. He even offered me the cover." Jade rudely wedged herself between Vincent and Lexi, nearly knocking the glass out of Lexi's hand. "You must have been so bored being out here all alone without anyone *interesting* to talk to." She looked over her shoulder. "You can leave now. Vincent is done babysitting you. Go find Leigh and the rest of the employees and talk about ... well, whatever it is you people talk about." She waved her hand dismissively at Lexi in an effort to shoo her away.

Lexi's glass hit the counter, hard. Vincent had snapped his jaw shut and glared at the back of Jade's head but said nothing to defend Lexi. Irritated, Lexi took a deep calming breath and fought the burning desire to tell Jade exactly where she could go.

"Yes, I better get back to my 'people.' I don't want to miss out on all the good gossip. You'd be amazed at the inside information I get to hear about jobs, campaigns, the latest scandals, what models are in and which ones are on their way *out*." Lexi fixed her gaze on Jade as the corner of her lips turned up mockingly. Without a word to Vincent, she turned on her heel and left the two of them at the bar, stunned by her outburst.

Lexi stormed through the room and tried to get her temper under control. Part of her wanted to march back over to them and lay into Vincent for allowing Jade to be so rude. A larger part of her wanted to toss Jade into the fountain in the lobby and hold her head under the water until she turned blue.

Just when she was about to go back and give Vincent a piece of her mind, someone gave her a hug around the waist. "Lexi! I missed you. You look pretty." She glanced down and found Madison clinging to her with a huge smile on her face. Lexi's spirits were instantly raised upon seeing her. She looked like a tiny princess. Anna and Erik stood beside her, smiling at their daughter.

Lexi crouched down and gave Madison a kiss on the cheek, her bad mood forgotten. "Let me look at you." She held out Madison's arms and twirled her around so her dress could flow and flap in the breeze. "You have to be the prettiest girl in the room tonight."

"Are you sure this dress doesn't make me look short?" Madison asked as she stood self-consciously on her tiptoes and pouted.

Lexi glanced over at Anna, who rolled her eyes and mouthed the word 'Jade' to Lexi. "No, Madison," Lexi reassured her. "Whoever told you that knows absolutely nothing about fashion. You look like you're at least eight years old, honey."

At those words, the small girl's frown became a radiant smile. She ran over to Erik and hopped up and down. "Dad, Dad. Lexi said I look like I am eight years old! Can you believe it?"

The tall blond gentleman scooped up his daughter and kissed her cheek. His handsome features lit up when his daughter was in his arms. "That Miss Lexi sounds like a smart woman. Now, how about you introduce me to your new friend who I've been hearing so much about?"

"There she is! She's the pretty lady over there." Madison pointed at Lexi and giggled when Lexi waved back at her.

Erik strode over with his hand extended and a warm smile on his face. "Hello, I'm Erik Caldwell, Anna's husband. It's wonderful to finally meet you. Madison hasn't stopped telling me about the secret stash of cookies you have over there at the office. And Anna might have mentioned you a few thousand times in the last week or so, as well."

"It's very nice to meet you too, Erik. I had a chance to see some of your photographs in the recent Hunter campaigns, and they are absolutely spectacular." Madison stretched her arms out to Lexi, and she happily picked the tiny girl up. "Madison, are you having fun with your mommy and daddy tonight?"

"Yes, but it's almost bed time. Daddy says I have to leave before the car turns into a pumpkin like Cinderella's did. I don't like pumpkins." She wrinkled her nose at the thought of sitting in a slimy pumpkin.

"Well, I'm glad I got to see you before you left." She leaned in and whispered in the little girl's ear. "Did you see the dessert table?"

Madison's eyes grew huge. "Mommy! Lexi and I are going to get some dessert. We'll be right back." She wiggled out of Lexi's arms and began pulling her toward the elaborate table full of sweets.

"Don't get anything on your dress, Maddie!" Anna called after them.

Lexi and Madison considered every single dessert on the table and picked three to try. The chocolate mousse was the unanimous favorite, so they had another. They grabbed an extra one for Anna and made their way back to Maddie's parents. When they arrived, Vincent and Jade had joined Anna and Erik. Jade had her usual scowl on her face as she pawed at Vincent. He, however, looked distracted as he scanned the room, appearing once again to be focused on business.

"Mommy, try this! Lexi and I ate two of them, it's so good." She thrust the little cup of mousse at her mother and smiled.

"Tsk, tsk," Jade shook her head from side to side. "Two desserts? Really? Keep that up, Madison, and you'll be big as a house."

Everyone turned and gawked at her incredulously. *Who on Earth tells a five-year-old she's going to be as big as a house? Jade, the psychotic skinny bitch does, of course.*

Without missing a beat, Lexi jumped to Madison's defense. "Madison, you're beautiful. Don't ever let anyone tell you differently." She gave Jade a dirty look and put herself protectively between the little girl and Jade's vicious mouth.

Anna looked like she was ready to strangle Jade, but Erik quickly put his hand on her arm and gave it a little squeeze. "Thank you, Lexi," Anna said quietly as she dug her spoon into the mousse and grinned. "You're right, honey. This is delicious! You know what? I think I would like another one too, just like you and Lexi. Can you show me where they are?" Anna took her daughter's hand and led her away, but not before she gave her husband a pointed look.

When Madison was safely out of earshot, Erik's smile faded, and he focused on Vincent. "Vincent, I don't know what the hell you are thinking," he hissed in his ear loud enough that Lexi could hear. Jade had since flitted off to no doubt rub elbows with the next influential person she could use in some way.

Vincent tensed. "Erik, enough. She didn't mean anything by it."

"Are you nuts? She's rude and obnoxious, as usual. Unless she does some amazing tricks in bed, I have no idea what you see in her." Erik didn't flinch when Vincent turned and the two stood nose to nose, the air thick with tension.

"Stay out of it, Erik. I'm tired of this conversation. If she says something you don't like, ignore her."

"My mother raised me to be a gentleman, but if she says one more rude thing to my daughter, your niece I might remind you, I'm going to forget everything I was taught and let her have it."

Before Vincent could respond, Jade returned in a rush and kissed him, leaving a crimson stain on his cheek from her lipstick. "Sorry, I saw a casting director, and I think he's going to call me with a part in his pilot. Isn't that great?"

"Fantastic." Vincent sounded less than enthusiastic, and stayed fixated on Erik as he wiped the smear of lipstick from his face. "Jade, we need to talk." Vincent took her by the elbow and led her off to a private corner where the two got into a rather heated exchange. Even though Vincent kept his voice low and his expression guarded, Jade was all drama with flailing arms and screeches loud enough for Lexi to hear its whiny timber. After a few minutes, she stormed away and Vincent sulked back to Erik's side looking miserable. Anna and Madison returned, and he bent down and hugged his niece fiercely.

"I love you, Maddie," he crooned to the small girl.

"I love you too, Uncle Vince." She kissed his nose and wrapped her arms around his neck.

"And you are the most beautiful girl at the party." He spun her around in his arms, smiling as she giggled.

"That's what Lexi said too."

Vincent stole a sheepish glance at Lexi. "Lexi is a very smart lady." He kept looking at her, pleading with his eyes for her to accept his pathetic attempt at an apology for standing by and letting Jade pick her apart. She knew apologies didn't come easy to him, so when he mouthed the words "I'm sorry," she nearly melted.

She watched him caress his niece's hair and could tell he actually felt pained at the thought of her tiny feelings being hurt. Erik watched the interaction between the two of them closely, ready to step in if Jade came within ten feet of his daughter again. Still wondering what the hell Vincent was doing with a viper like Jade, Lexi decided to show him the compassion he hadn't had the courtesy to show her.

"Can I get that in writing? The part about me being very smart?" Lexi gently teased, smiling when she saw Vincent let out the breath he had been holding.

"Absolutely."

"Uncle Vincent, can we please dance?" Madison asked sweetly. "I have to go home soon. The pumpkin is coming, and I haven't had a turn to dance with a prince yet."

It was easy to see that Vincent could deny her nothing. "I would love to. Let's show these people how it's done." He perched her on the top of his feet, and together they swayed and twirled, their dance looking perfectly choreographed.

"She is gorgeous," Lexi said to Erik. Anna had gone off to say her goodbyes to her mother.

"She is one of a kind. She makes every day an adventure for us. That's for sure," he chuckled. He reached out and slipped his hand around Lexi's arm. "May I have this dance?"

"What a great idea. Honey, take her out for a dance, then gather up Madison and we can go." Anna had returned and was ready to leave. She put her hands on Lexi's shoulders and nudged her toward Erik. "Go have some fun, Lexi."

Hesitantly, Lexi took Erik's hand and followed him onto the parquet flooring in the center of the room. Couples swayed and spun around them as they navigated themselves to an open space in the middle. Erik took one of Lexi's hands and placed it on his shoulder and took the other in his hand, then pulled her close to him as he wrapped his arm around her waist.

Immediately, Lexi felt something hard beneath her foot. "Sorry." Her cheeks flooded with a deep blush.

"Something tells me that you're used to being in charge. Why don't you let me lead, and I'll take care of you for a change?"

His warm smile and unexpectedly kind words melted a piece of Lexi's heart that she tried her best to keep hidden behind a sturdy wall. She was always the one to be in charge. After Marie died, she'd had to step up and mature faster than any of her friends. When Harry got sick, she took care of him by herself for the most part, and then after he died, she took care of herself, relying on no one as she tried to find her way in the world. She was the caregiver, the reliable one, self-sufficient. She was…alone, and if she thought about it too long, the sadness overwhelmed her. She swallowed back tears and buried her feelings of loneliness deep inside, focusing on what she had rather than all that she had lost in her short life.

"I'm sorry, did I say something wrong?" Erik saw her tear-filled eyes, and his brow puckered. "Anna will skin me alive if I upset you."

Lexi shook her head. "No, it's me. Just feeling sorry for myself, that's all. You have a beautiful family." She watched Vincent and Madison scoot past them and smiled.

"I am very blessed." Trying to lift her spirits, Erik changed the subject. "So, are you ready to kill my brother-in-law yet? Has he made you cry? Because if he ever does, from what I hear all you have to do is tell Sean, and Vincent will have a black eye. Elizabeth has warned him to be on his best behavior as well. She's watching him like a hawk. I suspect she has Leigh spying on him for her, and if he steps out of line, she'll rain down on him like the fires of hell."

Lexi laughed. "Vincent's not a bad guy. I don't know what the big deal is about him. He's not that scary." Erik's eyebrow rose in disbelief. "Really, all you have to do is stay one step ahead of him and you're fine. I simply make sure his world is arranged just how he likes it, and I have no problem handling him."

"But the yelling. Most of his other assistants left in tears."

"The only time he ever yelled at me was when I cleaned his office."

Erik laughed. "Oh, I heard about that one."

Lexi blushed. "I think most of San Francisco heard about it the way he carried on. He actually stomped his foot at me. Who does that? But he had a right to be upset. I messed with his space, and it wasn't my place. So I listened and learned, and now we work together in relative peace and harmony."

"It takes a strong woman to deal with my pigheaded brother-in-law."

"Or maybe someone just as pigheaded as he is." Lexi closed her eyes, and let Erik twirl her across the dance floor. He was an exquisite dancer. As the song wound down, he spun them over to Vincent and Madison so he could claim his daughter.

"Come on, darlin', it's time to go."

"Just one more dance, daddy?" Madison pouted and crossed her arms. "I haven't got to dance with you yet."

"Fine, one more dance. But first," he took Lexi's hand and placed it in Vincent's, "Uncle Vincent will have to take care of my dance partner for me. It wouldn't be gentlemanly to leave her alone on the dance floor. How does that sound?" Erik winked at Lexi.

"Perfect!" Madison clapped and climbed onto her father's feet. She looked hopefully between the pair. "Well, come on, dance."

Vincent naturally drew Lexi closer to him, wrapping his arm around her waist. Lexi put her hand on his shoulder to keep space between their bodies. As soon as they started to sway, Lexi trampled his foot.

"Sorry." She was too embarrassed to look him in the eye.

"Stand on his feet. He doesn't mind," Madison offered when she saw Lexi blushing.

"You don't have to do this, Vincent. I'm sure there's someone here you need to talk to. Besides, Jade will have a stroke if she sees us." Lexi tried to slip out of his grasp, but Vincent tightened his hold on her and smiled.

"Jade is off talking to someone, and after all the help you've given to me tonight, I have time for one dance with you ... and any bruises I may get as a result." His warm eyes swept over her face, his features softening. "I'm sorry about earlier, with Jade."

Lexi shrugged her shoulders, but couldn't break eye contact, mesmerized by him up close. "I can take care of myself when it comes to Jade."

Her feisty attitude made Vincent smile. "You certainly can. It's quite refreshing to see, actually." Vincent smiled apologetically. "Still, I should have said something to her. What she said to you was completely uncalled for. She didn't mean any of it."

Lexi threw back her head and laughed. "Oh, she most definitely meant every word of it, Vincent. I have no doubt of that."

"She's very insecure."

"She's very rude too." Lexi sighed. "You've had to make quite a few excuses for her tonight. Don't you ever get tired of it?" She searched his face, trying to get a read on what he could possibly see in Jade.

Vincent closed his eyes and nodded his head.

"Then why on Earth ..." Lexi let her voice trail off. It was not her place to launch into this conversation with Vincent. Their relationship could be described as tentative friends at best, and they were currently in the middle of a huge fundraiser where Vincent still had plenty of work left to do. Definitely not the place to talk about crazy girlfriends.

The two of them danced awkwardly in silence, looking anywhere but at one another. Lexi heard him softly humming the tune that the band was playing, perfectly harmonizing with the instruments. He lightly tapped his fingers on her back to the beat of the music, tickling her and giving her chills.

Needing a distraction, Lexi decided to make small talk on a very safe topic: work. "Have you been able to talk to a lot of people?" Lexi noticed Julian and Christina dancing right behind them.

"Yes, actually. I danced with Mrs. Warner, and she said I'd be hearing from her husband early next week. So when that call comes in, we'll work around their schedule to set up a meeting. I apologize, but you might have to do some rearranging of things."

"No problem, boss." Lexi gave him a mock salute.

"You're too far away." Vincent pulled her closer so that her cheek was nearly against his chest. "Much better. Now we don't have to yell." His chin brushed against the top of her head, and Lexi's heart raced.

He listed off who he had and had not spoken to yet, but Lexi was completely distracted. Dancing with him had nearly given her a heart attack when they were a foot apart, but having her body pressed against his rock hard chest was almost more than she could stand. The earthy smell of his cologne was intoxicating. It took every ounce of her self-control to not wrap her arms around his neck and snuggle close like she had dreamed of doing so many times. His hands felt like blast furnaces on her body, setting on fire everything they touched. A wonderful tingling sensation flowed throughout her body as they danced. She thanked God that her feet were cooperating so that she actually looked like she knew what she was doing on the dance floor.

She pulled her thoughts together and focused on the reason they were there—to work. Christina caught her eye and nodded in her direction. Lexi stood on her tiptoes and put her lips to Vincent's ear as they approached.

"Julian Stone, to your left. He has a soft spot for music, big Beatles fan. Use it."

"Got it," he whispered against her cheek just before he turned her toward the designer. A chill shot down Lexi's back as his hot breath rolled down her neck.

"Lexi." Christina and Julian came dancing up beside them, and Vincent stiffened.

"Relax, Vincent," she purred in his ear, then turned to greet the couple. "Christina, Julian, are you having a nice evening?"

"Absolutely." Julian grinned at Lexi before turning to her dance partner. "Vincent, right? I'm Julian Stone."

"Julian, nice to finally meet you. And I assume this beautiful woman is Christina? Lexi has told me so much about you. You look lovely this evening." Lexi gave him a subtle pat on the back to let him know he was doing well.

"Thank you, Vincent. The gala is spectacular. Thank you for inviting us. I think Hunter's raised a fortune tonight." Christina gushed about how delicious the food was and asked for the name of the party planner for future reference.

"Lexi can get you the names of everyone we used. I'll have her E-mail them to you, if that's all right."

"That would be great. Thanks. After the new line hits the runway, we're going to throw a big bash," Julian said. Lexi suspected he was baiting Vincent to see if he'd jump into shop talk or keep it light.

Vincent played it cool. He didn't launch into a million questions about the line or when it would be hitting the market, just like he hadn't gotten desperate and offered to bring the phone numbers over to Julian personally. He waited. Like a game of chess, the two men asked cautious questions, Julian trying to get Vincent to work information out of him, and Vincent being interested but not nosy. Lexi and Christina collectively sighed in relief when Vincent eased the conversation toward music and the two men became immersed in their discussion of the classics.

Finally, Julian laughed. "He's good, Lexi. You're right!" Julian held out his hand to Vincent. "Have Lexi call Christina next week, and we'll do lunch. You know what, screw lunch. Do you play basketball? I think better when I'm playing."

"Basketball it is. But don't expect me to let you win because I'm interested in working with you," Vincent said, earning another booming laugh from Julian.

"I wouldn't have it any other way, man. Great meeting you, Vince. Lexi, always a pleasure, my record goddess."

"Bye, guys. Christina, I'll talk to you soon."

She and Vincent watched the couple make their way to the bar. Julian was soon surrounded by admirers. Lexi was so excited, she couldn't help herself and hugged Vincent. "You did it! I can't believe the way you worked him. You're brilliant."

The smile on Vincent's face was electric. He held her tighter and buried his face in her hair as they danced. "We did it. Lexi, thank you. I couldn't have done it without you." He pulled back, but kept his face close. His lips were so inviting and just within reach. Lexi began nervously gnawing on her bottom lip to distract herself. Vincent continued to smile and stare at her.

"I'm sorry," he whispered.

"For what?"

"For everything, but most of all for not remembering you."

Lexi's breath hitched in her chest at his words. They had never talked about the fact that he didn't remember her. There really wasn't much to even say about it. It was a lifetime ago for both of them, so he didn't ask and she didn't offer, and that was how they had existed until now.

"How could I not notice you?" he whispered as he reached out and tucked a stray piece of hair behind her ear, his fingers gently brushing against her cheek.

All the blood in her body surged to her face. "Your mom said you were an unobservant boob if that helps." Lexi was trying to lighten the situation before her heart leapt out of her chest and he realized the effect his touch had on her.

He threw his head back and laughed, spinning them in a circle. "I guess I am. I'll try and work on that, okay?"

Lexi could have spent the next few moments over-thinking things and reminding herself to keep her distance from Vincent. She could have acknowledged that she had absolutely nothing to offer this successful, sexy man with a supermodel girlfriend, other than her organizational skills and talent for slipping him greasy burgers on the down low. Instead, for once she simply went with it and enjoyed the feeling of being in his arms. Even if it meant nothing to him, for that dance, she pretended it did.

But eventually, as the music slowed and came to an end, she drifted back to reality. Lexi swallowed, trying to clear her head, but the rumble of his laughter and the heat from his body overwhelmed every sense. He was too much. He was ... everything. She had to stop this train of thought before she was crushed all over again. What better way than to dredge up the past.

"It's not your fault you don't remember me. I was horribly shy." Lexi's chin dropped to her chest, allowing her hair to veil her face from his prying eyes.

"Got over the shyness, did you?" Vincent teased, lifting her chin so he could catch her eye. "Because anyone who stands up to Tony on her first day, stops him in his tracks, and threatens to fire him, then tells me when I'm being an ass ... well, that doesn't exactly sound like something a shy person would do."

"That shy girl is still in there, don't you worry. I've simply gotten better at faking my bravado."

"Well, I'll never tell," he said with a wink as he led her off the dance floor.

Leigh was there to greet them when they stepped back onto the carpet. "Lexi, who knew you were such a good dancer?" Vincent excused himself and headed over to Elizabeth.

"I can't dance to save my life. That was all Vincent." Lexi sighed and watched the guests still on the dance floor swirl around them. After a few minutes, she scanned the room and found Vincent and Elizabeth in what appeared to be a very serious conversation. His face was darkened again, all traces of amusement and fun gone. He appeared to be completely focused on business once again. When she followed their gaze, she found Paolo Marradesi conversing with Adria Parketti. Paolo's wife looked like she wanted to strangle Adria as she flirtatiously ran her hand down the front of Paolo's chest, giggling about something.

"Leigh, Vincent hasn't talked to Paolo yet, has he?" Leigh shook her head no. "Well, don't look now, but Adria Parketti is about to wrap her legs around his waist right in front of his wife. Good Lord, does the woman have no shame?"

Leigh laughed. "Adria? Have shame? You must be kidding."

"I'll be right back." Lexi hurried over to Vincent and Elizabeth and asked, "What's the plan?"

"No plan. No stalking. It's called being patient," Vincent snipped, obviously stressed out.

"I hate to break it to you, but you're running out of time. His wife keeps looking at her watch. She's ready to go home." Vincent raked his hand through his hair.

Elizabeth took a deep breath. "You have to get five minutes with him, Vincent, or we're screwed."

"Go ask his wife to dance," Lexi said as she nudged him and nodded her head toward Francesca Marradesi, who was burning holes into the back of Adria's head as she continued her shameless flirting.

Vincent looked at Lexi as if she'd sprouted a second head. "And that's going to help how?"

Lexi tapped her purse, indicating the note cards she carried with her. "She used to be a prima ballerina, Vincent, you read her bio. She probably loves to dance, but have you noticed she and Paolo haven't stepped on the dance floor all night?"

"No." Vincent crossed his arms like a petulant child. "I know you're new to all this, Lexi, but you don't just steal away the wife of a man of Paolo Marradesi's stature. It simply isn't done."

Elizabeth mulled it over in her head for a minute before reacting. "She's right. Go try and score a few points with Francesca. Be your charming self, and pray that in gratitude she introduces you to her husband."

"That, or Paolo will get jealous and storm the dance floor to reclaim his wife," Lexi added. "Either way, at least you'll get to talk to him. But let's hope it plays out more like Elizabeth said. And if you know any Italian, now would be a good time to use it. *Buona fortuna.*"

Vincent rolled his eyes at the women, took a deep breath, and confidently strode over to Francesca Marradesi. He respectfully bowed his head to Paolo, and then whispered something in Francesca's ear that put a huge smile on her face. She took his hand, and the pair glided onto the dance floor. Lexi noticed Adria Parketti tense when Vincent walked over, and now that he'd absconded with Francesca, she looked absolutely livid.

"I hope this works," Elizabeth murmured. In the next moment, she began cursing under her breath.

"What's wrong?" Lexi scanned the room to see what could be irritating Elizabeth so much. It didn't take long for Lexi to find the source. On the edge of the parquet floor stood Jade with her hands firmly planted on her hips, glaring at Vincent and Francesca waltzing together.

"We have to stop her, or she's going to go out there and make a scene." Elizabeth took a step toward Jade when she was stopped by a group of businessmen and their wives that wanted to thank her for a wonderful evening. Elizabeth was trapped by their small talk while Jade inched closer to Vincent.

Lexi immediately ran over to Leigh and enlisted her help. "Emergency situation. We need to make Jade disappear." Lexi pointed to Jade, who was now tapping her foot furiously.

"Finally! Sean knows a guy—he only has four fingers, but I hear he's good at what he does." When Leigh saw the desperation on Lexi's face, she dropped the act. "What can I do?"

"We just need her to leave Vincent alone for ten minutes. What can we distract her with?"

An evil grin spread across Leigh's face. "I know how to get her feathers riled up over something other than Vincent. Come with me." She took Lexi by the hand and hurried over to Jade, explaining her plan on the way. "Jade hates Martina Korikova. A few years ago they got into it backstage at a runway show in Milan. Martina called her short, low class, and fat, so Jade went nuts. From what I read in the tabloids, Jade went down the runway sporting a swollen eye from where Martina popped her one."

"What do the two of you want?" Jade snapped as soon as Leigh and Lexi stood beside her. "Are you going to dance together? Couldn't find any men willing to be your partners?" she sneered.

Lexi thanked God and every heavenly creature up above that Jade had conveniently disappeared from the ballroom earlier while she and Vincent shared their dance or there would have been another tantrum of Jade's to deal with.

"Always such a ray of sunshine, Jade," Leigh said. "Actually, I was coming over to give you a heads up that Martina was talking about you again, but if you don't want to hear it…"

Jade's head snapped around, a murderous glare in her eyes. "What? She's here? What did she say?"

"She was talking to this other skank. I think I recognized her from the Dolce runway show." Leigh winked discreetly at Lexi and continued. "She was saying something about you pursuing acting. I think she called you a short, no talent whore, but I might have misheard her."

"Right, I'm a whore. She's the one who dropped to her knees and gave the photographer a blow job right on set to get the cover of a men's magazine. Puh-lease! I'll show her short when I jam my stiletto up her bony ass. Where was she?"

Without missing a beat, Leigh continued. "She was out front, smoking as usual."

"I think I'll go have a little chat with the walking carcinogen." Jade pointed her perfectly manicured finger toward the large glass door at the back of the room. "I saw a few drunk guys out on the terrace. Maybe a couple of them are blitzed enough to want to dance with you." Jade smirked, and then stormed off toward the elevators without so much as a second glance at Vincent.

Leigh and Lexi high fived each other and gave Elizabeth a thumbs up. Meanwhile, Vincent and Francesca continued to spin around the dance floor. They were the picture of fluid beauty. Francesca waved flirtatiously at Paolo while her dress swirled around her curvy body. At first he seemed annoyed, but he couldn't stay angry when she never once took her eyes off her beloved husband during her graceful movements.

When the music ended, Francesca grabbed Vincent's face and kissed both of his cheeks. She then hooked her arm in his and escorted him over to Paolo, who now stood with his brother Dante, drinking champagne. Paolo kissed his wife, then thrust out his hand to Vincent. The men talked for a moment, and Lexi held her breath, watching facial expressions to get a feel for how the conversation was going. When Dante threw back his head in laughter at something Vincent had said, Lexi knew he had pulled it off.

Like a pro, Vincent didn't overstay his welcome. He graciously thanked his dance partner and started to walk away when Francesca stopped him and held out her hand. Vincent politely obliged her request and reached into his pocket and slipped his business card into her hand. He again bid the trio goodnight, then headed back toward Elizabeth with a victorious smile. Lexi watched a smiling Paolo take the card from Francesca and tuck it into his wallet.

Lexi was about to run over and congratulate Vincent on a job well done when Jade reappeared and latched onto him with a vengeance. She wrapped her spiderlike limbs around him and tried to coax him onto the dance floor, but Vincent refused. Jade began gesturing wildly, but her voice was surprisingly soft, and Lexi couldn't hear what she said. When Jade glared over her shoulder and pointed directly at Francesca, then Lexi, it was pretty obvious what they were talking about: her.

Wishing she could disappear, Lexi looped her arm through Leigh's. "You almost ready to leave?" she asked, praying her friend would say yes.

"Sure, let's just go say goodbye to everyone and then we can head out. I have an early breakfast date in the morning anyway."

The women said their goodbyes to the ladies they had been talking to earlier. Kim had already left, but Erica was still there, furiously texting someone and not at all relaxed like she had been earlier.

"We're out of here, Erica. Quit working so much. You're making us feel guilty. We need to do a girl's lunch someday this week."

Erica smiled. "That would be great. Let's shoot for later in the week. The Davey-boy is going to have me on the phone nonstop for the next three days harassing the nice people of San Francisco, and now apparently Italy. It never ends. See you ladies later."

As they walked away, Lexi grumbled, "Damn it."

"What?" Leigh asked.

"David got to Paolo too. Vincent isn't going to be happy about that."

Lexi easily found Vincent in the large ballroom. He stood off to the side, talking to a group of people she recognized from the hit list. At his side, Jade was talking the ear off of the television producer in the group. She watched Jade standing beside Vincent, and it became very clear that she enjoyed using his connections to her benefit at every opportunity. She was one of the most selfish and self-centered people Lexi had ever met.

When Jade made eye contact with Lexi across the room, her face turned cold and hard. Rather than give the woman a reason to make another scene, Lexi decided against going over to say goodbye. Instead, she grabbed her phone and texted Vincent.

I'm getting ready to leave. You need anything before I go? Note cards perhaps?

Lexi watched Vincent slide his phone out of his pocket and peek at her message. His hair fell into his face as he looked down, and his lips curled into a private smile. He lifted his head and scanned the room. Lexi's heart beat faster as he kept looking, searching for her.

When he finally caught her eye, he gave her a small salute and winked, indicating he was fine. Lexi's stomach flipped at the gesture, thrilled beyond words that they seemed to be making progress, becoming friends even. It was more than she could have ever hoped for—that this man whom she'd secretly adored all these years, this gruff, short tempered, untrusting man, would let her into his life.

Of course, she wanted to be much more than friends with Vincent, as hopeless as that was. All the feelings she had buried long ago crept to the surface and burrowed their way back into her mind and her heart. She wanted him to hold her in his arms and dance with her, not out of obligation or good manners, but out of desire and love. She wanted to be the one standing beside him as he talked to clients and brokered deals, supporting him, helping him. Jade slid her arms around his waist and kissed his cheek, and Lexi was snapped back to reality.

She was quiet on the ride home, lost deep in her own thoughts. She remembered the flutter of her heart when she danced with Vincent, the way her stomach flipped when he touched her and how right it felt to be there. She recalled his smile when she told him about Julian Stone, the things Elizabeth had said to her about Hunter needing Lexi. The memories played over and over in her head like a movie that she never wanted to forget.

"You all right?" Leigh asked, glancing over at Lexi in the darkness.

"I'm fine, just thinking." Lexi leaned her head against the window and watched as the lights of the city flew past her.

"You did a great job tonight. Vincent scored some major points with big clients thanks to you. You guys make a great team."

Lexi didn't answer at first. She sensed where Leigh was going to take the conversation and she couldn't go there, not now. Finally, she took a deep breath and sighed. "He's my boss, Leigh. I did my job tonight."

"Right." Lexi could see the slight curve of Leigh's lips in the darkness of the car. "Your *boss* looked like a really good dancer."

"Leigh..." Lexi warned.

"It was an observation, nothing more."

Lexi sighed again, hoping Leigh would drop it.

Leigh tried to leave it at that, but eventually broke. "You've gotta give me something, Lexi. I'm dying over here. There's something there whether you want to admit it or not. I could see it."

Before she knew what she was doing, Lexi blurted out her secret. "I went to high school with him and had a crush on him for two years, and he didn't even know my name. Anna had to tell him who I was that day she brought Madison by the office." She buried her face in her hands in humiliation. Anything that Leigh thought she saw was nothing more than Lexi projecting her puppy-dog-like admiration onto Vincent. She must have seemed like a fool mooning over the boss while he danced with her as a favor to a five-year-old.

To her credit, Leigh didn't launch into a million questions like Lexi feared she would. She finished the drive back to Lexi's place in silence. When she pulled up to the curb, she put her hand on Lexi's shoulder.

"So, how was it to finally dance with him?" Leigh asked softly.

Lexi's eyes filled with tears as she smiled back at her friend. "Perfect."

12

You danced with him?" Hope badgered far too early the next morning.
Lexi took a sip of the coffee Hope had slid across the table to her. "Yes, we
danced. His five-year-old niece asked him to dance with me, no big deal. He was
being polite." Lexi grabbed a blueberry muffin out of the small, white sack from
the local bakery. Hope had used it to bribe Lexi into opening the door for her.

"M-hmm." Hope rolled her eyes in disbelief at her friend. "Polite, sure."

"Do I need to remind you he has a girlfriend? Or that she's a flipping
supermodel, Hope?"

"Supermodel, my butt. From what you've told me, she's a raging bitch,
straight up. Forget her. I want the dirt. How close together did you two stand
when you danced? Did his hand creep down to your tush at all? Did he give
it a little squeeze?" Hope leaned over and pinched Lexi playfully.

Lexi gave Hope the evil eye. "Okay, *that* was more sexual than anything
Vincent tried while we were dancing. He was the perfect gentleman. Now do
you believe me that it was no big deal?"

"Get up." Hope yanked Lexi out of her chair and flipped on the radio.
She held her arms out to Lexi and commanded, "Show me how you danced."

"Hope, seriously, I think you need a date. Call Sean. He'd love to dance
with you or be pinched if you're feeling frisky. I just want to eat my muffin,
and then I need to shower. I have a ton of work to do." Lexi tried to walk

away, but Hope clamped her hand around Lexi's wrist and dragged her back, sweeping her up into her arms and pressing their bodies together.

"Did he hold you like this?" Hope asked as she slowly dipped her head toward Lexi and lightly dragged her lips along Lexi's throat.

"No, if he had I'd be in the hospital with a massive skull fracture because I would have dropped like a stone on that dance floor. Besides, he isn't as aggressive as you, Hope."

"Fine, I'll be you, and you can be the docile gentleman." Hope crooked her eyebrow at Lexi, letting her know she had no intention of backing down. "Humor me. I spent the evening drinking wine, watching *Steel Magnolias*, and staring at the picture you sent me. I am a pathetic, horny woman, so let me live vicariously through you and your close encounter with the hunky kind."

Lexi placed her hand over Hope's lips silencing her as soon as she knew which way the conversation was heading. "Do not go there, Hope. He's my boss, with a girlfriend."

"But you like him," Hope mumbled behind Lexi's fingers.

"*Liked* him. A lifetime ago."

Hope wiggled her tongue along Lexi's fingers, making her friend yank her hand away in disgust.

"We're friends, Hope, and that's more than I ever thought I'd have with him. So, can I just be happy with that rather than have you plant seeds in my head that'll only lead to more schoolgirl mooning? Been there done that, and it sucked." Lexi wiped her hand back and forth on her pajama pants to dry it.

"But what if—"

"There's no if. He's my boss. The end." Lexi walked back to the table and took a big sip of coffee. "I'm not wasting years of my life pining after Vincent Drake again."

Hope wrapped her arms around Lexi's shoulder and pulled her into a hug. "Honey, I don't want you to waste a second of your life. You've already missed out on so much. But let's be honest—your experience with men is...well, limited. I'm not saying the guy's in love with you or that you're going to get married, settle down, and have throngs of children all from one dance, but answer me this, how did it feel when he held you?" Lexi glared at her friend. "Really, Lexi. Did it feel awkward or uncomfortable, like he was invading your personal space and all you could think about was getting away from him? Did he smell bad, have an unsightly mole or excessive nose hair?" A small grin spread across her face as Lexi shyly shook her head no. "So how did it feel to be in the arms of Vincent Drake?"

Lexi bit her lip and thought about it for a second. "Comfortable?" she offered as her best explanation.

"Comfortable is good. Like you belonged there." Hope snickered when Lexi's mouth fell open. "You can't fight chemistry, Lexi. It's a natural thing between a man and a woman, an attraction, if you will. You can't fight nature."

"Thank you for the speech, Dr. Ruth, and I hate to burst your bubble, but Vincent isn't attracted to me. He's my friend. I gave up my schoolgirl fantasies years ago. This is the real world. I need to live in that, not my head, and sometimes reality sucks. Being friends works for me. I'll take that. That's enough."

Hope eyed her friend suspiciously. "Is it? You've spent years of your life wanting him, and this might be your second chance with him. Something in the cosmos brought you two back together—chance, fate, destiny, whatever you want to believe. So are you going to try and fight for whatever this could become, or settle for friendship because it's the safer option? Would being friends really be enough for you, Lexi?"

For the briefest second Lexi considered pursuing Vincent. Maybe Hope was right. The way he held her after he'd pulled her close to talk had felt more than friendly, but was that real, or simply her overactive imagination where Vincent was concerned? Fantasy versus reality. Could she trust herself to tell the difference? Probably not.

Taking a moment to put on a brave face, Lexi decided to let this dream die and finally smiled. "Friends is enough, Hope. It has to be."

✦

Monday morning, Lexi arrived at work earlier than usual because she had countless appointments to reschedule and contacts to follow up on after the gala. Vincent showed up at exactly the same time and stopped Lexi in her tracks by handing her a bagel with cream cheese and tall cup of coffee as they stepped into the elevator together. Surprised, Lexi wondered what she had done to warrant such a kind gesture.

"You're here early." Vincent smiled as she tucked her keys into her purse.

"My boss, he's a real slave driver, and I know he has a pile of calls for me to make so I thought I'd get an early start." She took a bite of the bagel then held it out and offered it to him, just to see what he'd do.

His lip twitched in revulsion. "No thanks, I had some egg whites before I left my apartment this morning."

Jade must have been there this morning, Lexi thought to herself. *How someone as big as Vincent survives on rabbit food is beyond me.*

Lexi wrinkled her nose. "Please tell me you tossed some cheese in there, maybe a few pieces of ham?"

"There's nothing wrong with plain egg whites," Vincent chided. "They're a healthy breakfast, not like the carb-ball slathered in cream cheese that you're enjoying this morning."

"Hey," Lexi's mouth fell open as the elevator doors opened and they both stepped out, "you brought me this calorie packed carb-ball."

"Only because I knew if I didn't, you'd spend the morning eating those Peanut M&Ms you have hidden in the top drawer of your desk." Vincent winked and held his arm out, ushering her down the hall toward his office, but Lexi refused to move.

"How did you know about my candy stash?"

Vincent innocently shrugged. "I needed tape and stumbled across your Willy Wonka drawer."

She looked over at Leigh who was now covering her mouth to keep from laughing out loud as she watched the exchange.

"Keep your hands out of my drawers, buddy." As soon as the words left Lexi's mouth, she wanted to suck them back in, but it was too late. Blush flooded her cheeks, and Leigh actually snorted from behind her desk.

Vincent, however, kept a straight face, which made it even worse. "I'll try and remember that, Alexandra." The sultry tone of his voice washed over her, instantly electrifying her body.

Suddenly, she needed some space between her and Vincent. "If you don't mind, I have work to do!" Lexi started to storm down the hall.

She didn't get far before Vincent caught up with her and whispered in her ear. "You need more licorice, by the way." Without waiting for her snarky comeback, he continued down the hall in front of her.

"You *ate* my licorice?" Lexi pointed an accusatory finger at him. "Mr. Egg Whites chowed a whole pound of licorice?"

Vincent stopped and turned unapologetically toward her. "The bag was open, so I'm sure it wasn't a full pound, and yes, I ate them. Haven't you ever taken a moment to read the packaging? It's a fat-free food."

Rolling her eyes, Lexi shoved her way around him, brushing against his chest as he blocked her path. A flash of him holding her immediately popped into her mind, but Lexi shook it off and continued to her desk.

She tucked her purse into her drawer, flipped open her laptop, and got ready to pull up Vincent's schedule for the day. As her fingers flew over the keyboard, he sat down at her desk. The apprehensive look on his face took her by surprise.

"Hey, I'm sorry about earlier." He ran his hand through his hair as he only did when he was nervous.

The thought of letting him sit there and stew for a minute crossed her mind, but her kind heart won out and she let him off the hook. "It was candy, Vincent. I was just kidding. A joke." His face remained serious as he stared at her as if trying to determine whether she was really telling the truth. Lexi let out an exasperated sigh. "Scout's honor." She held up three fingers and put her hand over her heart. "I swear I was just teasing you."

Finally, Vincent relaxed. "It won't happen again." He stood up and made his way to his office. "And if I didn't tell you on Saturday, thank you for all your help, Lexi."

She handed him a copy of his schedule. "No problem." A blush slowly crept into her cheeks at his words of thanks.

He pushed the door to his office open and glanced back over his shoulder. "Oh, and thanks for the dance, too." The wink that he gave her before he disappeared into his office nearly stopped her heart.

There was no way she could allow herself to think too much about what had just happened. Instead, she began working furiously, planning Vincent's week, lining up the phone calls she needed to make, taking information down to productions so they could begin the research on the new prospects. She did everything and anything she could to not let her imagination run away with her and over-think Vincent's words and actions.

It was almost noon before she came up for air and found herself sitting behind her desk with nothing to work on. Her peaceful moment, however, was soon interrupted.

"Lexi, Lexi, Lexi!" Leigh sprinted over to her with a bouquet of roses in her hand. She placed them on Lexi's desk and stepped away, grinning widely.

"Wow, those are gorgeous." Lexi chuckled as she ran her fingertips over the velvety buds. "Who sent Vincent flowers?"

"I'd like to know the same thing," a voice sneered from around the corner. Jade appeared, overdressed and as snotty as ever. A grimace shadowed her face as she yanked a flower from the vase, twirling it between her fingers. "Red roses. How...unimaginative."

"Give it back. It's not yours." Leigh yanked the flower from Jade's grasp, and one of the thorns sliced deep into Jade's finger. The yelp and loud string of profanities that came pouring out of Jade's mouth attracted Vincent's attention from behind his closed office door.

"What the hell is going on out here?"

Jade sucked on one finger and pointed at Leigh with an uninjured one. "Your phone girl decided to stab me. I think I need some antiseptic." She sat down on one of the chairs and rummaged through her purse until she pulled out a bottle of antibacterial hand sanitizer and poured a dollop into her hand. She swore loudly as the alcohol in the sanitizer burned, and then held her finger out for Vincent to examine.

He gave it a quick once over and sighed. "It's going to be fine, Jade. I don't think you'll lose the finger."

Jade was furious at his flippant tone. "Do I need to remind you that I'm a model, Vincent? This body is what pays the bills. The last thing I need is to have it marred by imperfections." She turned on Leigh. "I should sue you!"

Leigh ignored Jade and addressed Vincent. "Sorry, Mr. Drake. I was just bringing these flowers down here to—"

"Who sent me flowers?" Vincent yanked the white envelope from the beautiful bouquet and removed the white card inside.

"But, they're—" Leigh stepped closer, but was silenced by Vincent's hand in the air as he read.

He tucked the card back into the envelope, his lips set in a hard line. With a flick of his wrist, he held the card out to Lexi. "They're for you, Lexi." His voice was clipped.

She tugged the white square from his tight grasp and glanced down at it. The card was written in blue ink, and the instant she read it, she knew why Vincent was so agitated. The flowers were from David Reid.

Alexandra,

Sorry we were unable to tango on Saturday due to your pompous employer. My offer still stands. Leave Hunter and join up with the winning team over at Reid. You won't regret it.

Until we meet again,

David Reid, CEO

(555) 277-4653

"Who are they from?" Leigh peeked at the note. When she saw the signature, she gasped. "No way."

Jade reached up from her seat and snatched the card out of Lexi's hand. When her eyes skimmed the paper, her fury matched Vincent's. "You've got to be kidding me."

Vincent cleared his throat, the scowl still planted firmly on his face. "If it's not too much trouble, when you're done ogling your flowers, could I bother you to do some work?"

His biting words shocked Lexi and Leigh both, and the two women exchanged a surprised glance. "S-sure. What do you need me to do?" Lexi asked.

He looked over at Jade, who was still scowling at the tiny, white card. "Jade looks hungry. Why don't you grab us some lunch, and I'll make a list of things that need to be done while you're gone." He leaned over and kissed Jade on the cheek.

Jade's eyes lit up, and she rattled off her order. "I'll take a salad of field greens with no blue cheese, ex—"

"Extra sprouts and a bottle of water. I think I got it by now, thanks. And Vincent will take the same, of course." Lexi snatched her purse out of the drawer in her desk and glared at Vincent.

Jade rolled her eyes as she took Vincent's outstretched hand. "Good help is so hard to find," she sniped as they disappeared behind the office door.

"What the hell just happened?" Leigh asked as Lexi slammed her purse onto her desk.

"David Reid happened. Vincent hates him, and I just got a big bunch of flowers from him so somehow we must be in cahoots. That's how Vincent's paranoid mind works." Lexi sighed and tucked the bouquet into a corner of the room, hiding it as much as possible. "Back to square one," she sighed to herself as she grabbed her purse and tossed her jacket over her shoulders. "Stupid David Reid."

Leigh wrapped a reassuring arm around Lexi's shoulder as she led her down the hall toward the elevators. "Mr. Drake will snap out of it, Lexi. Just give him time."

✦

For the next few days, Vincent spoke very little to Lexi. Unless he was giving her an assignment or needed her to answer a work-related question, he stayed locked behind his office door or out of the office at meetings. He was short tempered and in a foul mood with everyone, especially Lexi. Things came to a head when he returned from a meeting with the people from Keller Pharmaceuticals. It obviously hadn't gone well.

As he stormed through the office, Lexi held out a stack of messages to him. "You have about five messages—"

Vincent didn't give her so much as a second glance, and the slam of his office door reverberated through the building.

"—that need to be returned by the end of the day, but guess I'll take care of them." Lexi picked up the phone and began making calls. She was waiting on hold with one of them when the office door flew open.

"Alexandra, get off the damn phone and come in here. Now."

The acidic tone in his voice made her temper flare. She set the receiver down slowly and took a deep breath before leaving her seat. Moving in slow motion to collect her thoughts, she picked up the pad of paper and a pencil and made her way into Vincent's office. By the time she crossed the threshold of his doorway and slipped into one of the chairs at the foot of his desk, she was ready to let him have it.

"Vincent—" she began, but he quickly put his hand up to silence her.

"We lost the Keller account. Adria Parketti is a pain in my ass." Vincent shuffled papers on his desk, searching for something specific.

Lexi tried to finish her thought. "I'm sorry we lost the account, but that's no excuse—"

Vincent held out a sheet of paper and began barking out orders. "Take this to my mother's office and tell her the Keller thing went badly, and have Sean cancel the prop order for the commercial. Get this information to him today before we end up losing our deposit for the location." He leaned forward, his face deadly serious. "We're going after Julian Stone, hard. I want this account.

Do you understand? Call and confirm the appointment. Maybe try and talk with him personally. Flirt a little. He seemed to like you at the gala. Hell, if he asks you to go on a date, do it. I need an in with Stone, so do whatever you have to and make it happen."

When Vincent's little tirade was over, Lexi waited with her teeth clenched in an effort to keep herself from jumping over the desk and wringing his neck.

Vincent stared back at Lexi. "Tell me you don't need me to repeat all of that."

"No, I got the message loud and clear." She stood up from the chair, her hands shaking with rage. "You know, Vincent, I get paid to be your assistant, to help you with whatever you need done no matter how rotten the request. It's my job, and I enjoy it most days. But show some manners. I happen to know your mother raised you better than that. So when you hint that I should to go screw Julian Stone so he'll hire Hunter Advertising, the least you can do is say please."

With tears brimming in her eyes, Lexi made a run for the door, but Vincent was faster. He pressed his hand against the smooth wood and held it firmly in place.

"Let me out of here, Vincent. I have nothing else to say to you."

He stood there for a minute, then let out a loud sigh. "Well *I* have something to say to *you*. I'm sorry. I was upset about the Keller thing, and I took it out on you. I apologize. You didn't deserve any of that." He put his hand on her shoulder and slowly ran it down her arm, finally taking her hand and giving it a squeeze.

The tears that had welled up in Lexi's eyes tumbled slowly down her cheeks. He brought his hand to her face and wiped them away with the pad of his thumb.

"God, I'm such a jerk."

"My thoughts exactly." Lexi willed herself to stop crying. But all she could hear in her head were the awful things Vincent had just said to her.

Vincent's fury gone, he gently cradled her face in both his hands, trying to keep up with the tears that continued to fall. "Please don't cry. You're breaking my heart here." His eyes searched hers, trying to figure out how to fix this. "I'm sorry, Lexi." He leaned against the door and ran both hands through his hair in frustration. "Take the afternoon off or stab me with that letter opener if it'll make you feel better."

Lexi's lip twitched slightly at the thought, but then she had a better idea. She reached in her pocket and pulled out her phone, ready to dial when a loud banging on the door scared her half to death.

"Who the hell is it?" Vincent snapped.

"Don't you dare take that tone with me, young man. Open the door."

Vincent cringed at the sound of his mother's voice.

"Sounds like you have a visitor." A smile tugged at Lexi's lips as she glanced down at her notepad and shook her head. "I wish I could stay, but I have a *long* list of things I have to get done right away."

Vincent snatched the notebook from her hand and crossed every single thing off the list. "Nope, your schedule just cleared. Please stay."

There was more banging on the door. "I can hear you in there!"

"I wish I could, but I need to go shopping for some sexy underwear if I'm going to convince Julian Stone to hire Hunter." She innocently batted her eyelashes at Vincent. "I'm taking you up on your offer, and I'll be out the rest of the afternoon. Oh, and you can have the honor of telling her about the Keller account. Have a nice chat with your mother."

Lexi threw open the door, nearly knocking Vincent over and stifled a laugh when she saw an irate Elizabeth leaning against the doorframe. "Good afternoon, Elizabeth," Lexi sang as she brushed past her and collected her purse from her desk.

As Lexi headed down the hall, she heard Elizabeth growl, "Why was Lexi crying? Vincent Giovanni Drake what did you do now? I'll fire *you* before I'll allow that girl to quit, so you better start talking and figure out how to fix this."

✦

By the time Lexi returned to work on Thursday, her head was clear. She was calmer and felt more in control of her life. The hour long pep talk Hope had given her the night before was just what she'd needed. Vincent had been a jerk, plain and simple. There was no excuse for the way he had spoken to her. Whatever his problem was, it was *his* problem, and she would not be his doormat. Lexi hoped his chat with Elizabeth had been very long and uncomfortable, and that he would mind his manners from now on.

At eight a.m. Vincent strolled past Lexi's desk, an hour late, and without a word, grabbed his schedule off the corner of her desk and disappeared into his office.

"Good morning, Vincent," Lexi muttered sarcastically to herself as she stared at his shut door and began talking to herself. "Good morning, Lexi. I hope you had a good evening. I'm sorry I was an idiot yesterday, please forgive me. It won't ever happen again."

"Speaking to the spirits again, Lexi?" Sean chuckled as he helped himself to a cup of coffee in the corner.

"Good morning," Lexi said more loudly than normal, glaring at Vincent who chose that moment to emerged from his office for a fresher cup of coffee than the one Lexi had placed on his desk an hour earlier. "What can I do for you, Sean?"

"I wanted to make sure you two were playing nice and that Vincent wasn't trying to pimp you out to potential clients again."

Vincent choked on his coffee and cast an accusatory glance in Lexi's direction.

"I didn't say a word, thank you." Lexi folded her arms across her chest and glared right back at him.

Sean clapped his hand on Vincent's shoulder. "You really fu—, I mean, really screwed up this time, didn't ya, Vince?"

"Did you want something, Sean?" Vincent asked through his clenched teeth.

"Nope, just saying good morning to the beautiful ladies of Hunter. You should try it sometime." He grinned widely and waggled his eyebrows in Lexi's direction. "Good morning, Lexi."

Lexi rolled her eyes and went back to work. "Goodbye, Sean."

"Oh, Vincent, I almost forgot. I talked to Lacey down in production, and they had a question on the Fredrik Khan ad."

The two men launched into a lengthy discussion about budgets and operational overhead that Lexi tuned out while she continued returning phone calls and rearranging Vincent's schedule to accommodate his new appointments. She was just about to leave and drop some papers off to Elizabeth when Leigh emerged from around the corner. When Lexi noticed what she was carrying, she almost grabbed her purse and headed straight for the elevator.

"Lexi, look at what you—" Leigh froze mid-sentence when she saw Vincent and Sean huddled in the corner, staring directly at her with great interest. "Um, here." She ruefully held up an exquisite bouquet of flowers.

Purple hyacinths spilled from the vase, the deep colored blooms filling the area with their rich scent. Between the violet flowers, white daisies peeked out, brightening up the richness of the hyacinths. The greenery scattered through the vase added to the exotic beauty of huge the arrangement.

Leigh stood before Lexi, looking like a deer caught in the headlights, the vase clenched tightly in her hands. The women held their breath and waited for the yelling to begin, but no one spoke.

"What's the big deal that Lexi got flowers?" Sean grabbed the vase from Leigh and plopped them onto the desk. "So, who are they from? Your boyfriend?"

These are beautiful, she thought to herself as she reached for the delicate blooms. Then she paused. *If they're from Reid, I'll kill him.*

Lexi gave Sean a droll stare. "I don't have a boyfriend. I have no idea who they're from." She stole a quick look in Vincent's direction as she held the tiny white envelop in her hand, her heart thundering in her chest as she prepared to open it.

"Purple hyacinth, interesting floral choice." Vincent's deep voice came from across the room and made her stomach do a little flip.

She slipped the card out of the envelope and read it.

Alexandra,
A man of few words, I will let the flowers speak for themselves.

Her brow knit together as she read the words repeatedly, her lips moving as she tried to figure out what the note meant.

"Well?" Sean asked.

"I have no idea who they're from."

"What does the card say?" Leigh peeked over Lexi's shoulder and read it quickly. Soon the same confused look fell across her face. "What the hell does *that* mean?"

Lexi shrugged. "No clue. Sean, is this your idea of a joke?" Sean slowly shook his head from side to side. She was intrigued by the flowers, the note, and the sender. But more than anything, she was relieved that they weren't from David Reid. She glanced across the room to find Vincent leaning against the wall, his arms folded across his chest with an unreadable expression on his face. "What?"

It was his turn to shrug. "Nothing." He pushed off the wall and strode across the room until he was right in front of the flowers. Everyone tensed as he reached out his large hand and softly stroked the fragile petals. As he headed back to his office he commented, "They look much more tasteful than those awful roses from Reid yesterday; that's all." Vincent glanced around at everyone still standing there, staring at the vase. "Am I the only one with work to do today?"

Leigh headed back to her desk, but Sean simply rolled his eyes when Vincent's door closed. "I better go get something done before he gets his panties in a bunch. Oh, any chance you would be willing to help a guy get a date?"

"Sure, you want me to make you a profile on an on-line dating site?" Lexi held her fingers poised over the keyboard and smiled.

"Do it and die." Sean grinned. "No, I want to go on a date with Hope."

"So, what do you want me to do about that? Tie her to a chair?"

"Now that sounds like fun." A devilish smirk washed over his chiseled features as Lexi glared at him. "Well, can you put in a good word for me? Maybe tell me what I need to do to get back into her good graces or simply how to get her to answer the phone when I call?"

Lexi laughed. "She's a stubborn woman. If she doesn't want to answer the phone, she won't, and I can't make her." Sean's shoulders sagged in disappointment. "However, if I were you," his head snapped up as he listened, "I'd suddenly have the urge to get something painted on the side of your new Ferrari. Doesn't have to be big, but there's no way she'd let anyone other than herself work on a Ferrari. The shop is known for its customer service, so she'd have to speak to you about your plans."

Sean mulled it over in his head for a few seconds, and then grinned. "I know exactly what I'm going to have done to it."

"Don't blow this. Two strikes with Hope and you're out. Forever."

Sean gave her a little salute, then flashed his dimples and pulled his cell phone out as he walked down the hall. Lexi caught the very beginning of his conversation. "Hello, yes. I'd like to bring in my Ferrari and discuss a custom paint job. I hear that you're the best. Yes, I would love to meet the owner. This afternoon? Sure."

Lexi chuckled to herself as she made some minor changes to Vincent's schedule for the rest of the week. "Good luck, Hope." She pecked away at her keyboard and smiled. "You're gonna need it, girlfriend."

As Lexi sat at her desk, her eyes kept being drawn back to the beautiful bouquet perched on the corner of her desk, brightening her day. It was gorgeous, there was no other way to describe it, and she was intrigued by the message. Knowing Vincent had his meeting with Julian Stone that day, Lexi thought there was a slight chance they were from Julian, but he was not a man of few words, just the opposite.

"So, I was doing a little research." Leigh came strolling around the corner, grinning.

"Do I want to hear this?"

"I think you do." She flopped into one of the chairs at Lexi's desk and sniffed the flowers next to her. "I went online."

"M-hmm..." Lexi quickly texted Christina to confirm Vincent and Julian's basketball game/meeting for that afternoon.

"And the flowers in the bouquet have different meanings." Leigh squirmed in her seat with excitement. "The daisies mean innocence, and the hyacinth means loveliness!"

Lexi raised her eyebrows skeptically.

"Really, go to a florist's website and it's all there in black and white. Of course, if you go to a different one, the same flowers mean something all together different. It's been a little frustrating trying to decipher the note, to tell you the truth." Leigh glared at the bouquet like it was purposely taking some sort of sick pleasure in mystifying her.

Lexi opened her mouth to beg her to end the hunt for the hidden meaning behind the flowers, but all rational thought stopped the second Vincent's office door swung open and he strolled out wearing long, black basketball shorts, a tight fitting 49er's T-shirt, and a pair of white high top sneakers. As if the casual attire wasn't enough to make Lexi's heart skip a beat, Vincent also had a baseball hat on his head, flipped backwards, and a pair of dark sunglasses covering his eyes, just like he'd worn all throughout high school. Suddenly, she was seventeen again, swooning in the hallway over the hunky Vincent Drake.

"Damn," Leigh murmured as Vincent flipped through the file in his hand, completely oblivious to being shamelessly ogled by the two women.

"Lexi," Vincent started as he reached for a pen off the top of her desk. "I need you to call Mr. Garcia about this contract." When he looked away from his stack of papers, he found Lexi and Leigh with their mouths hanging open in stunned silence. "What's wrong with the two of you?"

Leigh snapped out of her reverie first. "Sorry, I was just telling Lexi about the birthmark Sean has on his arm."

Vincent shook his head. "Him and that stupid birthmark. I still don't get how he can see a naked woman. It looks like snowman to me, and why on Earth would he tell everyone about it?"

Lexi took the papers he held out, her eyes fixed on his muscular biceps. Reflexively, she licked her lips and took a deep breath when he pulled off the sunglasses to look her in the eye.

"You do know the meeting isn't for two hours right, Vincent?"

"I know," he grinned, "but I'm going to get there early so I can get some practice time in before Julian shows up. I haven't played basketball in years, not since high school."

The smirk on his face made Lexi's heart skip a beat. She quickly tried to cover her stunned expression. "You're really going to try and beat him?"

"Of course. I want him to respect me, not think of me as a spineless coward." He laughed as Lexi shook her head in disbelief. Leaning forward, he covered her hand with his and gave it a small squeeze. "Trust me, I know what I'm doing on this one."

"Good luck, Mr. Drake. The Stone account would be such a catch for Hunter." Leigh smiled while she watched their interaction with great interest.

Vincent pulled his eyes away from Lexi and laughed confidently. "Consider it done." He stood up and glanced back at Lexi, who had let her hair fall in front of her face to cover her blush. "Please don't forget to call Mr. Garcia, Lexi."

Lexi nodded and wrote a quick reminder on a Post-it, then gasped. "I almost forgot!" She jumped out of her seat and squatted down behind her desk, rummaging through the large bag she had brought with her. She gingerly slid something out and handed it to Vincent.

"What is this?"

"What is this?" Lexi asked, shocked. "*This* is the Rolling Stones Japanese produced box set."

"Um, thank you?"

"It's not for you, goofball," she said, rolling her eyes. "It's for Julian. He's been dying to find a copy of it, so I thought it couldn't hurt to go to the meeting bearing gifts."

"Where'd you find it?" He gingerly turned it over in his hands, taking care not to damage it in any way.

"Another collector I know had one, but he wasn't willing to part with it, until now. I had to do a little sweet-talking, but he finally agreed."

"You're brilliant."

"Finally we agree on something!"

Without another word, he tucked the album under his arm and headed down the hallway.

"Good luck!" Leigh called after him.

"Let him win!" Lexi added, grinning to Leigh. They both started laughing when they heard his distant reply.

"Never!"

✦

Later that afternoon, Lexi was straightening up her desk, getting ready to leave for the day. She had spent most of the afternoon looking at the phone, hoping to hear something from Vincent about the meeting with Julian, but every time it rang it was someone else.

Her gaze drifted back to the gorgeous bouquet of flowers. She reached out her hand and ran her fingers gently over the soft pedals, then dipped her nose to smell their sweet fragrance. Each flower was in such perfect bloom that they almost looked fake. Lexi smiled and went back to work, desperately wanting to clear her desk before she left for the day. She headed into Vincent's office with a small stack of files, and as she crouched down, tucking things into the drawer, Vincent's office door swung open, and a beaming Vincent filled the doorway.

"Hey!" Lexi rose to her feet, anxious for information. "So, how did it go?"

The smile on Vincent's face told the entire story, but Lexi wanted to hear him say it. He walked right up to her and unexpectedly hoisted her up into his arms, her feet swinging freely in the air.

"We did it!" he laughed into her ear, his arms wrapped firmly around her waist as he twirled her around. "Can you believe it? I'm presenting to him the day after Reid!"

Lexi threw her arms around his neck before she could stop herself and hugged him back. "That's fantastic!" Her feet gently landed on the ground as he set her down, beaming.

Suddenly, she became aware of how close he was and the fact that his hair was in even more sexy disarray than usual from the basketball game, his hat nowhere to be found. Lexi's cheeks turned red when she realized she still had her arms wrapped around his neck. She slowly slid her hands down his chest, feeling the ripple of muscles just underneath the flimsy cotton fabric of his T-shirt, and then balled her fists up at her sides, willing them not to grab him by the shirt and pull his lips to hers.

"You know what the best part is?" Vincent grinned as he stepped away from her and sat back in his chair, taking a long drink from his water bottle.

"What?" Lexi tried to ignore the droplets of water that had spilled onto his neck.

"I won the game, twenty-one to eighteen. His outside shot was total crap."

Lexi smiled as her heart hammered in her chest. "Sounds like a successful afternoon then."

"And he loved the album. I gave it to him after we set up the meeting. That way it didn't look like I was trying to bribe him or anything shady. He actually gave me a message to pass on to you."

She rolled her eyes. "Well, this should be good."

Vincent stood up and moved closer to her, then took her hand in his.

"Vincent, what the heck?" Lexi almost fell over from the sight of him, looking down at her with a sexy twinkle in his eyes.

He held up a hand to stop her. "Julian says you are his queen." With a smile, he took Lexi's hand in his and pressed a kiss to her knuckles.

Lexi watched his lips meet her skin, their soft, heat brushing against her flesh, awakening every nerve ending in her body. When his eyes locked on hers, Lexi was lost, hopelessly enamored by Vincent Drake. Again. She saw his lips moving, but had no idea what he was saying because all she could think about was what his lips would feel like, not on her hand, but pressed tight against hers. What it would feel like if his hand slowly crept up her calf, glided up her thigh, then dipped under her skirt, his fingers brushing against her panties ever so lightly.

Color flooded her cheeks as she tried to calm her breathing and pull herself from the erotic thoughts flooding her mind. She regained control of herself long enough to catch the end of his baffling thank you speech in which she was referred to as something along the lines of "Album goddess whom all men should worship for eternity."

"So basically, Julian says thanks?"

Vincent chuckled and released her hand from his warm grasp. "Yes, he says thank you. Actually, we both do. Thank you, Lexi, for everything you do. I know I don't say it enough, and I know I give you a hard time when I'm in a bad mood or stressed out, but I really appreciate all your hard work."

Lexi opened and closed her mouth twice, trying to find the right words. Finally, she turned on her heel and started walking out the door.

"Oh, and Lexi?"

She stopped. "Yeah?"

"The purple hyacinths mean I'm sorry."

She stood in the doorway, mouth once again agape in shock. "Th-they're from you?" she stammered, clutching the door jamb for support.

Vincent winked. "My florist helped me make the bouquet this morning." He crossed his arms with a self-satisfied grin on his face. "Just wait until you see the bouquet of thank you flowers I send tomorrow."

· 13 ·

I t's open, Hope!" Lexi called from the bathroom as she put the finishing touches on her makeup.

"Mornin'." A very sleepy Hope leaned against the door jamb. "Do you need a few more minutes or are we good?"

Lexi dropped her brush and scooted past her, slipping her shoes on quickly. "No, I'm ready. Let's get moving. I need to get to work a little early today."

Hope rolled her eyes. "You say that every morning, Lexi. For the number of hours you spent there this last week, they definitely don't pay you enough."

"Oh, stop it. You know we have that big presentation tomorrow. Well, Vincent has a big presentation. I'm just—"

"Hopelessly in love with him?" Hope offered, earning a dirty look from Lexi.

"His assistant. And there will be a lot that has to get done today. *And* my salary is extremely generous."

"Yeah, you do it all for the money, Lexi. Keep telling yourself that." Hope tossed her purse over her shoulder and headed for the door while Lexi poured coffee into her travel mug. "By the way, your car should be done later today. Sorry we had to keep it an extra day, but parts for that thing are a real bitch to find sometimes."

"Not a problem. I appreciate the ride." Lexi locked her door, and they headed down to the parking garage.

With all of Hope's fast driving and shortcuts down alleys, they made it to the Barrington Building faster than usual, which thrilled Lexi.

"So we're still on for tonight? Dinner, dancing, and hot guys?" Hope asked as she put the car in park so Lexi could get out.

"Not sure about the guy part. I'll leave that up to you, but yeah. I have a change of clothes in my bag. Why don't you pick me up around six?"

"And you'll be ready to go?" Hope eyed her skeptically.

Lexi laughed. "Probably not, but come upstairs and drag me out kicking and screaming if you have to. Twenty-third floor, down the first hall, all the way to the back. Make a right and you'll see my desk."

"Is Captain Asshole back?" Hope asked nonchalantly, staring out the windshield.

"Sean?" Lexi spun around to look suspiciously at Hope. "How did you know he was out of town?"

Hope's cheeks turned pink, and she became very interested in a small scuff mark on her dashboard. "It just popped into my head. He might have mentioned something about it when he called the shop." She shrugged her shoulders like it was no big deal.

"So you talked to him again?" Lexi watched Hope fuss with the dashboard.

"Three days ago."

"Let me get this straight. He came to the shop the other day, and you blew him off—"

"I did not blow him off. I simply asked what he wanted done to the car, and he gave me some ridiculous answer about a blond, forties-style pinup girl." She rolled her eyes dramatically. "But really he had no idea. So I told him when he knew exactly what he wanted, he should come back," Hope said indignantly. "I'm a busy woman, Lexi. I don't have time to play his games. What does he think? That he can just flash those sexy dimples and I'll turn to goo? Please."

"So you sent him packing when he came to the shop the other day. Then he called you back?" Hope nodded her head slowly. "And what happened? Were you nice to him on the phone?" Lexi asked, almost afraid to hear the answer. The rage that flashed across Hope's face made her cringe.

"Was I nice? I was professional like I always am with paying customers. However, if he refers to me as 'babe' one more time, I'm yanking out his tongue and strangling him with it."

"Don't hold back. Tell me what you really think."

"He's an arrogant, sexist, pretty boy." Hope crossed her arms with a huff and glared out her window.

"And you *like* him." A huge smile exploded onto Lexi's face with that realization. "He's really nice, Hope! And I know he's interested in you, big time."

"He's a pig and an imbecile, but I'll still do a great job for him—on his car—because it's what I do. I'll treat him like any other customer." The nonchalant lilt of her voice told Lexi everything she needed to know.

"So, what did he decide he wanted on the car?"

"This time he decided he didn't want detailing. Instead he opted for a completely new paint job. The yellow 'isn't working for him.'"

"Since when?" Lexi furrowed her brow. "He thought the yellow was … how did he put it all last week? 'Totally kick ass.'"

Hope snickered to herself. "Well, I might have had something to do with that. I mentioned that it's common knowledge in the automobile industry that men who drive yellow sports cars have tiny … things. That didn't sit too well with him."

"Apparently. What color does he want it now?"

Hope grinned from ear to ear. "Sleek, sexy black."

"So you convinced Sean and his drop dead gorgeous dimples that he needed to be in a make-Hope-all-hot-and-bothered-because-she-has-a-thing-for-black-cars, black Ferrari?"

She shrugged innocently. "It's my job to tell the client if I think something will or will not work for them, and Sean is definitely not a teenie-wienie-yellow kinda guy."

Lexi nodded her head in agreement. "You got it bad, don't you? Just admit it. You know you want to." Lexi grinned at her friend.

Hope scowled and replied, "Go to work. Your darling Vincent is waiting for you, I'm sure. Maybe he'll even chase you around the desk a little today." Hope threw Lexi a sexy wink.

"Bitch," Lexi laughed as she climbed out of the car.

"And you love me for it. See you at six. Be ready for a night out on the town!" The tires screeched as she sped away and cut into heavy traffic. Lexi shook her head and made her way upstairs to begin her day.

Everything that could possibly go wrong that morning did. Vincent was late to work because Jade needed a last minute ride to the airport for a photo shoot, then he got stuck in a huge traffic jam on the freeway. When he finally arrived, he was ready to kill someone, so Lexi made sure to give him some time to himself before checking to see what he needed her to do.

After a long morning of making copies and phone calls, she had to go down to productions, a task she normally dreaded because it meant having to deal with Tony. Vincent let it slip, however, that Tony was gone for the day. When Lexi picked up the materials in productions, she was shocked. Asshole or not, Tony and his team did amazing work. The boards for the Stone presentation were ready and looked amazing. Lexi was admiring them at her desk when Vincent walked by.

"Did he fu—*mess* anything up this time?" He joined Lexi in examining the materials.

"Surprisingly, no," Lexi chuckled. "Maybe he's turning over a new leaf."

Vincent gave her a droll look. "More like he is lying in wait for his next attack. Trust me. Don't ever let your guard down around him."

"I wasn't planning on it." She peered up at Vincent's weary face. Elbowing him lightly, she asked, "How about I get you some lunch? What do you want?"

"I would kiss your feet for a big turkey sandwich from that New York deli on Fifth."

"A simple please would suffice, but if you insist, kiss away." She jokingly held out her foot to him and nearly fell onto her desk when he stepped closer like he was actually going to do it. "I was just kidding!" She staggered back, clutching the edge of her desk for dear life.

He laughed and dipped his head right next to hers. "So was I. I don't kiss feet." Before she could open her mouth to respond, his warm lips pressed against her cheek, and his husky voice whispered in her ear. "Thanks, Lexi."

Lexi closed her eyes and prayed that she would remember everything about this moment for the rest of her life: the soft feel of his lips, the heat of his breath against her neck, the silky strands of his hair that brushed against her cheek, the smell of his cologne, the enveloping warmth of his body as it loomed over her. She wanted to revel in the perfect memory for as long as possible, burning it into her mind.

Vincent noticed her sudden silence and watched her intently. His eyes dropped to her mouth and for a second he too seemed miles away, deeply lost in his own thoughts. When his tongue darted out and slowly stroked across the soft, pink skin of his lower lip, Lexi's body flushed with heat.

Trying to cover up her overwhelming lust, she used a little humor to deflect his attention.

"If I go all the way to Fifth at this time of day, you're buying *my* lunch too," Lexi teased as she bent over and grabbed her purse, then took a deep breath to calm her thundering heart, "and I'm starving."

Vincent pulled out his wallet and placed a fifty into Lexi's outstretched palm. He wrapped his much larger hand around hers and closed her fingers around the cash. "This should cover your little feeding frenzy. If not, let me know."

"I was only kidding." Lexi tried to give the money back, but he pushed her hand away.

"I'm not. Lunch is on me. And since you'll have change, if you should pass a donut shop …"

"A dozen powdered jelly?" Lexi laughed without thinking until Vincent's mouth fell open.

"How do you do that?" he asked incredulously.

"Do what?"

"Know exactly what I'm thinking?" His eyes locked on hers, watching her every move as she shifted uncomfortably in place.

"I remember watching you eat them before school." She glanced down at the carpet to hide her embarrassment. "I took a guess you still liked them."

Vincent reached out and gently lifted her chin up so he could see her face. "You know it kills me that I can't remember you."

Leigh came around the corner at that moment, sending Lexi scurrying across the room. "I'll go grab lunch. I'll be back as soon as I can, with traffic and all."

Leigh and Vincent watched her dart down the hall like a jackrabbit.

✦

The entire day went by in a flash. A little before six, Lexi got a text from Hope that she would be a late. Something about a Porsche owner with his head firmly planted up his ass. Lexi laughed and was actually relieved because Vincent was still in his office and had given her a laundry list of things that still needed to get done for tomorrow.

At seven, Lexi had just changed her clothes for her date with Hope when the printer jammed. She was about to crawl under her desk and drag it out when her phone rang. "Lexi White, can I help you?"

"Hey, Lexi, it's Christina. How are you?"

"I'm great. We're a little busy getting ready for a big presentation that my boss has tomorrow with this really famous fashion designer," Lexi teased as she eyed her makeup bag and glanced at the clock; Hope would be there soon. "What's up with you?"

"Nothing," she said in a hushed tone. "I just wanted to see how you guys were doing with the presentation. Everything ready to go?"

Lexi dropped her tone to match Christina's. "Why are we whispering about this?"

"Because I'm not supposed to be calling about these things, but I just want to make sure that everything's on schedule." Her voice became deadly serious. "He liked Reid's campaign."

Lexi felt like she was going to be sick. "How much did he like it?"

"A lot. It was good, all about being unique and expressing yourself."

Lexi's eyes immediately flew to the production boards sitting beside her. The main tag line for the ad was burned into her memory not only from the boards, but the PowerPoint and the mockup ads. Everything had those same two words on it: Unique expressions of self, by Julian Stone.

"Shit, shit, shit."

"No, no, don't say shit, Lexi. Say 'we can kick Reid's ass.' Tell me he's gonna look like dog food after you guys present tomorrow."

Lexi's mind was a million miles away, trying to figure out how she was going to break the news to Vincent that the presentation he had been slaving over had already been pitched to Julian.

"Lexi? Are you still there?" Christina's worried whispers snapped Lexi out of her trance.

"I'm here. We'll be there tomorrow, and Vincent's presentation *will* make David's look like dog food!" Lexi was on her feet pacing in front of her desk. "Christina, I love you, but I gotta go. I'll see you soon." Lexi tossed the phone onto her desk and flew into Vincent's office.

"What the hell?" Vincent's head shot up when the door crashed into the wall, rattling the framed pictures that hung nearby. "Wow, you look gorgeous."

She nearly melted into a puddle right there in the doorway of his office as he smiled at her. Shaking her head from side to side, she forced herself to remember the real reason she had come barreling into his office in the first place, and it wasn't to fish for a compliment.

"Thanks, but we have trouble, big trouble." Lexi began pacing across his office in her high heels, trying to figure out what they were going to do and how they could quickly tweak what they had and turn it into something wonderful, something that would knock Julian Stone's socks off.

"You're making me really nervous here. Is there someone with a gun in the lobby?"

Lexi shook her head no, but continued her rapid movements.

He slowly looked her up and down. "Stalker ex-boyfriend?"

Lexi stopped walking, glared at him, unamused, and then bit her lip as she resumed her walking.

"Have you spent any time in a psychiatric facility?" he asked, slowly reaching for the phone.

Lexi went to his desk and slammed her hand down over his. "Don't ask me how I know this because I will deny it until the day I die, but I just found out that David Reid gave a great presentation to Julian Stone today."

Vincent swore under his breath, then collected himself. "Okay, well, I'll just have to be better than him now, won't I? Nothing to worry about. I can do that. Reid is a walking social disorder."

"That wasn't the bad part. Apparently, his presentation centered on being 'unique' and 'expressing yourself.'" Lexi had barely finished the sentence, but Vincent was already on his feet.

"What did you say?"

"You heard me."

"There must be a mistake." He sat on the edge of his desk.

"I wish there was. My information is from a very reliable source."

Vincent raked his hands though his hair, tugging on the strands before releasing them from his grasp. Suddenly, his face lit up and he grabbed the phone. "Come on … come on … pick up. Someone …"

"Who are you calling?"

"Productions. I'm going to tell them all to stay, and we'll pull an all-nighter if necessary."

"Vincent, it's after seven. No one is down there. You know they run out the door at five o'clock sharp."

"Then get them on their cell phones and tell every one of them to get back in here or they're fired."

"Vincent, most of them left for the airport before lunch. You know Tony took the team to that conference, and that's why all the boards had to be done this morning."

"Do it!" he barked, at his wit's end. "Please, just try," he said in a much softer tone as he closed his eyes and clutched his head, deep in thought.

Lexi ran to her desk and scrolled through the employee logs, searching for phone numbers. She then began the uncomfortable task of calling his production department back in to work or even worse, firing them for not answering Vincent's orders. Phone call after phone call kicked to voice mail, not a single one of them picking up because they were all in the air.

She slammed down the receiver, knowing she wasn't going to be able to get anyone at this point. In sixteen hours, Vincent needed something intelligent to take to Stone, and what they currently had in their possession wasn't going to get them the account.

In the midst of the chaos that swirled around her, Lexi's BlackBerry began vibrating on her desk. There was a text from Hope.

> *Leaving the Crowbar. Be there in fifteen.*
> *H*

"Damn it. She's gonna kill me," Lexi said to no one in particular.

"Language, Miss White," a booming voice chided, "my virgin ears." Sean smugly grinned as he leaned against the wall beside her desk. "Damn, girl, you look hot."

"What do you want, cue ball? We're in full out crisis mode here. I don't have time for this."

"Man, you sound just like Vince. Creepy."

"Sean!"

"Who peed in your cereal?"

Lexi sighed. "Sorry. The Stone presentation. There's been a snag."

"Shit."

"My sentiment exactly."

"Anything I can do to help?"

Lexi sprang to her feet. "Yes! Vincent needs someone to run new pitches with him, brainstorm new ideas and hammer out a plan, and then make the new presentation. Everyone in productions has checked out for the night or left town, and to bring another team in at this hour and get them up to speed on this project would take too long. But you're here, so you can help him!"

"Hold up. I'm not the creative VP. I'm the one that gets the stuff for the ads. Vincent tells me what he wants, and I make it happen. I organize, I plan, I execute. I don't think up the little jingles or draw the cutesie pictures. Trust me, the only creativity I have is in the bedroom. Now, if it's *that* kinda campaign you're talkin' about, count me in."

Lexi flopped back down in her chair, completely dejected. "No, it's not that kind of campaign."

"If you think having me stay will help, I can. I don't have any plans. I was going to eat, and then head home and watch the game."

"A bite to eat. Shit!"

"There you go using that foul language again, Lexi. You know that talk is completely inappropriate for the workplace."

"Sean, shut up and listen. Hope will be here in ten minutes. I was supposed to go out to a nice dinner with her, then go dancing and watch her pick up guys." Lexi quickly appraised Sean in his black suit with a dark gray shirt underneath, open just enough to give a peek at his tan, muscular chest. "I need you to take her out and show her a good time." Sean opened his mouth to make a completely inappropriate comment, but before he could utter a word, Lexi cut him off. "And not *that* kind of good time either. This is it. This is your chance with her. Don't blow it!"

A dazzling smile broke across Sean's face. He straightened his posture, brushed the lint off his jacket, and winked at Lexi. "Gentleman Sean reporting for duty, miss."

"Just don't piss her off. Flatter her, charm her, romance her, but whatever you do, don't call her 'babe'!" Lexi called after his retreating form.

Taking a deep breath, Lexi got out of her seat and headed toward Vincent's office to give him the news about her failed attempt at bringing the productions team back into work. She knew he would be furious, but at this point there wasn't much they could do. There simply wasn't time for a tantrum. They needed to get to work. Lexi thought about calling Elizabeth, but she too was out of town. Running out of options, she bit the bullet and knocked on his door.

"Who's coming back?" Vincent eyed her as he rapidly tapped his pencil on the notebook in front of him.

"No one, Vincent. I called them all, but nobody picked up the phone."

"As usual." Vincent leaned back in his chair and looked at the ceiling.

"Sean was here. I asked if he would stay and help," Lexi said, second guessing her decision to send him out with Hope.

"Oh God, no. Sean and I cannot work together on this part of the project. We'd kill each other."

"I'd call Elizabeth, but she—"

Vincent interrupted with an exasperated sigh. "She left this morning. No, don't bother her. She isn't scheduled to come home until tomorrow night anyway. Well, hell, I'll just do it myself. I'll pull an all-nighter. I did this all the time in college. The stakes weren't as high though. I'll get everything hammered out and then hand it off to whoever strolls in from productions tomorrow. Tony should be back. It's the best I can do at this point." Lexi bit her lip, obviously worrying about him. "Go. You're all dressed up. You must have big plans."

Lexi abruptly turned on her heel and headed for the door. She paused and closed the door, then kicked her black heels into the corner of his office.

"I'm not leaving you here alone. God knows what state this office would be in when you got through with it. Besides, I already sent Sean out to dinner with Hope in my place."

"You really think that was wise?" Vincent grinned as he watched her pull her hair back into a ponytail and twist it into a knot behind her head.

Her light laughter filled the room. "Probably not, but it's encouraging that I haven't gotten a text threatening my life yet. You never know, sometimes you find the best things in the most unexpected places."

"So I hear."

 · 14 ·

Lexi grabbed a notepad and pen off Vincent's desk and sat down on the couch in the corner. They had one night to pull an entirely new Stone campaign together, so there wasn't a second to spare. "Okay, how do we do this?"

Vincent leaned back in his chair and spun in a slow circle, staring at the ceiling. "Well, first we make coffee, lots of coffee." He strolled right out of his office, and Lexi heard him clunking around with the coffeemaker. When he returned to the room, his sleeves were rolled up to his elbows and his tie was in his hand. He slowly flicked open his shirt at the collar.

"What were the other pitches you considered for this account? Was there anything good you didn't go with that maybe we can tweak one way or another?" Lexi asked hopefully.

Vincent shook his head and pulled a file out of his drawer, then sat down on the couch beside her, spreading the contents on the coffee table. "Stone was so hard to get a read on at the time; we didn't have much to go on. And now, after getting to know him a little, I can see it's all crap. He won't like any of it." His hands raked through his hair.

Lexi quickly skimmed through the papers on the table and agreed with Vincent's assessment of the situation. "Fine," she closed the folder and tossed it into the trashcan beside her, "we start fresh." She raised her pen to the paper. "Show me what you've got, Mister Vice President. Impress me."

Vincent gave her a cocky smile and started rattling off ideas that Lexi scribbled down as fast as he could speak. Every so often she added one or two of her own thoughts while Vincent paced the room, thinking.

Hours later, crumpled pieces of yellow paper littered the office floor. Others were taped to the dry erase board Vincent had dragged in from Elizabeth's office. He paced the room like a caged tiger, trying to come up with a tag line that felt right for the Stone project. On his five hundredth lap around the room, he nearly stumbled over Lexi, who was now sprawled out on the floor, flat on her back, her long, shapely legs running up the wall.

"What the hell are you doing?"

"Shhhh, I'm concentrating," Lexi whispered, holding a finger to her smiling lips. "Perspective is everything."

"We'll, I'm starving. Let's order something to eat. Screw perspective, I'm far more creative on a full stomach."

That perked Lexi up considerably. "Tell me you like Thai food."

"Never had it, actually." Vincent shrugged looking down as he loomed over her. "Is that what you want?"

Lexi quirked an eyebrow at him. "Do you like spicy food? If not, this might not be the thing for you."

Vincent rolled his eyes. "I think I can handle it."

"Okay," Lexi snickered, "then let's eat."

Vincent held out his hand and helped Lexi up from the floor. "Do you know a good place?" Lexi quickly rattled off a phone number. "Here," he thrust a phone at her, "you make the call."

"What do you want? Shrimp, pork, or chicken?"

"Surprise me." Vincent smugly smiled, challenging Lexi. "And make it spicy."

An hour later, boxes of food from a variety of entrees covered Vincent's desk. There were noodles, dips, and sauces, as well as chicken, pork, and shrimp dishes to choose from.

"I think we're getting closer, don't you?" Lexi asked as she grabbed a plate. She filled it high with spicy chicken and rice, then went back to the couch and stretched out. She was surprised when Vincent came and sat on the floor, leaning his back up against the couch in front of her.

"Yes, but let's take a break from the project talk until we're done eating. Rest and refuel."

"Done." Lexi took a heaping bite of food.

"Think it's a good sign we haven't heard from Sean or Hope yet?" Vincent chuckled as he set his plate onto his lap.

"I think it means so far Sean has had the good sense to keep his mouth shut. Either that, or she's killed him and is dumping his body into the bay as we speak." Vincent laughed out loud. "Don't let her size fool you. She knows how to wield a tire iron."

"Don't piss off Hope. Got it."

"He doesn't have a girlfriend, right?"

"No, he'd been seeing someone casually, but it wasn't going well at all. Then recently, I think it was the day we went to Crowbar, as a matter of fact, he officially broke it off with her."

Lexi hid a little smile. "Good to know."

Vincent looked over at Lexi and cautiously stabbed at curry shrimp. "So, tell me what you've been doing for the last ten years."

"It's a long, boring story. You really don't want to hear it." Lexi shoveled some rice into her mouth to try to avoid any further discussion of the topic, but Vincent persisted.

"Actually, I do. And since I'm your boss, you can't say no." Lexi playfully kicked his shoulder with her bare foot. "Anna said something about NYU."

"I made it through three glorious semesters." Lexi sighed.

"Did you like living in New York?"

"Loved every minute of it." Her eyes clouded with sadness. "I only wish I could have stayed longer."

Vincent watched the pain flit across Lexi's face as she became lost in her thoughts. He knew some of her story; Anna had filled him in. He placed his hand on her leg and gave it a reassuring squeeze. "I'm so sorry about your dad."

A single tear rolled down her cheek, but Lexi quickly wiped it away, unwilling to wallow in her sadness any longer. Harry wouldn't have wanted that for her. She placed her hand over Vincent's and held onto it for a second, relishing the contact. "Thanks."

"I think what you did, dropping out of school to take care of him, is easily the most selfless thing I have ever heard of someone doing."

"He is…he was my dad. There was no way in hell I was going to let him go through that alone." Lexi paused, chewing the mouthful of spicy chicken. "Even at the end, when he didn't remember who I was, *I* knew who I was, and I knew I was doing the right thing by him, so it was manageable."

Vincent gave her a sad smile, and then popped a piece of shrimp into his mouth. He tried to speak, but instead began sputtering, waving his hand in front of his mouth. "Hot!" He filled his mouth with ice from his drink, hoping to dull the pain, but his eyes started watering when no relief came.

Lexi stifled a laugh and ripped off a piece of bread, handing it to him. "You're the one that said to get it spicy. Just put this in your mouth for a few seconds and breathe, Vincent, breathe." She gently patted him on the back until his breathing slowed down.

"How do you eat this stuff?" Vincent wiped his eyes. "I think my taste buds were just incinerated."

"Are you always such a baby?"

"When I swallow something that has the same effects as Drano? Yeah."

Lexi threw another piece of bread at his head and seized the moment to change the topic of conversation to him. She pointed up at the diplomas hanging on his wall. "So after Stanford, you went to Columbia for grad school?"

"Yeah, from one end of the country to another." He went and rummaged through the rest of the boxes, looking for something safe to eat. "What else in here won't dissolve the lining of my stomach?"

Lexi groaned and got up off the couch to help him. "Here, eat this. It has an orange glaze on it, so it's sweet without the heat of the chilies." Vincent eyed her cautiously. "It's on the kids' menu at the restaurant so I *think* you can handle it."

"Smartass." Vincent popped a piece of pork into his mouth and grinned as he went and sat back down.

"It's part of my charm." Lexi joined him on the couch and watched him happily dig into the pork. "So, why the cross country move after undergrad?" The smile slipped from his face, and he stared at his plate intently. "Never mind." Lexi wished she hadn't brought up the subject.

"It's fine. I just needed to put some space between me and a few people." He laid his head back on the couch and studied the ceiling.

"So things didn't work out with Jennifer?" Lexi remembered that the golden couple of Riverdale High had both been accepted at Stanford, making everyone in town speculate that they'd be walking down the aisle eventually.

"Jennifer?" His head shot up and he laughed. "Oh Lord, no! Jennifer and I were over well before I graduated college. Hell, we were almost over by our high school graduation." He shook his head from side to side at the mention of her name.

"Really? You two always looked so happy together. You were the 'it' couple, you know." Vincent rolled his eyes. "I'm serious. Everyone wanted to be you guys."

"Yeah, well, things weren't always as they seemed." He became very quiet as he found himself lost in his own thoughts. "Being popular wasn't all it was cracked up to be."

"Yeah, rough life having everyone adore you, being the star of the football team, girls throwing themselves at you and being able to get away with murder by flashing a sexy smile. Sounds like hell." Lexi twirled a piece of chicken on her fork.

"Did you really think I had a sexy smile?" Vincent leaned closer and grinned from ear to ear, his pearly white teeth on full display as she inadvertently stroked his ego.

"I was a child. I didn't know any better," Lexi quipped. Vincent placed his hand over his heart, pretending to be hurt by her words. "Oh please, I'm sure Jennifer stroked your ego every chance she got."

Vincent snickered. "She was shallow. I can see that now. But at the time, I thought she was genuine. Lesson learned."

Lexi had to stifle a laugh. The similarities between Jade and Jennifer were endless. They both had that smile-sweetly-to-your-face-then-stab-you-in-the-back vibe about them. Lexi highly doubted that he had learned nearly as much as he thought, but she kept her opinion to herself. "Who do you keep in touch with from Riverdale?" she asked.

"No one. I was so ready to graduate, it wasn't even funny. I didn't care if I saw any of them ever again." Lexi raised an eyebrow at him in disbelief. "Really. All of my 'good friends' were totally fake. Because my family had money, they all wanted to be my buddy. Every single one of them wanted something from me and yet were ready to let me take the blame for their screw-ups the first chance they got."

Vincent got up off the couch and grabbed two bottles of water and handed one to Lexi. "Do you remember my graduation party?" he asked.

"I knew you had one, but I didn't go. My invitation must have been lost in the mail."

"Thanks, like I don't feel like enough of a jerk already." He shook his head. "Anyway, I wasn't going to have one, but all of my friends talked me into it. Mom and Dad took Anna to Los Angeles for the weekend to go shopping as her graduation gift, and I stayed behind. As soon as they left for the airport, people poured out of the woods around the house, beers in hand. By Sunday morning, the house was trashed. And do you know how many people stayed to help me clean it all up before my parents got home? None of them. They all emptied my parent's liquor cabinet, screwed each other in their beds, and ate every piece of food in the house, but no one could be bothered to stay and help me scrub the vomit out of the carpet or pick up the empties that were strewn about the yard."

"That's terrible." Lexi could see his jaw tense as he wallowed in the memory.

"They did that kind of thing all the time. They'd borrow my car, then return it with no gas and junk all over the floor, or a nice dent in it that they didn't expect me to notice. Over the summer, when my grandfather got sick, my parents came down here a lot on the weekends to check on him. It was like they had radar, and as soon as my parents left for the airport, people just appeared at my house, ready to party."

"I bet that got old fast," Lexi commented, and Vincent nodded his head in agreement. "How did they even know when your parents were leaving?"

"Jennifer."

"What a bitch."

Vincent laughed and took the empty plate from her hand, tossing it into the trash. "My thoughts exactly when I walked in on her and my roommate lathering one another in the shower my freshman year at Stanford."

Lexi choked on her water. "Oh God, what did you do?"

"I walked out of the room and knocked on every door I passed and told them two people were screwing in my bathroom. He and Jennifer were so occupied, it took a good five minutes before they even noticed they weren't alone." He glanced up at the clock then sat back down behind his desk and returned his attention to the papers in front of him as he prepared to get back to work. "High school was a totally artificial environment, nothing was genuine. It made college quite an eye opening experience in many ways. For example, I quickly found out that being the big fish in the Riverdale football pond was meaningless to college football scouts. They couldn't have cared less about the snot-nosed kid from some no-name town. Stanford was a harsh introduction to reality for Mr. Popular here."

Lexi watched him busy himself to avoid making eye contact with her. She knew better than anyone that appearances could be deceiving, but she never thought that applied to Vincent Drake. The guy who had everything at his fingertips was just an illusion.

In reality, he had been more like her than she ever could have imagined. He too had been ready to close the door on that chapter of his life as soon as the valedictorian speech ended. She thought back to their brief encounter on graduation day, and for a fleeting moment, she wondered: if she had offered him her hand, would he have taken it and left with her?

As she looked at the man sitting behind the desk ten feet from her, she knew it didn't matter. None of it was important now. It was like she said earlier—perspective was everything. And now she realized that popular and invisible were simply labels. They didn't do anything to really describe the people who wore them. They told nothing about their heart or soul.

"Back to work. What have we come up with that we actually like?" Vincent had asked that question five times already, and each time they axed a few more ideas. They'd whittled it down to just two or three things, but none of them were *the* idea they needed to catch Julian Stone's attention.

Lexi examined the scraps of paper that hung on the wall and tore them all down, shaking her head. "We need to go back to the beginning. Let's start fresh. Forget the old campaign, put it out of your mind. It's dead to us. What do we know about him?"

"He's young, hip, good looking?" He turned to Lexi who nodded in agreement. "His stuff is edgy, mysterious, and classically rebellious."

Lexi stopped jotting things down and mulled that over. "Explain classically rebellious to me." She jumped to her feet and tapped her pen on her hip as she listened to the smooth sound of Vincent's voice.

"Well, he's pushing the envelope. His stuff is reminiscent of James Dean with a *Rebel Without a Cause* kind of vibe, but modernized, don't you think? The way he weaves old elements with new."

Lexi abruptly stopped walking. "Old and new... weaving old with new!" She ran over to his desk and wedged herself between his chair and his computer. She quickly Googled James Dean and pulled up a few classic pictures of him from the fifties. "Keep talking." Lexi turned the screen so he would have a clear view.

"I don't know. I'm not a fashion guy."

Lexi rolled her eyes. Her fingers flew over the keyboard, and she continued to surf the net until a coy smile danced across her face. Music began pouring out of the computer speakers.

"What the hell is that?" Vincent asked.

Lexi pressed her slender finger to her lips, which curved up into a triumphant smile. Impatiently, Vincent listened to the song. He had never heard it before, but could pick up a familiar melody running behind the lyrics. He furrowed his brow and asked, "Is that the melody to ..."

"It's a classic song, with a new edge to it." Lexi nodded her head. "This was all over the radio eighteen months ago." She quickly pulled up four more songs in which the artists took the hook or the melody from a classic song and put their own twist on it. A light bulb went off in Vincent's head.

"Weaving old and new." Vincent was on his feet, running his hand through his hair as he stared out his window at the illuminated San Francisco skyline. "I can see the campaign. We use classic songs—Beatles and the Rolling Stones, of course," he turned and winked at Lexi, "in the background for the music. We can even do album covers plastered all over the backdrop of the photo shoot." Vincent's voice was excited, confident as he came to stand beside Lexi, who had moved into his desk chair and curled her legs underneath her as she listened, quickly taking notes.

"What if we took it further?" Lexi suggested. Vincent stopped walking and waited for her to continue. "Somehow spin the line and say that it's so classically modern that his pieces can be mixed and matched with those timeless pieces from your wardrobe—like the white T-shirt, the jeans, the leather jackets, the little black dresses—to make something old new again, just like these songs."

Vincent ran his palm along his stubbled jaw, thinking. Lexi watched as his head slowly started to bob up and down until he was nodding in agreement. "It's a risk, though, having us suggest that the public doesn't need to buy a whole Julian Stone outfit. His people might not like it."

"How many people do we see walking the streets looking like they are a head-to-toe ad for Chanel or Gucci? It looks lame, like they're trying too hard. One piece of Julian Stone clothing mixed with something from your own wardrobe says knowledge of fashion. Wear the clothes; don't let the clothes wear you."

"I know what you're saying, but I think we'll still catch flack from his reps."

Lexi stood up and stretched her arms over her head, trying to unknot the muscles of her back and shoulders. "Then we just have to make it so damn good that Julian falls in love with it and tells his people to go take a hike if they don't like it." As she extended her arms, her shirt crept up, and she felt a cool breeze as a tiny sliver of her abdomen was exposed.

She glanced over at Vincent to see him with a dazed, far away expression. "Vincent? Did you hear what I said?"

"No, sorry. I was thinking about something else."

Lexi's face dropped. "I was just trying to help. If my idea was off base, I apologize. You're the VP, I'll be quiet."

Vincent went over to the desk and placed his palms in the center of it, leaning across the surface until his face was inches from hers. "You know that you're utterly ridiculous, right? Your idea was great. I love the spin. Yes, it will be a little bit tougher to sell, but I can do it." He paused, his eyes darkening and becoming more intense as he stared at her. "You are an amazing woman, Alexandra White. Don't ever let anyone tell you differently. Not even me." His lips slowly curled up into a teasing smile.

They spent the next three hours outlining the proposal and framing the mockup of the ads. Shortly after midnight, they moved down to the productions room to construct the layouts for the large presentation boards. Vincent blasted classic Beatles and Rolling Stones tunes through the workstation for inspiration, but Lexi knew it was also to keep them awake as the night drew on.

A few hours later, Lexi salvaged what she could of the original PowerPoint presentation and made the necessary changes while Vincent worked on the presentation boards and materials at the drafting table. He was also sending E-mails in an effort to get permission to use the album covers, not only in the presentation, but also for the potential campaign. He meticulously organized the graphics packet, making sure it portrayed the same classically rebellious vibe they were going for with the presentation. He glanced over at Lexi when he heard her singing along to the song that was playing. Her head bobbed in beat with the music, her ponytail whipping from side to side in a playful way. As he waited for the packet to be finished, he strode over to the computer to check on her.

Lexi was cutting and pasting the new bullet points into the presentation when she felt him lean over her shoulder, his hand resting on the desk beside the keyboard as he peeked over her shoulder to see the screen.

"You missed the 's' here." His arm reached around her, his much larger body surrounding hers for a second. She was tired and wanted to lean her head back against his chest and settle into the warmth of his arms. Sleep deprivation only fueled her already overactive imagination. She stifled a yawn with the back of her hand and made the correction. His body shook with a deep rumble of laughter behind her.

"Sleepy?"

Lexi scowled. "I'm fine. Did you get the approval for the covers?"

He confidently shrugged his shoulders. "Of course. I told you I knew a guy."

Too tired to argue, Lexi held up her hand to stop him. "Good enough for me." She pulled the flash drive out of the computer and wearily made it to her feet. "I'm going back upstairs to pull in the new demographics package. I need the projection numbers and cost analysis, but it's on my laptop. If you need me, that's where I'll be." Lexi's eyes closed for a second as she took a few steps forward and crashed into something hard. She felt Vincent's arms wrap around her to keep her from falling.

"I think I better go with you so you don't end up wandering around on the wrong floor." He laced his fingers with hers and guided her toward the elevator. "Come on, honey, let's get some coffee in you."

She caught snippets of what he said, but she wasn't really listening. There was a playful twinkle in his eyes as he held her, a look that she adored and rarely got to see anymore. Lexi knew she was half out of her mind from lack of sleep, but her body was begging to touch him, to get closer, to feel every inch of him. She fought the urge to gently place her lips to the exposed skin of his chest and feather kisses up his neck. Delirium must have set in, because she could have sworn she heard him call her "honey."

She followed him down the hall, her eyes remaining focused on their interlocked hands. When she felt the pad of his thumb gently brush back and forth over her hand, but her pulse soared and her temperature rose with each pass of his finger. He tugged at her hand, pulling her into the tiny elevator with him.

"What time is it?" Lexi grabbed Vincent's wrist and wrenched his arm so she could read his watch. "Holy crap, three thirty a.m. already?" She quickly checked her reflection in the mirrored walls of the elevator. "Great, my hair looks like a shrub."

Vincent smoothed out a few of the stray strands. "There, perfect."

"Thanks." Her eyes pulled away from his and lifted up to watch the illuminated floor numbers on the elevator.

The large doors slid open and the couple slowly sauntered past Leigh's empty desk. It was odd to be in the office and have the hallways quiet and free of the normal hustle and bustle of Hunter Advertising. No ringing phones, no beeping intercoms, no laughter, just the quiet padding of their feet on the carpet.

"Why don't you go home, Lexi. You look exhausted."

She shrugged. "I can't. I don't have my car. Hope gave me a ride here this morning and was going to pick me up."

"I can give you a ride," Vincent offered. "It's the least I can do considering how much you helped me tonight."

"When you're ready to go home for the night, I'll take you up on that, but I can wait."

Vincent looked at the clock and shrugged. "Actually, I was just planning on crashing here. By the time I get home and get to bed, it'll just be time to wake up, so why bother? I can run you home. It's no problem."

Lexi leaned back in her desk chair and waved a dismissive hand at him. "Don't worry about it. I'm fine. There's still plenty of work to do. How about that coffee you promised?"

Grinning, Vincent went straight to the coffee machine and poured two cups, then handed the one with cream and sugar to an exhausted Lexi. "Here, drink this. It should help."

Lexi held the mug tightly in her hands, allowing the warmth of the coffee to spread through her body. The air conditioning of the office put a chill in the air at that hour of the morning. Vincent led Lexi into his office where her laptop was still lying on his couch. While she merged the files, Vincent found his suit jacket and draped it over her shoulders to help keep her warm.

Her hand came up and met his as it rested on her shoulder. "Thank you."

An hour later, Vincent began running through the new pitch. He only had a few hours to practice and had to get all traces of the old campaign out of his memory. Lexi stayed huddled under Vincent's jacket while as he presented. Occasionally, she corrected him or suggested he reword the phrasing to make it seem less stiff, remembering Julian's concern with Vincent. But for the most part, she sat back and watched a master work.

Of course, Lexi noticed, there was nothing stiff about Vincent as he strode back and forth across the room, passionately explaining the idea of the campaign and why he felt it was the right path for Julian to take. He exuded confidence and power when he spoke. Each gesture, each facial expression was designed to give emphasis to all the main points. Lexi remained captivated as she watched him move, and the deep tone of his voice washed over her like a caress. The sight of him in his element was extraordinary.

When he finished, Lexi sat stunned. "Vincent that was amazing. You're so natural with it after only a couple run-throughs."

Proud but exhausted, Vincent smiled and sat down next to her on the couch, his head tipping back and his eyes closing, but his smile never wavering. "Thanks. I think we did it, Lexi. This is so much better than the original. He has to love it." He yawned, then tapped his fingers on the arm of the couch. "I'm going to review the PowerPoint one more time. Why don't you get a little sleep?" He handed her a throw pillow then waited until she placed it under her head and closed her eyes.

"Fine," she said through a yawn, "but only because you're my boss and you ordered me to."

Vincent laughed as he walked to his desk. She was by far the most stubborn woman he had met in a long time, and yet somehow, she was getting under his skin. He found himself looking forward to moments like this when they would banter back and forth like old friends. "Like I could get you to do anything you didn't want to do."

He waited for her snarky comeback, but was met only by silence. When he turned around, he saw the gentle rise and fall of her chest accompanied by the sounds of her deep breathing. The beautiful Alexandra White was already fast asleep.

As she lay there, Vincent couldn't help but think about what a kind, selfless woman Lexi was. Who better than she to be jaded by the breaks she had been dealt her in life? And yet, through the death of her mother and then her father, which inevitably turned her life upside down, somehow Lexi came through it with her beautiful spirit intact.

He envied her—her strength, her perseverance, her grace, all of the tiny facets that made Lexi the most intriguing person he had ever met. How he wished he had her ability to be true to herself despite the rotten things life threw at her. But Vincent knew he was different, bitter and cynical because of the past, which he had unfortunately allowed to dictate who he was. While she was light and sunshine, he was nothing but clouds and darkness.

He flew through the slides of the PowerPoint, not really paying attention to them anymore, only wanting to shut his eyes for a few seconds for a power nap. After fighting the urge through the last few frames, he finally succumbed when a soft "Vincent" escaped Lexi's lips, drawing him to her side. He knelt beside her as she twitched in her sleep.

"Harry," she whimpered as her dreams continued, her body becoming more restless with each passing moment.

"Shhhh, it's okay. Harry's safe, don't worry." For some reason, her distress cut through Vincent, and he found himself compelled to try and comfort her. He ran his hand down the side of her face, his fingers lightly brushing the soft, creamy skin. Careful not to wake her, he sat down on the couch, patting her leg as he closed his eyes for the briefest of moments, hoping to get in a quick power nap before dawn. As he settled in and got comfortable, Lexi unconsciously curled up beside him like a kitten.

His head tipped back to rest on the couch, and a smile of masculine satisfaction played across his lips when she breathlessly said his name one last time. Then he drifted off to sleep.

· 15 ·

Madison's tiny feet zoomed across the plush carpet before she abruptly stopped. She turned to her mother, who stood in the doorway wide-eyed with shock.

"Mommy," Madison whispered, her head slightly tilted to the side, "is it nap time?"

Anna chuckled. "No, baby, it's not nap time. And I thought Leigh was making this up," she mumbled to herself as she stepped into the room.

"Is Uncle Vincent dead?"

"Well, he might be soon," Anna snickered, imagining what would have happened if Jade walked into the room and made this cozy discovery. Lexi's head was nestled against Vincent's chest, his arm draped protectively around her, holding his jacket in place over her body. The look of peaceful contentment on his face alone would have sent Jade into orbit.

"Why is Lexi laying on Uncle Vince?"

Anna quirked an eyebrow and wondered about that herself. "I think they had a lot of work to do last night." She glanced around the room and took in the presentation boards and scraps of paper littering the floor.

"Ooh, they stayed up past their bedtimes? Lucky."

At the sound of his niece's high pitched laughter, Vincent's eyes popped open and darted around the room, trying to locate the source of the noise.

"Who died?" A very disoriented Vincent stretched his arms high over his head and waited for his sister to answer. He paused only for a second to look down and find Lexi nestled at his side. A little stunned, he looked up at Anna and found her with her hands planted on her hips, grinning.

Madison's high-pitched voice brought him back to reality. "My pet fish Ariel died the other day, remember? Mommy said she gave him a burial at sea, but really she just flushed him down the potty." Madison crept closer to the couch. "Lexi, Lexi, wake up. Did you and Uncle Vince have a nice sleepover?"

Lexi stirred, but kept her eyes tightly closed. When she finally moved, she began patting Vincent's chest, as if trying to figure out what, or rather who, exactly she was curled up against. Anna snickered when she heard Lexi repeating "No, no, no."

"Morning, sunshine!" Anna sang as Lexi's eyes slowly opened to find three faces watching her closely, waiting for a reaction. Madison smiled as she crawled into Vincent's lap, nestling up on the other side of him and mirroring Lexi's position. Lexi looked scared while Anna remained silent, but she looked even more terrified when she dared to look up into Vincent's eyes.

"You snore like a freight train," Lexi said as she pushed off of him and perched herself on the opposite end of the couch, smoothing out her hair and tugging at the bottom of her wrinkled shirt.

"I do not," Vincent said indignantly as he placed a kiss on the top of Madison's head. "Anyway, you talk in your sleep." He cast a mischievous glance in her direction.

Lexi's face went white, and her eyes got huge, as if she remembered quite clearly the wildly vivid fantasy she had been frolicking in all night long. One that possibly involved her legs wrapped around Vincent in the back seat of a long, black limousine. Her cheeks flushed pink, not even wanting to imagine what she might have said, or God forbid, moaned in her sleep.

Vincent tried to give her a reassuring smile. "Don't worry. I couldn't understand a word of it. You just mumbled a lot."

Lexi let out the breath. She didn't have time to worry about the dream or if he was telling the truth once Madison began asking questions.

"So do you guys have sleepovers a lot?"

Anna snorted as her daughter's question made both Vincent and Lexi's cheeks turn red.

"No!" they said in unison.

"Oh," Madison's face fell. "Well, next time you have one, can I come?" The hopeful smile on her face was impossible to resist.

"Um, sure?" Lexi replied, looking to Vincent for some guidance, but he was busy glaring at Anna.

"You can be the chaperone, baby. Someone needs to keep an eye on these two, I think."

"Do you ever have sleepovers with Miss Jade and Lexi at the same time?"

Vincent's mouth fell open at his niece's innocent but probing question. Anna didn't even try to hide her amusement as Vincent sputtered in shock.

"Madison, who Uncle Vincent invites to his sleepovers is none of our business."

"Anna, you're not helping here." Vincent was interrupted when Lexi let out a yelp.

"Wait, what time is it?" Lexi glanced over at the window and for the first time noticed the bright sunshine streaming into the room. She was on her feet in a matter of seconds, Vincent's jacket falling to the floor at her feet.

"Shit! I mean shoot. Oh hell, sorry, Anna!" Vincent apologized and swept Madison into his arms, kissed her cheek, and handed her off to his sister.

"When the school calls about Maddie's language, I'm making *you* go in and meet with the principal, Vincent," Anna scolded, waving her finger at her brother, who was paying absolutely no attention.

"It's almost nine thirty. We have three hours until the presentation," Vincent said and sat down behind his desk to begin typing as Lexi ran around the room picking up all the wadded up pieces of paper.

"It will take you at least twenty minutes to get there," Lexi offered as she hastily stuffed the papers into the trashcan beside Vincent. "Traffic won't be a problem at this time of day. I used to work in the same part of town as his studio," she said in answer to Vincent's quizzical expression.

"We're just going to get out of your way. It looks like you have a lot to do here," Anna said as she carried Madison toward the door.

"Wait." Lexi dropped the last piece of trash into the can and stole Madison from Anna's arms. "We need to run a very important errand before you go." She winked at Madison and whispered something in her ear.

"Yes, Mom, it is very important. We need to, um, scout a location. Isn't that what Daddy does?" Lexi threw her head back and laughed out loud, Vincent joining in soon after.

"That's my girl, Madison," Vincent chuckled.

"Oh, go get a cookie, you two. Like I don't know that's where you're headed." Anna laughed, and then waved them out the door.

With Madison and Lexi gone, Vincent tried to busy himself behind his desk to avoid any further interrogation, but his twin wasn't having any of it. "So, do you want to tell me what the hell was going on in here?"

"We're working under a major time crunch, that's what's going on here. We had to completely redo the Stone presentation last night. Lexi found out that Reid gave a presentation that had a similar theme to ours, and I couldn't walk in there without something that would blow Reid out of the water." He pecked away at the keys on his keyboard, his eyes fixed on his computer screen. "What we came up with is even better than the original, I think."

Anna crossed her arms and cleared her throat to get Vincent's attention. "And this morning?"

"What about this morning?"

"Well, you two looked very ... *cozy* on the couch together."

Vincent rolled his eyes. "We were sleeping, Anna. Nothing happened. Lexi fell asleep on the couch around four this morning. I worked a few more hours then had to close my eyes for a minute for a power nap. Next thing I knew, you and Madison were standing there and launched into your version of the Spanish Inquisition."

Anna and Vincent stayed locked in a stare down of wills, waiting to see who would give in first. Anna, of course, won.

"She's my assistant."

"She's brilliant, beautiful, witty, and puts up with you and your shit."

"Language, Anna."

"Bite me, Vincent."

"What do you want me to say?" Vincent waited as Anna gnawed on her lip, trying to formulate the right words.

"Nothing, I just want you to be happy. Sue me."

"When this presentation is over and Stone hires Hunter, *then* I'll be happy." Vincent gathered up the presentation papers that were scattered on his desk.

"That's not what I meant, Vincent." Anna pouted as her brother made his way over to her.

"I know, Anna, and I'm fine, but thank you for worrying."

"I just think that you and Lex—"

"Uncle Vincent! I got you breakfast!" Madison flung herself through the door and handed Vincent a chocolate chip cookie.

"A cookie at this hour of the morning?" Vincent eyed the treat. "I wonder whose unhealthy version of breakfast this is."

Lexi gave Vincent a dirty look and yanked the cookie from his hand as she passed. While he watched, she took an exaggerated bite out of it and winked. "Deliciously unhealthy." Vincent opened his mouth to protest, but Lexi silenced him with a smug smile. "You snooze, you lose."

Madison snuggled up to her uncle. "Don't worry, Uncle Vince. I brought you an extra." She placed another tiny treat into his hand.

"Honey, we need to let them get back to work." Anna started to usher her daughter toward the door.

"Wait! Where are the invitations?" Madison demanded.

Lexi watched as Anna handed her daughter two blue envelopes from her purse. On the front, written in crayon, were Lexi's and Vincent's names and dozens of little flowers. Madison skipped over to Lexi and bounced up and down as she ripped open the paper and pulled out the card inside. "Can you come? Can you come?"

"A tea party? I would love to come to your tea party, Madison. Thank you for inviting me."

"Uncle Vince, you're coming, right? I have your hat all picked out." Madison grinned at her uncle, who bent down and kissed her on the cheek.

"I wouldn't miss it for the world. Are you going to make Lexi wear a hat too? I bet she would like a really fancy hat."

"Ooh, Madison, how about that pink one with the feathers all around it? We have the matching boa and everything," Anna chimed into the conversation, ignoring Lexi's murderous glare.

"When's the party, sweetie?" Lexi asked Madison, ignoring Vincent's chuckles.

"Tonight!" Madison twirled around the office, her cookie held high above her head as she spun.

"Oh, I might not be able to make it. I don't have a car today. I was supposed to pick it up last night." Anna watched Lexi's pained expression when she saw how sad her news had made Madison. "If there was anything I could do I would."

"Maybe another time then, Maddie." Anna tried to comfort her daughter.

"She'll be there," Vincent said as he pulled the flash drive from his computer and tossed it to Lexi. "I'll give her a ride, no problem."

Before Lexi could say a word, Madison squeaked in delight. "I love you, Uncle Vince! Thank you." She waved as Anna gently ushered her daughter out of the office. "See you later!"

"Bye, Maddie," Lexi and Vincent said at the same time as Anna closed the office door.

Lexi smiled and turned from the closed door. "You don't have to take me over to Anna's this afternoon. I'll call Hope and see if she can drop the car off for me."

Vincent shrugged. "It's no big deal."

Lexi glanced at her watch. "Do you want to run through the presentation one more time really fast? Or do you need to go home and change instead?"

"Well, first I have favor to ask." He eyed Lexi apprehensively, but her warm smile put him at ease. "Feel like coming to the Stone presentation with me? That way, if I get stuck or go off track, you can be there to set me straight."

"You want me to go?" Lexi stammered. "And talk?"

Vincent's smile made her stomach do that wonderful flip flop thing. "Yes, please?" The intensity of his eyes alone would have been enough to make her agree, but what he said next sealed the deal. "I need you, Lexi."

Unsure that her mouth would be able to produce coherent speech, she simply nodded her head.

"Fantastic. Why don't I drive you to your place and drop you off. Then I'll run to my apartment, shower and change, and then pick you up about forty-five minutes before the presentation. That should give us enough time to get there and get everything set up and maybe even run through it one more time before Julian shows up. Will that give you enough time to get ready?"

Lexi's brain shut down after hearing that Vincent would be coming to her apartment. Busy worrying about whether there was a pile of laundry on her couch and dirty dishes in her sink, she only half listened to what he was saying.

"That should be—"

"What the hell happened to my art room?" Tony roared as he burst through the door. Vincent's entire body tensed, his jaw clenched, and his eyes darkened with anger, but he remained cool as he spoke, his voice never faltering.

"*Your* art room?"

"There's stuff everywhere. Papers, prints, photographs. What the hell was wrong with the presentation that you had to mess with it and leave the place looking like a bomb went off? You signed off on everything. There should've been no edits necessary!" Tony's face was red by the time he ended his rant. It was only then that he noticed Lexi. An evil sneer crossed his face. "Or maybe it was *you* that messed everything up."

"Tony," Vincent growled, taking a step toward his cousin. "Enough. I was down in productions last night. I made the mess. I had this new idea for the Stone account, and I went for it. No one else was in town to help, and you were conveniently unable to be reached, so I handled it myself. I *apologize*," he ground out the last word through gritted teeth, "if the room is not as clean as you would like. I'd be happy to have someone clean it for you."

It took every bit of self-control Vincent had to make that statement, Lexi was certain of that. His hands were balled at his sides, his knuckles white from his tight grip. The muscles of his jaw visibly clenched and unclenched as he attempted to keep his fury in check.

Tony continued to glare at Vincent, then glanced over at Lexi in her wrinkled clothes and disheveled hair. His gaze turned back to Vincent, and he seemed to take note of his haggard appearance, something very out of character for his usually perfect cousin. That's when he asked in a snide voice, "So the two of you were here all night? *Together?*"

"I'm going to start printing out the packets and getting everything packed up. I'll be at my desk." With her gaze planted on her shoes, Lexi stepped out of the room and, in her hurry, didn't close the door all the way. From behind her desk she had a view of everything going on inside and could hear the argument continue.

Tony hardly waited for Lexi to leave the room before he started in again, "So you and Lexi, huh? I knew you two were hooking up."

With Lexi out of the room, Vincent apparently saw no reason to contain his anger any longer. He began laying into Tony without apprehension. "Listen, I'm going to say this once. You work for me. If I want to come down to productions and work on a campaign, I can do that. Would I have preferred to hand this off to you or one of your people? Yes. However, you sent them all to a conference the same time Jared took his team out of town with my mother *and* on the eve of a huge presentation, I might add. Pretty piss poor planning on your part, wouldn't you say? I wonder what Elizabeth would think? Doesn't show very good management skills, now does it?" Tony remained silent as Vincent continued to seethe. "But don't worry. Lexi did stay and help me with it, and this pitch is ten times better than the original. You better be careful, cousin, she might move up the corporate ladder faster than you."

"Fuck you."

"No, fuck *you*, Tony. And if I hear one little hateful word come from your mouth about Lexi again, you'll be sorry. Painfully sorry."

The anger in Vincent's voice made Lexi shudder.

"So protective of her. I wonder what Jade would think about you showing such loyalty to your assistant."

Vincent charged at Tony like a bullet, pinning him to the wall with a loud crash. His nose was millimeters away from Tony's. "Not another word or it will be your last."

The two men stayed locked together for a minute before Tony broke eye contact. "Get off me." He gave Vincent a shove, but like a brick wall, Vincent didn't budge.

"Do we understand each other?"

Tony refused to answer him. Instead, he wormed his way out of Vincent's grasp and stepped out of Lexi's view in the direction of the production boards and began critiquing everything.

"The photo layouts could be better. You needed to use the higher resolution when you merged the picture fields. Next time leave it to the professionals so you don't look like such an amateur. This one is on you, Vincent. You lose this account, and you have no one to blame but yourself. And personally, I would love for everyone to finally see that you aren't half as great as you think you are."

Lexi heard Tony's footsteps heading toward the door so she quickly busied herself, keeping her gaze down on her desk as he stormed past and slammed the door shut behind him.

Seconds later, Vincent had gathered up all the presentation materials and rushed out of his office with the production boards in his hand.

"You ready?" he asked Lexi as she bent behind her desk, scooping color copies out of her printer as fast as she could.

Lexi waved a single finger at him. "Last copy, then I'm good to go."

Vincent laid the materials down and quickly poured each of them a tall cup of coffee. By the time Lexi came from behind her desk, he had her coat draped over his arm. He gallantly held the jacket out so she could slip her arms inside. She stole one of the cups of coffee from the counter and headed down the hall, not even bothering to wait for Vincent.

In the elevator, Vincent began practicing the pitch, and they came up with a hand signal for Lexi to give if he slipped into too formal a tone, which he had a tendency to do when feeling stressed. Their voices echoed in the massive concrete parking garage as they continued discussing what points Vincent should emphasize. Lexi nearly dropped her briefcase when Vincent stopped at his car. In the parking space was a Matchbox-sized black Lotus convertible.

"What the hell is this?" she laughed, peering down at his undersized car.

He popped the trunk and carefully maneuvered the production boards inside with barely any room to spare. He slammed it shut and rolled his eyes. "It's a Lotus, Lexi."

"Yeah, but where's the rest of it?"

"Get in the car." Vincent held the door open for her and pointed to the seat.

"Does it run on triple A batteries?" Lexi snickered as he closed her door with a little more force than necessary.

He slid gracefully into his seat, the engine roaring to life with the turn of his key. He turned to her, his sunglasses in place, and revved the engine. Over the thundering noise he shouted, "No batteries, honey. It's all about power."

Even though the man was sexy as hell as he pulled out of the parking garage and onto the city streets, Lexi managed to keep her cool, refusing to stroke his ego where his car was concerned.

"Power shmower. Can you drive this thing or what? There's nothing worse than a guy with a fast car who can't drive it properly." She raised a challenging eyebrow in response to his incredulous glare.

"Hold on." He threw the car into gear, and they went screaming down the street.

Lexi tried not to focus on the way the muscles of his forearm clenched and coiled as he shifted gears. She tried to ignore the way he licked his lips and smiled as he whizzed past car after car. And more than anything, she tried to ignore the way his hips rocked slightly as he pumped the clutch in and out. There was no reason to dwell on the sensual confidence with which he drove the city streets, changing lanes and fluidly gliding along the road. Nothing good could come from fantasizing about those things, but the adrenaline rush as they whipped along the street made Lexi's body ache in a delicious way that she hadn't felt in a long time.

Unconsciously, Lexi fanned her hand in front of her face, trying to cool the flames that engulfed her body. Vincent, of course, noticed. "Are you hot? Do you want me to turn up the air conditioning?"

"No, no, I'm good," Lexi said, blushing. She took a few deep, calming breaths as she watched the buildings fly past the window. She maintained control until she felt a warm hand gently graze her thigh.

"Still think it's tiny?"

Before she could stop the words from flying from her mouth, she said, "I'm quite certain nothing of yours is tiny, Vincent." Her eyes nearly popped out of her head. "I said that out loud, didn't I."

Vincent laughed. "Yes, you did."

"Sleep deprivation, that's my excuse and I'm sticking with it." She sighed in relief and pointed out her window. "Oh look, there's my place. Pull over here." The car had barely stopped before Lexi leaped out and made a run for her door, desperate to put some distance between her and Vincent, but he jumped out and called after her.

"I'll be back in," he glanced at his watch, "an hour? Be ready when I get here."

She stayed on the sidewalk and gave a tiny wave as the car peeled out of the parking space. In a matter of seconds it disappeared down the street and out of view. Lexi shook her head, trying to clear out the very dangerous thoughts that rolled around in there. For the sake of her heart, she had to purge her erotic fantasies about Vincent. She leaned her head back as she rode the elevator to her floor, mentally trying to plan out her wardrobe for the presentation so she could save time after she jumped out of the shower. When she got to her apartment, she found a note taped just under the peephole.

Lexi,
You are in so much trouble with me. Get over to my place as soon as you read this.
Hope

"Ugh." Lexi didn't have time to deal with a tantruming Hope. She had just under an hour to get ready and clean her apartment before Vincent returned, and she couldn't be late. Carefully turning the knob, Lexi tried to silently slip into her apartment unnoticed.

"Where do you think you're going?" Hope's eagle eyes peeked out of her apartment door. "You weren't going to blow me off *again* and sneak inside, were you?"

"Hope, I have to leave for the Stone presentation with Vincent in an hour, so I don't have time."

"Oh, you have plenty of time." Hope linked her arm with her friend's and guided her into her apartment. "So Vincent's coming over? I assume he dropped you off, and going by your clothes, it looks like you two crazy kids spent the whole night together."

Lexi unhooked her arm from Hope and began putting the couple of dishes that were in the sink into the dishwasher. "We were working, Hope. I told you."

"No, you didn't tell me anything. The Neanderthal you sent downstairs to take me to dinner told me."

"I worked all night and then fell asleep on a couch. Boring. How was your evening with Sean? You're being very quiet about things, and I didn't even get an angry text from you."

Hope's mouth fell open. "Didn't get a text? Are you serious? Did you lose your phone or something? I texted you about twenty times!"

Confused, Lexi rummaged to the bottom of her purse where she found her BlackBerry. Twenty-one missed calls. Eighteen were from Hope and three were from Sean. She remembered that after she got Hope's text, she had set the phone to vibrate and tossed it into her bag. It must have fallen to the bottom, and with her hectic night, she completely forgot about it.

"Hope, I'm so sorr—"

"Save it. The night was … well, it wasn't a total bust."

Lexi laughed. "I'd say so after this 'OMG he's so flippin' hot!' text you sent at nine-oh-nine p.m."

"That wasn't from me. He stole the phone for a minute."

"M-hmm." Lexi scrolled through a few more explicit texts and snickered.

"Oh, give that to me. I was drinking last night. Half of those comments were made under the influence."

"Hey, I was just getting to the good ones about Sean's lips wrapped around an olive!" Lexi pouted.

"Okay, okay. I admit it! The guy is incredibly sexy and charming, and he makes me all hot and bothered when he calls me 'babe.' There, I admitted it. But he's still a pig and a jerk, and he's going to need to work on that before he gets to put his hands on this." Hope gestured her hands down her curvaceous body.

"Fair enough." Lexi hopped off the stool she had been sitting on and waved her friend into her room. "I have to get in the shower, but come tell me about your night."

While Lexi showered, Hope filled her in on all the details of her night with Sean. Lexi was impressed. It sounded like he had behaved like a perfect gentleman, although he had definitely turned on the charm. Hope had put on a brave face with him so he wouldn't know that his words and actions turned her insides to mush.

"So, wait—did you two dance at the club?" Lexi wrapped her hair up in a towel and strolled out of the bathroom in just her robe.

"Oh my God, Lexi, the man can move. He's big, but has rhythm and grace like you couldn't even imagine. The hip action alone…" Hope fell back onto the bed, fanning herself.

"Are you going to see him again?" Lexi flicked through her closet and pulled out a blue wrap dress. She held up a pair of silver heels to Hope, and when she got the thumbs up, she placed them on the bed.

"I have no idea."

"Did he kiss you goodnight?" Lexi yelled from inside the bathroom as she got dressed.

"On the cheek."

"His idea or yours?" Lexi asked as she ran her fingers through her hair to help it dry and stepped back into her bedroom.

"Mine. He still has to earn the lips."

Lexi was putting on mascara when her phone beeped with a text from Vincent.

What apartment number?

Lexi quickly texted back.

403—You better be leaving your place and not sitting in front of mine.

She stifled a laugh at his response.

I just took my car out of my pocket and am pulling onto the street now. Be there in a few.

"Oh great, he's on his way already. I need to hurry. Hope, how messy is the apartment out there?"

"What do you care? You aren't trying to impress him, are you?" She smirked at Lexi from the bed.

"No, but he's my boss and I don't want him to think that I live like a pig. Just go make sure the place is straightened up while I finish my makeup and dry my hair."

Hope left the room and began picking up the already clean apartment for her friend. Lexi frantically dried her hair and touched up her makeup. While getting ready, she kept running through the presentation in her head, mentally marking the points Vincent needed to drive home. She was so wrapped up in her thoughts that she didn't notice the voices in the other room until she was slipping her shoes onto her feet.

"This one is of her and Harry when she was seven. I personally like the blue frosting all around her mouth."

"Hope Lila Greyson!" Lexi came flying out of her room, ready to kill, but her breath left her lungs in a whoosh when she saw Vincent, showered, pressed and looking like a specimen of male perfection as he leaned his shoulder against her wall and examined her family pictures. When the smell of his cologne hit her, she had to hold onto a nearby chair to steady herself. Her reaction didn't go unnoticed.

"You okay, Lexi?" Hope asked, biting her cheek to keep from laughing. "I was just showing Vincent some of your pictures while he waited for you to finish getting ready."

"And I assume you showed him the naked baby pictures too?"

"Nice birthmark," Vincent chuckled until he saw Lexi's face pale. Then he threw up his hands innocently. "I was just kidding. She didn't show me anything. But, good guess about the birthmark, huh?" He rubbed the back of his neck and looked away, embarrassed.

"I'm sorry you had to wait. I'm ready." Lexi grabbed her purse and jacket and ignored Hope's cackling in the corner.

"No problem. I was actually a few minutes early." Vincent's warm smile instantly calmed Lexi's thundering heart.

"Hope, before I forget, I need a ride—"

"We talked about Madison's tea party while you were beautifying, and Vincent doesn't mind taking you." Hope snuck a wink in Lexi's direction. "So I'm going to get your car from the shop this afternoon and bring it up to his sister's place and pick you up there."

"If you're sure you don't mind, Vincent," Lexi said.

"I already gave her Anna's address. Oh, and Sean told me to send you his regards," he told Hope.

She quirked an eyebrow at Vincent in disbelief.

"Fine, he actually asked me to tell you that he can't get you out of his head, but I thought that sounded a little creepy, so I edited."

"Maybe you can teach the guy some gentlemanly manners." Hope smiled. "You seem to know how to treat a lady and make her swoon." Lexi glared at her from across the room.

"Sorry, Hope. Sean's… Sean. Love him or hate him, what you see is what you get. He's actually the most upfront and honest person I have ever met. If he thinks it, he says it." He gently ushered Lexi toward the door. "Oh, and he thinks you're incredibly sexy when you talk cars."

"Will he be at your sister's place tonight?" Vincent nodded his head. "And does he know I'm coming?" Hope beamed when Vincent slowly shook his head no.

"Perfect." Hope fell back onto the couch with a silly grin on her face. "Get out of here, you two, and good luck with the presentation."

Lexi peeked over her shoulder as Vincent held the door open for her. "Will you lock up?"

"Of course." Hope waved them out the door. "Good luck! Break a leg, or whatever I'm supposed to say for an advertising presentation. Basically, don't suck!"

Vincent laughed and closed the door behind him. "I can see why Sean's so smitten with her."

"Smitten?" Lexi giggled at his antiquated word while she leaned against the wall, waiting for him.

"Yes, smitten." He leaned his head closer to her. "It means to captivate, to affect someone strongly, or to fill someone," Lexi gulped audibly as his eyes darkened, "with love or longing."

Lexi blinked a few times, not saying anything. When she found her voice, she squeaked out, "Smitten is good."

"You're absurd sometimes, do you know that?" Vincent pushed away from the wall and headed for the elevator.

"So I've been told." Lexi pushed the button and waited for the doors to open. "Not to sound like a total girl, but do I look okay? I have no idea what one wears to a presentation. I hope this is acceptable."

"You look perfect. Professional. And I must say, that color looks beautiful on you."

Vincent's phone beeped. He glanced at the display, and then tucked it back into his pocket. The third time it happened he cursed under his breath.

"Is everything okay?" Lexi watched him become more and more agitated.

"It's fine. Nothing that concerns you." His wall had gone back up.

"Well, it looks like something. And since you're about to pitch one of the biggest campaigns of your career, maybe it will help if you get it off your chest so you can move on and make a decent presentation. But if I'm wrong, just tell me. No need to spare my feelings."

Vincent opened and shut his mouth three times as they stood beside his car before he finally said something. "Jade's pissed I didn't call her last night to make sure she arrived safely or answer any of her calls. I guess she left some messages with Leigh today too that I might have ignored."

Lexi remained silent and let him talk. The more he said, the more difficult it became to keep quiet and not voice her abysmal opinion of Jade.

"It's not like you didn't have a lot going on since she left, Vincent."

"I know," he said, throwing his hands into the air. "I'm working like crazy trying to make a name for myself, trying to show people that I am more than just the boss's son. And every time I have to pay attention to work rather than her, I catch grief." His hand raked through his hair. "I mean, when she has to leave for a week to do some ridiculous photo shoot or get ready for a runway show, I don't complain. I understand it's for her career. Why can't she extend me the same courtesy?"

"I'm sorry. That sounds incredibly difficult."

His phone beeped again, and this time he laughed then showed it to Lexi. "Great, now she's dragged you into it."

I know you're with that two bit whore of an assistant right now, you prick, because she isn't picking up your office line. Leigh is trying to cover, but I don't buy her lies, not for a second. Call me!

Lexi sighed. "Why don't you talk to her and explain what's going on?"

"Because, frankly, I don't have time, and I don't feel like it." He took a deep breath and smiled. "Thank you for letting me complain. Usually I bother Sean with this kind of stuff. I appreciate you listening, and I'm sure he will be grateful for the break from my ranting."

"You're under a lot of pressure, Vincent. And I'm sure she just misses you." Somehow Lexi managed to get the last part out without gagging.

Vincent snorted. "You, Alexandra White, are an amazing person." He brushed his thumb lightly over her cheek. "Sean usually just tells me to dump her skinny ass. Actually, he begs me to do it."

Lexi gave Vincent's hand a squeeze and tried to make him laugh. "Well, Sean is pretty smart. Maybe he knows best." His phone buzzed again, and this time when he took it out of his pocket Lexi grabbed it and stuck it in her purse. "Problem solved. Jade's been muzzled. Now, are you ready to give this presentation?"

"Yeah, I think we're ready."

· 16 ·

"You remembered to download the projection charts, right?" Lexi asked as she slid into the car. Holding her door open, Vincent poked his head in. "Yes, Lexi."

As he slowly walked around to his side of the car, another thought popped into her head. "The album covers! Did you print out the revised ones?" she shouted as he opened his door.

Vincent cast an amused smile in her direction as he put his key in the ignition. "Yes, Lexi."

"What about the—"

Vincent turned toward her, wrapped his arm around the back of her seat, and leaned in. She felt the warmth in his smile all the way down into the pit of her stomach. "I've done this a few times, you know. Don't worry. We have everything we need. Trust me."

Embarrassed, Lexi dipped her head and fidgeted with her seat belt strap. "I'm being silly, I'm sorry. I'm a little nervous."

"Don't apologize." He lifted her chin so he could look her in the eye. "It's my fault. I'm used to doing this alone, without a partner. I tend to be a control freak on these things. What I should have done was give you a list of everything I was bringing. You were just looking out for me. Thanks." He eased himself back into his seat and pulled into traffic, the loud purr of the engine turning the heads of the people on the street. "And don't be nervous. You know this presentation better than I do. Actually, I should just let you do the whole thing. You up for it?"

Lexi's mouth fell open, wide with shock, as Vincent patiently watched and waited for her answer. Her grip on the door handle tightened, her knuckles turning white from the intense pressure she was exerting. "Y-you ca-can't—"

He waited a few seconds as Lexi stammered, then tipped his head back in laughter. "I'm kidding. Breathe, Lexi, breathe."

Her hand slapped his shoulder repeatedly as she yelled at him. "That wasn't funny. It's all fun and games until Lexi throws up in your Lotus."

"You wouldn't dare."

"Try me."

"Sorry, I couldn't resist. Forgive me?"

Lexi crossed her arms and faked annoyance. "You just better get this account, pal, or I'm going to be pissed that I missed my night out with Hope trolling for hot guys." She watched his brows knit together, his lips turning down in a slight frown until she saved him with a smile. Only then did Vincent grin and roll his eyes, realizing that she was kidding.

He was the picture of calm as he drove through the streets of San Francisco. Lexi's stomach, however, flipped and flopped relentlessly with each smile or glance he cast in her direction. At first, she assumed it was because of the importance of the impending presentation, but the longer she stayed in the cramped space with Vincent, the more she realized that the presentation had nothing to do with it. He was gorgeous and sexy enough to make any woman's heart race, but it was more than that now that she knew him better. When he wasn't storming around the office, he was actually a lot of fun to be around. He was smart and clever, and the carefree banter back and forth between them felt so natural, like they'd been doing it for years.

Never in her life had Lexi felt so comfortable around a man or free to just be herself. That was just as appealing to her as Vincent's broad shoulders and killer smile. The more she was around him, the more she found herself wanting to be around him.

The feelings that she had taken great care to bury deep ten years ago when she walked out of Riverdale for NYU were now peeking out and springing to life again with each smile or touch from Vincent Drake. If she was being completely honest with herself, what scared her most was knowing that she was falling for him again, even more deeply, with absolutely no chance of ever having him.

"Are you all right, Lexi? You're so quiet. I really was kidding about the presentation thing. I'm sorry if I stressed you out. Honestly, this is the fun part of my job. I could give presentations all day." He had a boyish grin on his face as he explained his approach—he wasn't only selling his idea, but he was selling himself and his skills to the client. He could have a great idea, but it came down to presenting competence, control, and power when he walked in the room. Clients more often than not went with someone they felt comfortable with over the best pitch. If he could walk in there with a great idea and prove himself worthy to Julian, then according to Vincent it would be a done deal.

There was such confidence and intensity as he spoke that Lexi knew he was focused and ready for this. He was used to getting what he went after. This was who Vincent Drake was, the man he had become over the last ten years. His anger when he didn't get a client made much more sense to Lexi now because she understood that he took each loss personally. When he put his heart and soul into a project and placed himself out there for these clients and they rejected him, it hurt. How could it not?

"You love your job, don't you?" Lexi asked.

"I do. I won't lie; there are days that suck, and there are people who suck that make me want to scream." They exchanged a glance and both said "Tony" at the same time. "But to be able to be creative and innovative every day; it's exhilarating." The car glided to a stop in front of what appeared to be a recently remodeled three-story, brick warehouse with a door covered in black, wrought iron bars. The only bit of flair was the ornate detail of a letter S in the center of iron bars.

"Sixteen Reservation Drive. This is the place," Lexi confirmed.

Vincent opened the trunk and carefully removed the boards from the back of the car. "This looks like an interesting part of town." His eyes scanned the other buildings nearby. Different types of art galleries and design companies littered the street. "Cool architecture."

Lexi nodded her head in agreement as they walked down the sidewalk to Julian's door. "I've been to some of these galleries. The openings they throw are extravagant. There are also a number of musicians that live down at the end of block so there's always music playing as you walk around and window shop." Her eyes twinkled as she talked. "There's a shop around the corner that has the most beautiful pieces of blown glass. They're spectacular."

"I've lived here for years and never knew all of this was down here. I'll have to stop in that gallery sometime. Elizabeth loves unique pieces." He rang the bell twice and waited for someone to answer.

Christina flung open the door, her long, coppery hair rolling over her shoulders in big waves. "Lexi!" She threw her arms around Lexi's neck and pulled her in the door. "Oh, sorry. Hello, Vincent. I didn't forget about you."

"Good afternoon, Christina." Vincent extended his hand to her, and Christina released her grasp on Lexi and pulled Vincent into a tight hug.

She stepped back and smiled. "Listen, we only have a minute so let me be brief. I adore you guys, but I'm not stupid either, I've done my research. Your campaigns are great, financially successful for the clients, and innovative. The people who work with you adore you, and unless my research is mistaken, you have the highest percentage rate of repeat clients on the west coast. I want Julian to go with Hunter, but it's his call, not mine. So, I'm going to give you a little advice, and if you're the smart man that I believe you to be, you'll take it to heart.

"First, lose the formal 'Good afternoon' thing." Christina imitated his posture and cadence from a moment ago. "Talk to Julian like you would a friend. He prefers that to being terribly formal. Don't kiss his ass; don't play him. Tell him straight up why you are the group to go with and what you think you can do for him that no one else can."

Vincent remained silent and listened to Christina's laundry list. Lexi stood beside him, nodding her head in agreement.

"Last but not least, no matter what he says or does, stick to your guns. Show him you have confidence in your idea and your capabilities." Christina turned her attention to Lexi. "Can he pull this off?"

Lexi playfully shrugged her shoulders and glanced over at Vincent. Instead of launching into a long-winded explanation as to why he was the man for the job, he winked, and Lexi's face lit up with a quiet confidence. "Julian doesn't stand a chance."

"Perfect!" Christina clapped her hands together and pulled them inside. "Let me show you around while we wait for Julian."

The interior of the converted warehouse was spectacular. Honey colored hardwood floors and high ceilings made the space feel enormous. Christina led them through the rooms, giving them a sneak peek at the newest line. Seeing the designs and sketches all over the wall made Lexi smile to herself, remembering the mess Vincent's office had been the night before.

"Remind you of anything?" Vincent whispered in her ear, his chest pressing lightly against her back.

"Yeah, Julian is as big of a slob as you when he's working."

"Maybe the two of you can bond over your lack of organizational skills." Christina added, overhearing their conversation. "Do you know how many times I've cleaned this room top to bottom only to have him come back and complain?" She turned to Lexi with a look of exasperation. "Men!"

"I think you two were separated at birth," Vincent teased.

"Zip it, Vincent," they said in unison.

He threw up his hands in surrender and wisely kept his mouth shut as Christina linked arms with Lexi and led her into Julian's office. The walls of his office were lined with hundreds of albums. At first it appeared to be wallpaper, but each cover rested on a clear plexiglass shelf and was covered in plastic. From floor to ceiling, the amazing collection was on display. Lexi pointed to one of the walls and mouthed "He's going to love our idea," then turned her attention back to Christina, who was pointing out Julian's more treasured albums, which were framed and hung along the hallway to the conference room.

As Christina continued the tour, Lexi tried to pay attention to what she said, but she was distracted by Vincent. She felt his eyes on her, watching her every move as they wandered through the apartment, but whenever she looked in his direction, his eyes quickly flicked away. To make his odd behavior more confusing, his demeanor completely changed the moment they stepped into the conference room.

"The two of you can get your things settled in here, and I'll go see what's taking His Royal Highness and company so long."

"Thank you, Christina," Lexi said as she began rummaging through her bag, pulling out different pieces of the presentation. She glanced over at Vincent when he didn't say anything and found him standing across the room, his mouth drawn into a tight line. "Are you all right?"

"I'm fine," he said shortly, striding over to the long conference table and getting his laptop hooked up to the projector.

"Wait, what just happened? Are you mad because I monopolized Christina the whole time? I'm sorry. She took my arm and was showing me around. I didn't want to be rude."

"You're fine, Lexi." He ducked his head to figure out where to plug in the flash drive. When he stood back up, Lexi was right beside him, her eyes starting to brim with tears.

"Would you be more comfortable if I waited in the lobby? I don't mind. I really shouldn't be here, anyway. I'm just your assistant."

His aloof posture immediately softened. He regularly dealt with snarling competitors, hostile businessmen, angry advertisers, but it appeared that a hint of misery in Lexi's usually sparkling eyes could bring him to his knees. "Why do I keep making you cry?" He ran his hand roughly through his hair. "I'm sorry. I was being a jerk. I guess I got a little nervous. Please don't go anywhere. I really do need you here." He took her hand in his and gave it a reassuring squeeze.

Lexi took a deep breath. Getting so weepy and emotional around him all the time only proved that his opinion meant way more to her than it should. She wanted to do a good job, she wanted him to respect her and her abilities, but every time he shut down like that, Lexi took it personally. If she really wanted to be respected, she needed to stop crying, or Vincent would see her as the girl she had been, not the woman she had become.

To cover for her ridiculous behavior, Lexi tried to be snarky. "Did you get it all out of your system? The being nervous and being an jerk thing? Because next time, I'm kicking you in the shins."

"Do it, please." He looked into her eyes and saw the tears had thankfully disappeared. "So are we good?"

"Well, *I'm* good, not sure about you, but you better be. I can hear Julian walking down the hall." Lexi gave him a shove in the shoulder. "Loosen up, Vince."

"I hate that name."

"You let Maddie call you Vince."

"That's because she's cute when she says it."

Lexi put her hand over her heart and feigned sadness. "And I'm not cute?"

Rather than answer with words, Vincent's eyes slowly traveled over her, lingering on the gentle curve of her hips and then her lips before returning to her eyes. She nervously fidgeted during his silent appraisal. When she didn't think she could stand the quiet a second longer, Vincent gave her a slow and sexy smile. "You're beyond cute."

Just then the door flew open and Julian strode in, his booming laughter startling Lexi. She let out a tiny squeak and very conspicuously took three large steps away from Vincent. Julian paused and exchanged a quick glance with a grinning Christina.

"We interrupting something?" he asked.

Lexi's cheeks flooded with color when she saw the knowing grin on Julian's face. Vincent didn't miss a beat. He strode over and tapped fists with Julian to say hello.

"Nope, we were just discussing beautiful women." He took a quick peek back at Lexi, and then extended his hand to the two men who had followed Julian into the room. "I'm Vincent Drake."

"Sal Irvin," the man beside Julian said as he shook Vincent's extended hand. "Julian and I've been friends since we were kids."

"And now he's my business manager. He's one bossy son of a gun too. This guy here is Peter, my cousin."

"I got all the good looks in the family." Peter tipped his head in Lexi's direction and grinned when she chuckled at his joke.

"Nice to meet both of you. Have you recovered from our game yet? Your ankle healed?" Vincent motioned to Julian's left foot.

"Um, yeah. I limped around for a day or two, but it's better now." He shrugged his large shoulders and leaned against the wall.

"When were you limping? You've been fine," Christina scoffed as she listened in on the last part of the conversation.

"It was sore. I twisted it while we were playing. That's why I lost." Christina rolled her eyes at Julian and shook her head. "Did you show Vincent my new toy?" Julian asked.

"No, I figured you'd want to do that yourself. That is, if your ankle is okay to walk on."

Julian shook his head at Vincent. "Women. I'll never understand them." He motioned to the door. "Come on. Let me show you something before we do the presentation, if that's okay. Then afterwards, maybe we'll do a little two-on-two game." The four men walked out, leaving Christina and Lexi giggling at the conference table.

"What's the toy?" Lexi asked.

"The idiot just put in a basketball court outside, complete with the Sacramento Kings logo at center court. You don't even want to know how much he had to pay for the right to use it." Christina flipped through the packet that was sitting on the table, peeking at the information.

"Holy hell. He's going to love this!" She jumped to her feet, hugging Lexi. "Come on, Vincent. Sell it, baby." She held her hands up in a silent prayer.

"He will, don't worry. He was amazing during the run-throughs. I think he'll knock Julian's socks off."

"Good, he better. If I have to work with that creeper Reid, I'll never forgive him." The phone in the corner of the room rang. Christina excused herself and grabbed the receiver. "Stone designs. Can I help you?" Lexi watched her friend's face wrinkle up with displeasure. "My name is Christina, and I'm Mr. Stone's assistant. And *you* are?"

There was a long pause during which Christina's brows furrowed. "Jade who? Is Mr. Stone expecting your call?"

No, no, no, it can't be! Lexi screamed in her head and paled. *What the hell is that psycho up to now?*

"Well, Mr. Stone is about to start a meeting. No, he cannot talk to you first!" Christina said in a clipped tone, her irritation growing. "What about Vincent Drake?"

Oh my God! In a panic, Lexi began flapping her arms wildly to get Christina's attention.

"Please hold," Christina snapped into the phone before pressing her hand over the receiver to talk to Lexi. "This woman is nuts. She's left three messages this week alone."

"Jade, the model Jade?"

"According to her, she's the supermodel Jade, and now she's throwing Vincent's name around left and right. You know anything about this?"

Lexi cautiously asked a few questions. "What does she want?"

"To talk to Julian about the new campaign."

"But you don't even know what campaign you're using yet."

"She claims to be very versatile and can pull off whatever look we need. I've ignored her until now. Who is she, and how does Vincent know her?" Christina put her ear to the phone and laughed. "She's screaming at me to get back on the phone."

"She's, um, kinda his girlfriend."

"Kinda?" Christina asked, her interest piqued.

"Well, she *is* his girlfriend."

"Oh, and he wants her to be in the campaign?" Christina eyed Lexi suspiciously.

"God, no! I mean, we didn't talk about it, but he isn't designing this ad so Jade can star in it if that's what you're wondering."

"Good, because that wouldn't fly." Christina put her ear back to the phone and said in a professional, but patronizing tone, "I'll be right with you, honey." Christina snickered when Jade began squawking again.

"What do we do now?" Christina asked.

Lexi thought about it, and no matter what, this wasn't going to end well. Either Jade would talk to Julian and blow the presentation, or someone would have to tell Jade to take a hike and deal with the fallout. Given the people present in the room, Lexi was the only one for the job.

"Give me the phone."

"Are you sure? She's got fangs, this one."

"It's the talons you have to watch out for with her." Lexi grabbed the phone from Christina and took a deep breath. "Jade."

"Who the hell is this?" she snapped.

"It's Lexi."

"Why am I talking to you? And what the hell are you doing at Julian Stone's studio?"

"Jade, we only have a few minutes. Would you like to tell me what you're doing, calling a client and offering your services while you throw Vincent's name around? Do you know how this will look to Julian if he knows you called right before the presentation? Or after?" Lexi was shaking she was so mad. "Vincent worked his tail off for this."

"Don't you dare tell me about Vincent, you little witch! I think I know Vincent better than you ever will. Put Stone's assistant back on the phone," Jade screeched.

"No. He and Vincent—" Lexi took a calming breath when Jade interrupted. "Screw you!"

"Listen, Vincent doesn't need this headache."

"Stop saying his name!"

"Jade, calm down, you might break a nail."

"Calm down? Oh, I'm calm. I'll be even calmer when Vincent finally fires you."

"If he fires me over this, then so be it. But I'm not going to let you ruin this presentation for him." Christina gave Lexi a high five of encouragement.

"Look at you. Protecting Vincent, how sweet. What do you think he needs protecting from? Me? Or better yet, do you think he needs *anything* from you?"

"He's quite capable of taking care of himself."

A light bulb must have suddenly gone off in Jade's twisted head. "You like him. Why didn't I see this before? You have a crush on him! Silly girl. Vincent's a powerful man with influential, cultured friends. He would *never* want a simple girl like you on his arm. You don't fit in with him or his life. Quit dreaming," Jade cackled into the phone.

"This conversation is over, Jade. You're irrational and obviously missed a dose of your happy pills, so I'm going to let whatever you were ranting about slide this time. But if you ever talk to me like that again, I'm not going to bite my tongue, and I'll let you know exactly what I think of you."

"How dare you!"

"No, how dare *you*. How dare you talk to me that way. How dare you try and use your relationship with Vincent to get yourself a job even if it means ruining his chance at a campaign. You're just plain cruel." Christina jumped up and down with glee at Lexi's tirade while Jade was stunned into silence. Lexi seized the opening to drive the final stake through her dead, shriveled heart. "Now, go smile pretty for the camera or whatever it is you do." She dropped her voice lower until it was almost a purr. "And don't worry. I'll take *good* care of Vincent while you're gone."

As the receiver slammed down, Christina lunged at Lexi and hugged her tight. "That was awesome! Remind me not to piss you off."

Lexi sank into the nearest chair and clasped her hands together so that Christina wouldn't see how badly she was shaking. She may have won that one, small battle with Jade, but in doing so, she had just started a war of epic proportions. And it was a war she stood no chance of winning.

"That was such a bad idea," Lexi said as she tilted her head back and stared at the ceiling.

"What was a bad idea?" Vincent asked as he strolled through the door, Julian and his two friends right behind him.

Lexi gave Christina a warning look to keep her mouth shut about what had just happened. She wanted Vincent to get through the presentation before he found out about Jade's asinine behavior. "Not eating something before I came here. I was a little light headed, but I'm much better now."

Vincent came over with a concerned expression and stood beside her chair. "You sure you're okay? You do look a little pale." He stroked slowly along her arm, making every place he touched tingle.

"I'm good." Lexi stood up so Vincent wouldn't notice the blush that suddenly rushed into her cheeks.

"Vincent, Lexi, can I get you anything before I leave? Water, coffee, juice?" Christina interrupted as Julian, Sal, and Peter took their seats at the far end of the enormous glass conference table, their hands immediately digging into the bowl of candy that sat there.

Lexi shook her head no while Vincent offered a quick "No thanks." He went to the front of the room and stood where the PowerPoint presentation was being projected onto the wall.

"Have a good meeting." Christina winked at Vincent and made her way to the door.

"Tina, you wanna stay?" Julian asked, motioning to the chair beside him.

"No, I've got some work to do. I'll hold your calls so you aren't interrupted." She cast a sly glance to Lexi, who smiled in appreciation and passed out presentation packets to the men.

Lexi held her breath as the men flipped through the pages, waiting for some sort of reaction. When she saw Julian's head bob up and down, she cast an encouraging smile to Vincent, who also watched the men, no doubt taking note of each subtle body movement. Julian and Sal huddled together for a second, pointing back and forth on one another's papers, but their facial expressions were impossible to read.

Julian set his papers down on the table and leaned back in his chair, his fingers locked behind his head. Casually he said, "All right, Vince, impress me."

Vincent's presentation was pure magic. He spoke with confidence and personality. Julian and his entourage sat quietly as Vincent gave the presentation, never taking their eyes off of him. They occasionally leaned forward in their chairs, most often to get a better view when Vincent went over the artwork for the print ads. Julian brought up a concern about getting the licenses to use the covers, and Vincent quickly extinguished it when he proudly shared that he had already taken care of the licensure and permissions for any albums used in this presentation. Peter, who had been very quiet up until then, murmured his approval.

Lexi was amazed with the presentation and was certain she had a goofy, adoring grin on her face the entire time. Vincent was so personable and charming that she couldn't take her eyes off him. It was as if he was speaking directly to each individual in the room. The few times his eyes sought her out and lingered, Lexi's blood raced through her veins. She would give him an encouraging smile, letting him know he was on the right track. The gorgeous smile that resulted on his face each time made Lexi's stomach flip with excitement.

As the presentation wrapped up, Julian remained eerily quiet. He looked repeatedly from Vincent to the papers in front of him, saying nothing. Finally, he glanced over at Peter, and then spoke. "I don't like it."

Vincent remained stoic at the front of the room, not letting Julian see any visible reaction to his words. Lexi's heart sank, but she took Vincent's lead and remained expressionless.

"What are you concerned about?" Vincent asked.

"I think people are going to find the old and new mix lame. Right now, it's all about being hot or a trendsetter," Sal offered, Julian's head nodding in agreement.

"I disagree," Vincent said, his voice firm and unwavering. "There are so many people who know nothing about fashion. They buy a head-to-toe look from a design house and think that just because they are decked out in a label, they are fashion forward, when really, they all look cookie cutter."

Lexi held her breath as Julian shifted in his seat. "I get what you're trying to do, Vince. But I'm the designer. I made the clothes. I decided which pieces went together to make the looks. No offense, but what do you know about designing a line? And in essence, that's what you've done, redesigned my entire line."

"The pieces in your collection are incredibly strong, each one being able to stand on its own and make a statement." Vincent glanced again at Lexi for reassurance that he was on the right track.

"I agree," Lexi chimed in. "I'm certain when you designed the line originally, a number of these pieces were put together differently in the planning stages. Then as things began to take shape, you saw that this top worked better with this pair of pants, or this shirt paired with this jacket was better. You're known for the versatility of your line, and the pieces mix beautifully within your label and outside of it."

Vincent jumped back into the conversation. "That's what we want to show-case, the way your line has a timeless, classic edge to it. So many designers are trend motivated, but you aren't. Your line is a new take on a classic, and by encouraging people to pair it with what they already have and love, it makes it far more marketable to a wider cross section of the population."

Lexi and Vincent held their breath as Julian silently sat in his chair, digesting all that had been thrown at him. The two exchanged a silent dialogue, Vincent shrugging, indicating his uncertainty, Lexi nodding, letting him know that she believed in him.

Julian pushed the presentation papers away from him and toward the center of the table. "Well, this meeting is over." He stood up, Sal and Peter following suit, and moved toward the door. He peeked over his shoulder and added with a grin, "I like your backbone, Vince, and I love the idea. I just wanted to see how vigorously you would defend it. I'm sold. Let's celebrate Hunter getting the account with a quick game of two-on-two. The suit better not slow you down, Drake."

Lexi knew Vincent couldn't visibly cheer to celebrate the win. He had to keep his composure no matter how badly he wanted to pump his fist into the air. So instead, he reached out to the one person with whom he wouldn't have to use words to communicate, the one person who knew how much this meant to him, and squeezed her hand with all his might. The firm squeeze he got back from Lexi's trembling hand made him smile. She had been just as nervous as he was, and yet she followed his lead, kept her cool, and defended their idea magnificently. They were a great team.

An hour later, after the most argued game of two-on-two in history, Lexi and Vincent were finally ready to leave Julian's place. "I'll call you next week, Christina," Lexi called over her shoulder as they walked out of the studio.

As Vincent slid beside her in the Lotus, Lexi couldn't keep still. "Are we clear?" she asked when they were half a block down the road.

"Yep."

"We did it!" Lexi screamed in the car, feet pounding on the floor in celebration. Vincent joined in her excitement and high fived her repeatedly. "Oh my God, I almost passed out when he said he didn't like it, but then you went into our motivation and I knew we had him. I know this probably sounds lame, but I'm so proud of you, Vincent. You really were amazing in there." When she stopped talking, she realized that her hands were wrapped around his arm, her smiling face within inches of his in the cramped space of the car. Still giddy, she gave his arm an excited shake, then sat back in her seat and let it all sink in. Julian Stone had liked their campaign enough to hire them on the spot.

Vincent reached over and laced his fingers with hers. The two sat there in a very comfortable silence, each reliving the high points of the day in their head. When Vincent began rubbing gentle circles along Lexi's hand, she turned her head toward him and smiled.

"I'm glad we're friends after all these years," Lexi said softly.

Vincent reached out and cupped her cheek, his eyes full of tenderness as he spoke. "My life is better with you in it."

Lexi let his overwhelmingly kind words sink in. She adored him, there was no point in pretending she didn't, and at this moment she didn't even care that her heart would eventually get trampled. She was so happy, she decided to seize the moment and celebrate their victory. "Can I ask you a huge favor?" She turned the full power of her brown eyes on him, her long lashes fluttering like a butterfly's wings.

"Anything," he said, sounding as if there was no way he would be able to refuse her today.

She poked at the roof of the car. "Take the top down for me?"

A wide grin spread across his face. "Seriously? I assumed it was a standard girl thing that you all hate convertibles—it messes with the hair and everything. At least that's what Jade always says." He reached over and pressed the button that sent the gears churning to retract the top of the car.

As it disappeared, Lexi felt the pleasant heat of the sunshine beating down on her skin. "In case you haven't noticed, Jade and I are pretty much polar opposites. We're nothing alike." Lexi rolled her window down, put on her sunglasses and shook her head, letting the wind rush through her long hair as Vincent sped down the road.

"I've noticed."

· 17 ·

The drive to Anna's house was exactly what Lexi and Vincent needed to wind down from the excitement of the Stone presentation. The beautiful scenery and the ability to simply be without need for conversation were refreshing. On more than one occasion, Vincent peeked over at Lexi and simply watched her hair swirl in the breeze. The soft and silky strands brushed against him as the wind caught hold of them, and once Vincent even reached out and twirled a stray lock between his fingers before setting it free again.

Lexi's smile was wide as Vincent pointed things out to her along the coast, like a pod of dolphins swimming just offshore or a spectacular sailboat skipping over the waves. The scenery was picturesque and the company sublime.

Instead of stopping, they enjoyed each other's company for as long as they could, taking a leisurely drive up the coast before doubling back toward Anna's house in time for Madison's tea party. Lexi asked Vincent to stop at a little shop along the way so she could get a gift for Madison, because she refused to arrive empty handed.

For Lexi, the entire afternoon was like a dream. She felt like pinching herself every few minutes just to make sure it was real—from the presentation to getting the account to the wonderful drive with Vincent. She couldn't have asked for a more perfect day. The speed of the car, the whipping wind, and the smell of the ocean all accentuated the wild day they had just experienced together. Vincent's company somehow had a strangely calming effect on her. By the time the car rolled down Anna's long driveway, Lexi was more content and happy than she had been in a long time.

Vincent slowly backed up to park, his arm wrapping around the back of Lexi's seat until he maneuvered the car into its spot. After he turned off the engine, he crowded close to Lexi and pulled a few of her more wild hairs back over her shoulder. Even with his efforts, her hair was still sexy and windblown.

"That was amazing, Vincent. I had so much fun today. Thank you." Without thinking, Lexi leaned over and gave him a quick peck on the cheek and a brilliant smile, then escaped from the car, running off to meet Anna, who was waving from the front porch with Maddie.

Caught completely off guard, Vincent sat in the car, still able to feel the heat from her lips on his cheek. He hadn't felt stunned by a kiss since grade school, and yet, here he was, grinning like a fool. Seared into his memory was not only the kiss, but also the feel of her body, or more specifically, her breasts, pressed against his arm when she leaned in for the kiss. But he couldn't allow himself to dwell on that or he would have another, much *bigger* problem all together. His body was already becoming too responsive when Lexi was near. The last thing he wanted was to look like a horny teenage boy in front of her. He took a few deep breaths, then put the top up and locked the doors to the Lotus, twice, just to kill a little more time before he had to face Anna's questioning stare.

As he walked toward the house, Vincent knew he wasn't the right man for Lexi and that things could and would never progress to anything more that friendship between them. He needed to stay away from her. He was too cynical, too jaded to ever have someone as special as Lexi in his life. She deserved better... but whenever she was near, Vincent couldn't help but think about how exciting his life would be with the fiery Lexi White in it.

"Hello, brother dear." Anna wrapped her much smaller arm in his as he passed. "A little birdie told me that you and Lexi scored the Stone account. Mom will be so proud of you two. She's on her way, you know."

"I can't wait to tell her. The presentation went really well. He hired us on the spot." Vincent tried to take a step toward the house and was stopped again by Anna, who wore a smug grin. "What now?"

"Oh nothing, I just thought you'd like to know you have a little lipstick on your cheek." she said in a teasing voice and smudged the stain with her thumb while Vincent stood there, not saying a word. "Interesting. It looks a lot like the color Lexi's wearing." Vincent returned her knowing grin by messing up her hair.

"You big ogre, not the hair! Madison, your uncle's here to play."

Madison crashed into him, wrapping her arms around his thigh.

"Uncle Vince! Did you see Lexi's here for the tea party too?" Maddie tugged his arm and dragged him over to the kitchen table where Lexi was sitting, talking to Erik.

He crooked his finger at Maddie and whispered in her ear. "I gave her a ride. And guess what? She likes to ride around with the top down on my car, just like someone else I know."

Maddie cupped her tiny hand around Vincent's ear as the pair continued exchanging secrets. "I like her, Uncle Vince. Did you see this bracelet she brought me?"

Vincent smiled as Madison showed off the tiny silver hearts that hung between the emerald colored crystals of the bracelet. "It's beautiful, Maddie, just like you." He placed a tiny kiss on her nose and followed her over to the kitchen table.

Lexi smiled as she watched Vincent sit down and pull Madison onto his lap. With a chuckle, Anna brought over a bag and held it out to her daughter. Madison rummaged through it before pulling out the biggest, pinkest, most disgustingly feather-laden hat. Lexi cringed.

"That one would be perfect for her," Vincent quickly said with a wicked grin on his face.

"No, silly, this one is for you. Lexi's allergic to feathers. She told me when she got here."

Lexi smirked triumphantly across the table as Maddie planted the hat on top of Vincent's head, the feathers falling in front of his eyes. The way the sunlight sparkled off the rhinestones that outlined the hat sent Lexi into hysterics. "Vincent, you look fantastic."

"Keep laughing, Alexandra, keep laughing." Vincent stole the bag out of Madison's hand and dug through until he pulled out a hat. "This one is perfect for Lexi." In his hand was a huge, floppy ten gallon hat. As Vincent placed it on Lexi's head, she could barely see the table in front of her.

"Well, that's usually Daddy's cowboy hat for tea parties. But, sure, Lexi, you can wear it and be a cowgirl!" Madison clapped happily while Lexi pushed up the brim of the hat to glare at Vincent in all his feathered glory.

"I hate you," Lexi hissed so only Vincent could hear her.

Vincent leaned in even closer, pretending to adjust her hat. "No you don't." He gave her a sinful wink that made her cheeks turn pink.

Lexi was saved from any more embarrassment by, of all people, Sean.

"Real pretty, Vincent," Sean boomed from the doorway. "You got a nice dress to go with that hat?" He gave Anna a hug and shook Erik's hand. "Did Vincent drink all the tea again?"

"Uncle Sean!" Madison launched herself into his outstretched arms. Sean swung her around in circles as her feet dangled above the ground. "We haven't started yet. I was waiting for you. Look, I put extra cookies out because you're always so hungry."

"You're the best girlfriend ever, Maddie." Sean kissed her cheek while Erik choked on his ladyfinger.

"Girlfriend?" Erik choked. "She's never dating. And if she ever tries, I'm doing target practice in the front yard, dressed in full camos, when the little bastard pulls into the driveway."

Erik's rumblings about phone calls from boyfriends made Lexi think of Jade and the awful phone conversation they'd had a few hours earlier. She had forgotten all about it with the excitement of the presentation, but now she was swamped with guilt for not confessing sooner. She lightly touched Vince's arm.

"I have to talk to you about something." Vincent's smile immediately fell when he heard Lexi's serious tone.

"I get the feeling it's not going to make me happy."

"No, there's nothing happy about it; that's for sure. But I need to explain—"

Vincent held up his hand and cut her off. "Is it a matter of life and death?" Lexi thought about it then shook her head side to side. "Then can we just talk about it tomorrow. I don't want to ruin Maddie's tea party by being in a bad mood."

Lexi watched the sweet girl run around and pass out napkins to all her guests. She was thrilled to have them all there, one big, happy family. There was no way Lexi would ruin that for her, so she agreed to table her confession until later. But first thing tomorrow, she would tell Vincent everything and accept the fallout.

Madison clapped her hands as she skipped across the room. "I better get more cookies on the big plate thing. And I need to find a hat for Uncle Sean. It's almost time to start. I'll be back."

Sean sauntered up to the table and took the empty seat between Vincent and Lexi. "So, the entire office is a buzzing about the two of you."

"You should know better than to listen to the crap they spew about me in the lounge," Vincent said as he leaned back in his chair, pretending to be unaffected by Sean's jabs.

"I don't know. This was kinda juicy gossip. I actually hope it's true."

Lexi didn't even want to imagine what they were saying about her and Vincent spending the night together at the office. Between that and the blow up with Tony, the rumor mill had plenty of fresh fodder to work with. She was certain it must be some horrible lie that Tony had concocted, like Lexi was pregnant with Vincent's love child and after his money. Then an even more horrible thought popped into her head—Jade. The unresolved conversation between the two of them could be the source of the gossip. And if it was Jade spreading the rumor, Lexi knew it would be more horrible than anything she could ever envision.

"I think you need to stay out of it, Sean," Vincent growled.

"How can I stay out of it if I'm directly involved?" Sean asked, looking back and forth between Lexi and Vincent incredulously.

"Listen, we spent the night together working, Sean. Nothing happened. Yes, we slept on the couch toget—"

Sean's raucous laughter interrupted Vincent's speech. "I was talking about landing the Stone account, dude! What were *you* talking about? You slept together? Do you two have something to confess? I'm all ears!" He happily tapped his fingers on the table, anxiously awaiting more of the details on their night together.

Lexi wished the ground would open up and swallow her whole at that moment. She knew the mere suggestion that she and Vincent had slept together was insane. *The only place he'd ever want to sleep with me is in my overactive imagination. He has a gorgeous girlfriend; he's an established member of the community and a brilliant advertising executive.* Lexi understood that he was way out of her league. A tiny angel swooped in at that moment and saved her from her thoughts.

"Time for the tea party to start!" Maddie declared as she returned to the room with Anna, who was now wearing a sparkling silver halo and carrying a fresh pot of tea. Madison placed a large, flamboyant hat shaped like an overflowing fruit basket on Sean's bald head.

"Come on, Maddie. Don't you have a police man hat in there or a baseball cap, something less girlie? Lexi, want to trade?" Lexi happily shook her head no. Suddenly, the giant cowboy hat didn't seem so ridiculous anymore.

Anna walked over to her husband and tossed Erik what appeared to be a dunce hat with large plastic ears attached to it. "Daddy, I found your Dopey hat!"

"Oh, goodie," Erik said unenthusiastically. "I thought it was lost forever. Wherever did you find it?" He shot Anna a dirty look.

"Mommy found it in the garage. It must have got lost in there when you were playing with it," Madison said as she filled the tiny cups on the table and began passing them out to her guests.

"Fantastic," Erik grumbled while his wife giggled.

Lexi laughed every time Vincent moved, because more feathers would cascade down from his hat and land in his tea. When he caught Lexi laughing, he picked up the pink nightmares and blew them in her direction. Sean lost a few grapes every time he bent down to sip his tea, and the occasional banana sprang free and tumbled onto the table, making Maddie laugh.

The tea party was in full swing. Madison was a wonderful hostess, leading the group in songs and telling stories. She even convinced Sean and Vincent to arm wrestle for the last chocolate chip cookie.

As Sean victoriously wiped the crumbs from his chin, a sultry voice halted him. "Whoa, when you guys have a tea party, you really go all out, don't ya?"

Standing in the doorway was the fiery Hope Greyson, leaning against the door jamb, her long black hair spilling over her shoulders looking like she just stepped out of the pages of a magazine. Sean spun around so fast, he nearly fell out of his chair. Grapes spilled off the top of his hat and scattered everywhere.

"The door was open so I let myself in. I hope that was okay."

"Of course!" Anna chirped, watching with great interest as Sean tried to collect himself.

"Hope?" he squeaked.

"Yes, the name's Hope. Please remember that." She held out her hand to Madison and took a seat at the table. "Hi, Madison. I'm Lexi's friend, Hope."

"You look like Princess Jasmine," Madison said in wonder as she stared at Hope's black hair and perfectly manicured fingers.

"I know I'm late, but do I still get a hat?" Hope smiled.

"Oh, yes. Here pick out whatever one you want."

"Hey," all the other adults at the table pouted.

"Cool!" Hope yanked a pirate hat out of the bag and put it on her head. "I don't suppose you've got an eye patch to go with this?" She grinned happily when Madison found one. "Awesome."

"You had a pirate hat in there all this time?" Sean whined. "I'd make a good pirate. Why do I have to be the fruit?"

"Because she said so, and it's her tea party. Now quit whining and pass the tea," Hope snipped back at Sean, silencing him. Madison excused herself from the table to go search for a magic wand she insisted she needed. When Sean opened up his mouth to complain again, Hope nudged his shoulder. "Quit being a baby. It's just fruit."

Vincent and Erik stood up and took the break in the festivities as an opportunity to sneak a beer from the refrigerator. They leaned against the counter and chuckled as Sean continued to stare at Hope.

"I like this woman." Anna reached her hand across the table. "Hi, Hope. I'm Anna Caldwell. Nice to finally meet you. I've heard lots about you from Sean."

Hope shook her hand and snorted. "I'm not his girlfriend, and we haven't slept together nor do I plan on it, no matter *what* he might have told you." She looked over her shoulder to make sure Madison wasn't back yet and continued in a hushed voice. "However, my breasts are spectacular. That much I'm sure he mentioned ... and got right," Hope said with a sassy grin as she wrapped her free arm around Lexi.

"Oh my God, I love you." Anna giggled.

"Hope? Really, what the hell are you doing here? Did you miss me, babe?" Sean reached for her, but Hope swatted his hand away like a fly.

"What did I tell you about the touching? Hands off, caveman."

"Careful, or I might have to throw you over my shoulder and show you just how much of a caveman I really am," he purred back at her, his large body getting as close as possible to Hope without actually touching her.

"Oh my," Anna snickered as she watched Hope sit nose to nose with Sean, and not even flinch. Anna covered her mouth to hide her laughter while Vincent and Erik shook their heads at Sean.

Lexi, however, patiently waited for the comeback.

Hope sat back in her chair and gave him a long, slow appraisal from head to toe, then shrugged. "Your club isn't big enough to tame me, *babe*."

Madison breezed into the room as everyone exploded with laughter. "Time for the magic show!" Madison kept all the adults busy for the next forty-five minutes with her tricks and an impromptu game of charades. The girls destroyed the boys' team, mainly because Erik was the worst charades player of all time and all they did was argue when it was their turn.

"This," Erik gestured his hands wildly at his sides, "is *not* flying, Sean. I was bicycling my arms. The word was bicycle."

"You were flapping your wings, man, or having a seizure, or being electrocuted. Nothing about that says bicycle. Madison, your dad stinks at this game. Can we be done?"

"I think that's a great idea. I need to give Maddie her bath anyway and start getting her ready for bed. Make yourselves comfortable, and I'll be right back." Anna excused herself upstairs with Madison right behind her.

"Lexi, the car runs like a dream now. That noise was a belt. I changed it and fixed the leaking hose. She's as good as new. I had to keep it the extra day because the moron sent me the wrong part." Hope tossed the keys to Lexi.

"You're the best." Lexi gave her friend a big hug.

"So what kind of car do you drive?" Vincent asked from right behind her. "I'm dying to see what the girl who called my car a toy thinks is a worthy automobile."

Lexi slipped the keys into his hand and gestured toward the door. "Go see for yourself."

Vincent made it as far as the door when he stopped short and said, "I know that car."

Everyone walked outside and stared at Lexi's gorgeous silver '67 Chevy Camaro with racing stripes. She grinned proudly as they ran over to get a closer look.

"Did you restore this?" Sean asked Hope incredulously. His mouth fell open when she nodded her head.

"This was your dad's car." Vincent ran his hand over the curve of the hood. "I remember him driving around town in this all the time."

"So you remember my dad's car, but not me? Great. That does wonders for a girl's self-esteem. Thanks, Vincent." Lexi laughed, opening the door.

"Your baby's back and in perfect working condition, thanks to yours truly." Hope grinned as Sean continued to walk around the car, his mouth still agape. "I messed with the engine again while I was waiting for the belt to get delivered. Give it a start."

Lexi stole the key from Vincent and hopped in the car, letting the engine roar to life. The resulting purr sounded like heaven and always made her think of Harry. She ran her hands lovingly over the steering wheel and smiled. She hardly noticed when Vincent climbed into the car beside her.

"I want your car."

"What? Your little Matchbox car not doing it for you anymore now that you've seen a fine, performance machine like this?" she teased, laughing as he ran his hands over the dashboard.

"My car is still faster, but this is just gorgeous."

"Excuse me? Faster? I don't think so. Listen to this." Lexi slammed her foot down on the gas. The engine thundered, making her teeth rattle from the vibration. "Hope put so much horsepower in this thing it would eat your car for breakfast."

"Can I drive it? Can I drive it?" Sean popped his head in the window, a hopeful look in his eye.

The only other person Lexi ever let drive the car was Hope. It was the last piece of Harry she had, and that's why she put so much time and care into it. Sean was a good man and would understand. "It was my dad's, Sean. It's all I have left of him. Be careful, and I have one condition." She climbed out of the driver's seat so he could get in. Vincent vacated the passenger's side at the same time. "Hope has to go with you to make sure you don't do anything stupid."

"Agreed!" He crooked his finger at Hope and tapped the seat beside him. "Come on, baby, let's roll."

"Lexi," Hope snarled as she walked by her friend, "if he puts his hand on my knee while he's driving…"

"You'll love every second of it," Lexi whispered and gave her a push toward the car. "Have fun, you two. No making out in my car, please." Lexi waved and ignored Hope flipping her the bird as they went screaming down the driveway.

"Your car wins," Vincent chuckled as they walked back to the house and sat down on the porch swing together. Erik went inside to check on Anna and Madison while Lexi and Vincent watched the sun set behind the tall trees at the edge of the yard.

"There's nothing wrong with your car, Vincent. I was just teasing you earlier. So, you remember Harry's car?"

Vincent smiled sheepishly. "I used to see it at the diner every day when I drove home from school. One day, I stopped to get a better look at it, and your dad must have seen me through the window. He came out, and I thought he was going to yell at me, but instead he popped the hood and told me about the engine. I didn't understand half of what he was saying." He looked over at Lexi, who had tears streaming down her face. "I'm sorry, I didn't mean to make you cry."

Lexi always had a hard time talking about Harry, but to hear Vincent talk about him in such a kind and loving way was more than her heart could handle. She buried her face in her hands and wept.

"Shh, it's okay, Lexi. I'm sorry. I shouldn't have brought it up." Vincent pulled her against his chest and let her cry. He held her and rocked them gently on the swing, doing his best to soothe her.

"No, I'm sorry," Lexi whispered against his chest. She felt ridiculous, sobbing in front of him and clinging to his shirt for dear life, but to have his arms wrapped around her felt like home. For the first time in a while, she felt loved and cared for. More than that, she felt protected, something that up until then, only Harry had been able to do. "I'm such a wimp."

Vincent's expression hardened. "You are most certainly not a wimp. You're one of the strongest women I've ever met. Look at what you've been through and still you walk around with a smile on your face, bringing joy to everyone around you." Lexi made a small grunt of disbelief. "I'm serious. What about the presentation? That new campaign? It was all you. Your ideas were the centerpiece of it, and you stayed in that office all night, helping me when I was acting like a complete bastard. You, Alexandra White, are amazing."

Lexi was captivated by the sound of his voice. He spoke with such power, such certainty, that she couldn't question it. She found herself lost in his eyes, which showed the honesty of his words. He wasn't feeding her a line; he wasn't simply being kind and telling her what she needed to hear. He was speaking from his heart, and Lexi was overwhelmed by it.

She was hyperaware of him, picking up on even the slightest movement, like the way his shoulder bumped into her, or the way his forearm slid against hers. She doubted the contact was accidental. With great care, like she was a fragile china doll, Vincent reached up and wiped the remaining tears from her cheeks with the pad of his thumb, his fingers lingering on her face. Between his touch, his eyes, and his heartfelt words, Lexi felt herself falling again, falling for the man who had held her heart all these years, even if he'd had no idea.

Vincent leaned in closer, his eyes still on hers, never wavering. He dipped his face, brushing his cheek against hers, not once, but twice. Lexi's whole body tensed, waiting to see what would happen next. She felt his lips lightly graze the corner of her mouth, and then the spell he had on her was broken by the loud crunch of tires on the driveway. Vincent pulled away from her, putting a safe distance between them but still looking guilty as sin.

A very tired Elizabeth and Robert Drake climbed out of the car and waved. Vincent and Lexi jumped up from the porch swing and hurried over to help them with their bags. "Hello, kids! How are you?" Elizabeth hugged them both and gave them each a motherly kiss on the cheek. "I hear you had a big day today."

Robert came around the car, and Lexi introduced herself. "Hello, Mr. Drake, you probably don't remember me, but I'm Lexi White. Nice to see you again."

"Lexi, dear! My wife's been talking about you nonstop. I'm sorry I didn't get to talk to you at the gala and welcome you to Hunter, but she kept me busy. Vincent, congratulations on landing Stone. We're so proud of you. Your mother tried to change her flight three times this morning to get home to help you after Jared checked his voicemail and told her what had happened. American Airlines will never be the same again. I'm sure we'll be stopped by security and subjected to a full body cavity search every time we fly in and out of Miami."

Elizabeth rolled her eyes. "I wasn't that bad. You're always exaggerating. The woman wasn't listening to me when I told her it was urgent."

Robert wrapped his arm around his wife as he led her to the house. "Oh, she was listening. Everyone in Terminal A was listening, dear. Your voice carries."

"Grandma! Grandpa!" Madison appeared at the bottom of the stairs dressed in her silky pink pajamas, saving Robert from his wife.

"Hello, angel face. Look, Grandpa and I bought you lots of presents. He has the bag in the family room. Go see what he's got."

Madison flew off after Robert to check out her bounty. Elizabeth, however, cornered Lexi and Vincent with a knowing grin. "So, tell me everything."

Lexi's face paled, wondering just how much Elizabeth had seen when she pulled into the driveway. It must have looked awful, Lexi in Vincent's arms, his face against hers. Elizabeth probably thought she was a tramp for throwing herself at a man with girlfriend. Lexi's cheeks flamed red as she stared at the toe of her shoe, unable to look Elizabeth in the face. Vincent, too, was suddenly dumbstruck.

"About the presentation," Elizabeth prompted as she glanced back and forth between the guilty-looking pair standing in front of her.

"Oh, it went very well. Julian thought it was perfect. He loved Lexi's print ad. I think that's what sold him on the idea." Vincent smiled proudly at his partner in crime.

"He's being too kind, really, Elizabeth. He came up with the overall concept. I just followed his lead."

"You worked all night on the new project, and then gave a spotless presentation? You must be exhausted. You two make quite a team. The person who hired Lexi is one smart cookie, if I do say so myself. Maybe Mom really did know best, huh, Vincent?"

Lexi chuckled as Vincent scowled at his mother.

"Just say 'Thank you, Mother,' and I'll consider us even." Elizabeth waited with folded arms, tapping her foot.

"Thank you, Mother." Vincent ground out the words through his clenched jaw.

"Thank you, Elizabeth, for hiring me, and giving me the pleasure of working with this ray of sunshine every day," Lexi sang and quickly placed a kiss on Elizabeth's cheek before chasing after Madison, trying to tickle the tiny girl.

"Madison, bed time."

"But, Mom..."

"No arguing. Let's go."

"Can Lexi read me a story, please?" she asked, looking at Lexi with a huge grin on her face. "Or can you and Uncle Vince do another sleepover, but this time at my house?"

Elizabeth mumbled a shocked "Oh my."

"Maddie, Lexi and I didn't—"

Lexi glared at Vincent. "She's five, Vincent. Do you really want to explain *that* to her?" She turned her attention back to Maddie. "How about you pick out a book, and I'll read it to you up in bed. I can't sleep over, because I have to get Miss Hope home soon. She gets cranky if she's up too late."

"And we wouldn't want that now, would we?" Sean snickered as he walked in the front door of the house, Hope right behind him.

Lexi eyed Hope, who had a funny look on her face. "Is my car still in one piece?"

"Never better." Sean grinned as he tossed the keys back to Lexi and gave Hope a sideways glance.

"Arrogant fool," Hope griped, and then joined Elizabeth and Robert on the couch.

Before Lexi could go ask her friend why she seemed embarrassed, Madison came flying down the stairs with a large book in her hands. "Let's go, Lexi. I know just the book. Uncle Vincent, are you going to come too?"

"I'll be there in a minute, honey. You two go on upstairs and get started." Vincent smiled as Madison gave everyone a hug and a kiss and said goodnight. Then she slipped her hand in Lexi's and led her to her room.

Madison's room was done in pale pinks with a mural of a meadow littered with purple flowers and grazing horses. Off in the distance stood a beautiful castle. The sun washed over the whole scene, giving it a warm, happy feel.

"Wow, Madison, this room is awesome."

The little girl crawled into the center of her large, white canopy bed and patted the mattress beside her. "Come lay down, Lexi!"

Lexi drew back the white bedspread and Madison snuggled under the fluffy fabric. Once Madison was comfortable, Lexi lay down on top of the comforter beside her and picked up the book.

"*Beauty and the Beast?*" Lexi smiled.

"Yes! Because *you* are in it. Well, her name is Belle, but I call her Lexi now. And Uncle Vincent is the Beast!" Madison exploded into a fit of giggles and quickly had Lexi laughing right alongside her.

All childlike giddiness vanished when Lexi felt a heated stare from the doorway. Vincent was leaning against the doorframe, watching them laugh and be silly. He occasionally glanced Madison's way, but mostly his eyes stayed locked on Lexi while a secretive smile crept across his lips.

"Do I even want to know what you two are giggling about?" His deep voice washed over Lexi, and she had to look away as he approached the bed. When she felt the bed dip from his weight as he climbed in beside Maddie, and inches away from Lexi, her heart began beating wildly.

"You're the Beast." Maddie waved the book in his face.

"The Beast? What about Prince Charming? I think I'm more charming than beastly, wouldn't you say, Lexi?"

Slowly, Lexi turned in his direction. On the other side of Madison, Vincent lazily stretched out on top of the covers, his long, muscular legs extending all the way to the end of the bed. He propped his elbow up on the pillow while his hand supported his head. He playfully grinned at Lexi, waiting for her to agree.

"I plead the fifth on that one." Lexi laughed. "I enjoy my job too much to risk it."

Vincent rolled back onto the pillow, clutching his heart. "Maddie, Lexi thinks I'm beastly."

His niece kissed his cheek. "Yes, but just like Belle in the book, she loves you anyway. Now come on, we have to read!"

Once again, Lexi blushed at Madison's innocent words. Her assessment was spot on. Even with Vincent's flaws, Lexi still found him to be the most wonderful man she had ever met, and it was slowly killing her inside.

Madison saved Lexi from her thoughts by launching into her version of Disney's *Beauty and the Beast*. "So let's skip the beginning. Uncle Vincent is cursed by that mean lady who turns him into the grumpy beast."

Lexi nearly laughed as she imagined Jade as the mean lady Madison was describing. Vincent propped himself back up and rolled his eyes, still denying he was anything like the beast.

"And we can skip the singing stuff, unless you want to sing this song, Lexi?" Lexi's face whitened as Madison pointed at the lyrics on the page.

"Oh, I think Lexi should have to sing, Maddie." Vincent chuckled and egged the little girl on, earning himself the evil eye from Lexi.

"Just remember who makes your coffee every morning, Vincent. And gets your lunch. You really want to risk getting on my bad side? You can kiss all those burgers goodbye, pal." Lexi smiled at Madison. "Honey, why don't you sing the song? I bet you would do a wonderful job."

Madison broke into song, looking back and forth from Vincent to Lexi as she sang, not missing a single word. After the musical interlude, she had Lexi read the book. She used different voices for each of the characters, which thrilled Maddie to no end. Vincent took over a few of the household characters, doing a spot on French accent that made Lexi swoon.

When Belle and the Beast finally met in the story, Vincent read the parts of the Beast with a low, gruff voice that softened the more he was around Belle. Lexi turned the page, and Madison clapped with delight.

"This is my favorite part in the whole book!" She crawled out from under the covers and jumped on the bed. "You two get to dance!"

"Oh, honey, I don't know," Lexi stammered, having no idea how she was going to get out of this one. There was no way she could be in Vincent's arms again without him seeing the feelings she harbored for him. But Vincent was already on his feet and walking around to her side of the bed. "Oh, we don't really have to."

Ignoring her completely, Vincent gave a gentlemanly bow to Lexi and extended his large hand. "May I have this dance, Belle?" he asked in character. When Lexi paused, he gave her a playful wink.

Lexi looked at Maddie clapping her hands in wide-eyed anticipation, then glanced at Vincent patiently waiting for her to accept his offer. It was completely unfair of him to use it his irresistible wink like this, but before Lexi knew it, her legs were shifting off the bed, and she felt the soft carpet under her feet. She slipped her tiny hand into Vincent's and took an unsure step in his direction. He gently pulled her into the center of the room and brushed his lips over her knuckles before sweeping her up into his arms.

Madison began singing right on cue. "Tale as old as time..."

Dancing with Vincent in front of all those people at the gala had made Lexi self-conscious, but that was nothing compared to dancing with him alone in Madison's room. The intimacy of it, the way he cradled her in his arms so gently, with only the eyes of a child on them, and the radiant smile on his face as he spun her around the room was overwhelming. The warmth from his body spread out around hers, his contact like tiny flames licking against her skin.

Lexi focused on her breathing the entire dance, trying desperately to not get lost in his eyes, but failing miserably. She watched the way his irises sparkled as he glanced over at Maddie, blowing her a kiss, and then twirled Lexi in circles. For those two minutes, Lexi felt like she was actually living out a fairy tale.

"Okay, now you two kiss!" Madison proclaimed from her bed as the song ended, bouncing with excitement.

Lexi froze. "N-no, that's not in the book." She craned her neck to look at the pages, searching for any indication of a kiss.

"But that's when Belle and the Beast start to fall in love," Madison said with a deep frown.

"Yes, honey, but we can't just kiss. Uncle Vincent he's my ... my ..."

"Friend," Vincent offered, tugging on Lexi's arm, trying to calm her down. "We're friends, aren't we?" He leaned in closer and whispered, "Are you worried that if we kiss we might start to fall in love?"

Way ahead of you on that one, mister, Lexi thought to herself, wondering how she would ever find her way back from this. "Actually, I'm afraid this will just be another reason for Jade to gouge my eyes out next time she sees me," Lexi said through a tight smile, trying to keep Madison from hearing.

"Never mind," Madison said sadly, her excitement quickly replaced with disappointment as she sat down on her bed.

"Maddie, the problem is people just can't go around kissing," Vincent tried to explain.

The sight of her sadly pouting broke Lexi's heart. She didn't want her hang up to be the reason the little girl's big night ended on a sad note, so she did the only thing she could. "Let's do it."

Vincent's head whipped in her direction, his eyebrows rose skeptically. "Are you sure? Because I don't want you to be uncomfortable."

"Vincent, shut up and kiss me."

He took her hand and slowly spun her in one final, torturously slow turn. When she was facing him, he wrapped one arm around her waist, while the other cupped the back of her neck, his fingers wrapping around her long hair as he held her in place.

Lexi's heart screamed to life in her chest as his face approached hers. She was certain he could feel her trembling in his arms, but she was helpless to stop her body's reaction to their impending kiss. This was something she had dreamed of, fantasized about, and hoped for all those years ago, and it was about to happen.

His lips were soft as they brushed against hers, better than anything she had ever imagined. He was gentle, but completely in control of the kiss. At first he applied only light pressure, but then something changed and his mouth moved more forcefully over hers, hungrily even. She felt his grip on her hair tighten as his lips took control of hers, teasing and guiding her into a more heated kiss.

Lexi was thankful he had a good grip on her, because her knees turned to Jell-O when she felt his warm tongue graze against her lower lip. Her body melted to his, her soft curves molding against hard muscles like perfectly matching puzzle pieces. Without warning, Lexi's arms wrapped around his neck, and she opened her mouth, allowing him to slide in and taste her. Her tongue tentatively made contact with his, but she still allowed him to set the pace. She had been kissed many times before, but never had she felt it move through her body like an electric current, awakening every cell in its path, the way Vincent's kiss did. In those few seconds, she had never felt more alive. As he deepened the kiss, a tiny giggle from Madison snapped Lexi right back into reality and out of the erotic fantasy that was playing out in her head.

She forcefully pushed Vincent away and covered her mouth with her hand. "What did I do?" she murmured, half to herself, half to Vincent. The look on his face mirrored hers, his chest heaving as he tried to catch his ragged breath.

"Lexi, wait." Vincent reached out and tried to grab her arm, but Lexi stepped away.

"That was the best kiss ever!" Maddie fell back on her bed laughing.

You have no idea, Lexi thought to herself. Her heart thundered in her chest, and she felt like she couldn't catch her breath. She needed to get out of there. She desperately needed to be as far away from Vincent as possible. The other side of the Earth even seemed too close at that moment. With unsteady legs, she took a tentative step towards the door, trying to ignore the taste of Vincent on her lips and fresh memory of his chest against hers.

"Maddie, I have to go now. It's late. Vincent can finish reading to you." She didn't even wait to hear the girl's response before she ran out the door and down the steps.

Lexi sped past Sean at the bottom of the steps. "We need to go," she mouthed across the room to Hope, tears starting to fill her eyes.

Hope gave nothing away to Elizabeth or Robert who were sitting in chairs beside her. She gracefully stood up from the couch and gathered up Lexi's purse as her friend paced by the front door. "Thank you for a lovely evening," Hope said to Anna, giving a small nod with her eyebrow raised in Lexi's direction to let her know something was up.

Anna wrapped her arms around Hope. "It was wonderful meeting you," she said and then whispered something to Hope.

Lexi did her best to cover her distress as she hugged Robert and Elizabeth and waved to Anna over her shoulder. "Thanks for having us, Anna. Sorry we have to run. Vincent's upstairs finishing the story with Maddie."

"Bye, Lexi!" They all called after her as she practically ran out the front door with Hope trailing behind her.

"What did Vincent do now?" Vincent heard Sean ask as he rushed down the stairs looking for Lexi.

"I don't know." Anna turned just in time to see Vincent come flying down, his eyes scanning the room frantically.

"Where's Lexi? I have to talk to her."

Sean pointed his thumb at the front door. "She just left, man. Ran out of here like a bat outta hell. You have any idea why that is?"

Elizabeth intently watched from across the room with Robert, waiting to hear Vincent's response. "Let's give them some space to talk. He needs Sean. He's the closest thing to a brother he has right now," Robert said. Vincent gave a grateful nod as his father led Elizabeth into the kitchen.

Vincent refused to look Sean in the eye. A noise outside caught his attention, and he focused on watching Lexi as she climbed into the passenger's seat of her car, visibly upset. He pushed open the door and stood on the porch to watch the car speed away.

Sean came up behind him and put his hand on Vincent's shoulder. "You want to talk about it?"

"I have no idea where to start."

Vincent's posture tensed, his arms folded across his chest in a blatant leave-me-alone gesture. Not scared off, Sean asked casually, "Can I just make an observation then?" Sean watched Vincent's eyes flicker over to his, waiting for what was coming next. "You like her."

"She's my friend." Vincent leaned back against the rail of the porch and sighed.

"I'm not talking about in a friendly kinda way, man." He watched Vincent busy himself by picking chipped paint off the wood beside him. "I've seen the way you look at her. At the gala, at the office when she's busy on the computer. Hell, tonight at the tea party, I've never seen you laugh so much."

Vincent raked his hands through his hair before rubbing them over his face. "It's complicated."

"No, it's not. You like her, she likes you. And she does, in case you haven't noticed. She gets this cute little grin on her face when you walk in the room, and she watches you when you aren't looking, all the time." Vincent rolled his eyes but Sean ignored him and continued. "What's so damn complicated? Explain it to me."

"Oh, I don't know—Jade."

"Screw Jade," Sean said, sitting down on the swing.

"Lexi's nice and I'm not."

"So be nicer." Sean rolled his shoulders.

"She has a good heart." Vincent hopped up on the railing near the swing and leaned against the post beside him.

"And so do you."

"I don't know if I can trust her," Vincent said in a serious voice.

"And you trust Jade? Are you insane?" Sean stopped the swing and leaned toward Vincent. "Why are you still with her? She makes you miserable far more than she makes you happy."

That was the question Vincent had been asking himself for months now. The only good things about Jade he could think of after a while were the facts that she traveled a lot and that even though she was a pain, he knew what to expect from her. She was predictable and safe. He would never allow her close enough to hurt him, and she frankly didn't want to be that close to him either. She liked being with Vincent because of who he was and he knew that. She was shallow and petty, caring about a man's status far more than his soul.

"I know what to expect with her. And I can keep her at arm's length so she can't screw me over. With Lexi, I don't think I could do that. I'd want too much."

"So you're choosing to be miserable over being happy?"

"I'm choosing to be safe over sorry."

Sean got up off the swing with pity in his eyes. "You have to let all that baggage go eventually, Vincent. Before it ruins you. Yes, people screwed you over in the past, but it's in the past. Don't let them continue doing it to you by keeping you from someone who might make you truly happy. You're scared."

Vincent hopped off the rail and began pacing the deck. "I'm not scared, Sean. I'm just not ready to trust someone completely again, if ever. I did with Adria and others before her and look what happened."

"Adria was a bitch and a money grubber who wanted power and her own company. She was and still is a sadistic shrew who has probably screwed men out of all sorts of things. It's what she does. She spreads her legs to get what she wants. But that was years ago. Your life has nothing to do with her anymore, so don't let her take something else away from you. Just think about it, please."

There was deep sadness in Vincent's eyes as he smiled at his friend. "I'll think about it."

"Good, because I like Lexi. She's a kick in the pants and I think that's exactly what you need, someone who isn't all gaga over you because you're this big shot and you have money. She sees you for you, Vincent. And she still likes you. That's pretty amazing, man."

They laughed and looked out over the full moon as it hung low in the sky. "She is amazing." Vincent grinned at Sean who nodded his head wholeheartedly in agreement.

"And she has a kickass car." Sean elbowed Vincent in the side. "Stop over-thinking things, man."

"Kinda hard not to. She's my assistant."

"Well, hell, there is that, but work around it." He held open the door to the house and let Vincent step inside. "So what happened up there? Did you say something stupid again?"

"No, that's your style." Vincent shrugged his shoulders. "I kissed her."

Anna and her parents walked into the room just in time to hear Vincent's big confession, then all hell broke loose.

"You did what?"

"That's great!"

"Oh, boy..."

"Shit."

Their reactions bombarded him from every direction, and Vincent slowly nodded in agreement with all of it. "My thoughts exactly."

· 19 ·

"You kissed him?" Hope squawked as she nearly went off the road in shock. "Stop saying it!" Lexi moaned from the passenger's seat beside her friend. "I'm so stupid. What's wrong with me?"

"Honey," Hope reached over and squeezed Lexi's hand, "it was just a kiss."

"I kissed my boss, Hope," she sobbed, "and to *him* I'm sure it was just a kiss, but to me it was..."

"It's okay. I swear it will be okay."

For the rest of the ride home, Lexi remained silent, her head pressed against the glass of the window as she watched the scenery fly by. By the time they reached the apartment, Lexi had no more tears left to shed. She crawled from the car and retreated into the safety of her home. Hope followed her inside and helped get her friend settled.

"Let me make you some tea. It'll help." Hope rummaged around for the kettle and heated the water while Lexi changed into a pair of comfy pajamas.

By the time Lexi sat down on the couch, Hope was there with a cup of tea and a hug.

"This is a disaster, Hope. I have no idea what I am going to do. I kissed him. It was no peck on the cheek. It was a full on, make out kiss. Every time I close my eyes I can see him; I can feel him." Lexi rubbed her fingertips across her lips with panic in her eyes. "I need to make these feelings go away. I won't be that pathetic girl I was in high school again."

"You aren't pathetic."

Lexi snorted and rolled her eyes. "I smuggle a grown man cheeseburgers just to see the way his eyes light up when he spies the bag in my hand. I make him a cup of coffee every morning, even though he's more than capable of doing it himself, just so he thanks me in his husky morning voice. Hell, if my desk wasn't right outside his office I'd probably be coming up with lame reasons to walk by his door just to catch a glimpse of him. I'm pathetic with a capital P." She slowly sipped her tea and settled back on the couch.

"Well," Hope said nonchalantly, "based on what I saw, you aren't the only one sporting a little crush. He's interested in you too."

"Please." Lexi put her mug down on the coffee table and tucked her legs under her as she rolled her eyes.

"Are you really that blind? The man sat there and blew feathers at you all night, which in case you misunderstood, was shameless flirting on his part. And don't think I didn't notice the two of you all huddled close together, whispering back and forth. Anna nearly fell out of her seat watching you guys. Even Sean said something about it."

"Oh, God." Lexi pressed her hand to her stomach in an effort to stop the rolling she felt inside. "What did he say? Do I even want to know? Did it involve condoms?"

Hope laughed. "You need to calm down. It wasn't bad. He thinks you're good for Vincent. You make him smile; everyone says so."

"Everyone?" Lexi squeaked out in horror. "I have to quit. I can't go back there knowing people are talking about me like that. I thought I was doing a good job hiding my ridiculous crush." She covered her face with her hands.

Hope smoothed the hair out of her friend's face and rested her hand on Lexi's shoulder. "Is that what it is, just a crush?"

"Stop it. Don't make me say it. I can't."

Hope let the question die and replaced it with a much juicier one. "Is he a good kisser?" she asked with a wicked smile. "He looks like he could curl a girl's toes. That dark, brooding thing he has going on is pretty sexy."

For the first time since they had left Anna's house, Lexi laughed. "The man could teach a college level course on kissing." She fanned her heated cheeeks as she remembered how the soft, gentle kiss turned into so much more.

"Was there tongue?"

"Hope!" Lexi scolded.

"I just need to know exactly what kind of kiss your *boss* gave you."

Twisting her fingers together, Lexi whispered, "He gave me the best kiss of my life. I felt it under my skin, Hope. And then I wrapped my arms around his neck and practically mauled him ... in front of Madison." Lexi smacked herself in the head. "Anna will never let me near her daughter again."

"Who initiated the tongue?" Hope's question stopped Lexi's ranting.

"Excuse me?"

"Whose tongue went in whose mouth first? That's a crucial bit of information."

Lexi thought about it for a minute and blushed. "I guess it was his tongue in my mouth. I still don't understand why that matters."

"Because that means *he* kissed *you*. Think about it. He was okay with the whole idea from the beginning, right? He wanted to kiss you, and what could've been an innocent little peck, he turned into a Gene Simmons-like display of oral showmanship." Hope grinned.

"I French kissed my boss!" Lexi wailed as she buried her face in the pillow. "That's just so wrong. How am I going to face him tomorrow when all I'll be able to do is blush like an idiot or stare at his lips and remember the sexy chest rumble thing he did as he kissed me? Either way, it's too late. I'm so screwed."

Hope scooted closer to her friend and cradled her arm over Lexi's shoulders. "I know it all seems like a total disaster right now, but you'll be fine. You're an amazing and wonderful person, and if he can't see that about you then he isn't worth your time. I know that's not what you want to hear, but it's true. If it's meant to be, it will all work out somehow, no matter how impossible it all seems right now. You can't mess with fate."

Rarely did the hard-nosed Hope get spiritual. If she wanted something, she went for it. She made her future happen and didn't wait around for things like fate and destiny, so her show of that little bit of faith in the cosmos made Lexi smile. It reminded her of something Marie would have said, telling her to trust in fate and destiny to lead her down the right path because some things were out of her control. The universe had plans for everyone according to Marie. Lexi just wished she knew if hers included Vincent.

"Is there anything I can do to make you feel better?" Hope asked as she rubbed Lexi's back.

After a few seconds, a mischievous smile swept across Lexi's face. "As a matter of fact, yes, you can. Tell me about your drive with Sean."

A strangled sound came out of Hope as her tea went down the wrong pipe. "Someone's obviously feeling better," she choked out. When her coughing fit subsided, she said indignantly, "I have no idea what you're talking about."

Lexi rolled her puffy eyes, desperate to get the focus off of her. "Don't think for one second I missed that goofy look on your face when you came back in the house, young lady."

"We aren't talking about me. We were discussing your epic crush on Vincent."

"Yeah, but this topic is so much more fun." She pointed at Hope's face. "Aww, look, you're blushing."

"Stop it! I am not!" She whipped a mirror out of her purse and checked her reflection. "Crap, I am. That son of a bitch. I think he cast some sort of voodoo spell on me."

There was no stopping the smug grin on Lexi's face. "So, was it an *interesting* drive?"

"Damn it, stop the interrogation!" Hope slammed her head down on the table. "We made out. I'm weak. I'm a weak, weak woman. I think you should stage an intervention for me."

A full belly laugh rolled out of Lexi, and with great pleasure, she turned Hope's own words back onto her for maximum embarrassment. "So, was there tongue?"

Hope's long black hair whipped over her shoulder as she raised her chin and answered Lexi's embarrassing question head on, trying to save face. "Yes, there was tongue. Lots and lots of tongue. And the tongue action was *not* limited to my mouth."

"What?" Lexi shrieked in shock.

Hope shrugged. "A lady doesn't kiss and tell."

"Bull," Lexi laughed and then hugged Hope. "I'm not even going to ask where else his tongue was."

The women shared a knowing look. "That's probably for the best." Hope winked at her friend.

"Thanks for cheering me up. I appreciate you listening to me and my whining."

"I love you, Lexi. And I'm always here for you."

"Unless you're making out with Sean, that is."

The two women stayed up late, with Hope trying unsuccessfully to keep Lexi's mind off of Vincent Drake. Just after midnight, Lexi decided she was going to call off work tomorrow so she could clear her head. Vincent had meetings later that day, anyway, so she would just be sitting at her desk, wallowing in her humiliation, and she could do that just as well at home. She called Hunter and left a brief message for Leigh. In the morning, she would text Vincent and let him know she wasn't feeling well and wouldn't be back until the following day. That would give her one more day to clear her head before she faced him.

After a restless night's sleep, Lexi focused her energies on cleaning her apartment, immersing herself in that rather than dwelling on her memories of the night before. She savagely tried to scour away her feelings for Vincent as she scrubbed her place. Her BlackBerry remained eerily silent all day, which was fine with her. She would rather not risk hearing the deep, sexy timbre of his voice on her mental health day. Within the safety of her apartment, she simply focused on anything and everything that was *not* Vincent Drake.

By the time she was done with her rampage, her bathroom floors gleamed, every scrap of clothing was washed, folded and put away, cups and glasses were arranged by height, and food was sorted by the time of day in which it was eaten. Her home could have been photographed for *Architectural Digest* it was that pristine.

Hours later, Lexi ventured out of the house and found herself at the one place that always made her feel better: her bench. It was nothing extravagant, a tiny haven in a bustling city, but it felt like it had been hers from the very first time she sat down on the gently splintering wood, with tears in her eyes, missing her father. She couldn't explain what it was about being near the water that calmed her, but it made her feel content and hopeful. Being there reminded Lexi that life goes on, and in the end, somehow, everything would be okay. As the sun started to set, Lexi peered out over the water one last time, and then headed home.

Emotionally and physically exhausted, Lexi fell into bed that night, happy that for at least a few hours her brain had remained a Vincent-free zone. Her dreams, however, were a different story.

✦

Her morning coffee was interrupted by Hope's loud voice. "Jesus, Lexi. Next time you need to purge yourself of a man, I'm taking you to the garage and letting you clean the shit out of it. The place is an absolute hole. Oh my God, did you alphabetize your entire DVD collection? There have to be—"

"Two hundred and fourteen movies," Lexi said smugly as she took a sip from her mug. "And eighty-five CDs; don't forget those."

Hope shook her head as she surveyed the rest of the apartment. When she poked her head into the bathroom, she noticed that Lexi had even folded the end toilet paper into a little triangle just like they did at fancy hotels. Thoroughly amazed, she plopped onto the stool beside Lexi and shook her head. "Have you expelled your demons? Are you ready to go back to work?"

"Ready to get back to work? Yes. Am I ready to see Vincent? Absolutely not." Lexi waved her BlackBerry at Hope. "I have ten missed calls from him."

"What the hell did he want?" She snatched the phone, but Lexi immediately grabbed it back and slipped it into her purse.

"I have no idea. He never left a message. I'll find out when I get there." Lexi pushed herself up from the table and slipped the strap of her purse up and over her arm. "Wish me luck."

"Good luck." Hope followed her to the door and walked across the hall to her place. "Oh, and no making out in the elevator over there at Hunter. Tell Vincent to keep his lips to himself." She snickered as she disappeared into her apartment.

"It's not funny, Hope!" Lexi yelled at the closed door. She had to smile when she heard her friend's muffled voice from behind the door.

"Yes it is!" The door opened a crack, revealing a smiling Hope. "You can either laugh or cry. You did all your crying yesterday. It's time to move on to laughing. Go to work and call me when you get home."

Lexi took a deep breath as she stepped into the elevator at the Barrington Building. The muffin she had eaten on her way into work was not sitting well. When the door opened and she finally saw Leigh's smiling face, she felt better.

"Lexi! How are you feeling?" Leigh came around her desk to give her a hug. "Was it the flu or something? We missed you yesterday."

"Thanks, I'm fine," Lexi said softly as she avoided Leigh's question and glanced over at the desk. "Does he have any messages this morning?"

Leigh made a face and shook her head. "Actually, he already got them. He came in early today, and I should warn you, he's on the war path."

"Fantastic." Lexi's shoulders slumped. "I better go see what crawled up his behind today."

"Oh, that's easy. Jade's with him."

Lexi froze in middle of the hall, now really wishing he had either left her a message or that she had picked up the phone when he had called. For all she knew, she could be walking into a hornet's nest. "Jade's back?" She tried to sound casual, but her pale complexion gave away her shock.

"Yeah, her broomstick landed early this morning. He must have picked her up at the airport and brought her here."

"Wonderful. Well, off to my execution. It was nice knowing you, Leigh."

"Wait. Something's up. What's going on with you and Jade?" Leigh eyed her suspiciously and waited, but when Lexi didn't answer, she continued. "Well, whatever it is, I got my money on you." She winked at Lexi, making her smile. "I suggest a long flight of stairs with alligators waiting at the bottom. Just give her a little push. Oh, and make sure you get a good shot in for me, preferably in the face."

"You're so bad," Lexi laughed as she walked down the hall, feeling much better than she had a few minutes ago.

"If you need your fists wrapped, I'm your corner girl!" Leigh called after her.

"I'm surrounded by crazy women." Lexi laughed to herself as she rounded the corner, but what she found at her desk made her hiss. "Speaking of which …"

"Well, well, well, look who it is. Come here to moon over my boyfriend some more?"

Jade's feet were propped up on the desk as she flipped through a stack of folders. She didn't even flinch when Lexi stalked over and tugged the file out of her hand.

"Good morning, Jade. How was your trip?" Lexi tried to be polite, but was unable to unclench her jaw to speak to the woman.

"You didn't answer my question. Here to ogle Vincent?" Jade sneered.

Screw polite, Lexi thought. She just wanted her to go away. "Actually, I came here to work, Jade. That's what most people do. We can't all be jet-setting supermodels." She waved her hand at the desk. "Do you mind?"

Jade rolled her eyes and swung her legs off the desk, but stayed in Lexi's chair, her arms folded tightly across her surgically-enhanced chest. "As a matter of fact, I do." She placed her hands flat on Lexi's desk, her posture letting Lexi know things were about to get ugly. Her voice had a steel edge to it. "Let me tell you something. Vincent will never want you, so give it up. You can chase him all you want. I don't even care. Just remember, I'm the one he comes home to, it's my body he touches at night, and it's my name he calls out when we're making love, so don't think for one single second that he's even going to notice you exist, Lexi. You're insignificant, at best."

Remaining stoic, Lexi took Jade's insults in stride, feeling in a way that she deserved them. She *did* harbor romantic feelings for Vincent when he was already in a relationship, and she did kiss another woman's boyfriend, even if that woman was the wretched Jade. Both of those sins alone made her deserving of this tongue lashing and more. She stood by and let Jade seethe in the chair a moment longer before attempting to respond.

"I'm not after Vincent." Her voice was strong and steady.

Jade snorted in disbelief at Lexi's blatant lie. She stood up and perched herself on the edge of the desk, looking down her nose at Lexi. "Yes, you are. Don't lie to me and don't play games. Much better women than you have thrown themselves at him, and he hasn't given them a second glance. You don't stand a chance."

Something inside Lexi snapped. "If I really don't stand a chance, then why all the posturing, Jade? You must be feeling at least a little threatened to be reading me the riot act like this." Lexi's calmness seemed to infuriate Jade even more.

She pushed off the desk and stood toe-to-toe with Lexi. "Just to be clear, I told Vincent everything that happened with Stone, and he's not happy with the way things were handled. Not happy at all. And don't think I've forgotten a single word that you said."

"Well, neither have I. What exactly were you doing calling Julian? Do you often call Vincent's clients trying to get a job? I thought people were knocking down your door trying to get you to model for them."

"You need to stop talking now." Jade's eyes narrowed to slits as she glared at Lexi. "Who the hell do you think you are to talk to me this way?"

Lexi glanced at Vincent's closed door, a flicker of self-doubt washing over her. She could hear him talking in a raised voice. Jade just snickered as his voice grew louder.

"Are you insane?" Vincent shouted. "No, that's not acceptable. She's been here a few weeks and you think she's ready for that? Absolutely not. I won't allow it."

A thud sounded, as if something had slammed onto the desk.

"That promotion is not going to happen. That's final."

"Aww, too bad, Lexi."

Lexi's heart sank with every word as she realized she was the subject of the angry conversation. Jade seemed pleased as she walked over and poured herself a cup of coffee as Vincent continued his ranting.

"I know it was unprofessional. I'm dealing with it, I assure you."

"See, I told you he was pissed at you for trying to mess with my career," Jade said with a sneer.

Lexi desperately tried to hold herself together, but the emotionless tone that was creeping into Vincent's voice nearly brought her to tears. Jade kept a close watch on her, probably watching for anything she could use to launch into her next attack.

"This conversation's not over," Vincent growled.

After the distinct sound of the phone slamming down onto the cradle, an eerie silence fell over the office. Vincent's door flew open, and Lexi simply stood there and stared at him, unable to move.

"G-good morning, Vincent," she stammered, trying to settle her pounding heart.

Vincent looked from Lexi to Jade and back again. "What's going on out here?"

"Nothing, baby. Just a little girl talk." Jade slithered over to Vincent and wrapped her arms around his waist, her eyes locked on Lexi. Vincent hardly acknowledged Jade was touching him.

"Well, I have a lot to catch up on." Lexi tucked her purse in her drawer, sat down at her desk, and began taking inventory of the folders that had piled up, ignoring the couple wrapped in an embrace only three feet away.

"Jade, I need to talk to Lexi. Will you excuse us?"

The temperature dropped a few degrees as an icy chill settled on the room. Jade unwrapped her arms from around Vincent, furious, but remaining in control. "So sorry if I'm in the way. I didn't mean to inconvenience you and *Lexi*." Her name hung in the air, and Jade's unusual calm made the hairs on Lexi's arm stand on end.

"Jade," Vincent finally turned away from Lexi.

Throwing her hand into his face, Jade cut him off. "Save it, Vincent. You and your dear Lexi talk about whatever it is you need to discuss. I have a phone call I need to make. I need to talk to my agent." On her way out of the room, Jade cast a dirty look in Lexi's direction, letting her know she wasn't finished.

Once Jade left, Lexi tried to keep it causal. "How'd the Walker meeting go yesterday?"

"He hired that buffoon, Reid. But you would've known that, had you answered your phone," Vincent snapped.

"About that, I'm sor—"

Vincent stepped closer and took the top file off her desk and began looking through it, dismissing her comment with a wave of his hand. "You were sick, whatever." He started walking away, and Lexi thought the conversation was over, but she was mistaken. "My office, please." Vincent paused outside the door, ushering her in.

Lexi's heart flew up into her throat as she stood up and followed him, and her hands trembled as she clutched a pen and pad of paper. She had grabbed them at the last second hoping the conversation was going to be about work and not about what had happened between them at Anna's.

"Have a seat." The air rushed out of her lungs as soon as her butt hit the plush cushion of the seat. "We need to talk."

If Vincent spoke in one more clipped sentence, Lexi was going to scream. Annoyed, she snapped, "Fine, *Mr.* Drake, what do you need?"

"Cut the Mr. Drake crap, *Miss* White, unless you want to have this conversation as employer and employee. Of course, you know what tends to happen when my assistants piss me off. I thought we could talk as friends."

Friends. The word stung as it spilled from his lips. Were they even really friends? Did friends torpedo a friend's promotions? Did friends take out their anger out on each other? Did friends accuse one another? No, they trusted each other, and Lexi seriously questioned whether Vincent was even capable of trusting her at this point. Her mind kept replaying the snippets of his phone conversation in which he'd undermined her abilities, and in that moment she realized that she didn't know if she could trust Vincent.

Never in her life had Lexi wanted to slap someone so badly. "So talk, *friend.* You obviously have something to say."

"Actually, I was hoping you could explain when you were going to tell me about your little phone call with Jade?"

If she wasn't angry before, she was now. "I tried to tell you, *Vincent.* At your sister's house, I said I had to talk to you about something, and you said if it was going to put you in a bad mood to wait. Obviously, I was right about the bad mood part, so I did what you asked and waited."

"And you couldn't tell me any of this before you ran out of there that night? Do you have any idea the shit storm I walked into with Jade because of that?"

"Wait a minute, let me get this straight—did you *know* she was going to call Julian? Did you want her talking to him minutes before we walked in there to present to him? In your expert opinion, was that actually a good idea?"

Vincent raked his hand through his hair and sank back into his chair. "I had no idea she had any contact with Stone at all. And yes, it was a horrible idea. You and I both know that. But when my girlfriend calls a client in the middle of a presentation and you take the call and get in the middle of everything, telling her to take a hike … it wasn't your place to interrupt that call."

"It might not have been my place, but it was my job. And more importantly, it was the right thing to do." Lexi crossed her arms and jutted her chin out defiantly.

"Jade's fit to be tied."

A muzzle sounds good to me, Lexi thought to herself before responding to Vincent. "Gee, I hadn't noticed. I thought all the nasty things she said to me out there were her way of saying hello."

"Cut her some slack." When Lexi rose to her feet in protest, he blurted, "She thinks you and I are having an affair."

"Cut her some slack? You've got to be kidding. She was wrong to call. I don't care what the reason, the timing sucked. And she most definitely is wrong about us having an af-aff," Lexi paled, her fury replaced quickly with mortification. "Why does she think that? Wait. Y-you didn't tell her about th-the…"

"About what?"

Her eyes slammed shut, unable to look him in the face as she said the words. "Did you tell her we kissed?"

A loud cough came from Vincent, and Lexi's eyes flew open in time to see his shocked expression. "Are you kidding? I don't have a death wish, and I doubt you do either. Besides, why would I tell her that? It was no big deal."

And with those five little words, Lexi was crushed. The same kiss that she had described to Hope as the best in her life, he called no big deal. She had felt sparks between them while Vincent felt … nothing. Lexi cursed herself for even daring to think in her wildest dreams that the kiss might have meant something more to him.

She had to get out of the room and far away from him, so she stood up and began walking toward the door. Vincent opened his mouth to say something, but quickly shut it.

"Is there anything else? I think I'm all talked out," Lexi said.

With a sigh, Vincent held a file out to her. "My mother needs a copy of this, including the PowerPoint."

"Okay." When she reached out to take the file from his hand, he clutched it, refusing to let go until she finally met his gaze. "What now?" she sighed, emotionally exhausted.

"I'm sorry if I upset you." His words were soft and gentle, his eyes apologetic.

There was no way for Lexi to have any idea what the apology was for exactly. He had said and done so many upsetting things that she had lost count. She was furious at herself for being a coward, for not telling him what happened with Jade, but that didn't excuse his behavior. She was mad at him for everything, but mostly for being Vincent.

It seemed like a lifetime ago that she was sitting on that swing with him, her stomach filled with butterflies as she wondered if he was actually going to kiss her. And then later, when she was wrapped in his arms, sharing the most perfect kiss she would ever know, the world seemed like a much different place. But now, in this office with Jade lurking in the shadows, she found herself growing tired of his hot and cold treatment.

"Which time, Vincent?" Lexi shook her head sadly as she took the file and walked out of his office, slamming the door shut behind her.

Not even bothering to stop at her desk, Lexi walked right to the restroom and locked the door, needing just a few minutes to clear her head. There was far too much Vincent Drake rolling around in her brain for her to get anything done. The man was the master of mixed messages. He pulled her into his office and they had a discussion over a tiny phone incident, but the big topic of them kissing was completely dismissed. Then, right when she was ready to punch him out, he apologized. A girl could get emotional whiplash around this man. Could Lexi survive that?

She let the cold water run into the sink, chilling her hands as it flowed between her fingers. She splashed a small amount on her face in an effort to shock Vincent from her system. The mirror loomed in front of her, revealing a tired, weary woman that Lexi hated looking at.

"Get over it, Lexi," she lectured herself out loud. "You did it once, you can do it again. Move on, find out where you really belong in the world." She glared at herself. "And if you let Jade treat you like gum stuck to the bottom of her shoe again, I'm kicking your ass!"

Rejuvenated after scolding herself in the bathroom, Lexi grabbed the file and made her way to Elizabeth's office. She'd only been down to Elizabeth's office a few times. It was nestled back in the corner of the floor, away from the daily ruckus of the office. Behind the large, ornate desk, Laurence, Elizabeth's secretary, greeted her with a warm smile. He was an older gentleman with salt and pepper hair. He had been with Hunter for over twenty-five years and was a wonderful story-teller with plenty to share from his years with the company.

"Miss Lexi, how wonderful to see you. To what do I owe the pleasure?"

The area outside Elizabeth's office was very similar to where Lexi worked, with print ads lining the walls. The clients and products in the ads here, however, were very different. The work Elizabeth did was always so classically done, her attention to detail apparent in every shot. While Vincent was more about the big picture of a campaign message, Elizabeth tried to evoke emotion, not only with the things they said in the ad, but in the setting and body language.

"Good morning, Laurence. Vincent asked me to give this to Mrs. Dee. How are you today?" Lexi sat down in a chair and set the file on her lap.

"I'm very well. Thank you for asking. Mrs. Drake is just finishing up an overseas phone call and then she'll be right with you."

"That's fine. I'm in no rush." There was something about the tone of her voice that caught Laurence's attention.

"How's Mr. Drake?" he asked cautiously. Lexi's eye roll response made him laugh. "That well? You know by now not to take his ranting personally, right?"

"Oh, this one was very personal," Lexi said under her breath.

"There's no excuse for poor behavior, but there might be a reason. Did you hear he lost the Walker account? With all of these clients choosing other firms, Elizabeth's afraid he thinks he's losing his touch."

"When did Walker tell him? He just had his meeting yesterday." Lexi slouched back in her chair.

"From what I heard, it was at the end of the meeting. He said Vincent didn't impress him enough. Whatever that means."

The door to Elizabeth's office opened, and she poked her head out. "Laurence, I need to speak with ... Lexi. Just the lady I was looking for. Come in, dear." Her warm smile made Lexi temporarily forget the awful start to her day.

"Vincent wanted me to give you this." Lexi handed the file to Elizabeth.

Elizabeth flipped through the pages and smiled. "Yes, we'll definitely need this. Laurence, hold my calls please."

Lexi was awestruck each time she walked into Elizabeth's office. The huge panes of glass that intersected at the corner gave a breathtaking view of the city. Every day she had the city to look out at, to dream over, to make her smile. Tiny cars drove past on the network of roads below, and little dots of people scattered around as they moved through their daily lives on the streets of San Francisco.

Elizabeth sat down in a plush leather chair and set her bottle of water onto the tiny table beside it. She beckoned Lexi into the chair beside her and opened the folder, flipping through the contents and pulling out a few sheets before smiling at her.

"How are you today?" A frown suddenly appeared on Elizabeth's face. "You've been crying."

"No, I just splashed a little water on my face. I'm fine." Elizabeth saw everything, noticed every detail about people. Nothing got past Elizabeth Drake, no matter how hard Lexi tried.

Elizabeth sighed. "I know my phone call put him in a bad mood, but there was no reason to take it out on you." Elizabeth tapped her nails on the arm of the chair. "I'm going to have a long talk with my son."

"No, please don't do that. My issues with Vincent today actually had nothing to do with the phone call. We argued about something entirely different."

That caught Elizabeth's attention. "Did he even mention my call?"

"No, but I might have overheard a little bit of his end of the conversation, and when we were at the end of our *discussion,* he handed me this and told me to bring it to you." Lexi shrugged her shoulders and glanced out the window where she could see an airplane soaring through the cloudless sky.

"Well, since he was too much of a coward or too pig headed to tell you, I guess I will."

Lexi felt her nerves kick into high gear. Something was off. Her senses told her this wasn't an insignificant discussion they were about to have. "O-okay. What d-do you want to talk about?"

Without hesitation, Elizabeth placed her hand on Lexi's. "Relax dear, it's not bad. I wouldn't lure you into my office and fire you out of the blue. That's not my style."

An irrational thought popped into Lexi's head as she thought back to the angry conversation she'd caught bits and pieces of. "Did Vincent ask you to fire me?"

"No, he didn't. And for the record, *I* hired you so I'm the only one who can fire you. In the past, I've made the mistake of letting him pick his assistants and then he fired them, but your job is actually much more secure than even Vincent realizes, so don't you worry, dear."

"I'm sorry. I have no idea why I'm so emotional today."

"It's fine, dear. Everything is fine. The reason I wanted to talk to you is I have a proposition, if you're game. I think it would be a great opportunity, and I hope you will consider it."

The hint of excitement in Elizabeth's voice was contagious, and before long Lexi found herself on the edge of her seat.

"What you and Vincent did with the Stone account was nothing short of amazing. It would have been amazing even if it was the original presentation, but knowing that you two put that together the night before, it was astonishing."

Lexi blushed at the praise. "Thank you."

"I want you to know that Vincent told me just how much of that presentation was your idea." She sipped her water, watching Lexi's expression of surprise. "He may be a hotheaded jerk, but he gives credit where credit is due, and to hear him speak about it, you deserve a great deal of credit for that presentation, so thank you. You really helped land an important account for the company."

After the drama of the morning, Lexi was shocked to know that Vincent had been so honest with Elizabeth, especially when he didn't need to be. He could have allowed her to think that all Lexi did were the typical assistant duties: running copies, taking notes, and feeding him while he created the fabulous presentation concepts. But instead, he'd praised her input and made sure Elizabeth knew about it. Of course, that was totally opposite of everything Lexi had overheard him saying that morning.

A frustrated sigh escaped from Lexi. "Your son's the most confusing man I have ever met."

"I know."

"I'm sorry," Lexi said, shaking her head. "I didn't mean to interrupt."

"Let me cut to the chase. I like you. I think you're a natural at this, and your ability to read people and situations is invaluable. Sean also told me that you did some freelance ad work for Hope's shop, the Crowbar. I did a little research, and again I have to say am thoroughly impressed with your work. The concept, the style was perfect for what you were trying to achieve and the demographic you were trying to reach."

Lexi felt the rush of blood to her cheeks as they flamed red. "Thank you," she said timidly, "it was no big deal."

"On the contrary, it is a very big deal. Those ads were brilliant, and the way you marketed the shop showed great ingenuity. Even Vincent remembered the ads that ran, as did Robert. They stuck with two men who truthfully can't find the mustard in the refrigerator even when it's looking them in the face, so for them to take notice is high praise." Elizabeth laughed then became very serious. "Can I put all my cards on the table and have a very off-the-record conversation with you?"

Without pause, Lexi answered. "I'd never betray your confidence, Elizabeth."

"I know that, dear. Thank you." She slipped off her heels and casually folded her legs under her. "I wanted to give you a promotion."

The suspicions she had earlier were confirmed with Elizabeth's admission. She noticed that she said "wanted," past tense. Rather than saying anything, she simply nodded and let her continue.

"You have amazing potential, Lexi, which I don't think you even realize. That presentation I gave you that Friday in the copy room—do you remember?" Again Lexi nodded but remained silent. "It was a test of sorts. I saw what you had been studying in college, and I wanted to see if you still had it in you after being out of the loop for so long. Not only did you find the errors I purposely made, but some of the rearrangement you did to my final product was so fantastic, I used it in the actual presentation. Eight years away from your studies and yet you jumped back in the mix and impressed me, which I have to say is not an easy thing to do."

The compliment overwhelmed Lexi. "I—I don't know what to say. You're too kind." Tears welled in her eyes.

"Be clear, I'm not being kind, Lexi. People adore you. They respond to you. I can't tell you how many clients I've talked to since the gala who have asked how you are doing. They remember you because you have this inexplicable spark. I know Vincent has explained that a good part of what we do is sell ourselves to clients, and you're already mastering that. The area I think you need to work on is your confidence. *You* need to believe that you're as good as I know you are."

There was no point in trying to hide how overwhelmed she was anymore, and for the second time that day, tears fell down Lexi's cheeks. "You make me feel like I can do anything, Elizabeth. And it's been such a long time since I thought about chasing my dreams."

"I want that for you, dear. I want to see you blossom and grow. You've waited so long." Unable to stand it a minute longer, Elizabeth pulled the crying girl into her arms and offered her whatever motherly comfort she could.

A few minutes passed, during which Lexi desperately tried to let what Elizabeth said sink in. Her praise, her confidence meant the world to Lexi. After the emotional rollercoaster she had been on for the last forty-eight hours, Lexi wasn't sure how much more she could take.

"So where do we go from here? I heard Vincent say he didn't want me to get the promotion." She took the tissue Elizabeth offered and dabbed it under each of her eyes.

Out of the blue, Elizabeth chuckled. "That might be how it sounded dear, but I assure you, Vincent knows you're destined for more than being his assistant forever. He wasn't opposed to your promotion. He was however, vehemently opposed to where I wanted to send you."

Now Lexi's curiosity was piqued. "And where exactly were you going to send me?"

She sat back and sighed. "Productions."

"Why does Vincent care if I go work in productions?"

"I think who you would have been working with upset him more than where you would have been working," Elizabeth admitted.

"Tony."

"Yes, he was adamant that you were not ready to have Tony as your supervisor."

Suddenly, Lexi was annoyed by Vincent's meddling. "I can handle Tony, I assure you."

The fiery response made Elizabeth laugh out loud. "Oh, I know you can. My nephew can be quite difficult, but I've heard that on more than one occasion, you put him in his place."

"I was just doing what Vincent told me to do."

"And therein lies the problem. My nephew and my son don't get along. My brother and I inherited the company when my father died, however, when he married his fourth wife, Billy decided it was too much of a bother to be tied down to one place, so he sold it to me with the condition that his son have a job. Tony and Vincent were the same age, both out of college and looking to start careers. I accepted the terms and became president of the company. Vincent and Tony never got along because Tony made everything a competition between them. On paper, Tony was a better student, with perfect grades, but Vincent was more well-rounded and creative."

Lexi curled up in the chair and held her mug tightly in her hands as Elizabeth continued.

"It was obvious from the beginning that Tony was great when given an idea, at executing the plan and creating spectacular presentations. But Vincent excelled at creating the big ideas. When he isn't being crabby, he can be quite charming, as I'm sure you've noticed." The knowing smile Elizabeth threw in her direction made Lexi's cheeks turn pink.

"A real Jekyll and Hyde that one," Lexi giggled.

"He gets the charm from his father and the temper from me," Elizabeth laughed. "When two of the original chief executives retired from Hunter, I had to make replacements. Vincent and Sean were attached at the hip after they graduated. Truly, I think that boy ate at our house every Sunday for a year. Sean's degree was in business management, and he was a natural with the staff. No one blinked when I promoted him to business manager and eventually VP to run that side of the office. It wasn't until I had to make a promotion on the creative side that everything went to hell."

It was easy to see this all had been difficult for Elizabeth to talk about. Her family was very important to her, and she hated seeing anyone hurt.

"I was damned if I did and damned if I didn't on this one. Someone needed to move up the ladder. I had Vincent who was creative with an impeccable work ethic, the one who could come up with the ideas and charm the clients, or Tony, who had a brilliant mind and an eye for the art and details of it, but his ideas were poor. Give him an idea, and he could execute it with precision. But ask him to come up with the concept himself and it was a disaster. There was no choice. Vincent got the VP position, and Tony was made head of productions. He became this nasty, vengeful man who to this day has a giant chip on his shoulder where Vincent is concerned."

All the pieces fell into place for Lexi. "And Vincent was afraid if I was moved to productions that Tony would go after me because of the fact that I worked for him."

"His concern was that Tony would take out his anger at him on you, that he would either give you a hard time or not give you a chance to show what you could do and stifle you." Elizabeth grinned. "My son feels very protective of you, in case you hadn't noticed."

"I can take care of myself." Lexi raised her chin confidently into the air, not wanting anything from Vincent at that moment.

"Yes, you can. But sometimes it's nice to have someone looking out for you as well." Elizabeth patted her hand.

"Do you still think I should go to productions? I think it'd be an amazing opportunity, and I'd take the job in a heartbeat without complaint. Tony and I could come to an understanding." The promotion was not something she was willing to let Vincent or anyone take away from her just because he thought she couldn't handle herself.

"Believe it or not, after some reflection, I agree with Vincent. Productions isn't the place for you." Lexi opened her mouth to protest, but Elizabeth stopped her. "You're an idea person Lexi, a big picture kinda girl, like me." Elizabeth beamed. "I don't want to groom you to make boards and presentation materials. I want to groom you to be a creative director like Vincent was before he became a VP. Here's the problem—you have the most potential, but the least amount of experience or credentials of anyone on staff. I can't just promote you on a gut feeling."

Lexi's dream of coming up with her own campaign ideas faded into the distance.

"What we need is for you to get some experience under your belt, covertly. Get you involved in different campaigns so you can give your input and make a name for yourself all on your own. Everyone around you will naturally see the same things I do. I want you to absorb everything that is going on around you from someone who has been through it before and quickly worked their way up through the ranks. Besides, who better to learn from than the best?" She cocked an eyebrow at Lexi, awaiting her reaction.

"So I get to work with you?"

Elizabeth clapped her hands and threw back her head in laughter. "Lexi, I adore you. Why must my son be a moron?"

"I can come up with a list if you'd like," Lexi offered, a genuine smile crossing her lips for the first time all day. "In all seriousness, what are you proposing?"

"I want you to be Vincent's partner on the Stone account. It's as much yours as it is his, anyway. Everyone in the office knows the two of you worked together on it, and I don't think anyone will raise an eyebrow if you're involved with it. There's another account I will want you in on the planning stages of, once we secure a meeting with the client. Again, you'd be working with Vincent on that one. He knows the job from the bottom up and he has great insights he could share with you. I think the two of you make a dynamite team, and we need to turn our luck around a little. We've been turned down by quite a few clients lately."

The offer was very generous considering Lexi had no qualifications, no experience, and couldn't compete with the people around her in many ways. But she did have great ideas and knew how to execute them. No matter how angry she was at him, she had to admit Vincent was a genius when it came to forming an ad campaign. He could teach her so many things, but could they work together? Vincent often made her feel like she was a burden.

"Have you even discussed this with him? I'm not sure he wants to work with me."

Elizabeth shook her head from side to side in disagreement. "He most definitely wants to work with you, dear. This part was his idea, actually."

Lexi remembered the latest conversation she'd had with Jade. "Well, he might feel differently now. Jade said—"

"I don't care what Jade says. She's not on staff here, last time I checked. Maybe I should remind her of that fact too." Elizabeth lowered her voice, the edge disappearing and being replaced with stern, motherly suggestion. "I think this is a great idea. It's great for Hunter and great for you. The chemistry you and Vincent have will lead to great things. Trust me, a mother knows."

Part of Lexi wanted to scream yes and say the hell with the fallout of working side by side with her heart's desire, she could handle it. This was a once in a lifetime chance. But another part of her screamed for her to say no, to protect herself from the certain doom that would surely come if she spent more time working that closely with him. She was only human, after all, and he was irresistible.

Elizabeth rose to her feet and went back to her desk. "This is your call, Lexi. You don't have to tell me now. I think you should discuss this with Vincent before you make up your mind."

"I'll let you know by Monday," Lexi promised. "I cannot thank you enough for this offer, Elizabeth. It was very generous of you."

"It was all Vincent's idea," Elizabeth said emphatically. "He sees something in you too."

If only Lexi could figure out what that something was.

· 21 ·

Vincent leaned back in his leather desk chair as he looked out the window. The ornate lines of the cityscape entranced him and allowed him to mentally escape from the disastrous day he was having, even if it was only for a short while.

He'd never intended to start a fight with Lexi that morning. He'd wanted to apologize for kissing her at Anna's and make sure she wasn't still upset with him. The kiss...things weren't supposed to get so heated between them, but when he felt the softness of her lips, the way her body molded perfectly against his, something snapped. For some inexplicable reason, every cell in his body screamed at him to pull her closer and wrap her in his arms, so he did.

The deep feelings of lust and desire that engulfed him when they kissed had caught him off guard. He knew on some level, even though he didn't want to admit it, that he was very attracted to Lexi. Even Sean saw it. But how could he not be? She was breathtakingly gorgeous in a shy and unassuming kind of way, but it was what was inside of her that was truly exquisite. For the first time in a long while, Vincent had met someone he wanted to believe in, that he thought was perhaps genuine rather than someone who only told people what they wanted to hear, waiting for the right time to strike. Unfortunately for Vincent, an air of uncertainty remained. His rocky past made him unwilling to let her in, because he knew it could be his undoing.

The rapid exit Lexi had made from Anna's house took away their chance to talk about the kiss, not that he knew what the hell he would have said. When the topic had come up during their heated conversation that morning, he'd shrugged it off and said it was no big deal. That was a lie, but what made it worse was the devastated look he saw on Lexi's face as the words escaped his lips. No woman wanted to hear that her kisses were less than memorable, and he immediately regretted having insulted her. So once again, she'd retreated. And now she was hiding in his mother's office.

Vincent climbed out of his chair and began rifling through his desk drawer, looking for something, *anything* that would keep his mind off of Lexi White. The longer his thoughts dwelled on her, the more confused he became. What he wanted with his heart and what he wanted with his head were in constant conflict when she was around, and it was driving him crazy.

The file of the Lewis account found its way into Vincent's hand. He began reading through the meeting notes, trying to spark an idea for a direction for the project. Deep in thought, he was startled when the office door flew open.

"Sorry I was gone so long, baby. This was a really important call."

Vincent stifled a groan when Jade strode in without knocking for the umpteenth time. He cursed himself for not taking her back to her apartment this morning and just being late for work. He would never get anything done at this rate.

She flopped herself onto his couch, swinging her feet onto the coffee table. When her heel caught on a small bud vase and it crashed to the floor, spilling water and flowers everywhere, Vincent heard Sean's voice whisper through his head:

Screw Jade.

"What's with all the damn flowers?" She carelessly scooped the buds up and crammed them haphazardly into the vase before setting it back on the table. She made no effort to clean the large water stain on the carpet. Instead she reached into her bag for her phone so she could check her E-mail.

"It's a decoration. My mother thinks they make the room look warmer so she has them brought in fresh every other day."

"They make the place look like a funeral home if you ask me," Jade muttered, crinkling her nose in disgust at the beautiful buds. "So, what are we doing today?" Jade asked with an utterly bored look on her face.

"*We* aren't doing anything. *I* need to make a few idea notes on an account." Vincent's voice trailed off as he fell back into deep thought about the campaign. An idea struck him, and without thinking, he asked the question. "Is Lexi at her desk?"

Jade's head couldn't have whipped toward him faster if he'd told her he was selling everything, shaving his head, and becoming a Tibetan monk. "You did not just ask me about *her*."

This time Vincent did groan out loud. "Jade, I'm not in the mood for this. Was she at her desk or not? That's all I'm asking. I need to have her do something for me."

"And I bet she'd be happy to oblige you anything you asked, *Mr. Drake*."

"Do we have to do this again?"

"Supergirl wasn't at her desk. She's probably off kissing someone else's ass. Try not to get too jealous."

"Why do you have to act this way, Jade? She's never done anything to you," Vincent asked in a tired voice.

"Are you kidding?" Jade was on her feet, her hands waving wildly as she spoke. "That little bitch talked shit about me to Julian Stone, and now he won't return my calls. This is my career she's messing with, my livelihood. What the hell, Vincent? I'm your girlfriend, in case you've forgotten. I would think you should be pissed at *her* for screwing with my life."

"I know who you are."

"Well, maybe you need to see who she is. I called that office at their request. My agent got a message that Stone wanted to talk to me. I called twice. Once I left a message and this was the second call. Whatever she said, that wench of Stone's…"

"Christina," Vincent offered through gritted teeth as he pinched the bridge of his nose.

"Yeah, that Christina bitch put me on hold, then got all snippy. The next thing I know, I'm talking to Lexi, who is bitching me out for calling."

"It was an important day, Jade. We had been up all night."

"I don't need to be reminded that the two of you spent the night together, thank you very much." Jade walked to the window and glared out over the city.

"For the millionth time, we were working. She's my employee. We do have to work together on occasion. Are you telling me you weren't up all night at least once while you were on your latest trip? And were there other men in the vicinity? Of course you were, and you were probably at a nightclub, drinking and dancing every night. I'll bet I can go on-line right now and find photographs of you stumbling into a taxi at dawn. But I'm not giving you a hard time, so why am I being accused of something I most certainly did not do?" Vincent was on his feet now, angrily stuffing a file into the tall cabinet.

"I don't like her, and I don't trust her. And for the record, I hate the way she looks at you." Her arms were crossed tightly over her chest.

Jade's all-consuming paranoia was getting old. She didn't trust Lexi? What a joke. The real problem was that she didn't trust him. People were drawn to Lexi's radiant personality, whereas Jade repelled humanity. Lexi was everything Jade was not, and then some. For a minute he wondered if Jade could see that he was developing genuine feelings for Lexi. Was he was that transparent, or was this just her general insanity rearing its ugly head again?

Lexi had never done a thing to Jade other than stand up to her instead of cowering at her feet. That was one of the things Vincent admired most about Lexi—the fact that she wouldn't let Jade intimidate her.

He also wasn't exactly sure that Jade was telling the truth on this whole phone call incident. Julian had never once mentioned Jade when he described the look he'd prefer for the models in the print ads. As a matter of fact, he wanted to do something completely away from Jade's severe, high society look. If he had contacted Jade's agent and was actively pursuing her, that would have come up during the meeting. Sean's words again floated into his head.

Screw Jade.

Jade's screeching pulled Vincent from his thoughts. "You have to be blind not to see that she wants you. Her eyes are always on you, like you're the source of the air she breathes. She gets this puke-inducing grin on her face when you thank her or tell her she did something right." Jade crept closer to him, her finger pointing in his direction as she spoke. "When you have your back turned, her eyes are all over your body, and the little stolen glances and smiles between the two of you are downright disgusting. I get the feeling you're quite enjoying all the attention from the Girl Wonder too. Doesn't Hunter have a no fraternizing policy?"

"For the last time, we are *not* fraternizing." Vincent's voice was cool and icy, his fury bubbling under the surface. If he lost his temper, he knew he would be confirming Jade's suspicions about his interest in Lexi and just how much he had thought about fraternizing with Lexi as he made the long, lonely drive home from Anna's that night.

There was a swift knock on the door, interrupting the argument.

"Come in."

"Vincent, I need to talk to yo—" Lexi stormed into the room and stopped mid-sentence when she saw Jade perched with her hand on her hips in the center of the room. "I'm sorry, I'm interrupting."

"Why do you do that? Why do you let her call you Vincent when every other person in this office has to call you Mr. Drake? What makes *her* so special?" Jade snapped.

Without acknowledging Jade, he turned his attention solely to Lexi. "Would you mind excusing us, please? But don't run off, I need to talk to you when we're done in here." The warm tone of his voice and his smile caught Lexi totally off guard and made Jade fume all the more. She dared a quick glance in Jade's direction to find her eyes blackened with hate as she glared back at Lexi.

"Um, okay, sure. I—I'll be at my desk, *Vincent*." She raised an eyebrow at Jade in challenge then quietly left the room.

"Did you see *that*?" Jade screeched as the door closed.

Vincent shrugged and picked up his coffee. "You started it, and she just finished it." He knew he was goading Jade into a fight, one that would end badly, but maybe he was ready for that.

"Why do you always defend her?" She inched closer to him, scrutinizing his expression. "You like her."

"She's my friend, Jade. We went to high school together."

"Oh please. You had no idea who she was, so don't act like it's some long lost Lifetime Television reunion special. What could you possibly see in her? Is it her chunky body? Do you like your women plump? Or is it her little doe eyes and the way she bats her eyelashes adoringly at you, worshiping the ground you walk on? Tell me, Vincent, what is it about the little mouse that gets you all hot and bothered?"

"Stop it, Jade," Vincent warned.

"Why should I? I was just asking a question."

"Careful what you ask for. You might not like the answer." Vincent's face was rigid, his jaw clenched as he watched Jade seethe with anger.

"She's not even attractive," Jade mumbled as she checked her reflection in the window and combed her fingers through her hair.

"Jade." He couldn't wait any longer and tried to start the difficult conversation, but Jade was granted a small reprieve when her phone rang.

Irritated that in the middle of an argument she would answer the phone, Vincent sat down and spun his chair, turning his back to her. He had no interest in a single word she was saying. He simply wanted her to go away. As she clamored on and on in hushed tones and then louder cackles of laughter, he turned to face his desk and decided to busy himself. He replied to an E-mail, all the while mentally preparing the complex speech he would give Jade when she hung up. It was time to part company.

"Are you sure about that?" He heard Jade say in a raised tone. She gasped and held up a single finger to Vincent when he met her gaze. She continued listening intently to the mystery person on the phone. "Thanks for letting me know. Sure, I'll ring you later. Ciao, baby." She dramatically snapped the phone shut and sat down in one of the chairs beside Vincent's desk.

He turned off his monitor and sat back in his chair, steeling himself for her latest drama. "Jade, I really think it's time we—"

"Vincent, we need to talk," Jade interrupted.

He could tell she would not stop until she had her say, so he deferred to her. "So talk."

"I think you have a mole here at Hunter."

She kept talking, but Vincent wasn't listening. His brain stopped functioning the moment he heard the word mole. Any thoughts he had of breaking up with Jade were pushed aside as his mind worked to process this shocking information. A mole, a spy, a traitor. Someone in a position of trust was betraying his family. A list of suspects immediately popped into his head, and his cousin was at the top in big, bold letters. Jade's whiny voice kept droning on and on, interrupting his train of thought. Finally, he held up his hand and yelled, "Enough!"

Jade froze with her mouth open, mid-word.

"Why do you say that?" Vincent bit out each word as he leaned forward across the desk, his intense gaze daring her to try and withhold any information from him.

"W-well like I said, that call I just took, it was from Lauren, one of the girls I was down in Jamaica with these last few days."

"And what the hell does this Lauren know about Hunter?" Vincent snapped, not caring about being calm or polite.

"Listen, this is all hush-hush." Jade got out of her chair and sat on the edge of his desk, tipping her head to reveal her big secret. "So, Lauren is sleeping with someone fairly high up over at Reid. The girl's a whore, spends most of her time on her knees if you know what I mean." Vincent's lack of a response and infuriated glare made Jade shift uncomfortably. "She wouldn't tell me who exactly, because she knows we're dating and doesn't want to get the guy in trouble. At least I think it's a guy. She could be bi; you never know these days."

Vincent rolled his hand at her, encouraging her to get to the point. "And?"

"I'm getting to it," she snapped right back at him. "While we were in the hot tub, she let something slip about how her agent got her the gig with Tony Walker for the print ads of his national shoe line last week."

"She had the job that long ago? This happened the first day you arrived in Jamaica? How was that possible? We hadn't…"

"You hadn't even given your final presentation. It gets worse. She was complaining about it because she has to go to *Alaska* for a week to do the shoot."

Vincent's entire body coiled, his muscles clenching as he tried to control his anger. "Alaska? Snow? Reid's idea was centered around a winter shoot too?"

Jade nodded her head. "As soon as she talked about Alaska, I was suspicious because I saw your mock ups that night at your apartment. I remembered you'd talked about snow acting as the clean palate of it all. None of it made sense, but then I got to thinking, what if there was someone leaking information to Reid."

Overcome with anger, Vincent began pacing the room like a caged panther. The power he showed with each graceful stride made him look deadly. "Who's feeding them the information?"

"She didn't know. She never admitted they were being fed information. I pumped her full of tequila that night to get her to talk. She kept claiming she didn't know anything about who came up with the Walker idea, and after five shots, I tend to believe her."

"So, what was that call about?"

"Oh, well, when she got home, her boyfriend, being the thoughtful guy he is, wanted to spend some time alone with her because *he* had missed his girlfriend who had been gone for three days. After he," Jade made a gagging noise, "welcomed her home, she dragged a little more info out of him. Men are so easy to get information out of after sex."

Unamused, Vincent punched his fist into the top of his desk. "What did she say, Jade?"

"She said two days before they were set to give the Stone presentation, David walked in and demanded everything be changed. Her boyfriend was pissed because they all had to scramble for forty-eight hours straight making the changes he orchestrated."

A colorful string of profanities flew from Vincent. "He's done this twice. This is going to end, now." He grabbed the phone and began furiously pecking on the numbers.

"Wait," Jade ripped the phone out of his hand and slammed the receiver back into the cradle.

"Damn it, Jade."

"What good is it going to do for you to go off half-cocked and basically let him know you're aware of his bullshit? It will stop for a while, but you won't ever figure out who here at Hunter is screwing you." She squeezed his hand encouragingly. "Whoever this is isn't very smart or subtle. I think we can flush them out pretty easily. Let me help you."

Vincent removed his hand from hers and fell back into his chair, feeling like he had just been kicked in the stomach. Whoever this was had to be stopped, and surprising as it was, Jade was right. If he let his temper get the better of him, he would never be able to figure out the source of the leaks. "I need to think about how to approach this."

An evil grin spread across Jade's face. "No worries, baby. I have an idea."

Lexi sat at her desk, trying to keep busy, but every few minutes she glanced at Vincent's door, wondering what the hell was going on in there. Jade had been visibly pissed when Lexi walked into Vincent's office, and thanks to Lexi's smart mouth, was even more infuriated when she left.

So much had happened, and it wasn't even noon yet. Lexi and Vincent had a lot to talk about. She wanted to know exactly what his feelings were about her working with him on the Stone account. He might have thought it was a good idea yesterday, but maybe after sleeping on it he would regret the suggestion.

If that wasn't enough to agitate Lexi, there was the lingering topic of the kiss. The topic didn't feel closed, but what more could she even say about it? "Thanks for making me hot in all the right places with one kiss?" or even worse, "Kiss me again?" There was no way she'd ever be able to discuss the topic with him openly and honestly because to do so would reveal how much she cared about him. Once she did that, she would just look desperate.

There were times when the small touches they shared, their playful banter, the way his eyes darkened while he spoke to her, or the way they lingered on her lips made her think that maybe he felt something for her too. In those situations, she would get a glimpse into what it would be like to be loved by Vincent Drake, and it felt wonderful. She let herself imagine the two of them working together, side by side, and the connection that would grow between them. Their budding friendship could deepen and turn into something more, something she had only dared to dream about until now. The naughty part of Lexi wondered what would happen if she, for once, went after her heart's desire.

While she waited for Vincent, she worked on everything that had piled up with her being gone the day before. She had just clicked open a message when she heard a familiar voice. "Hey, Lexi!"

Christina stood in the doorway with her long, auburn hair pulled back into a sleek ponytail. Under her arm was tucked a shiny, black motorcycle helmet. Lexi found herself feeling genuinely happy for the first time that day.

"Christina, what are you doing here?"

"Are you telling me you didn't get my E-mail?"

Blush flooded Lexi's cheeks as she glanced over at the monitor. "I was home sick yesterday and have been running around like a lunatic since I walked in the door this morning. I was just about to check it now."

"It was no big deal. I wanted to see if you were free for lunch."

"Lunch with you, sounds fantastic." Lexi desperately wanted to get away from the office and have a little girl talk with someone who might actually understand what she was going through.

"Well, it was supposed to be lunch with just me, however, when Julian found out I was having lunch with you, he wanted to come, and then when Peter heard," she flashed Lexi a cheeky smile, "he wanted to tag along too. Something about wanting to see you again."

Lexi couldn't miss the teasing way she mentioned Peter. Christina was playing matchmaker.

"What's with that?" Lexi asked, eyeing the helmet Christina had tucked under her arm.

"We brought their bikes. Ever been on a motorcycle before?" Christina smiled wickedly at Lexi, tapping her nails against the top of the helmet.

"Seriously? I think it's just what the doctor ordered." She glanced down at the clock. "I do need to talk to Vincent, though, before I go, or at least make sure I can get ten minutes with him when I get back."

"No problem. Let me run downstairs and let the guys know. They can race to the pier and back. That should occupy them for a few minutes and let them get that need for speed thing out of their system." Christina winked and took off down the hall toward the elevator.

Lexi tidied up her desk as she waited for Vincent to finish up with Jade so she could let him know she was leaving for a while. After five minutes, she was ready to risk interrupting them again when the door opened and Jade's short mop of brown hair peeked out.

"I'm hungry."

"I don't work for you," Lexi said, not even looking away from her BlackBerry.

"Fine, your hero Vincent's hungry."

"Has he suddenly been rendered incapable of speech?"

"I've just about had it with you."

Lexi gracefully stood up from behind her desk and walked over to Jade with not a bit of amusement on her face. "That makes two of us."

Before Jade could say anything, Vincent appeared in the doorway. "Jade, your phone's ringing." He stepped aside so she could retreat into his office, out of the way. "Hi," he said to Lexi, closing the door behind him, and thereby muffling Jade's gossip-mongering.

"Hi," Lexi replied, for a second getting lost in his green eyes at such close proximity.

"I'm sorry about before." He said it so fast, she almost missed it. Raking his hand through his hair, he sighed. "What I said before was ... inaccurate."

"My head hurts, Vincent."

"I know I hurt your feelings before, and that was not my intention." He leaned his shoulder into the wall beside her.

"And what was your intention? Just tell me. I'm a big girl, I can take it." Lexi steeled herself for his answer. Telling herself not to cry, she held her breath and waited.

"What I wanted to say was—"

"Lexi! Hey, Vincent." Christina and Julian came down the hall with Peter right behind. "You ready to get lunch?"

Julian walked over and shook Vincent's hand. "Hey, man, you mind if we borrow Lexi for a little bit? Tina wanted to take her to lunch, and Peter and I kinda decided to crash their girl time."

Vincent looked down at Lexi, who refused to meet his eye. Instead, she focused her attention on the potted plant beside her. "S-Sure, Lexi can go to lunch." He nodded his head at the helmets, his brows knitted together in concern. "Motorcycles?"

"Yeah, I got a new bike and thought I'd take Lexi for a ride." Peter's stance was one of complete male arrogance.

"Helmets are required by law in California. I assume you have an extra?"

Lexi glared at Vincent, incredulous at his questioning of Peter. She glanced back and forth between the two men, watching them posture and scowl at one another. A giggle escaped from Christina just before she buried her face against Julian's shoulder, earning her a glare from Lexi as well.

"Don't worry, Vince, I'll take good care of your girl."

Furious, Lexi waved her hand at both of them. "Hi, I'm standing right here." She elbowed Vincent and pulled him away from the group. "What the hell do you think you're doing?"

"I don't like that guy," Vincent whispered back.

"I don't remember asking your opinion."

"Oh come on, like you didn't see him staring at you during the presentation, undressing you with his eyes. Look at him. He can't wait to get you wrapped around him on that bike."

"You have lost your mind," Lexi snapped, glancing back at their guests and smiling politely as she and Vincent continued their hushed discussion.

"No, I haven't. He wants you."

"He wants lunch, Vincent. And maybe he wants to show off his motorcycle a little. I think I can handle it."

Vincent gave her a patronizing smile. "Have fun on your date, then."

"It's not a date; it's lunch. And so what if it is a date? I don't remember joining a convent. Believe it or not, Vincent, I do enjoy the company of men. I do have a pulse."

"He's not your type. He isn't right for you." Peter stood across the room, checking out his reflection in the glass of one of their framed print ads.

"Don't you have a girlfriend to go check on?"

"Enjoy your lunch," Vincent growled and stepped away from her, approaching his office door. He flashed a dazzling smile and a wave back at Christina, Julian, and Peter, and then disappeared into his office slamming the door shut behind him.

"What's his problem?" Peter asked as he held out Lexi's coat for her.

Lexi shrugged. "His girlfriend just got back into town, and she tends to suck the fun out of everything and everyone in a five mile radius." She tossed her purse over her arm and followed Christina and Julian to the elevator.

"Enjoy yourselves." Leigh grinned from behind her desk. She pointed at Peter when he had his back turned and flashed Lexi a big thumbs up.

Peter smiled at Lexi and whispered in her ear, "Thanks for letting us crash your lunch with Christina."

His massive shoulders and chest brushed against her back as he ushered her into the open elevator doors. The heat from his body felt good as he stood behind her on the elevator, close but not crowding. A shiver went down Lexi's spine when his fingers gently pushed a stray piece of hair out of her face. "N-no problem."

As they stepped off the elevator, Lexi's phone went off. Without even thinking, she slipped it out of her pocket and glanced at the tiny screen. Her heart flew into her throat as she read the words. To anyone else, it would seem like an aberrant message, a mistake. But Lexi, who had been replaying Vincent's earlier words over and over again in her head, knew exactly what it meant.

It was a very big deal.

She froze in the lobby, the sun streaming in through the large, glass windows. People moved past her, jumping in and out of the elevators on their way to appointments. Lexi simply stood there, rereading the message as if her life depended on it.

Their kiss was a big deal in a good way or a bad way? If it was such a big deal, then why was Jade still wrapped around him like an anaconda? Why had he bit Lexi's head off all morning, and why did he just act like a complete prick in front of Peter? There was no understanding this man, no matter how hard she tried. He only created more questions that would forever go unanswered.

He couldn't just say something like that and leave it hanging out there between them. What did it even mean? Did he want her? Her pulse soared at the mere thought, but was stopped by the ache in her heart when she remembered seeing him with Jade today. Until he made up his mind about what this thing between him and Lexi meant, she wasn't going to put her life on hold. She had been there done that.

"Everything okay, Lexi?" Christina asked as she wrapped an arm around her friend's shoulders. "We don't have to do this. It seems like you and Vincent might have some … unfinished business." Christina recognized what was going on between them.

Frustrated tears welled in Lexi's eyes as she stuffed her phone back into her pocket. She refused to let them fall and took Christina's hand, leading her toward the door. She could see Julian and Peter beside their bikes, the chrome of their motorcycles shining in the sun. "Vincent and I have no business. Let's go to lunch."

Peter held an outstretched hand to her, a handsome smile welcoming her to his side. "You ready to have some fun, babe?" He brushed her hair out of her face and slid the helmet over her head, giving it a little tap to make sure it was on tight.

Lexi smiled. "Absolutely."

Peter strode over to the bike and hoisted one leg over the beast, straddling the seat. "Jump on, babe. And hold on tight."

Tentatively, Lexi approached the bike. It was big and intimidating, almost as intimidating as the confident, sexy man who was on it. But Lexi needed this. She needed to clear her head and feel alive. She was tired of sitting around waiting for life to happen. She wanted to be out there living. Sitting at her desk, working her fingers to the bone and waiting on Vincent was no way to live. She needed fun. She needed to feel desired, even if it was only for an hour.

Her heart clamored with excitement as she climbed onto the bike. She gingerly wrapped her arms around Peter. The closeness and intimacy felt awkward since she didn't know him very well. His body shook as he chuckled, then Lexi heard his voice through the head set in her helmet.

"I drive fast, babe. You need to hold on tighter. Don't worry, you won't hurt me. And if you do, I'll probably like it." Peter took her hands and pulled them more tightly around his chest. Lexi's fingers danced over the hard outline of his muscles, holding on, but also exploring what he had going on under that T-shirt. "Ready?" he asked, revving the engine. When Peter saw Lexi nod her head, they took off from the curb and went flying down the street with Christina and Julian at their side.

The lunch was exactly what Lexi needed. Peter was sweet and flirted shamelessly with her. The blatant interest from a man was nice compared to the mixed signals she had to decipher from Vincent. Peter was all man and had no qualms about telling Lexi that he wanted to see her again.

The moment she stepped off the elevator, Leigh nearly tackled her, wanting every detail. "Who was the hottie? Obviously a friend of Julian's, but what's his story? Did you like him? Did you give him your phone number? What did you eat?"

"Whoa," Lexi held up her hands at her friend and laughed, "take a breath, woman."

"He was tall, dark, and handsome—don't you dare decide to play modest. My love life's in the toilet currently, and I need to live vicariously through you. Start talking."

Lexi leaned against the granite counter of her desk and grinned like a school girl. "His name is Peter, and he's very sweet and confident. The man is also the biggest flirt, which I kind of enjoyed. He works for Julian, and they've been friends since birth, I guess. I did give him my phone number, and we went to Celsius for lunch. I had the chicken with mushrooms and capers."

"Does he have a brother?" Leigh asked hopefully.

"I'll check next time I talk to him." Lexi glanced down the hall that led to Vincent's office, suddenly apprehensive about taking another step. "Is she still here?"

"Yep. She's screwing up his whole day. He's in a fantastic mood. Why he doesn't ship her skinny butt home, I have no idea."

Vincent's office door was open, and Lexi heard Jade complaining about being bored. Lexi sat down at her desk and got to work. The entire Stone file was sitting there on top of everything else with a Post-it that said "please review" in Elizabeth's handwriting. Lexi grinned, knowing that Elizabeth was trying to get her to say yes to her offer with this little enticement. Curious, Lexi went over the contract details and added the suggested dates on the timeline to Vincent's calendar.

Jade appeared in the doorway with what was becoming her typical scowl. "Ugh, you're back?"

"Yes, I do work here." Lexi rolled her eyes and went back to her calendar.

"You were gone a long time for lunch. I hope you don't think you're getting paid for the extra half hour you took." Jade crammed the empty carryout bags into the small trashcan beside Lexi's desk.

Lexi was in a great mood after her lunch and wasn't about to let Jade ruin it. "I'm sorry, but do you sign my paychecks now? What business is it of yours how long I take for lunch?"

"I think Vincent would be very interested to know."

In a sickly sweet voice Lexi said, "Aww, Vincent's interested in what I do? That's so nice of him."

When Jade heard Vincent talking on the phone, she crept closer to Lexi and responded. "Just admit it, you little wench, admit that you want him. I'll respect you more if you have the nerve to say it to my face."

"Vincent's an amazing man, Jade. He's smart, sexy, and kind once you get to know him. What woman wouldn't want him? I'm sure thousands of women fantasize all the time about the feel of his lips or his touch and how gentle of a lover he would be." Lexi's voice was a soft purr as she spoke, the caressing tone only incensing Jade more.

"I knew it," she pointed an accusing finger at Lexi. "I knew you wanted him. You will never have him. If it's the last thing I do, I'll keep you away from him. You are trash and don't deserve a man like Vincent. You could never make him happy."

Jade meant for her words to hurt Lexi, to cut her, but they didn't. If anything, they made Lexi see her for the truly weak and desperate woman she was. Her relationship with Vincent wasn't nearly as strong as she put out to the world. If it was, she wouldn't be this insecure and attacking Lexi every chance she got. Lexi actually began to feel sorry for Jade. Until she opened her mouth again.

"You're all alone, Lexi. You have no one who loves you and never will."

"Jade!" Vincent snapped form the doorway, having heard the last bit of the conversation.

Lexi glanced in his direction and saw the horror on his face at Jade's words. He was mortified. For some odd reason, that made Lexi happy. She could see that he cared in his own dysfunctional, immature, and scarred way, and that made her happy.

The decision she made next wasn't about Vincent anymore, and it wasn't about Jade. It was about Lexi and what she wanted, what she needed. For the first time in a long time, Lexi had options. She had things to learn and a life to lead. There was only one way to make that happen, and she wanted to go for it, even if it was risky. She had to try. In front of both of them, she picked up the phone and pushed a three digit extension.

"Elizabeth, it's Lexi. I'll take the job." After a few excited words from Elizabeth, Lexi put the receiver in the cradle and turned her attention to Jade with a smile. "Go away, Jade." Lexi waved her fingers at the irate woman, dismissing her.

"You little…"

"I really don't feel like arguing with you anymore. Vincent is your boyfriend, you've made that abundantly clear, and I'm not about to be the other woman." She glanced over at Vincent, making sure he was listening too. "So you have nothing to worry about from me, Jade. I won't come between the two of you." Lexi leaned closer to Jade so she could have a private word with her. "But, if you're a fool and screw things up with him, I can promise you the second you break up, all bets are off, sweetie."

· 22 ·

Lexi padded around her apartment, wandering aimlessly from her bedroom to the kitchen with her large cup of coffee firmly in hand. She ran her hand over the cool, smooth surface of the granite countertop, brushing a few stray crumbs onto the floor. Paperwork from the office sat within arm's reach, but Lexi was too distracted to focus on it. So much had happened since Lexi had accepted Elizabeth's offer a few days earlier.

Elizabeth began checking in with Lexi, often asking if she needed anything, while Vincent went into full teacher mode. He was perfectly professional, and his focus set the tone for the meetings. There was a purpose behind every detail he shared so he expected her to pay attention.

Often during these meetings with Vincent, Lexi would find herself getting lost in the melodic sound of his voice. It was impossible not to be mesmerized by him when he talked about the various projects. He always made sure Lexi understood the whys and hows of each scenario before moving on to something new. When he was done, she knew so much about them that she could explain the reasoning behind each color palette, even if it was only based on an obscure comment about the color blue always catching the client's eye. A tiny piece of information like that, when used the right way, was another tool to ensure a successful campaign. Vincent could talk in-depth about these things, but when it came to his life and his feelings, Lexi had never met a more closed-off person.

It was a very big deal.

His words raced through her head numerous times a day, distracting her from whatever she was working on as she again tried to decipher the meaning. In perfect Vincent fashion, he never explained himself or even acknowledged he had sent the text. It was never discussed. For him, it was as if it never happened. For Lexi, however, it was the subject of many of her dreams and the reason behind more than one sleepless night.

Lexi knew he was flawed, horribly so. She wasn't a naive teenager anymore who thought he walked on water. She saw him for the man he was. Behind his severe, controlling, and arrogant behavior was a kind, loving man who pushed people away to keep them from hurting him. But he was intelligent, sweet, and funny once you broke through the façade he had created. She knew his softer side, and that, more than anything, was what she craved.

She also knew Jade was just waiting for the perfect opportunity to rip her to shreds. In the past, that might have made her shut down or run, but now Lexi wasn't afraid, nor was she willing to give up the life she was finally making. Jade would just have to find a way to deal with the fact that she and Vincent worked together, and Vincent would have to figure out what he wanted, because she was growing tired of his mixed messages. She wasn't going to sit around and wait for him any longer. If Vincent ever decided he wanted her, he would have to break up with Jade and open himself up to Lexi, not just the parts he was willing to share, all of him. Until he was ready to do that, Jade could have him.

That didn't mean that every time he walked into a room her heart rate wouldn't go up, or when he leaned over her shoulder and his chest pressed tightly against her back she wouldn't have to fight the urge to turn her head to the side and trail kisses up his neck. She couldn't stop the way her body reacted when he was near any more than she could change the electricity that arced between them until one of them got spooked by the intense feelings and left the room. What she could change was the way she watched life go by and ignored other men and basically let herself be a romantic hermit.

Peter was a pleasant distraction. He made her feel beautiful and attractive. She knew he wasn't really her type; he was a little too wrapped up in himself. But even knowing that, she had to admit that all the attention he gave her was very good for her ego. And the way Vincent's jaw clenched whenever Peter's name came up in conversation was an added bonus. Part of her hoped it was jealousy that put that scowl on his face, but with Vincent, she never really knew what was going on in his head.

Frustrated that she was once again dwelling on a man she might never understand, she slipped out her door, hoping the headlines of the morning newspaper would provide a much needed distraction. As she bent and scooped the bundle up from the floor, she heard Hope's door click open, and when she saw who stepped out, the newspaper that had been in her hand fell to the ground with a loud thud.

"Later, Hope." Sean turned around, and when he saw Lexi gaping at him in just her T-shirt and underwear, he gave her a sexy wink and strode down the hall with a definite spring in his step.

"Nice outfit, Lex. You really should wear that to work one day. I bet Vincent would love it." His low chuckle disappeared as he stepped into the waiting elevator.

Wasting no time, Lexi sprang across the hall and opened Hope's door. She heard the light clanking of dishes being loaded into the dishwasher. When the door shut behind Lexi, Hope's voice purred from the other room.

"Did you forget something, baby?"

"Yeah, I forgot the conversation where you told me that you and Sean were having sleepovers." Lexi leaned against the refrigerator and grinned as a cookie sheet slipped out of Hope's hands and crashed onto the tile floor.

"Crap!" Hope scrambled and tucked it into the dishwasher before finally facing Lexi's highly amused gaze. "Oh, damn it, I thought I could just do it once and get it out of my system and never have to tell you about it, but I'm hooked." She fell into a chair at her tiny table and put her head down, embarrassed. "It's an illness."

"Big, bad Hope has fallen. I never thought I'd live to see the day."

Hope grabbed a napkin off the table, balled it up and flung it at Lexi's head. "You've only known me for five months, you dork."

"I'm just saying, I've never seen you lose your cool, especially over a guy," Lexi teased as she took a seat beside her friend.

"Honestly, I have no idea what happens to me when he's around. I get all hot and want to strip off my clothes and rub myself against him." She slapped her hand over her mouth, embarrassed that she had shared so much. "Anyway, he wanted to get a drink last night, and I said fine, no biggie. I brought Marco and Tony with me, figuring they'd scare the hell out of him, I'd laugh, and it'd all be good. And ya know what happened? The two turncoats liked him! He schmoozed them. They were carrying on, laughing, and left me alone with Sean after one beer. When has Marco only had one beer at a bar? He must've paid them off, all I can figure." She gently banged her head on the table. "And then Sean did that husky thing with his voice, and he asked me to dance. I should have known better, but he's just so big and strong and … *gah*!"

Lexi laughed as she watched Hope fan her face.

"Then with the lights and the music … the man basically made love to me right there on the dance floor. His hips were moving, and his hands were wandering, and I just melted into some girlie pile of goo." She hung her head in shame. "I might've giggled."

Lexi covered her mouth and made a dramatic gasp at Hope's confession. "You giggled?"

"Bite me," Hope snarled with a twinkle in her eye.

"I'm guessing Sean beat me to it," Lexi said, pointing at a small red mark on the top of Hope's breast that peeked out from the deep V in her camisole.

"Damn it!" Hope clutched the neckline in her hand. "I'll kill him."

"Hope Greyson, you've got it bad." Lexi shook her head from side to side. "So, how was it?" There was no keeping the curious grin off Lexi's face no matter how hard she tried.

There was a moment of silence as Hope closed her eyes and smiled. "There are no words for how amazing it was. He was everywhere, wrapped around me like a second skin by the time we closed the apartment door. And the man is all muscle. For the first time, I liked feeling small beside a man. He took control, and it was so damn sexy." She pulled her lower lip between her teeth as she thought back on the night's events. "I have a feeling every other man on earth will pale in comparison."

"Holy cow," Lexi muttered, still shocked by how deeply Hope was affected by him.

Hope waved a hand in the air. "Enough about me. How was work the last few days? Sean told me about your promotion."

"Was that before or after he gave you that love bite?"

"How's Vincent? Kiss him again lately?" Hope asked pointedly, knowing it would shut Lexi up.

Ignoring her, Lexi answered her original question. "Work's been fine. It's amazing how much goes into the campaigns that you never see. Vincent's a master of negotiations. The way he works with people to get what he wants is awe inspiring. And the ideas he comes up with are brilliant. Some are cutting edge, and yet he can also do more classic approaches. His mind is really amazing."

"You are aware that you're gushing, right?"

"He's also the moron who is still dating Jade."

"What's the deal with the two of them? I mean, the guy kisses your face off one day, texts you that it was a big deal to him, whatever the hell that means, and then he stays with the vilest creature to walk the planet. What the hell is that about?"

Lexi held up her hands in surrender. "I have no clue. And it's been weird ever since that day we had it out."

"You mean the day you told her if she broke up with Vincent you were going after him? Sean loved that story, by the way."

"You did *not* tell him I said that!"

"I sure did. I need to know someone in that place has your back when the shrew is around."

Lexi rolled her eyes. "Well, thanks. But for whatever reason, I think Jade's been handled. She really doesn't even acknowledge that I'm alive anymore. She and Vincent got in a horrible fight that day. Now she doesn't say a word to me. Don't get me wrong, if looks could kill, I'd be dead ten times over, but her mouth has stayed surprisingly shut lately."

"Give her a few more days, and I'm sure she'll show her true colors again." Hope stood up and refilled her coffee. "So, what are you doing today?"

"Not much. I think I might head into work for a few hours."

Hope quirked an eyebrow at Lexi. "On a Saturday? Any chance Vincent is going to be there?"

Lexi shrugged her shoulders. "I hope not. There are a few things I want to go over without him staring over my shoulder." As her chair scraped across the floor, Hope laughed.

"Oh, somehow I don't think you mind that at all, especially if he's wearing that cologne you love so much."

With one hand on the door, Lexi turned around and glared. "I hate you."

"I love you too. Have a good day." Hope kissed her fingertips and blew a kiss in Lexi's direction.

"Go put on a turtleneck, you hussy." When the door shut, Lexi was still laughing.

✦

Vincent sat at his desk, scouring through the Marradesi file again. The date of their initial meeting with Paolo was fast approaching, and Vincent wanted to make sure he knew every minute detail about the company.

As he flipped through the papers, he found a Post-it with a small notation in Lexi's angular script, and an inadvertent smile spread across his face.

European or American?

That was all the tiny note said, but seeing it made Vincent's chest swell with pride. Lexi was already thinking about things like presentation style, seeing the differences in the markets here and abroad. Her attention to detail was amazing. She was like a sponge, absorbing everything he shared with her. They had spent countless hours over the last few days huddled around his desk going over demographic charts and budgeting projections or at a work station down in productions discussing color and presentation style.

His fingers grazed the edge of the yellow square wistfully. Lexi. His pulse quickened at just the thought of her. It was her grace and unassuming beauty that Vincent craved, and it was her gentle spirit that made him want to wrap his arms around her and never let go. He was beginning to realize how much he wanted her.

Even with the stress of knowing that someone in the company was betraying them, Vincent couldn't help but look forward to his afternoon meetings with Lexi. He could get through the most painful of mornings if he knew for sure that after lunch she was going to peek her head through his doorway. Her long brown hair would fall over her shoulder as she walked inside, clutching her legal pad and pen in hand, like the eager student she was.

His cell phone vibrated on the desk. Jade. How four small letters could bring such a sour taste to his mouth was astonishing. He had cared about her at one time, but now all he could do was see the hateful things she said and did to the people he cared most about and compare her to Lexi and her selfless ways. There was no competition. Jade lost every time.

When they had met months ago, Vincent had found a woman who wanted him but didn't need him refreshing. She was successful on her own and was highly focused on her career; therefore, she wasn't dependent on him. Her job required her to travel extensively, so their relationship occurred in small doses.

About the time she started getting on his nerves, she would jet off to some exotic location for a week. When she returned, everything went back to normal, not because he had forgiven her, but because he was absorbed in other things and had long forgotten the source of the argument.

His family hated her. They would never tell him that to his face, and he may have been oblivious, but he wasn't stupid. Whenever Jade walked into a room, Anna and Elizabeth would get identical pucker-lipped scowls on their faces. They never had lengthy conversations with Jade, only speaking to her when absolutely necessary, and Jade was the constant butt of Sean's jokes. Erik, who had worked with her professionally on photo shoots long before Vincent met her, had warned him to stay away from the infamous Jade, but he didn't listen.

A few nights ago he had finally been ready to break up with her and end his misery, but as soon as she suggested the possibility of a mole at Hunter, he knew he was screwed and had to keep her around. Jade knew everyone in the business. Her connections ran deep. Her model friends were sleeping with the most influential men in the business, and they spent the majority of their time on location smoking, drinking, and spilling their dirty little secrets. Jade would be an invaluable source of information no matter how much Vincent hated to admit it. And so she stayed.

Lexi made it clear she wouldn't be pulled into the middle of their unraveling relationship, and he admired her for that. Vincent had blurred the professional line between the two of them enough. He should never have kissed her, no matter how much he wanted to. Lexi deserved better than that. She deserved a man who was committed to her one hundred percent of the time. Now that he had to keep Jade in his pocket, all hopes of developing something more with Lexi would have to wait. He only prayed she would still be there when he was finally free.

The phone continued to dance across his desk until he finally pressed 'ignore,' knowing that Jade would leave a lengthy and profanity-laden voicemail. "Go shopping, Jade." Vincent muttered at his phone as he slid it into the drawer for safekeeping. He glanced at his watch and realized it was already lunchtime. He had been in the office for hours and spent a majority of that time daydreaming of Lexi. When his stomach growled, Vincent gave in and headed over to Lexi's desk and began rummaging through the drawers for the carryout menu from Archie's.

"What did she do, take it home with her?" he mumbled as he wiggled on the locked center drawer of Lexi's desk, having turned up nothing in the other three. "Why the hell is this locked?"

"To keep my boss out. He's a real nosey guy, and for some reason he can't keep his hands off my drawers." Lexi grinned as she sat down on the edge of her desk, her eyes twinkling with amusement at Vincent's frustration. She tossed a bag of food at him, and the familiar blue lettering on the plain white sack made his mouth water.

"I swear to God, I don't know how you do it." He sat down in her chair and ripped the bag open, pulling the sandwich from the bag and taking a huge bite without hesitation. "You're the best."

"Yeah, well, don't get used to it. You got lucky. On the way over I had a hunch you'd be here today. Remember, Elizabeth edited my job duties and getting your sorry butt lunch is off my daily 'to do' list."

Vincent grinned as he washed down the burger with a big swig of milkshake. He licked a bit of the chocolate drink from the corner of his mouth, his tongue fascinating Lexi. "Don't you worry about me. I'm a resourceful guy."

"Who have you suckered into being your new greasy beef supplier?" Lexi's hand went to her hip instinctively as she waited for his answer.

"Leigh will get me whatever I want, but she makes me buy her lunch too."

"Damn, I wish I had thought of that." Lexi shook her head from side to side. "Hey, you're getting mustard on my keyboard! Go mess up your own desk."

He rolled his eyes and wrapped the paper around his burger before he tossed it back into the bag. "Don't get me wrong, I'm thrilled to see you, but why are you here on a Saturday?"

She didn't answer, but raised an eyebrow in challenge and turned it back on him. "And why are you here?"

"The Marradesi thing. And you?"

"Research," Lexi said nonchalantly as she pushed him out of her chair and sat down.

"What are you researching?" he asked suspiciously.

"Nothing," Lexi said as she slipped a file to the bottom of a larger pile, hiding it.

Curious, Vincent grabbed the entire pile before she could stop him. When he opened the folder, he paused, his brows furrowed together in confusion. "Me? You're researching me?"

"Give me that." She was on her feet and snatched the papers from his hand, putting them behind her back. "I was just looking at old campaigns that you've done. Just to get an idea what kind of things you like in a design."

"And the magazine article from when I was voted bachelor of the year?"

Lexi rolled her eyes. "It's a cute picture of you. I thought I'd hang it on my wall next to my 1995 *Tiger Beat* cover of Leonardo DiCaprio."

"I'm way hotter than him," Vincent deadpanned.

"Um, hello? He's saving the environment, going green. What are you doing, Mr. Cheeseburger with Extra Bacon?"

"I have far better abs than him." He began to playfully creep the hem of his T-shirt up over the waistband of his jeans.

He watched Lexi's eyes grow wide, but they never left his body. Knowing she would watch whatever show he was willing to give made his blood run like molten fire through his veins. What he wouldn't give to feel her hands on his body. When Lexi nibbled on her bottom lip, Vincent had to stifle a groan. The woman had no idea the effect she was having on him as she sat there, innocently watching and enticing him. Wanting to see how far she'd let his teasing go, he slipped his thumb onto the waistband of his jeans and tugged them down an inch, revealing a sliver more skin. When her eyes bugged out of her head, he chuckled to himself, knowing she had reached her limit.

With a squeak, Lexi grabbed his wrist and held his hand in place, acting as if she was revolted by the display. "Spare me the peep show."

The wicked smile on his face made Lexi tremble. "Your loss." He gave her hand a squeeze and pointed back at the file. "Seriously, what are you looking for in there?"

"Everyone has something that's theirs in whatever they design. Elizabeth is the details, the meshing together of the tiniest parts. Fabrics and background props are as important as the message. In yours, you're all about the idea and selling the overall concept as clearly and succinctly as possible. I guess part of me is wondering what my 'thing' will be if I ever get to design a campaign on my own."

Without thinking, Vincent blurted out, "Passion."

"Excuse me?"

"Well, it's just that from working with you and seeing the ads you did for Hope, if I had to label what piece of yourself you put in the things you create, it's passion. In your ads, people can feel the excitement, they can feel this air of wanting, and it's the passion you create which draws them to whatever you're selling. It's incredibly attractive." He ran his hand through his hair nervously as he wondered if he'd said too much. He tried to keep his comments solely about her work, but then she batted her sultry eyes at him and he was lost. "Your work, I mean."

A snarky grin appeared on her face. "Of course, the work."

The coy curl of her lips had him captivated. He knew how soft her lips were, and he knew that he was right. Lexi was full of fire and passion. He had felt it when they kissed, and he couldn't stop thinking about it. Even now, in the middle of the office during a casual conversation, he could feel it building between them. The desire, the need to touch her was getting to be unbearable. One hand balled into a tight fist, and he jammed it into the pocket of his jeans, but the other took on a life of its own and reached out for what it wanted. He played with a lock of her long brown hair before brushing it back over her shoulder. A smile escaped his lips when he saw Lexi shiver at his touch.

"Oh, thank goodness you're both here!" Elizabeth came rushing around the corner, breaking the trance, and bringing them back to reality. "Wait, Lexi, what are you doing here on Saturday? Vincent has no life, I expect it of him, but you must have something better to do." Her eyes danced between the pair, picking up on the chemistry flowing between them.

Lexi glanced at Vincent, smiled, and said, "Actually there's no place I'd rather be on a rainy Saturday. So, what's up?"

Elizabeth motioned to Vincent's office and followed them inside. Vincent stood off to the side, allowing his mother to sit at the desk. Lexi sat in one of the chairs in front of the desk, her knee bouncing gently with excitement.

"The date of the Marradesi meeting has been moved up. It's this week. Paolo just called. They'll be in town for an opening, and he told me he was anxious to talk to the man who charmed his wife at the gala, so it looks like you're up, Vincent."

He confidently nodded his head. "That's fine. I've been researching them for weeks. I'm interested to talk to them and find out what direction they want to take."

"I'm glad to hear that, because I want Lexi at the meeting, and I want her to design the campaign with you from beginning to end." Elizabeth waited for the argument from her son, but Lexi chimed in first.

"Elizabeth, this is a huge client. I'm happy to just watch Vincent work. I really don't think…"

"I agree. Not that she doesn't have wonderful ideas, but she's never been in a negotiation before, let alone one this high profile." Vincent began pacing back and forth across the room.

Elizabeth cleared her throat and looked pointedly at her son. "And what exactly do you know about makeup, Vincent? Or the way women feel about makeup? You have the marketing part down, but I have a feeling they're looking for the best niche for them in the American cosmetics market, and from there they'll go global. This needs a woman's touch; I can feel it." She crossed her arms and sat back in his leather chair. "It's her or me. Pick your poison."

"Her!" Vincent said emphatically.

"You!" Lexi said at the same time.

"I'll try not to be offended by how quickly I was cast aside by my own son." Elizabeth pretended to wipe a tear, but her warm smile overpowered any dramatics. "Lexi, you can do this." There was no doubt, no convincing, just a clear statement of fact from Elizabeth.

"I can do this," Lexi whispered to herself. A warm hand gave her shoulder a squeeze.

"*We* can do this." Vincent's hand lingered on her shoulder, and Lexi reached up, grasping it for dear life, hoping his confidence would wash away her self-doubt.

"So, now what?" Lexi's voice was still shaky as she asked the question.

Elizabeth clapped her hands together and then handed each of them a folder. "Well, I hope you didn't have a date or anything this evening because we have a lot to work on."

Lexi's cheeks immediately reddened, and she grimaced. "I think I better go make a phone call."

Vincent stiffened and watched Lexi exit the room. By the time he bothered to look back at Elizabeth, she had her hands folded sweetly on the desk and smiled angelically at him.

"Are you sure about this? Because if this is you playing matchmaker, you picked one hell of a client to put at risk."

"I know I'm right. And this is all about business. I'd never risk the Marradesi account. Honestly, the two of you together are magic, even if you can't see that yet." With a knowing smile, she stood up, patted his cheek, and headed for the door. "A mother knows," she said cryptically. "Enjoy your evening. And you can thank me for this later."

Lexi came back into Vincent's office after wrapping up her phone call and began studying the file Elizabeth had left for her.

"Was he mad?" Vincent asked without even looking up from the paper he was jotting notes on.

"Who?"

"Peter." He peered over the top of the paper, carefully gauging her reaction. A chuckle slipped from her lips. "Oh, I think he's fine."

"If you have plans…" Vincent tried to do the right thing and give her space even though he wanted nothing more than to keep her close.

"Vincent, trust me. Peter will be fine. He's nice and makes me feel sexy and desirable, but can I tell you a secret?" She crooked her finger and leaned toward the desk as Vincent did the same. "I highly doubt he'll ever love someone as much as he loves himself."

There was no stopping the belly laugh that Vincent felt coming. "He gives Narcissus a real run for his money?"

"This is terrible, and I shouldn't be telling you this, but he took me to a gallery opening Friday night. It was modern art, which I enjoy, but some of it I just don't get. Anyway, one of the artists graffitied a trash dumpster and named it *The Globalization of Evil*. Another took Styrofoam cups, arranged them in circle, colored one red, and named it *The Tenth Circle of Hell*. This one woman basically hung a bunch of mirrors and called it *Contemplation of Self*. I thought the name fit because as I looked at it, I definitely thought 'what the hell am I doing here?' but when I turned to see Peter's reaction, he was busy winking at himself in the mirror. He did it all night. No matter where he was in the room, he looked at the mirror, saw his reflection, and winked."

She broke out into an uncontrollable fit of giggles. Vincent doubled over with his head lying on the desk as his entire body shook with laughter. He gasped for breath after a few seconds. "Great, now I'm going to have that in my head every time I see him, thanks."

"Glad to help." Lexi sat back in her chair and smiled while Vincent laughed.

"What?" Vincent asked when he caught her staring.

"It's just nice to see you laugh. You've seemed stressed the last few days, like something is bothering you."

He began moving around the room, trying to figure out how to answer. Finally, he dug his hands into the pockets of his jeans, stared at the floor and sighed. "Yeah, something is going on, but I can't talk about it right now."

"Professional or personal?" Lexi asked a little uncertainly.

"I guess a little of both, but mainly professional. The personal will work itself out." He leaned back on the edge of the desk and smiled apologetically. "I'll tell you soon."

He could see by her expression that she wasn't buying it, but she let it go, for now. "Well, I'm here if you need me."

"Thanks." Vincent smiled and relaxed a bit. "You have no idea what that means to me."

An awkward silence fell between them. "So, are we okay then?" she asked, waving her hand back and forth between the two of them.

He stood up and leaned toward her, then kissed the top of her head. "Always."

· 23 ·

The rest of the weekend was spent scouring the cosmetic industry's current ads and comparing them to the things that Marradesi had been doing in Europe. Vincent and Lexi weren't going to pitch anything at this initial meeting, but they could get an idea of where they wanted to go with the presentation and test the waters to get a feel for how receptive the client would be to it.

Jade, having another of her I-am-the-center-of-the-universe moments, had been furious that Vincent had to work so much over the weekend, but she would have really been upset if she knew Lexi was there with him. He had wisely left that part out. Sunday she went with a few of her friends to have a facial, hoping to find out more about the Hunter leak, but returned empty handed.

Monday came up on Vincent quickly. He and Lexi had been at the office past nine o'clock Sunday night before and were back at it a few hours later.

"Good morning, Leigh." Vincent gave her a tired smile as he passed her desk.

"Jeez, you look as tired as Lexi today. What's up with the two of you?"

His first reaction was to tell her exactly what they had been working on, but then he remembered that someone was giving information to his competitors. Until he knew who that person was, he needed to remain more tightlipped.

"Just a bunch of busy work. Did Lexi tell you to block out the afternoon for both of us?"

"Of course she did. So, where are you buying my lunch from today?"

Vincent laughed. "Today you're on your own, I'm afraid. I think I owe Lexi a decent meal."

"Have a good day. And try and get a good night's sleep tonight, please."

"Yes, Mother." He shook his head as he walked to his office.

Exhausted as he was, he suddenly found himself wide awake when he turned the corner toward his office. Lexi stood a few feet away at the coffee maker, looking like an absolute vision in blue.

Her outfit was simple and reserved, a feminine take on a suit, but the side slit in the skirt gave just a hint of the alluring things that were hidden underneath. Her sleek, black heels made her shapely legs seem to go on for miles.

She balanced precariously on her tiptoes trying to reach a new box of coffee filters. Even in the heels, her tiny frame was still a few inches too short. Vincent snuck up behind her and reached up over her shoulder to help.

"Here you go, Shorty."

Lexi's face wrinkled in annoyance. "It's the damn heels. I hate them."

Vincent's gaze raked over her body, slowly drinking in her curves. "I have to say, I'm quite partial to you in those shoes."

"Thank you, Mr. Fashion. Please tell me I'm appropriately dressed for this meeting today. My bedroom looks like the closet threw up in the middle of the floor." She did a little spin then tucked the filter into the pot and added the coffee grounds.

"You look beautiful and professional."

"Where are we meeting them again?" She threw away the old filter and headed back to her desk.

"We're having lunch at that new restaurant, Bravo. Paolo's nephew owns the place, from what I understand."

Lexi sank down into her chair. "I'm nervous."

"Breathe, Lexi. It's just a meeting. We go, we talk, and we leave." His fingers gently stroked her hair in encouragement. "And for the record, throwing up is typically frowned upon at these things."

◆

We go, we talk, and we leave. Lexi repeated the phrase in her head as she finished her morning work and prepared the few materials they were taking to the meeting.

By noon, she was ready to crawl out of her skin. She had reorganized her desk twice and spent twenty minutes aligning the coffee mugs so all of the handles were perfectly parallel. Vincent, however, continued to breeze through his day, the picture of relaxation. He glided in and out of his office casually, made smartass comments to Lexi, and then disappeared back behind his door.

Lexi was printing off the final fact sheet about Hunter when Sean turned the corner and crashed into her.

"Howdy, Miss Polka Dot Panties," he snickered.

"I catch you doing the Walk of Shame and you're making fun of *me?*"

His broad shoulders shrugged. "Did you know your hair looks like hell in the morning? I think some men," he glanced over at Vincent's door, "would find it very sexy. And the polka dots too."

He was obviously trying to deflect the conversation from himself by irritating Lexi, but she wouldn't fall for it. "So, you and Hope." A huge grin swept across his face, his cheeks tinting the slightest shade of pink. "Are you blushing? Goodness, now I've seen everything!"

"A gentleman doesn't kiss and tell." There was an air of sincerity as he said the words, which warmed Lexi's heart.

"Good, and you better not either, or Hope will roast your balls on a spit."

Sean wrapped his arms around her and pulled her to his chest. "Your friend's an amazing woman. I promise I would never do anything to disrespect her." He placed a kiss on Lexi's forehead and squeezed her tight.

"Thanks, Sean. Hope's like a sister to me."

"Now let me see you." He held Lexi out at arm's length and surveyed her outfit. "Our little Lexi, all grown up. You look like a mini Vincent, only cuter." Lexi quickly stuck her tongue out at him.

"Hey, I heard that," Vincent grumbled from his doorway. He went to the coat rack and pulled off Lexi's jacket. "Stop grabbing her. We have to leave in a minute."

Sean got a mischievous look on his face. "So, Vincent, what do you think about polka dots?"

The file in Lexi's hand slipped from her fingers, sending papers flying in every direction. "Damn it!" She dropped to her hands and knees to gather them.

Vincent knelt beside her, collecting the last few items. He held his hand out and helped her back to her feet. As she stood up and brushed off her skirt, she noticed Sean watching their interaction with great interest. She didn't miss the smug smile he sent in Vincent's direction either.

"Thanks." Lexi dipped her head to hide her embarrassment.

"You seem so tense today, Lexi. Maybe you should find a way to release some of it. Vincent, do you have any suggestions?"

Now it was Vincent's turn to drop something. Lexi's jacket slipped through his fingers, and Lexi noticed the flustered expression on his face as he snatched the coat from the ground and held it in front of him. "Sean..." Vincent growled.

Seemingly pleased that he had been able to fluster both of them to the point of speechlessness, Sean gave a cheeky salute and headed back to his office. "My work here is done. Good luck with that meeting, guys. You two kids have fun."

"What the hell was *that* all about?" Lexi prayed Vincent hadn't picked up on Sean's teasing.

"I have no idea, but I'm guessing you're not worried about the meeting anymore." He shifted in place, still clutching the jacket in front of him.

"Screw the meeting. Sean's scarier than Marradesi any day."

Vincent laughed and relaxed, wrapping the jacket over her shoulders. Lexi grabbed her bag and tucked the files safely inside. "Ready to go?" she asked.

The picture of confidence, Vincent placed his hand on the small of her back and began leading her toward the elevator. "Absolutely. Let's do this."

* * *

When they pulled up to Bravo, the valets all whistled as Lexi's car rolled to a stop. A group of them crowded around, all wanting to get a better look at the classic automobile. Lexi had let Vincent drive, keeping her promise and figuring it would be a good idea to keep him as relaxed as possible. Nothing put a smile on his face like driving fast.

"What's the horsepower on this?"

"You the original owner?"

"Who did the restoration?"

The young men peppered Vincent with questions as he climbed out of the driver's side door. Vincent made his way around the car to take Lexi's hand. "It isn't mine. It's the lady's. You'll have to ask her."

Lexi smiled and began answering the litany of questions. "Four hundred horsepower engine last time I checked, but my mechanic likes to tweak things without telling me, so it's probably more by now. My father was the original owner, and Hope Greyson over at the Crowbar did the restoration. Now if you'll excuse us, we have a lunch date." With a flip of her hair, she headed toward the restaurant.

Vincent glanced over at the valets and found them all staring at the gentle sway of her hips. He turned darkly to the men. "And Bob," he said, reading one of the gawkers' nametag, "if anything happens to her car, I'm holding you personally responsible. Do we understand each other?"

A small tug on his arm drew his attention back to Lexi. "You didn't have to threaten the guy," she said with a laugh.

Vincent chuckled when he heard Bob demand to be the one to park the car since "his ass was on the line for it," and he knew her car would be well taken care of while they ate.

Inside the restaurant, they felt like they were standing in a plaza in the middle of Italy. The rough cobblestone floor and rich colors of the fabrics were authentic in a homey, rustic way. Music played, and people spoke in Italian at every turn. Each element added to the experience.

"Mr. Drake, Miss White, *buon giorno. Benvenuto al Bravo*," a stocky man with short black hair said with a slight bow. "I'm Angelo. Allow me to show you to Mr. Marradesi's table. They just arrived as well."

Angelo led them through the restaurant, pointing out different antiques that his grandmother asked him to bring over from Italy. Lexi stopped twice to take a closer look at some of the family photographs. Her bright smile and genuine interest in what Angelo was saying endeared her to him immediately. He tucked her under his arm and gave her the full tour. Vincent followed behind them, smiling.

The aromas wafting through the air were mouth-watering. The trio passed large groups of people sharing everything on the table, from pasta to chicken and veal dishes. Employees breezed by with large trays of pizza in their hands, the cheese still bubbling. The garlic smelled like heaven.

The atmosphere was one of laughter and the clinking of glasses. It felt more like a relative's house than a restaurant, which was no small feat considering the size of the place. It seemed as if the rooms went on forever, yet the ambiance remained cozy.

Angelo led them to a private table situated at the back of the restaurant with no one else seated nearby. Paolo and Francesca sat beside one another at the large, round table. His arm was thrown around the back of her chair as she smiled and whispered something to him. Dante sat on the other side of Francesca and was talking to the wine steward. The steward nodded his head in agreement and then stepped aside so Angelo could seat Vincent and Lexi.

"Vincent, Lexi!" Paolo rose to his feet, shaking Vincent's hand and then kissing both of Lexi's cheeks. "Welcome to Bravo. It's wonderful to see you again, Vincent. You remember my wife, Francesca?" The gorgeous woman gracefully stood up from her seat and demurely offered Vincent her hand.

"Mrs. Marradesi, it's a pleasure to see you again. You look beautiful as ever."

She threw her head back and laughed. "Ah, Vincent Drake. Such a charmer. I told you before, please call me Francesca. " Her hand came up and gave his cheek a playful pat. Then she turned her attention to Lexi and offered her a warm smile. "Lexi, darling, *come va?*" Her hands clasped around Lexi's as she pulled her close and kissed her cheeks.

"Very nice to meet you, Mrs. Marradesi."

"Francesca," she corrected Lexi with a smile. "I meant to tell you at the gala, your dress was extraordinary."

Vincent's hand found the small of Lexi's back and pressed gently, encouraging her to relax.

Even though she was not good at taking compliments, especially from someone as well known in the fashion world as Francesca Marradesi, she adapted. "Thank you very much, Francesca. It was my mother's."

"And you both remember my brother." Dante simply stood up and gave a little nod to welcome both Lexi and Vincent before returning to his seat beside Francesca.

Vincent reached for the chair next to Dante and held it for Lexi, allowing him to sit between her and Paolo.

"Welcome to Bravo. My nephew has planned a wonderful dining experience for us. I hope you're hungry." Pride filled Paolo's voice as he smiled up at Angelo.

"This is a fantastic restaurant. How long have you been open?" Vincent asked as he took in the small details of the room, like the wrought iron accents and the gorgeous fresco on the wall beside their table.

"Four months," Angelo said, beaming.

"My nephew designed everything from floor to ceiling. He based the decor on my mother's house in Sicily, and a number of the recipes that we will be enjoying are hers. You must try the spicy calamari salad. It was her specialty."

Lexi gave Vincent a little kick under the table, knowing he was squeamish when it came to spicy foods ever since the Thai incident. "Sounds delicious."

Vincent kept a perfect smile plastered on his face. The only indication Lexi had that the word spicy even registered with him was the tiny kick back.

With great pride, Angelo listed all the one-of-a-kind dishes he was going to prepare for them this afternoon, and then returned to the kitchen.

While they waited for the food, Paolo told numerous stories from his childhood about the trouble he and Dante used to get into, driving their poor mother crazy. Often they were chased around the villa with pots and pans, not only by their mother but the women of the neighborhood as well. Apparently, they were quite the cads, breaking hearts and becoming known as "those Marradesi boys." Mothers warned their daughters to stay away from them, and fathers often threatened to kill. Francesca grew up in a town nearby, and the reputation of the brothers had traveled the miles to where she lived. So one day, when she heard that the infamous Paolo Marradesi was coming to town, a saucy seventeen-year-old Francesca put on her best dress and made sure he noticed her the moment he walked into the local market.

Food began filling the table—pasta, calamari salad, and antipasto served in courses. Each portion was small enough to allow them to taste everything offered. When Vincent's calamari salad arrived, he pushed it around the plate to make it look like he had eaten it. Lexi noticed and took mercy on him, eating hers quickly then playfully picking pieces off of his plate to lessen the eating load.

"Can I have a bite?" she grinned at Vincent.

"Didn't you just eat a whole plate of squid?" He played along with her ruse.

"I think a few of mine fell off onto your plate. Oh, look, that one was mine... and that one too. Wow. A lot of them escaped." Lexi began jabbing her fork into the stretchy rings.

Vincent rolled his eyes dramatically at Paolo, who watched the whole exchange with great amusement.

"A woman who likes to eat, now that's my kind of girl," Paolo teased as Lexi stole another piece from Vincent and he watched Francesca do the same thing with his last bite of squid. The women shrugged and savored the flavor of the calamari, unashamed.

The conversation flowed easily among the group. Lexi and Vincent both understood that eating and socializing came first, business second. Rather than try and muscle the conversation in that direction prematurely, they happily shared stories about their childhoods and families with their guests. Dante remained quiet, but the occasional smile escaped his lips.

Amidst the discussions, the Marradesis occasionally commented to each other in their native language. During one particularly lengthy exchange, Lexi bumped her knee into Vincent's under the table. When he turned to see what was up, she smiled and put her hand on his forearm, tapping her finger repeatedly. He took the hint and wrapped his arm around the back of her chair then made a point of leaning closer. He took the opportunity to whisper in her ear.

"What's up?"

Keeping a serene smile on her face she softly said, "Do you understand any Italian?" When he subtly shook his head no, she sighed. "Lucky for you, I do." When Vincent raised an eyebrow in disbelief, Lexi rolled her eyes. "I studied a lot of things to pass the time while Harry was sick. Italian happened to be one of them." She turned toward Vincent a little more and pointed to the fresco on the other side of the room as if that was the topic of their private chat. "From what I can tell, they like us, even Dante. Paolo is concerned about our age, so act mature, please."

"I can do mature. What else?"

"They feel comfortable around us, especially Francesca, so keep charming her."

Absentmindedly, Vincent's fingers trailed down Lexi's bare arm. "If there's anything else I need to know…"

Lexi smiled sweetly at him. "I'll just kick you again. It can be our secret code."

"I think I'm starting to get a bruise," Vincent chided. "Can't we do something like tap our fingers on the table?"

"Baby."

As they chuckled, he and Lexi looked across the table and found Francesca watching them carefully. She leaned into Paolo and a single word passed between them. *Amanti.*

"Lovers," Lexi whispered, but Vincent heard it clear as day. She gently tried to shift her body language and move away from Vincent, but as he turned and spoke to Dante, he shifted his chair closer to hers, not allowing her an escape. He saw Francesca's secretive smile turn into a full blown grin when Lexi's eyes met hers. She casually tipped her wine glass at Lexi in approval.

After they had gorged themselves on the main course, a tray of sweets arrived at the table. "I hope you saved room for dessert, Lexi," Paolo teased with a wink.

"I always have room for dessert, especially something as delicious as this." Lexi took another big bite of the extravagant Italian cake in front of her. "This is the best tiramisu I have ever eaten. What did you soak the lady fingers in? It isn't rum."

Angelo beamed proudly at her astute palette. Paolo and Dante laughed as their nephew rambled on about his preparation method from start to finish for his premier dessert. Lexi politely nodded her head and listened to every detail.

When Angelo finally stepped away from the table, Francesca laughed out loud. "I'm sorry, dear. We should have warned you that Angelo is very passionate about his cooking. Once you get him started, well, he can be impossible to stop."

"He's lovely," Lexi replied. "I just hope I can remember everything he said. I want to make this for my friend."

As the dessert dishes were being cleared, Vincent sensed the shift in atmosphere among the group. Paolo and Dante became more serious, preparing for the business side of the meal. Even Francesca toned things down, whispering more frequently in Italian with Paolo. When he felt Lexi's leg battering against his, he knew something was up. She passed him a piece of paper from her bag and began pointing to random words, giving him an excuse to huddle closer so Lexi could whisper information.

"It's Francesca."

"What is?"

"She's the person you better present to. She's going to make the final decision. Does she own the company or something?"

"She is the majority stockholder, but Paolo is listed as the owner in any papers you read." Vincent traced his pen on the page aimlessly to make it look like he was busy.

"She likes you. I know you can do this, but don't speak exclusively to Paolo and Dante when you discuss things. Make sure you ask her opinion on everything, ask for her viewpoint. A woman like Francesca Marradesi doesn't like to be ignored."

Her astute assessments of people impressed Vincent more than he could ever say. She read everything about everyone around her, knowing what to press and where to tread lightly. At times it scared the living hell out of him when he wondered how much she probably knew about him and his feelings only from her observations. Things that he tried so hard to keep hidden were exposed to Lexi.

She had been amazing all through lunch, interacting with Francesca, asking all the right questions. Vincent had been teaching her how small bits of seemingly inconsequential information would be monumental in their business. Their professional partnership was a good one, he could see that. Lexi was the sweetness to his more rigid, formal stance. She drew the people in with her radiance, and he kept them there with his business savvy. Lexi pulled off her part, now it was time for Vincent to work his magic.

"Thanks for the heads up," he whispered, his eyes locking on hers.

"No problem, partner. Go make us look good."

Paolo sipped his espresso, and then leaned back in his chair. "Tell us about Hunter, Vincent. Why are you the right company for us?"

"Hunter Advertising is the company for you for a number of reasons, Paolo. I believe we have the right team in place to design and execute a successful campaign here in the States to make Marradesi Cosmetics a household name. I can supply you with a number of references, from small business owners to multibillion dollar corporations. All were pleased with our final product. We have range, we have big ideas, and I believe we have the passion," he smiled at Lexi and continued, "to make this work."

Vincent paused to gauge their reaction. Dante rubbed his chin thoughtfully, and Francesca watched Vincent, her posture rigid, but not unhappy. What Vincent didn't realize was that he had Paolo eating out of the palm of his hand. He just had to work Francesca.

"That's a little about us. If you don't mind, I'd like to find out a few things about your company to get a feel for where you might like to see this campaign go. Francesca, I know your company is concerned with finding a niche in the American market. Can you tell me where Marradesi Cosmetics has made its home in the European market?"

The words had no sooner left his lips than a slow smile spread across Francesca's face. He watched her glance at Paolo and give a little nod before she began answering Vincent's question at length. She was a woman with definite ideas. She talked a lot about Europe and what worked there, but she also understood that advertising in the US was a different matter altogether. She didn't give any ideas about where she wanted the new campaign to go; she preferred for them to develop a few proposals from which to choose.

"Lexi," Dante started slowly, "I was wondering if you could tell us more about yourself. We're familiar with Vincent's work, but you seem to be new to Hunter. I'm curious where *you* see this campaign going, in general, if you don't mind me putting you on the spot."

There it was—a test. Dante had done his homework. He knew Lexi was an unknown in the industry. He wanted her to prove her worth on the fly.

Just when the color began to leave Lexi's face, Vincent gave her a playful kick under the table. She glanced up at him, both of them knowing that if she said the wrong thing it could cost them the client. He nudged her foot under the table one final time, trying to wash away her self-doubt.

"Come on, Lexi, I'd love to hear what you think," Vincent said and he smiled confidently at Dante. "She's been spot on so far." Vincent raised an eyebrow and waited for her to do what he knew she was capable of. She just needed to believe it.

"W-well, I think that from your past campaigns, you were marketed as an avant-garde brand in Europe where women tend to use more makeup product in general, but specifically the edgy, brighter color choices and hues for eyes and lips which your line spotlights. American women are not as fashion forward as the woman in Europe or into trends, but we all want to be. My suggestion would be to market the line in a different direction here, make it less intimidating, if that makes sense?" Francesca gave a little nod of understanding. "It can still be edgy, but market it as attainable beauty rather than being high fashion. It's all about making the woman feel better about herself, not overwhelmed with color palates and product."

Silence fell over the table. Vincent leaned back in his chair, smiling like a proud papa. But Lexi's eyes scanned between Paolo, Francesca, and Dante, who had all begun whispering amongst themselves in Italian.

"You were brilliant," Vincent whispered, his warm breath tickling her neck. When he saw tears welling in her eyes, Vincent gave her shoulder a squeeze. "Breathe."

"I like you," Francesca offered out of nowhere. "You remind me of myself. I apologize for Dante. I think it was rude to put you on the spot. In his defense, he can be a bit overprotective, and I assure you, he meant well. But you handled it beautifully." The air rushed out of Lexi's lungs in relief.

Paolo shrugged as he nodded toward Francesca. "It's her company. She's the boss. I just write the checks. " Dante gave the smallest of nods and remained silent.

"I would very much like to see what the two of you come up with for Marradesi Cosmetics. I would be honored if you would present us with your idea in a few weeks."

Vincent rose to his feet and pulled a stunned Lexi up from her chair. They had done it.

"I thank you for meeting with us, and I know we will be able to come up with something fantastic for you." Vincent turned to listen to the conversation Paolo and Dante were having about the next meeting, but he couldn't help but eavesdrop on Lexi and Francesca.

"Well done, Alexandra." Francesca wrapped her arms around a very shocked Lexi. "That brother-in-law of mine can be a pain, but you, you didn't waver. You just spoke from your heart. It was honest and very observant. I had a feeling you were up for this challenge, but men…you know them. They doubt more than they trust."

Vincent watched Lexi out of the corner of his eye, and when she looked over at him, he winked. Even in the middle of all the intense negotiations, he wanted to make sure she was all right.

"*Quell'uomo ha amore nei suoi occhi,*" Francesca muttered to no one in particular. Lexi's head snapped to attention, her face flushing red.

"He has love in his eyes?" Lexi gasped. "No, no he doesn't. We're friends."

Hearing Lexi's words, Vincent froze, now giving their conversation his complete attention.

Francesca eyed Lexi suspiciously. "*Capite l'italiano?*"

"*Si,*" Lexi whispered, cringing that her secret was out. Vincent hoped Francesca wouldn't be upset when she realized Lexi had been privy to everything they'd said.

A wicked smile curled Francesca's perfectly painted lips. "Clever girl. Oh, I like you even more now." She glanced back at Vincent and smiled. "And I stand by what I said. That man has love in his eyes. You might not believe it, and he might not know it, but it's true. I can see these things."

Lexi looked quickly at Vincent to find him watching her again. Her face flooded with color when their eyes met. Vincent hoped his face didn't look as shocked as he felt. Francesca's observation echoed in his head.

He has love in his eyes.

Vincent was broken from his stupor when Francesca announced, "Dante, Paolo, *andiamo.* I have an appointment at the spa."

Unconsciously, Vincent wrapped an arm around Lexi's waist, his hand settling on her hip as they began to say their goodbyes. It wasn't until he saw Francesca playfully elbow Lexi and nod her head at his hand that he realized what he had done.

"Alexandra, I look forward to talking with you soon. Please call me if there is anything I can do or if you have any questions." Paolo handed her a small card with his personal phone number on it as well as Francesca's. "Vincent, great to see you."

Dante shook Vincent's hand then took Lexi's and kissed her knuckles. "Brava, Alexandra."

"It was wonderful meeting all of you. We will definitely be in touch soon," Lexi offered in return.

On the way out of the restaurant, Vincent and Lexi stopped in the kitchen and thanked Angelo for the special lunch he had prepared. He thanked them for coming and told them any time they came to Bravo there would be a table for them. Lexi gave him a kiss on the cheek, which made him blush, and then Vincent led her outside.

She leaned against the rough, brick wall as they waited for her car to be pulled around. Vincent stood in front of this amazing woman, his huge smile still firmly in place. He was so impressed with the way she had handled herself. Neither of them had expected that question from Dante, and yet Lexi, who was completely new to the process, took it in stride and gave the perfect answer. She didn't corner them into a design; she left it vague, but gave them a specific direction to work with, and one the client liked.

As she rested against the wall, her toes tapped from the adrenaline that was certainly coursing through her body. He could see the gears going in her head as she replayed the meeting, still unsure of herself.

Vincent was overcome with the need to wrap his arms around her and hold her. He wanted to cradle her soft body against his and whisper into her hair how proud he was of her and tell her what a great job she had done in there. He wanted a lot of things with Lexi, but most he couldn't have at the moment. Not until he tied up a few loose ends.

"I think they kind of liked me," she said hesitantly, as if not sure she believed it herself.

"Kind of liked you?" Vincent asked incredulously. "Lexi, they loved you. When I was talking to Paolo, all he did was ask questions about you."

"Did they really love me, or are you just being nice?" Her eyes were hopeful like those of a child making a wish that might actually come true. It was her innocence, her good heart, and her untainted view of things that made her such a beacon for Vincent.

Vincent sighed. Tired of fighting his feelings, he took her hand and pulled her toward him, relishing the feel of her softness against him. He slipped his arms around her waist and pressed his forehead to hers. "Everyone loves you, Lexi. You just don't always see it."

· 24 ·

Lexi and Vincent settled into a comfortable rhythm. She spent hours scouring files and taking notes on what information she needed from Vincent. As he passed by her desk, he snatched the sticky notes and brought her the items without her even having to ask. Working together was easy, predictable, and effortless.

Things made sense to Lexi for once in her life. She had a fantastic job and was doing things she had always dreamed of, all the while working with a gorgeous man who she was lucky enough to call a good friend. He laughed with her all the time and seemed to be genuinely happier when she was around. If he was in a rotten mood at work, everyone nominated Lexi to give him bad news because she was the only person he didn't lash out at. The way he looked out for her in the office and helped her learn the ropes was way beyond what Elizabeth had outlined, but he never complained. If anything, he found more reasons for them to be together, staying late at the office or sharing late night phone calls that always ended in a discussion of what the other was watching on television.

Everything was great between them until Jade showed up. Whenever Lexi saw Jade wrapped around Vincent, a piece of her heart died. Lexi's favorite days were those when Jade was safely out of town on a shoot or at the spa with her friends, because it meant peace and quiet, and truthfully, a happier Vincent. When Jade walked in the office, his whole demeanor changed. His smile became forced, his posture tightened, and even the tone of his voice became cooler. Jade couldn't see the difference in him because this was the side of himself that he always presented to her, but Lexi knew the real Vincent Drake. The man who wiped her tears and teased her about her sweet tooth. Secretly, Lexi was thrilled he never let Jade see that side of him.

No matter how hard she tried, it was impossible to ignore the way he made her heart thunder every time he was near. There was no denying that the crush she had developed so many years ago was back full force and wasn't going away. And all the casual pats on her arm, his hand brushing innocently against hers, his devilish grin when he teased her, and the sparkle in his eye when he talked to her only made those feelings grow stronger.

All of the attention from Vincent made her wonder if the feeling was mutual. Did he actually feel anything for her, or was she just a welcome distraction from his failing relationship with Jade? Francesca Marradesi's words flitted into her head. *That man has love in his eyes.* Lexi wondered what she saw between them. She and Vincent were friends, and they enjoyed one another's company, but Lexi couldn't let herself believe Vincent might have feelings for her, not the same kind she had for him. That was only a dream.

At least things seemed to be moving along smoothly on the business end, but Lexi sensed that trouble was brewing. For two days, Vincent had slowly paraded employees into his office, and they all left with the same, hard, suspicious look on their faces. Nothing on his schedule explained the mysterious meetings. Lexi finally broke down one morning and checked with Leigh, thinking she must have missed a memo or something, when she heard Tony was invited up. Unfortunately, Leigh was just as clueless as Lexi, and all they could do was stare at each other wondering what Vincent was up to.

It was midmorning when Tony slithered down the hall. "Ah, if it isn't Alexandra, the Girl Wonder. Walk on water lately?" He took a seat and leaned toward her desk, straining to get a glimpse at what she was working on. "What are you doing snooping through the Majestic file?" His lips twisted in distaste as he pompously sat back and waited for the answer.

Without blinking, Lexi closed the file and cocked an eyebrow at Tony. "What I do isn't any of your business. Is Vincent even expecting you?" She knew darn well he was, but she wanted to make the arrogant pig squirm.

"Who are you? His guard dog? Somehow I'm not at all afraid. I'm guessing your bark is far worse than your bite. However, if you really want to bite me, that can be arranged."

Lexi tapped her pen on the desk, ignoring every disgusting word that fell from his mouth. "Is he expecting you?" Lexi enunciated each word with painstaking clarity, fighting the urge to reach across the desk and throttle him.

"People have been talking, you know," Tony said with a sinister grin on his face, "about you and my dear cousin. Mainly about how close the two of you are. Late nights at the office, all those private lunches behind closed doors." He waggled his eyebrows suggestively and waited for Lexi to react.

"Ignorant gossip doesn't interest me, nor do the petty people who spread it." Lexi glared back at Tony, her body language like that of a panther, coiled and ready to attack.

"You better watch yourself, little girl. It would be a shame if—" He was interrupted mid-threat when Vincent's door opened.

"Tony, not another word. Get in here." Vincent stepped out and ushered him inside. He closed the door without so much as a glance in Lexi's direction.

Twenty minutes later, Tony left Vincent's office, furious. Lexi gave Vincent his space, assuming he was probably in a similar frame of mind after the meeting with his worm of a cousin.

Over the course of the morning, three more staff members trickled into Vincent's office for these unannounced meetings. Each left looking far less happy than when they went in, and none said a word as they passed Lexi's desk.

Even Sean was summoned. "So, Lexi," he said as he slid into a chair and pulled it up close to her desk, "what's going on with all the cloak and dagger bullshit?"

"I wish I knew. He's had half the office traipsing through here today and his schedule is blank, so I'm as much in the dark as you."

Sean's brow furrowed. "That's weird. He tells you everything." Just then, Vincent appeared like an apparition in the distance and signaled for Sean to join him. "Later."

Lexi waved and watched the two vanish behind the door.

Stupid hunk of wood. I bet if I took it off the hinges, he wouldn't have a clue how to put it back on, she thought to herself, then returned to work.

A while later, the door opened with a loud crack and as Sean left, the jovial man she knew and loved was gone. Instead, a silent ball of fury walked past. Lexi tried to get his attention and see if he was all right, but he didn't even acknowledge her as he whipped his cell phone out of his pocket and continued down the hall.

Something was going on at Hunter, something very bad. Lexi had no idea what it might be, but from Sean's reaction, the reason for these meetings wasn't good. Part of her was hurt that Vincent didn't confide in her, but until he did, there was nothing she could do to help, so she went back to work.

◆

Just after lunch, Lexi checked on Vincent, to see what he was working on. Her gentle knock on the door momentarily broke his concentration.

"What do you need?" The surface of his desk was covered with papers, and he scribbled furiously onto a notepad as he glanced back and forth between the computer screen and his pile of papers.

"Nothing," she said as she walked in and peeked over his shoulder. "Marradesi account?"

He sighed and tossed his pen onto the desk. "Yeah, I'm trying to work on it, but every time I sit down and try to come up with the focus of the ad, everything sounds forced."

Lexi quickly scanned down his list. She grabbed the pencil out of his hand and began working off his paper, making notes and crossing things off. Her hair hung over her shoulder, and Vincent felt her soft curves pressed against his back and side as she leaned over him. He tried not to stare at the rounded swell of her breasts that were only inches away, or the way her cleavage peeked out every time she turned to say something to him, but he was helpless. She was perfection, and she didn't even know it.

Vincent forced himself to be a gentleman and keep his eyes on the paper, but he couldn't stop the way his body reacted to her perfume, to the heat from her body, or the way he wanted to touch her. His fantasies had grown more vivid in the last few days, most involving Lexi draped over his desk. But nothing could come of it, not now anyway. The issue of the mole still hung over his head, and he had to do whatever he could to figure out who it was. That involved a number of things he despised doing, including keeping Jade around a while longer. He had already set some things in motion and still had a few loose ends to tie up, ones that he dreaded.

"Okay, right here? Women don't want their makeup to be the reason they're pretty. That implies we're a bunch of ugly hags and the makeup will fix it." Lexi crossed off the idea and laughed. "We all want to think we're gorgeous and the makeup only accentuates it."

Vincent nodded his head in agreement and hoped she'd continue. Instead, she stood up and arched her back, her breasts thrusting out, shirt hiking up and her body making an erotic curve as her arms stretched high over her head.

"Absolutely beautiful." The words fell from his mouth before he could stop himself. Lexi froze, her arms still in the air as she quirked an eyebrow at him and smiled.

"Excuse me?"

"Oh, just repeating what you said. Women want to feel absolutely beautiful."

Smooth, he thought to himself. *Why not ask her to take the shirt off for research while you're at it?*

Lexi laughed and hopped up onto the desk, facing him. "I know. We're infuriating creatures, women. Half the time I don't understand them myself." Her hand came to rest on Vincent's shoulder. "Want to do a little brainstorming? I can grab my handy dandy yellow legal pad and we can mess up your office a little."

"Sure." Vincent wasn't sure what it would accomplish, he was too drained and unfocused, but at this point he didn't care, he simply wanted to be around her. He would have agreed to learn needle point if it kept that smile on her face.

"Be right back." She hopped off the desk and ran out the door. He sank back in his chair with a groan, his hands scrubbing over his face. Vincent felt like scum every time he ogled her. It wasn't fair. The mixed signals he was sending weren't fair to her, and allowing his feelings to grow when there was nothing he could do about it at the moment wasn't fair to him. Even Jade didn't deserve this. He was still beating himself up when Lexi walked through the door. She took her usual perch on the couch and sat, pen poised to take notes.

"Dazzle me, boss." She always started these brainstorming sessions the same way, with just a hint of a challenge in her voice to spur Vincent's creativity. Little did she know she was stirring so much more in him these days.

For two hours they tried to nail down a more specific direction for the Marradesi account, and every time they thought they had it, the market research didn't support the idea. Vincent grew more frustrated with his creative block.

Lexi sat on the couch with her legs folded under her, gnawing on her pencil. Vincent enjoyed watching her work and learning little things about her every day. Her forehead always wrinkled when she was deep in concentration. Occasionally she twisted her hair around a pencil and used it as a makeshift clip as she scanned pages of information late into the afternoon because she hated it when her hair fell into her face as she was reading. There were times when he simply stood in his doorway and watched her work. She fascinated him, and he wanted her more than he had ever wanted a woman before. She made him happy in ways even he didn't understand.

All he could do was hope that when the smoke cleared and the mole had been identified, Lexi would still be there. But deep down, he knew that might not happen, and that was beginning to scare the hell out of him. Would she wait for him?

A groan escaped his lips as he raked a hand through his hair. Immediately, he was back on his feet and walking off his sexual tension, trying to think of anything but her. "Repeat that last one, about the modern woman thing." He was distracted by his thoughts, and Lexi must have picked up on it.

She abruptly jumped up and said, "Let's go."

"What?" Vincent stopped mid-step.

"Come on. We are going on a field trip. We need a change of scenery. Move it."

"I just need to work through this a while longer. You can go if you need to."

"You're coming with me," Lexi insisted. Vincent opened his mouth to protest, but Lexi put her foot down. "It's not open for discussion." Her hands were planted on her hips, striking a very Anna-like pose. When he reached for his suit jacket Lexi shook her head. "Leave it."

Vincent playfully offered her his elbow and she slipped her arm around his, her fingers wrapping around his bicep. "Where to, madame?" he asked.

"It's a surprise." There was a definite twinkle in her eye as she ushered Vincent out of the office and toward the elevators.

"Where are you two running off to?" Leigh asked as she peeked up from her desk, trying not to smile.

"I'm being kidnapped. If I don't return, avenge me, please."

"Yeah, I'll get right on that." Leigh winked at Lexi. "Have fun. If Jade calls?"

Vincent stepped into the elevator and grinned. "Tell her I'm—"

"Playing hooky with Lexi?" Leigh asked hopefully as Lexi groaned.

Vincent gave her an unamused look. "No, how about I'm in a research meeting and can't be interrupted under any circumstances."

Leigh clapped her hands together and saluted Vincent. "Will do, boss! Have fun."

Vincent and Lexi were soon on a trolley, the wind blowing through their hair. They were heading for Fisherman's Wharf. When they reached their stop, Vincent climbed off first then held his hand out to Lexi so he could help her down. She relished the contact as she stepped into his arms and felt his hand settle on the small of her back as he began to lead her out of the crowd.

"Where to? I am but your simple hostage."

Lexi rolled her eyes and took his hand. "Come on. You're such a baby. Most people would be thrilled to skip out of work early on such a beautiful day." She tugged him down the street, then stopped to point at a large sign in the air.

"Ghirardelli?" Vincent asked.

"Exactly. You should know by now, chocolate makes everything better."

On their stroll through Ghirardelli Square, Vincent would occasionally pull her hand and lead her over to a nearby store window. His touch was warm, strong and familiar, like they had been communicating this way for years. He could have led her off the edge of the pier and Lexi would have followed. His laughter was like music to her ears, and when she felt him relax, she knew she made the right decision in getting him out of the office.

At the counter in Ghirardelli's, Lexi sampled a few flavors before finally choosing. She even ordered for Vincent.

"Hey, I just wanted a single scoop of sorbet," he protested.

"Sorbet," Lexi scoffed. "Health nut. Don't listen to him. He needs the espresso chip. He just doesn't know it yet." The woman behind the counter nodded in understanding and filled his waffle cone with massive scoops of ice cream.

"You know," Vincent purred in her ear, "I kinda like you bossing me around."

Fortunately, Lexi didn't have her cone in her hand yet or it would have fallen to the ground with an embarrassing splat. She dug her nails into the counter as she struggled to hold herself upright when her knees began to buckle. There was no hiding the shiver that went down her spine when his warm breath grazed her neck. The low rumble of his chest beside her told her he noticed as well. "Cold?" he asked with an air of male satisfaction before he wrapped his arm around her shoulders and tucked her against his side.

With a trembling hand, Lexi reached for her cone. "M-hmm," Lexi mumbled with a mouthful of Rocky Road, lost in his sexy eyes.

"I'll keep you warm," he offered, pulling her even closer. His tongue slipped out from between his lips, and he gently lapped at his ice cream. The way his tongue and lips moved should have been illegal.

Lexi's mind went deep into one of her most vivid fantasies, and her heart began to pound against her ribs. She was certain the flames erupting throughout her body were going to vaporize the ice cream in her hand. He started to lead her to a booth, where she knew they would sit side to side, very intimately. If his thigh rubbed against hers or if she had to watch him lick that cone another second, Lexi knew she would explode.

"Let's eat outside," she exclaimed loud enough that people turned to stare.

Vincent shrugged. "Fine with me. Where to?"

"I know a spot."

Once outside, Lexi could breathe again. There was more space, more air that was not full of his scent or his heat. Just plain old fishy-smell-off-the-bay air. She drew a deep breath into her lungs and willed her heart to stop slamming into her ribcage.

In the distance, a small path meandered down toward the water. Whenever she needed to get away from everything and just think, this was where Lexi went. The last time she had been there, it was Vincent who had plagued her thoughts and sent her fleeing to her refuge, her private sanctuary. And now, she was about to share it with him. The bench under her favorite tree was empty, so she happily took a seat in its shade and gazed out onto the water.

"The view here is beautiful," Vincent commented as he continued eating his ice cream.

"This is my favorite place in the city." Lexi broke off a small piece of her cone and tossed it to a nearby squirrel. "I come here all the time to think."

"It's very relaxing," Vincent agreed.

"It's the water," Lexi murmured. "It reminds me of home. Harry took me fishing more times than I can count. He loved the water. I like to come here and just feel close to him. I know it sounds crazy."

Vincent's hand found hers and gave it a squeeze. "It's not crazy at all. You miss him."

"It helps me keep things in perspective, and sometimes it helps me forget. Whenever I think things are too much, I come here. No matter what is going on or how bad it seems, when I sit on this bench, I'm reminded that the water continues to flow, the waves keep crashing on the shore, and life goes on around me."

They sat for a while, enjoying a comfortable silence while finishing their ice cream and watching the people walk by. Vincent snaked his arm around the back of the bench and Lexi leaned against him, taking this moment to savor the experience of sharing this place with him. For those few moments, there was no Jade, there was no Hunter Advertising. There was only Vincent and Lexi.

"Can I ask you a question? You don't have to answer it if you don't want to," Vincent asked as he stroked her hair gently.

Lexi swatted him playfully on the chest. "I'm not telling you my bra size."

"It's thirty-four C."

Lexi's mouth fell open in shock as her face turned red. "How the hell did you know that?"

"It's a gift." Vincent grinned from ear to ear. "Now can I ask my question?"

"It can't be worse than that. Shoot."

"How do you remember so much about me from high school?"

"I was wrong. I think I'd like to use my pass. Next question please?"

Vincent's eyes were pleading. "Come on. Please? Fill me in. I can't remember anything. Did we have a bunch of classes together or something?"

"Or something," Lexi said quickly, praying he'd let it go. But of course he didn't.

"Did Anna tell you, back then, I mean? I know you guys did yearbook together. Did she tell you all about her obnoxious brother?"

"No."

"So then how di—"

"I had a crush on you in high school, you idiot." The words flew out, and there was no way to suck them back into her mouth.

"Really?" Vincent's eyebrows rose high in surprise. When Lexi nodded, completely mortified at her admission, it seemed he couldn't stop the stunning smile that spread across his face. "Really?"

Lexi again nodded her head in humiliation.

"Like how big of a crush? I mean, did you know my locker number and my schedule?"

"Locker number seventy-three. We had four classes together, but one of them was study hall. You'd go to the vending machines and get peanut butter crackers every day and a package of donuts. You always ate lunch outside, never in the cafeteria."

"Did you doodle my name on your books too?"

"I'm going to kill you now."

"You weren't my secret admirer senior year who wrote poetry and slipped it into my locker were you?"

Lexi punched his arm. "Get real."

"Oh, thank God, because she was kinda scary. At least I think it was a she."

"I was more of a watch-you-from-afar kind of girl."

"I can't believe you had a crush on me."

Lexi could feel his amusement over the situation. He kept smiling and chuckling to himself, no matter how hard he tried to play it cool. Lexi was dying to know if he found her crush ridiculous or endearing, but her nerves were getting the better of her. In a panic, she jumped to her feet.

"God, I can't believe I admitted that. I'm going to go drown myself in the bay now." She hurried toward the water.

Laughing, Vincent quickly chased after her, grabbing her around the waist and swinging her into the air. Her laughter filled his ears until he placed her safely on the ground and held her tightly against his chest.

"You're always running away from me."

Her coy but honest reply caught both of them off guard. "Maybe I just like having you chase after me." Lexi loved the feel of his arms around her. Nothing would ever compare to the perfection of Vincent Drake, no matter how long she lived. He was it, her everything. If only he felt the same way.

Lexi's trance was broken by ringing church bells off in the distance. "Come on, it's late. We better get back before Leigh either sends out a search party or offers to help me hide your body." Lexi laughed as she tossed her napkin into a nearby trashcan. She started to walk toward the trolley when Vincent stopped her.

"Thank you for this." He brushed her hair back over her shoulder, his fingers lingering along the collar of her shirt. "Somehow, you always know just what I need."

"Any time you need to be kidnapped, I'm your girl."

He laughed. "Yeah, you sure are." His arm settled around her shoulders, and they walked to the trolley stop, ready to get back to work on the Marradesi account with newfound focus and determination.

· 25 ·

Two days had passed since Vincent's kidnapping, and he and Lexi had been working nonstop on the Marradesi campaign. They were still working on a number of good ideas, but what they didn't have was that one great idea that they could look at and say "that's the one." According to Vincent, they would know in their gut when it was right, so they kept plugging away with the designs.

Lexi arrived at work early that morning and got to work. She had woken up from a bizarre dream involving a goat named Jade wearing blue eye shadow and figured it was easier to just go in and start working rather than try to fall back asleep. She was surprised to find Vincent already in his office. He was on the phone, which made sense, because when he had overseas calls to make he would come in early. From the tone of his voice, Lexi guessed he was talking to either Paolo or Francesca. She heard him use a few of the Italian phrases she had taught him and smiled.

His muffled voice eventually quieted, and he walked out of his office. "It's six in the morning. What are you doing here?" he asked as he poured a cup of coffee and set it on her desk.

"Thanks." She took a sip and wrapped her hands around the heated mug. "I kept having nightmares about the campaign. Jade was a goat. All I know is I couldn't sleep, so I came in to try and get some work done. Were you on the phone with Paolo?"

Vincent sat down in one of her chairs and stretched out. "Yes, he was letting me know about a few problems they've had in the European market that he wants to try and avoid here."

"Great," Lexi mumbled.

"Exactly. Let me go over them with you real quick, then I have to run out for a while, but I'll be back before lunch."

They huddled around her desk for an hour before Vincent had to leave. He kindly left his office door open so Lexi could get the files and reports she needed from inside. After her fifth trip, it seemed easier to just stay and work from his couch, so she curled up on the black leather and went back to work. She was just beginning to develop a new campaign idea when the door opened.

"What the hell are *you* doing in here?" Jade's whiny snarl made Lexi's head snap up. It was the most Jade had said to her in almost a week.

"Working."

"You do have a desk, you know. Out there." She pointed her thumb toward the door.

"I do? Gee, thanks, I had no idea," Lexi continued scribbling on her notepad. "Do you need something?"

"Yes. You, gone. Vincent needs his office back."

"Vincent doesn't mind. We work together in here all the time." It was a low blow, but Lexi was not in the mood for Jade's pouting.

"Well, I mind, so get out!"

"Jade." Vincent's cutting tone made both of them jump. "Apologize."

"You've got to be kidding," Jade shrieked. "I asked her to leave, and she gave me attitude. How about she apologizes to me?"

Lexi was uncomfortable being witness to their argument so she gathered up her things from the small table and stood up to make her exit. "I have a ton of work, so I'll be at my desk if you need me. Excuse me." She gave Vincent an apologetic smile.

"No one here needs you!" Jade seethed as Lexi went through the door. "Stop glaring at me, Vincent. I told you I don't like her."

Lexi returned to her desk, and their raised voices carried on for a half hour. Then there was silence. Lexi felt terrible. She knew her smart mouth had caused the argument, but she couldn't help herself. Jade brought out the worst in her.

It was nearly lunchtime, and there was no sign that Vincent or Jade were coming out of his office any time soon. Still feeling guilty, Lexi made up her mind to be nice. She tapped on the door and decided to see if she could grab them lunch when she went downstairs for hers.

"Come in," Vincent said softly.

When Lexi pushed the door open she saw the two of them sitting very intimately on the couch. Jade had her arm around his shoulders and was playing with the buttons on the front of his shirt. Vincent's head was close to hers as he whispered something that made Jade smile.

Lexi's stomach dropped at the sight of them. They were a couple. There was a familiarity between them, one that Lexi couldn't deny. They had a history, a relationship, memories together. Lexi could understand Jade's hostility. If she had someone as wonderful as Vincent, she would fight for him with everything she had. The problem was, he wasn't Lexi's to have, and that suddenly became very clear.

"Sorry to interrupt, I was going to get lunch in a bit and wanted to see if you wanted me to bring you something back." Lexi's words came out in a rush, her discomfort with the situation obvious.

Vincent quickly sat up and separated himself from Jade. "You don't have to do that. We're fine."

Jade's red lips pressed into a perfectly smug snarl. "Vincent got us a private table at La Tavola."

"Oh, well, you guys have a nice lunch." Lexi sputtered random niceties, fighting the urge to run out of the room.

"Do you want to join us?" Vincent offered out of the blue. It was like something out of the Twilight Zone. Lexi's eyes got huge in shock, and Jade sucked in a breath so fast she nearly inhaled her tongue.

"What?" Jade's smug façade was replaced by blatant rage.

"I think that would be a very bad idea." Lexi shook her head from side to side in disbelief that he would even make that offer.

He rubbed the back of his neck nervously. "I guess you're right."

Lexi had never felt more uncomfortable in all her life. "I'm gonna go."

"Good idea," Jade snipped quickly.

Vincent's eyes were apologetic and embarrassed. "Thanks, Lexi."

"Sure." Lexi closed the door and traipsed back to her desk, still shocked. She logged off her computer to go to lunch when someone whirled into the room.

"Lexi!" Anna smiled and wrapped her arms around Lexi's neck. "How are you? You look tired. Is my brother being a tyrant again?" She took a few steps toward the door. "I can go kick his ass if you want."

"Be careful if you go in there. He might invite you out to lunch with him and Jade."

"Ick!"

"That's what I said." Lexi chuckled as Anna's eyes nearly popped out of her head.

"He didn't."

"Oh, he did."

"He's an idiot." Anna shook her head from side to side.

"Agreed. So, what brings you here, Mrs. Caldwell?"

"Well, I was going to talk to him about something, but he obviously doesn't have his faculties about him, so you wanna grab lunch instead?" Her wide smile told Lexi she wouldn't be taking no for an answer.

The thought of getting out of the office was more appealing than words could express. Lexi needed to be away from Jade, ASAP. And if she was being honest, some girl time with Anna might be just what the doctor ordered to help her clear her head. "I'd love to."

"Where do you want to go?"

"Anywhere but La Tavola," Lexi insisted.

Anna giggled. "Jade's so predictable. She would like that hoity-toity, celebrity hang out." Anna snickered. "Don't tell anybody, but our neighbor owns an exterminating business, and they had a rat the size of a cat in that place last month."

Lexi stifled a giggle. "How does Thai sound? I know a great place."

"Perfect." Anna grinned. "Let me pop in and say hi to Vincent before we go." In true Anna fashion, without knocking, she stormed his office door. "Hi Vi—oh, good Lord, my eyes," she whined. "For God's sake, get a room for that stuff. I'm taking Lexi to lunch. She won't be back for a while, so don't bitch about her being gone." She slammed the door shut, turned to Lexi and giggled.

"Dare I ask?" Lexi snickered as she grabbed her purse.

"What? Oh, they weren't doing anything. I just say that every time I see him with Jade. It annoys her to no end. Just the sight of her in general makes me ill." She linked her arm in Lexi's, and the two women headed for the elevator.

"Have I told you recently how much I missed you?"

Leigh smiled from behind her desk. "Kidnapping Mrs. Caldwell today, Lexi? You know she kidnapped Vincent the other day." Leigh winked at Anna.

"Did she?" Anna turned to Lexi and grinned. "Were handcuffs used?" Lexi's cheeks flamed red as Leigh cackled. "Never mind. You can tell me all about it over lunch."

"I take back what I said about missing you." Lexi stalked into the elevator to escape her laughing friends.

"No you don't," Anna sang as she pressed the button for the lobby.

"Fine, I missed you. But I'm not talking about Vincent."

With an impish grin on her face, Anna looked up at the illuminated numbers above the elevator doors. "We shall see."

✦

"Table for two," Lexi said softly to the hostess at Osha. The smell of rich spices made her stomach growl.

The women were escorted to a quiet booth in the back corner, away from the busy lunch crowd. The rich reds and oranges of the restaurant gave it a cozy but exotic feel. Sleek, streamlined tables and chairs put a modern twist on things.

Anna smiled as she slid into her seat beside Lexi. "This place is gorgeous. You eat here a lot?"

"Not really. Hope hates Thai food, and I'm not big on dining alone. Of course, I have been known to talk them into making me something to go from time to time." Lexi opened her menu.

Anna made her decision quickly and slapped her menu onto the table top. "So, I'm dying to hear about you kidnapping my brother."

Lexi groaned. "It was no big deal, Anna. And I told you, I'm not talking about Vincent."

Anna huffed. "Fine, let's talk about work. Oops, you work with Vincent. New topic. Let's talk about dating. That should be safe. Are you seeing anyone?"

Lexi choked on her iced tea at Anna's question. "Um, no, I guess not. I went out with Peter a few times. He works with Julian Stone. He was nice, but not my type."

That piqued Anna's interest. "Really? Not your type?" She leaned closer. "So tell me, Lexi. What exactly is your type?"

"Well, I don't know. I never thought about it." That was a lie, she always thought about it. Unfortunately, the answer to the question was unequivocally

Vincent, and there was no way in hell she was telling Anna that. So instead, she tried to play dumb and hoped that Anna would lose interest in the topic.

The grin on Anna's face scared her to death. "Fine, we'll start small. Do you like tall men or short?"

"Tall." Lexi began scanning the restaurant for the emergency exits.

"Interesting. Okay, what about build? Do you like a muscular man like Sean or say someone thinner like Erik?"

"Um, I don't know. I guess Erik-ish." Lexi sucked down a big swig of her iced tea and contemplated pulling the fire alarm.

"M-hmm." Anna tapped her finger on her chin and thought about her next questions. "Open book or puzzle?"

"Puzzle," Lexi gritted out when she saw Anna's exuberant smile.

"Okay, strong silent type or outgoing center of attention?"

"Silent. I like the silent type, Anna. You might want to try that right now."

"Pfft." Anna waved her hand dismissively into the air. "Unlike my *brother*," she winked, "I don't do silent, sorry."

Lexi glanced over her shoulder and wondered if she could make it to the door before Anna caught up with her. She'd have to take a cab back to the office, but it would be worth it if she could avoid the Spanish Inquisition. "So, how is Madison?" Lexi desperately tried to change the topic.

"She's wonderful. Do you like blonds?"

"No." Lexi buried her hands in her face, sensing she was going in for the kill.

"Eye color?" Lexi peeked through her fingers and gave her a warning glare. "I'll answer for you—green."

"Anna, listen..."

The waitress brought their appetizer just then, and Lexi was thankful for the interruption in conversation. She stabbed a bite of their chicken appetizer, dipped it into the spicy sauce, and then popped it into her mouth.

"Are you in love with my brother?"

Lexi choked on the tiny hunk of chicken. It flew out of her mouth and onto the white tablecloth beside her. The curry, of course, went right up her nose and tears streamed down her face as she gulped for air.

"Too spicy?" Anna asked innocently as she picked at the chicken on her plate.

"Wh-what," Lexi took a sip to wash the rest of the wasabi out of her system, but she knew her cheeks were still fire engine red, "what did you say?"

"It's a simple question."

"Are you crazy?" Lexi fanned herself with her napkin. "Is it hot in here?"

Anna shook her head wordlessly and continued grinning, waiting for Lexi to answer.

"I had a crush on him in high school, Anna. That was ages ago."

"That's nothing new. I knew that back then. You zoned out every time he walked by. But I didn't ask about high school. I'm asking about now. Right now. Are you in love with Vincent?"

"He has a girlfriend. One who at this second is still wrapped around him like spandex on a hooker and would love nothing more than to obliterate me from the planet Earth."

Anna took a long sip of her tea. "She's on her way out."

"Really?" Lexi asked in disbelief. "Because they looked pretty tight this morning, and I keep finding them huddled together in these intimate conversations."

It was Anna's turn to look uncomfortable. "Things aren't always what they seem."

"Explain that."

"I can't. And besides, this isn't about Vincent. It's about you."

"It's about me? Then fine. I'm done talking. Let's talk about you for a while. How's Erik?"

Anna went along with Lexi's demands. "He's wonderful. He just came home from a shoot down in Cabo. Next month, we're going to Key West for a week. Mom and Dad are going to watch Madison for us. I'm really looking forward to it."

"Sounds like fun."

The waitress came over, and they placed their lunch orders. They each got something they'd never tried before and decided to share. Just when Lexi started to relax, Anna's phone chirped.

"Sorry, it might be Maddie," she said as she reached into her purse. Her momentary concern was replaced with a smug grin. "Well, isn't that sweet."

"What did Maddie say?" Lexi laughed as she took another bite of tuna.

"Actually, it's not from Maddie. It's from my brother." She flipped the phone around and showed Lexi the message.

You'd better be on your best behavior, Anna. You aren't annoying Lexi, are you?

"He's so protective of you."

"No, I just think he knows you too well." Lexi laughed and tried to downplay the message.

"I wonder what Jade was doing when he sent this? Odd that he would be thinking of you when he's out to lunch with his," Anna made a gagging sound, "girlfriend, don't ya think?"

"Anna," Lexi pleaded.

"I know. You don't want to talk about it. So, how about listening?"

When Lexi didn't object, Anna took a deep breath and launched into what she had been dying to say. "Do you love him? I really want to know the answer, but truthfully, it doesn't matter. You've changed him, Lexi. He's such a different man than he was before you started at Hunter. The only people he would ever smile and be himself around were Madison and Sean before you. He was angry all the time. And miserable. He made the rest of us want to stab ourselves some days."

"I don't see how I had anything to do with it."

"When he's with you, he's happy. That day at my house, we all saw it. When he's not with you, excuse my language, but he's a pissy little shit. And if Jade's around? Good Lord, that woman's a perpetual raincloud. Of course, she is the source of all things evil in the world."

"Okay, I have a question. Why on earth is he with Jade in the first place? He's gorgeous. He could have any woman he wanted."

"Any woman? Wait, you think he's gorgeous?" Anna leaned forward hopefully, but Lexi threw a decorative radish at her.

"Focus, Anna. Answer the question, you troublemaker."

"My guess? She gives great blo—"

"Don't say it. I'm eating."

"Fine," Anna huffed. "Her oral skills aside, I think she's someone he knows he'll never love." She stabbed her noodles and spun them around her fork.

"So he picks his relationships based on—"

"Based on who can't hurt him. If he never loves her, she can't break his heart. He went through a terrible break up with Adria. He swore he'd never do that again."

Lexi dropped her fork. "Adria Parketti?"

Anna nodded her head.

"I had no idea they dated. What happened between them? Can I ask? If you aren't comfortable …"

"It's fine, God knows he'll never tell you, and it's kind of important information for someone who lo—someone who works with him to know." Anna took a deep breath and began the story. "They met in college and were the bright stars of their class, a real design powerhouse. Adria wanted him to stay out east and have the two of them open an East Coast offshoot of Hunter that they could run themselves, basically use the Hunter contacts for their own gain. As it got closer to graduation, Vincent decided he wanted to come back home to learn the ropes from Mom. She had years of experience and wisdom our grandfather had passed down to her, so it seemed logical. Logical to everyone, that is, except Adria. She lost it when she found out."

"How long had they been together?"

"Almost two years at that point. I overheard my parents say that he had asked my mom for grandma's ring to give her after graduation. That night, they got into a huge fight, and Vincent left everything in his apartment behind, got on a plane, and came home, with only the ring and the clothes on his back."

"Poor guy." Lexi could easily imagine a conniving Adria throwing a fit and being a real piece of work.

"A few weeks later, Adria slinked into town, begging Vincent to forgive her. She even kissed up to my mother in an effort to get a job at Hunter. Long story short, he forgave her, like an idiot, Mom hired her, and Adria worked hard … for a while. Once she made enough contacts in the business, she left without a word and started her own company, taking as many Hunter clients as possible. Vincent was devastated."

"What a bitch." Lexi had seen firsthand how heartless, selfish, and deplorable Adria Parketti could be.

Anna laughed. "That's the understatement of the century. After that, he really didn't date anyone for a long time. He'd take different women to events and things like that, but Jade is the first one he's put up with long-term."

"Jade," Lexi winced just at saying her name. "I want to strangle her. And for the record, she's shady."

"Oh, I know."

The two women sat quietly, each in their own thoughts as the waitress poured them coffee. Lexi blew gently across the top of her mug and took a sip.

"So, back to my question," Anna prodded again, seeing if Lexi was ready to answer her yet. "Do you love Vincent?"

"What do you think?" Lexi turned it around so she could avoid answering.

"I think you love him so much it scares you to death. I think you love him more than anyone outside his family ever has and that you're the one person he can count on in this world to have his best interest at heart. Even above your own."

Lexi sighed. "Let's just say, hypothetically, that you're right. What good would it do? Am I supposed to wait, day after day, and watch him and Jade frolic together through life and hope someday he will snap out of it and kick her to the curb? Can you imagine how hard it is to see them together and wish it was me?" Lexi's eyes welled with tears. "When she's gone, he's so wonderful to me, and I think maybe, just maybe, he feels something for me. And then Jade flies back into town on her broomstick, and I go back to being invisible."

"Lexi, you're most definitely not invisible." Anna pulled out her phone again and waved it at her across the table. "Even if he doesn't show it, you're always on his mind."

"On his mind and in his heart are two totally different things," Lexi said sadly.

"He said you have the most beautiful smile," Anna offered. "And he loves arguing with you."

Lexi rolled her eyes. "He'd say the same about you."

"True, but he didn't kiss me like he kissed you at my house either."

Lexi went white as sheet. "You know about that?"

"Yep."

"Who else knows?"

"Everyone in my family. Vincent told us about it that night."

"Oh God, this is all just too much. I feel like I'm on this emotional roller-coaster every day. I wonder if happy Vincent or angry Vincent will show up. I wonder if Jade's going to be there and treat me like gum stuck to the bottom of her shoe, or is today a good day—one where Vincent will be playful and relaxed. Will his hand somehow find a way to brush against mine every chance he gets? Will he sweep the hair over my shoulder and brush the pad of his thumb over my cheek? Will he look at me and smile, making my stomach flutter and my blood race through my veins? I love him so much it hurts, Anna."

Anna's eyes lit up at Lexi's pained admission, but she contained her jubilance. "Why don't you come to my house for a picnic this weekend, and we'll eat some food, relax, and talk about this more." Lexi opened her mouth to protest, but Anna cut her off. "Vincent and Jade won't be there. She has a something in

Denver over the weekend and Vincent's going with her, so it'll just be the family. Madison would love to see you. She's been asking about you."

Lexi scowled at Anna, trying to hide her smile. "Not fair using Maddie to get me to come."

"I never said I was a fair woman." Anna reached for the check and slipped the waitress her credit card before Lexi could make a move. "My treat. It's the least I can do for the woman who is going to save my brother."

"Anna."

All playfulness gone, Anna grabbed her hand. "Tell me what you want. Don't tell me what think you deserve, or what's impossible, none of those excuses. What do you want, Lexi White?"

Lexi knew what she wanted; there was never any question. But thinking it in her head and saying it out loud were two totally different things. In her head it was a fantasy, a dream that wasn't based in real life. But once she said the words, it would be out there. It would be real. She thought carefully about it, then took a deep breath and whispered, "V-Vincent." When she said it, she felt like a weight was finally lifted off her shoulders. It felt good. A little louder she said, "I want Vincent." Then she corrected herself slightly. "I want Vincent to want me too."

"Excellent." Anna grabbed her purse, and together she and Lexi walked out the door of the restaurant. As they waited for the valet, Anna turned to her and grinned. "Now that you've admitted it, tell me, what the hell are you going to do about it?"

"I'm going to find out if dreams really do come true."

26

Honey, you've been running around all morning. It's a cookout. We do this at least twice a month, why are you vibrating around the house like this? You're making me nervous." Erik cornered Anna as she wiped down the table on the deck for the second time.

"I just want everything to be perfect." Anna adjusted the centerpiece, pulling off the dead leaves and tossing them onto the grass behind her.

Erik eyed his wife suspiciously. "What did you do now?"

"I'm offended at the accusation. I didn't do anything."

"Really? Because you've been acting weird for a few days now." He watched her straighten the place settings and napkins—again. "Like the cat that's swallowed the canary."

She took a deep breath and answered. "Listen, Lexi's been having a rough time of it lately. Don't ask me why because I'm not telling." She held up her hands at Erik for emphasis. "And, in case you forgot, the last time she came over, Vincent nearly sucked her face off, then acted like a boob, and she left in tears. I just want her to see we are nice, normal people. I want her to cheer up a little and feel at home when she's with us. Is that so wrong?"

Erik still wasn't convinced, but he tried shutting his mouth and went back to cleaning the grill. "No, not if you're telling the truth. But I get the feeling—"

"Mommmmy!" Madison screamed from inside. "Telephone. It's Uncle Vince."

Anna's eyebrows shot up, knowing Vincent and Jade had left town that morning. "I wonder what he wants." She looked down the driveway. "Oh, honey, Mom and Dad just got here. Go help them. Dad's going to try and drag that cooler over here all by himself."

They could hear Elizabeth yelling. "Just ask one of the boys to help you. That thing is full of ice. Erik can do it."

"I got it," Robert insisted as he balanced the large cooler precariously on the trunk of the car.

"Throw out your back and you're sleeping on the couch, tough guy," Elizabeth warned, and then took off toward the house. "Or, if you have a heart attack and die, I'm going to *kill* you. Erik, go help your father-in-law before he's sprawled out in your lawn and we have to call the squad."

With a chuckle and a wave of her hand, Anna ushered Erik outside to help Robert maneuver the cooler to the back porch. When the men finally made it into the house, Anna and Elizabeth were huddled together in the kitchen. "What did Vincent want?"

"Oh." Anna clapped her hands together and bounced in place. "I almost forgot. He's coming over."

"He sent Jade to Denver on her own? Thank God!" Sean smiled widely walking through the door.

"No, he's bringing her." Her upper lip rose in a snarl.

A chorus of "Ugh"s rang out through the room.

"So much for your plans of Lexi having a nice time," Erik said.

"Why can't Jade just go away? I told Vincent we can find the mole without her." Anna began violently chopping a pile of carrots.

"Is he even any closer to finding this jerkoff—I mean jerk?" Sean asked as he snagged one of Anna's carrot slices. "Doesn't seem like she's helping all that much."

Elizabeth sighed. "She claims to know someone at Reid who is watching things on that end. Vincent, I think, feels like this is his mess to clean up, that he should have figured it out before Jade of all people."

"Well, I have a feeling his big plan is going to backfire. There are too many things up in the air and a long list of suspects." Sean took a long drink from his beer. "I still think we should slam people into chairs, put a spotlight on them, and use a good old lie detector. Works in the movies."

"And it's not admissible in court. Not to mention it goes against their civil rights, dear." Elizabeth rolled her eyes and slapped his hand as he tried to steal some of Madison's strawberries, then she left the room in search of her grand-daughter. Robert followed after her.

Erik grabbed a beer and sat down on a stool between Sean and Anna. "What are we going to do about Vincent?"

Sean chuckled. "You mean how do we get Jade to get her claws out of him?"

"Exactly." He looked over at his wife, who was being extremely tight lipped. "Anna, do you have an opinion on this one?"

"You know I hate that woman with every cell in my body. She is a soul-sucking leech who is dating Vincent for her own gain and sponging off his notoriety in the community. I told you on their first date that she was trouble." Anna pointed an accusing finger at Sean. "But no, you said, and I quote, 'She's a hot. Let him have his fun,' end quote."

"In my defense," Sean held up his hands innocently, "I hadn't heard her speak when I made that comment. I was basing it solely on the hotness of her rack. Had I known the screeching bansheelike tone of her voice, I would have suggested he throw holy water on her."

They all turned when a car screeched into the driveway. Erik went over to the window and laughed. "Um, what did you do to piss off Hope now?"

Sean sprang to his feet. Anna elbowed Erik out of the way so she could watch the show. Hope was at Sean's Jeep, dumping things out of a paper bag and onto the hood of his car. She stepped back, assessed her work, then picked up something black and gently dangled it from the antenna. She headed for the house with a proud swagger in her step.

"Is that your..." Erik stared, open mouthed.

"...underwear?" Anna finished, giggling.

"Yeah, she kinda hates it when I leave my clothes on the floor."

Hope strolled in and greeted Erik and Anna, but ignored Sean completely. "Hi, Hope."

"Hello, swine." She grabbed the beer Erik offered, popped the top, and took a swig, still refusing to look at Sean.

"I forgot," he pleaded.

"Bull. You remembered to bring the beer here. You remembered to TiVo that soccer game. But the laundry—that you had to step over to get to the bathroom—you forgot, right? Please."

"Baby."

"Don't *baby* me or there will be more than your underwear hanging from that antenna out there. *Capisce?* I know people."

Sean grinned and wrapped his arms around Hope. "You know I love it when you go all Sopranos on me, right? You're so sexy when you're mad."

Hope elbowed him in the gut. "So that's why you piss me off all the time?"

"Yep."

"Swine."

"Oink, oink." He nuzzled her neck and gave her behind a hard smack.

"I have no idea why I hang around you." She went over and sat down. "Thanks for inviting me, Anna."

"Thanks for the entertainment. So, when is Lexi getting here? I thought you two would ride over together."

"We were going to, but she went into the office this morning and never came back. She called and said she'd meet me here. I can't wait until they finish this cosmetics ad. She's driving me nuts!"

"Yeah, Vincent's been a real joy too. They have good ideas, but they don't have a spectacular one that will blow the roof off of it, and that's what's driving him crazy. He's such a perfectionist." Sean rolled his eyes.

"Poor Lexi spent her Saturday at the office and now she has to come here and deal with the she-viper."

"Wait, Jade's coming? I thought they were out of town." Hope quirked an eyebrow at Sean, but his somber expression told the tale. "Awesome!" A wide grin spread on her face.

Erik choked. "You're excited about seeing Jade? I think he might have driven you mad."

"Oh, I have been dying to meet this witch. If she steps out of line with my girl, I might just have to take her out."

Sean turned to Erik and grabbed his arm. "Man, please tell me you have Maddie's baby pool and a boatload of Jell-O," he pleaded with Erik, earning a dirty look from both Hope and Anna. "Jeez, it was just a suggestion."

"So, what do I need to know about her before she gets here?"

"She's psychotic."

"She's the devil incarnate."

"Her breasts are lopsided," Erik offered with a shrug. "I have photographed her, ya know. We had to touch them up for the cover we worked on."

They were all still laughing when Elizabeth walked back into the house. Robert stayed outside with Madison, pushing her on the swing. "Hello, Hope, good to see you again. Do I even want to know what you're all hysterical about?" She gave Hope a quick hug and went back to the sink to gather up the corn that needed to be peeled.

Through his laughter Sean told her, "Jade's breasts."

Elizabeth's eyes grew huge then she shook her head and laughed. "I'm going back outside with your father and Maddie. They're talking about caterpillars. That's more my speed. She wants to know if she can go in the pool, Anna."

"Sure, Mom, that's fine. Her swimsuit's in the pool house along with towels if you and Dad want to go in too."

When the laughter finally died down, they were back at square one. "How long until the walking buzzkill arrives?" Sean asked, wrapping his arm around Hope's shoulders and kissing the top of her head.

"Vincent said they're gonna be late, of course. Apparently, their flight was delayed because of mechanical trouble and by the time they would have gotten out there, they would have missed the red carpet. Jade threw a hissy fit at the airport and said there was no point in even going now, so they came home."

"It's all about the red carpet with her, isn't it? I wonder if she has one leading up to her door." Erik snickered.

"Why does he go out with her? I mean, Lexi would be so much better for him," Hope said, shaking her head.

"Wait, does Lexi even like Vincent?" Sean asked, truly surprised. "I know *he* has a little crush on *her*. They did suck face and all, but I didn't know she felt the same way."

Erik laughed out loud at him. "You and Vincent are so blind sometimes." He leaned down and whispered to Sean. "And for the record, it's no little crush. I get the feeling his crush is a rather big one."

Anna stood up when she heard another car pull in the driveway. A second later, a loud scream came from the backyard. "Lexi's here!" Madison's squeals of delight were followed by loud splashing noise.

"Hi, Maddie! Having fun in the pool?" Lexi's voice came in through the open window. Anna smiled as she watched Lexi hug the soaking wet little girl who had launched herself into her arms. She carried her toward the water where Robert and Elizabeth were waiting.

"She's such a good person," Anna said wistfully as she turned away from the window, a look of determination on her face. "We need to get rid of Jade."

"I got duct tape in the car," Hope offered.

"I know a guy," Sean smirked.

"We just need Vincent to make a move," Anna said. The backdoor opened and Lexi's head popped in, her long brown hair falling over her shoulders, sunglasses perched on top of her head. She was wearing a black string bikini with a towel wrapped around her waist.

"Hi, guys. Anna, do you need any help? Maddie has kinda kidnapped me and wants me to swim." Lexi smiled and waved at Hope, nodding toward the cars. "Nice work, by the way."

"Thanks."

"Go swim. I've got everything under control." Anna waved her hand and ushered her back outside.

"Is anyone else coming in the pool?" Lexi asked before she ducked back outside.

"We'll be out in a few minutes." Anna grinned.

Erik and Sean snickered. "This should be interesting."

"What's so funny?" Anna asked, looking back and forth between the two.

Sean shrugged. "Nothing, we just can't wait to see Vincent's face when he gets a load of Lexi in that bikini, or Jade's for that matter." The pair high fived each other and laughed.

"Come on." Anna laced her arm with Erik's. "Let's go save poor Lexi from our daughter and have some fun before Satan's whore arrives."

The pool was cool and refreshing, a wonderful contrast to the humidity of the sunny afternoon. Madison kept everyone entertained with her flips, dives, and cannonballs, loving the attention of the doting adults. Sean and Erik took turns throwing her high into the air so she could splash down in the pool, a wave spilling over the side and drenching the girls where they were trying to sunbathe. After a few death threats, the men got out of the water and started the grill.

"Who wants a margarita?" Anna asked as she held the kitchen door open. Lexi's and Hope's hands shot up immediately, and Elizabeth's joined theirs after some thought. "I'm not making a virgin one for you, Mom. You're having tequila. I don't even care if you dance on the table this time."

Anna began prepping the glasses with salt. As she cut the limes into wedges, she heard doors slam out front. "Cue the wicked witch music," she mumbled.

Anna opened the side door to greet her brother and his girlfriend.

"Oh Lord, margaritas? I hope you're making Mom a virgin." Vincent came in and kissed Anna on the cheek, handing her a bottle of wine. Jade was yapping on her phone and gave a bored, two fingered wave from the doorway.

"I can't turn back the hands of time. Mom's days as a virgin are long gone." He helped her put the finishing touches on the drinks before Anna thrust the glasses into his hands. "Go give these to Hope and Lexi. They're out by the pool." He craned his neck to look out the back window. "She's in the black string bikini, in case you couldn't tell." Anna nudged him in the shoulder and tried not to laugh when his eyebrows shot up in surprise.

"Jade," Vincent tried repeatedly to invite her out back but she waved him off and went back out onto the driveway, probably for better reception. "Never mind, then. Anything else you want me to take out?"

"Nope." Anna grinned.

Vincent balanced the drinks and took the first one to Hope, who was sitting in the shade, flipping through a magazine. She pointed toward Lexi, who was lying on her back in the sun, her skin glistening with the shimmer of suntan oil and sweat. Her black sunglasses were pulled down over her eyes, a perfect little pout on her lips.

Vincent slowly walked up behind her, his body casting a long shadow over her as she lay in the lounge chair. He knew she was beautiful, but had no idea just how spectacular her body was until he saw it lying before him like an offering. Every inch of her skin was perfect, like porcelain as it contrasted the dark color of her swimsuit. The swells of her breasts and the curves of her hips screamed to be touched. As he stood there, frozen in place, he fought the urge to reach out and run his hands over her skin, just to feel the softness under his fingertips.

"Sean, Jesus, you're like a solar eclipse. Move, I'm trying to get so—" Lexi whipped off her sunglasses and spun around, squinting her eyes from the bright sunlight until she saw Vincent smiling at her. "Vincent." His name came out in a rush of breath. "Wh-what are you…"

"Change of plans." He offered her the drink from his hand. "Your drink, miss."

Lexi took the drink and set it down on the small table beside her. "Nice cabana service Anna has here," she joked. He slid onto the lounge chair beside her and stole her sunglasses off her head.

"What did I miss?" he asked as Maddie came running over to him and crawled into his lap.

"You missed my cannonballs, Uncle Vincent. I got Grandma all wet," Madison bragged.

"I'm so sorry I missed that." He kissed the top of his niece's head.

"Did you bring your swimsuit?" Maddie asked hopefully.

"Yep."

"Go change and I'll show you again." Madison hopped back onto the ground, tossed her towel on the deck, and jumped into the water. "Come on, Uncle Vincent, hurry."

Lexi laughed. "You better hurry, or she's going to start jumping and you'll be wet anyway."

Vincent smiled at Lexi and slipped her sunglasses back over her eyes. "Thanks for letting me borrow these." He brushed his fingers over her cheek, then took off for the pool house, stripping off his shirt as he walked away. He didn't see Lexi and Hope mouth "nice" to each other when he disappeared through the doorway.

He quickly changed and joined his niece in the pool. Soon her laughter rang out followed by an enormous splash. A fraction of a second later, a huge wave of water slammed into Lexi's chair. She bolted straight up and brushed the dripping hair from her face.

"Oh, Lexi, I'm sorry," Vincent said as he quickly swam to the edge of the pool, pulling himself out and trying not to laugh. "I swear I didn't mean to get you wet."

Lexi opened her eyes and found a bare-chested Vincent standing before her, dripping and glistening with water. She seemed to temporarily loose her ability to speak, but shook her head from side to side, bringing herself out of her daze. "No worries, it's a pool party. People get wet." She craned her neck around his body. "Go, Madison's waiting for you."

Vincent squatted down beside her chair and put his hand on her bare thigh. "I really am sorry."

Lexi flipped her sunglasses up so he could see her eyes and know she was being sincere. "I know. Really, it's fine. I'm not going to melt. Go swim."

"Thanks. You really are the best." He gave her leg a squeeze and turned to face the pool.

Madison bounced up and down in the water, describing what kind of jump she wanted him to do. Just as Vincent leaned toward the pool to hear Madison better, Lexi gave him a big shove in the back and sent him flying into the pool with a splash.

When he surfaced, Sean was howling. "Nice scream, Vince."

"That was a perfect belly flop, Uncle Vincent," Madison offered, giggling as he wiped the water from his face.

Lexi stood at the edge of the pool, grinning proudly. "I didn't know you could fly."

In one massive lunge, Vincent flung himself at the edge of the pool and grabbed her ankle, holding her in place. "You wanna fly too, Lexi?" He grinned and gave a sharp tug on her foot. Lexi leaned dangerously far over the water, but regained her balance at the last second.

"Vincent Drake, you let her go this instant." Elizabeth's voice cut through the laughter.

"But, Mom, she pushed me."

"Vincent, you will not fling one of our guests into the pool. Let her go."

"Yeah, Vincent, let me go." Lexi playfully wiggled her ankle in circles trying to escape. "Your mom said so."

"This isn't fair," Vincent grumbled as he let go. Lexi couldn't resist sticking her tongue out at him. When he pulled his hand back to splash her, she screamed and ran back toward Elizabeth's chair and hid.

"Don't you dare, or your company car will be mine, young man."

Vincent and Madison finished up their time in the pool and climbed into a pair of chairs and dried off in the sun. Anna, Hope, and Lexi began setting out the food as Sean and Erik pulled it off the grill.

"Vincent, you better have sunscreen on or you'll be the poster boy for skin cancer," Jade's voice screeched from the doorway. She had finally ended her phone call and decided to join the rest of them. She wore a long sleeved swim cover up, an oversized hat, and large sunglasses to prevent a single ray of sun from touching her skin.

"He's a grown man. I think he can handle this himself," Anna snarled, in no mood for Jade and her dramatics.

"Ten minutes worth of ultraviolet exposure ages your skin a year. You might not care about how he looks, but I do."

"You little—" Hope grabbed Anna by the arm and held her in place. When Anna regained her composure she smiled. "You're absolutely right, Jade. Lexi, would you be a dear and go rub some lotion on my brother? I wouldn't want him to burn."

"I'd love to," Lexi grabbed the sunscreen and glanced over at Vincent. "Think I should get his chest too?"

"Absolutely." Anna grinned as Jade's teeth clamped shut.

"Lucky for you," Lexi said a moment later as she placed the lotion back on the table, never breaking eye contact with Jade, "I have more class than that."

"Here, Jade, go graze on some salad. There's a nice shady spot way over there." Hope pointed to the opposite side of the pool.

"Want a wiener, Jadey?" Sean asked, suggestively dangling a hot dog from the end of a pair of tongs as Jade walked past.

As the thick stick of beef bobbed in her face, Jade snarled. "Keep your wieners to yourself."

"Let me know if you change your mind, Jadey. I'll save this big juicy one just for you."

Vincent wandered over to talk to Jade, but she waved him away and pulled out a magazine and began flipping through the pages with a scowl on her face. Vincent rolled his eyes and grabbed a plate of food. Lexi tossed him a cold beer to go along with it.

"Thanks." He leaned back against the rail beside her and began eating.

"No problem," Lexi said softly. "So, why are you even here? I thought you two were heading out of town for the weekend."

He shook his head. "We were ready to leave, but the flight was delayed. Jade had a tantrum at the airport, and then there was no point in going. So, we came over here instead. I'm glad we did." He nudged her with his leg and smiled.

A beautiful smile spread across her face. "I'm glad you're here too." As they stood together in comfortable silence, a camera clicked and Lexi's head whipped around to find Erik, grinning from across the deck. "Does he always do that?"

"Snap covert pictures at family functions? Yeah. You'll get used to it after a while." Vincent held up two fingers behind Lexi's head and gave her bunny ears as Erik snapped his next shot.

Lexi glanced over at Jade and saw her snarling in their direction. "You better go sit with The Mummy. She looks a little testy."

Vincent leaned over and whispered in her ear, "She's always testy," and then walked away.

✦

The rest of the afternoon went smoothly. Madison took Lexi on a walk through Anna's garden, pointing out all the vegetables they had planted and which ones she liked and which ones she didn't. Erik continued lurking, snapping pictures now and then. Vincent and Jade sat in the shade, Vincent reading the newspaper and Jade reapplying her many layers of makeup and perfecting her hair.

Finally, it was time for dessert, and Lexi and Hope went inside to help Anna with the pies she had made.

"Here, can you cut this one and then just put them onto these plates." Anna handed Lexi a large knife and a serving piece to scoop out the pie. "I made a cherry, an apple, and a blueberry."

"Are you sure you want me to do this? I tend to be all thumbs on these things." Lexi cautiously picked up the knife and plunged it into the cherry pie.

"It's pie, not brain surgery," Erik teased, his camera at the ready to get a clear shot when Lexi made a fool of herself.

"I want a big piece," Sean yelled as he strode into the kitchen with a picture perfect Jade and a hungry Vincent following close behind.

Lexi cut the pie and put a generous piece onto a plate for Sean. She grinned triumphantly as she handed it to him, ridiculously proud that it was still in one piece and not on the floor.

"What's this?" Sean wrinkled his nose at it. "That's a mouse-sized piece. I need nourishment, woman."

"Glutton," Jade hissed from the corner, loud enough for Hope to hear it.

"Why don't you go forage around the backyard for some sticks or something healthy to munch on, Jade?" Hope glared at her, daring Jade to say another word. When Jade opened her mouth to reply, Hope took a step toward her and she shut it with a squeak and grabbed Vincent's arm for support. "I'm watching you," Hope snarled in her direction.

"Here, I'll get you a man-sized piece." Hope grabbed the knife from Lexi and quickly cut a huge hunk of pie for Sean. As she tried to balance it on the tiny serving piece, it flipped up into the air and splattered onto the floor at her feet. Lexi and Hope threw back their heads and laughed. Erik rapidly snapped pictures of the entire incident.

"Oh my, let me get something to clean that up with," Elizabeth said as she reached for the roll of paper towels.

"I got it, Elizabeth, but thank you. I'm the idiot who dropped it." Hope blushed and grabbed the towels from her so she could get the mess off of Anna's floor as soon as possible. "Quit your laughing, Sean, and help me." She grabbed his arm and dragged him onto the floor.

"Tell me you got a shot of the pie in the air," Vincent said as he came over to see the pictures Erik had shot. Everyone except Jade stood huddled around his camera for a peek.

"Let me just put them on my laptop," Erik said as he pulled over his computer and slipped the memory card in. The pictures quickly downloaded and had everyone in stitches again. "I'll blow this one up for you, Hope." Erik pointed to one where Hope's mouth was hanging open in shock as the pie sailed past her.

"Gee thanks." She rolled her eyes and grabbed a plate of pie that Anna had cut up for them. "Maddie, let's go eat our pie on the porch!"

"Can I come too?" Sean asked, trailing behind the pair.

"I'm not sharing my pie, Uncle Sean," Madison teased. When he playfully growled at her, she ran out the door laughing.

Jade's phone chirped, and she vanished again, leaving Vincent to his pie, which he enjoyed so much he began cutting another.

"Tsk, tsk," Lexi offered from across the kitchen as she caught him slipping the generous piece of apple pie onto his plate.

"Pie makes me happy." He shrugged unapologetically.

"Mm-hmm." Lexi watched him savor every bite while keeping one eye out for Jade. "Chicken," she whispered at him as he hid the pie when Jade glanced in the window.

"Erik, dear, these pictures are lovely," Elizabeth said loudly from across the room as she kept flipping through them on his computer.

"I got some good ones of you and Dad by the pool. They're a little further back, let me show you." Erik went over to help Elizabeth.

"So, any brilliance on Marradesi?" Vincent asked as he put his empty plate in the sink. "Sean said you went into the office today."

"I did, but no. I just feel like we're missing something, you know? Something right in front of our faces." Lexi folded her arms across her chest and leaned against the counter, looking at Vincent.

"Do you think we should scrap what we have and just start over?"

"Again?" Lexi asked in surprise. "I don't think we have enough time to do a floor-to-ceiling revamping of this one. Don't forget we have Julian's fashion show coming up. We need to finish his last minute stuff before then."

Vincent sighed. "You're right. It's just so frustrating because I know it's not there yet."

Lexi put an encouraging arm around his shoulder. "Don't worry, you'll get it. I have faith in you."

They both seemed to pause and savor the brief physical contact until they were pulled from their spell by Elizabeth's cheerful squeal. "Do you see it?" She smacked Erik in the arm.

He pointed at the screen. "The carefree smiles, the background figure, one adoring, one furious. I see where you're going with it."

"And look, everyday beauty wins out over this." Elizabeth flicked her finger at the screen and was giddy as she waved Vincent and Lexi over. When they were standing behind her, she moved her hand and unveiled the picture.

The photo must have been taken seconds after the pie hit the ground because the slice wasn't anywhere in the shot. Lexi and Hope were beautiful, natural, with their hair flowing loosely over their shoulders and carefree smiles on their faces. In the background were Vincent and Jade. Vincent had a secretive smile and his eyes locked on Lexi, his face full of adoring wonder. Lexi felt her cheeks blush as she stared at the shot. Next to Vincent was Jade, the picture of trend-inspired perfection. Every hair was in place, her eyes lined and lips painted flawlessly, and yet she may as well have been invisible. Everything about Vincent's body language showed how drawn he was to Lexi. Jade stood completely alone in the group.

"This?" Lexi squeaked out, holding a shaky finger at the screen. "What is it?"

"The new Marradesi campaign," Vincent murmured as his breath left him. "This is *it*."

Elizabeth turned around like a proud mama. "Good boy, you see it, right? Think big picture."

"The power of natural beauty, inner beauty. Effortless perfection. Trends come and go, but bring out the beauty from within. So naturally beautiful that the men won't even see the other women in the room, no matter how put together and made-up, only you. Not overdone or fake; real and true, just like the women who wear it. Perfect, just like you." His eyes left the screen and went to Lexi, who was standing open-mouthed beside him.

"Yes," Elizabeth exclaimed. "I think Paolo and Francesca will love it. In Europe they are the 'it' brand, known for being avant-garde, but I think here in the States they want to go in another direction." Elizabeth got up and grabbed paper, and she and Vincent walked off to the table.

Lexi heard them talking, but her eyes stayed fixed on the computer screen in front of her as she studied the picture. She and Hope were laughing in the foreground, and Jade was lurking in the background, pissed off, big surprise. But Lexi couldn't stop staring at Vincent's face in the picture. He was looking at her, not her and Hope together, just her, like she was the only person on Earth.

Erik looked over his shoulder and noticed what Lexi was staring at. He put his hand on her arm. "The camera never lies. I know you can see it. He will too, someday."

Tears welled into Lexi's eyes but she refused to let them fall. "Sure, Erik," she said, unconvinced.

"Really?" He arched his eyebrow and began flipping through more pictures that he had taken today. "Maybe you should look at the rest of these." There was one of Lexi and Madison in the garden. Over Lexi's shoulder, there was Vincent, standing at the edge of the deck, watching her. There was another from when Lexi was making a plate for Robert, and Vincent watched her adoringly as she kissed Robert on the cheek. The last one was her sunbathing while Vincent was on the other side of the pool, peeking at her over the top of his newspaper. The look in his eyes was not playful or adoring, it was lustful and hungry, the way a man looks at a woman he wants in his bed.

"Now do you see it?"

Erik flipped to one last picture. It was the two of them standing against the rail of the deck, eating and laughing. Their bodies were touching, their faces turned toward one another. They were, in that picture, the perfect couple. "*This* is what I see when I look at the two of you." Erik smiled. "And it's beautiful."

Lexi didn't trust herself to speak, so she simply nodded. Then she heard Vincent call out to her.

"Lexi, I need you."

27

Monday morning, Lexi arrived at Hunter ready to work. They finally knew where they were going with the Marradesi account, and after numerous E-mails back and forth on Sunday, she and Vincent were focused and ready to work out the remaining details.

Jade had had a fit when she saw the picture that Elizabeth insisted be the focus of the campaign, and when Sean pointed out that at least she'd get to be in the print ad, she went storming to Vincent's car. She stayed there and pouted until Vincent came out and took her home.

As Lexi poured herself a cup of coffee, Vincent snuck up behind her.

"Lexi, I need you."

"Jesus, give me a heart attack, why don't ya? I swear I'm going to tie a bell around your neck." She saw what was in his hand and nearly passed out. "What the hell is that?"

"This?" Vincent held up a poster sized blowup of Erik's photograph. "It's for the presentation boards."

"Can't we reshoot it with professional models?"

"Eventually, yes, but we're in a crunch, so no, not right now. We use this and go with it. Once they sign as clients, we'll talk about it, but I think you and Hope look absolutely beautiful. Besides, professional models would look too posed."

Lexi stared at the picture again, trying not to focus on the way Vincent was looking at her in it. It was too much to take in. "Fine, but keep it in your office. That thing creeps me out."

Laughing, Vincent went into his office to get settled in. Lexi began returning E-mails. There were quite a few for Vincent from Julian and Christina about the upcoming fashion show. This week was going to be a busy one for everyone at Hunter.

In the middle of the day, Vincent stuck his head out the door. "Lexi, when you get a minute, I need to talk to you about something important." His teasing tone from earlier in the day was gone. It was all-business Vincent asking for her time. His features were tightly drawn, tension radiating off of him.

A sense of dread washed over Lexi. "Sure, give me a second to finish this up."

"Actually, I need to speak with you now, and if that's the Excalibur file on your desk, bring it with you." He pointed at the pile of papers beside her hand and held the door open wide.

Lexi logged off of the computer, grabbed her desk keys and the file, and sat down on Vincent's couch, waiting for the bad news. Her stomach dropped when he began pacing the room. Pacing was never a good thing where Vincent was concerned. When he sat down beside her, Lexi felt like she might throw up.

"Did I do something wrong?" she asked.

"What?" Vincent was caught off guard by her question. "No, of course not."

"Really, you can tell me, Vincent. I can take it. No need to sugar coat things. If I did something—"

Very abruptly, Vincent exploded. "Not everything is about you, Lexi."

"Okay, thanks for biting my head off." Lexi's eyes threatened to fill with tears, but she turned her face toward the window so Vincent wouldn't see.

"Damn it." Vincent tipped his head back to look at the ceiling. He took a deep breath and told her the truth. "Someone at Hunter is leaking our ideas to the competition and costing us millions in accounts."

Lexi's head spun so quickly she was surprised her neck didn't snap. "What? Who? Tony?" She immediately slammed her hand over her mouth, unable to believe she'd accused his cousin of corporate thievery.

"I wish I could say you're wrong, but I honestly have no idea." He was back on his feet and began his usual path across the office, and then spun and retraced his steps.

"Do you have any idea which accounts?"

"Well, I think we both know they tried on the Stone account, but we got lucky on that one. Then there was the Keller account, and I'm going to venture a guess that we lost the Garcia account over it too. God, do you know how stupid I looked every time I walked into an office and gave what appeared to be a recycled presentation?" Vincent clenched his hands into fists and thrust them deep into his pockets as if to keep from punching the wall.

"Let's think about this." All Vincent's pacing made Lexi nervous, so she too began walking her own route around the room, occasionally bumping into Vincent, who was deep in thought. "Can I ask how you found this out? Who's the source?"

Vincent had a guilty look on his face as he answered. "That really doesn't matter. The fact is the information is good." Lexi watched him shrug then continue around his desk, closing that topic.

Suddenly all the meetings the previous week made sense to Lexi. He'd been fishing for information. "So, what do you need me to do? How can I help you?" she immediately asked.

"I really don't deserve you," Vincent muttered as he sat down at his desk and put his face in his hands. He took a deep breath and his head popped up. "Give me the file."

Lexi slid into a nearby chair and handed him the Excalibur file.

"This client might seem like small potatoes right now, but I happen to know that Mr. Johnson has connections, and this line of watches is getting huge celebrity buzz and is looking to go very big very fast. He's a family friend, so I really want to hit this out of the park for him. If we can snag this account now and look a little bit to the future in the presentation, this could be a huge money maker for Hunter. But we have to blow everyone away with our campaign."

Lexi's brow furrowed together in confusion. "I'm not following. What does this client have to do with catching the mole?"

Vincent sighed. "I want you to work on this, only you and me. I can't risk anyone leaking this information. Not the long term plans of Excalibur or our concepts, none of it. Only three people know about Excalibur's big plans. Two of the three are sitting in this room. Mr. Johnson is the other."

Lexi examined the file he handed her. In it was his initial presentation plan. The idea was brilliant. She quickly scanned the documents and understood the direction he wanted to take this project. "What do we need for the initial meeting?"

"I have a PowerPoint in there. I need you to fact check it and clean it up. I've stared at it too long, and I know it's sloppy in places. It needs a fresh set of eyes on it. If you think something needs to be changed, just do it. We aren't going to do a full presentation. He wants a brief concept outline and a small mock up ad, which I will work on myself." He shrugged when Lexi looked at him in surprise. "Fewer eyes on this the better."

"When do we need this done by?"

"Sunday." Vincent smiled apologetically when Lexi's face went white. "Really, I've done most of the leg work on this, I just need you to polish it up and make it better. And keep a lid on it. Everything stays locked up tight."

"I can handle that. Who else is presenting to him? Are Parketti or Reid?" Lexi asked, trying to get a handle on what direction this mole might be coming from.

"I know Reid is, and I bet Adria will also be presenting since she met him years ago when we were dating. He liked her then, so I assume she has weaseled into this as well."

"And we've lost accounts to both of them, right, not just Reid?" Lexi was on her feet, tapping her pencil against her thigh as she walked the room.

"Yeah. Like I said, whoever this is, is giving information to a number of sources. It's not like Person A here at Hunter is feeding everything to Person B at Reid. Whoever this is has lots of shady contacts and is working them to the fullest." He began rubbing his temples slowly.

The exhaustion she had been seeing in his face all week suddenly made sense. She couldn't imagine the amount of stress he was under with all of this happening at the same time as the launch of the Stone campaign and while they were still trying to nail down Marradesi.

"I'm sorry," Lexi said softly as she watched Vincent lean back in his chair and stare at the ceiling. He looked so hollow, so stressed.

"For what?" He shot up out of his chair and walked over to the window.

She went over and stood beside him. "Because this has to be awful, wondering who has been lying to your face."

He turned and peered into her eyes, his own full of sadness. "I really should be used to it by now, but yeah, it's the worst, because it could be anybody." Vincent turned his head back toward the window, pressing his forehead against the glass.

"I'm going to get to work on this and give you some space." She rubbed her hand across his back. "If you need me, let me know."

He reached out and grabbed her hand before she walked away and squeezed it as if his life depended on it. "Thanks."

Lexi went out to her desk and got right to work on the Excalibur account, wanting to make sure everything was perfect for Vincent. There was no way in hell she was letting this one get away from them. He had been so gracious in teaching her everything he knew. She was overwhelmed by his generosity and wanted to do this for him and in some small way repay him for everything.

It was well into the afternoon, and Lexi was starting to feel a headache coming on when Tony strutted into the room. "What, no cape today, Supergirl?"

It was hard to resist slapping the smug grin off his face. His behavior was always so suspicious that she wanted to pin him to the ground and force him to confess. Even more horrific was that he was doing this to his own family. How he could do that to such good people baffled Lexi.

As subtly as possible, she flipped off her monitor and hid the stack of papers she had been working on. She felt Tony's beady eyes following her every movement. "Do you have an appointment?" she asked, making sure she sounded as unenthused as she felt.

"When are you going to get it through that thick head of yours that I don't need an appointment?" He angrily held up the boards in his hand. "These are my appointment card with him whenever I feel like it. You better remember that, or else."

"Or else what?" Lexi rose to her feet and planted her hand on her hip. "Are you threatening me? What exactly are you going to do?"

Tony glanced down at the file she had tried to hide. "What's that? Were you doodling my cousin's name in a heart? Everyone knows you have the hots for him." He looked her up and down, his lips pulled into a lecherous sneer. "You've got a great body, I'll give you that, and the whole Girl Friday thing is probably really hot for Vincent, but Jade's some stiff competition. She *is* a supermodel."

"So I've heard," Lexi said through gritted teeth.

"I'm just saying she fights dirty. Wonder what she'd do if she knew you were going after her man."

"Jade's paranoia is nothing new. She isn't a very rational individual."

Tony raised his eyebrows in surprise. "Look at you, openly talking trash about Jade. My, you must really feel comfortable in your position here to talk so freely against Vincent's girlfriend. That, or you're already screwing him."

"How I feel about Jade has nothing to do with my work at Hunter, which is all Vincent's interested in, and he's given me an assignment which I need to work on, so this conversation is over."

Tony tucked the presentation boards under his arm and leaned over her desk. "Watch yourself, Lexi. That pretty little mouth of yours just might get you into a whole world of trouble."

She grabbed the phone to buzz Vincent, but Tony was faster. As Vincent's phone rang, Tony knocked on the door. "Vincent, it's me."

"Tony," Lexi hissed into the phone, hoping Vincent heard and would hide any confidential information, then hung up.

"What?" Tony swung around hearing his name.

"Um, would you like some coffee?" Lexi asked, quickly trying to cover.

"As if I'd drink anything *you* made for me. I'm not looking to be poisoned."

Lexi shrugged. "Suit yourself." She glanced at her desk, hoping enough time had passed. "Vincent will see you now."

Five minutes after Tony went inside Vincent's office, he left without another word to Lexi. Vincent stepped out not long after and made another cup of coffee. "So, Tony was exceptionally snippy just now."

"Good." Lexi shuffled the papers around on her desk, and then looked up and found Vincent standing over her, smiling. "What? I piss off Tony somehow and that cheers you up?"

"It's the little things you do that mean the most."

Lexi stuck her finger in her mouth and pretended to gag. "Thank you, Mr. Hallmark."

"Are you in the middle of something important, or can I grab you for a few minutes?"

"Mr. Drake, I don't think that would be appropriate," Lexi laughed.

He rolled his eyes. "Get in my office, now."

"Yes, boss." Lexi saluted and turned off her computer. She slipped any important files into her drawer and locked them up tight, then followed him into his office.

Vincent sat down behind his desk, Lexi taking her usual spot on the couch. "Did you have a chance to look at anything Tony brought up or did you just spend your time verbally abusing him?"

"Are you serious? Do you know what he said to me?" Lexi jumped to her feet, furious that he would accuse her of that until she saw his satisfied grin.

She stalked over to his desk and snatched up the boards. "Don't make me have to hurt you today, pal. What am I looking at? Oh God, more pictures of me? I bet my face is on the dart board down in productions."

"If it wasn't before, I'm sure it is now," Vincent teased.

"Shut it. Okay, what do you want me to see here?"

"I need to begin scripting the presentation with some inspiration from this picture. So, look at it and tell me what you see."

"My hair is stringy, I hate the blouse I'm wearing, and, wow, Hope's breasts look spectacular!"

"Really?" Vincent craned his neck to look at the picture, and Lexi smacked him on the head with the board.

"Such a man."

"One hundred percent testosterone, baby." Vincent grinned wickedly at her, his darkened eyes lingering on her lips just long enough to make her blush. "Now that we've established my manliness, back to the picture."

"Your hair looks nice."

"Again, stay away from the obvious and look deeper. What's there in the background of it all?"

"A really pissed off Jade."

Vincent gave her a droll stare. "I need emotions. What does it evoke, what do you see?"

"A really pissed off Jade."

"Okay, let's start there. The woman in the background is pissed off. Why?" Vincent started taking notes on his paper, watching Lexi's head cock to the side as she examined the photo.

"Um, because she's perfect yet isn't the center of attention." Lexi heard his pen scribble across the paper.

"Keep going. Who would you say *is* the center of attention in the picture?"

"Well, Ho—I mean, the two women in the foreground seem to be getting the most attention.

Vincent's head popped up. "Really? Is that what you see?"

"Sure, look how they are the focus of the picture, front and center, shoulder to shoulder." Lexi pointed to the two of them so Vincent could understand what she was talking about.

He thoughtfully ran his hand over his chin, then went over to the couch and sat down beside Lexi, taking the picture from her. She held her breath as she felt his arm slide around the back of the couch behind her. He leaned closer and held the picture between the two of them. "When I look at it, I only see one person as the center of attention in this photograph." His voice was low, his warm breath caressing her cheek.

His body was everywhere, the warmth he generated blanketing her as she sat beside him. She felt strangely protected. "Well, you're pretty central in the picture too, I'll give you that, but I think—" She stopped speaking when she felt his free hand wrap around her shoulder and brush up and down her arm.

"Lexi," His darkened eyes pierced hers. "Not the man. He's completely secondary in this. The focus of the picture is the beautiful brunette, right here." She half expected so see his finger pointing at Jade, but when she saw her face as the one he was talking about, her eyes grew huge with surprise.

"Me?"

"She is the star of this photo. The man doesn't even see anyone but her. Look at him. His eyes are fixated on her face. He's watching her every movement, he probably has been from the moment he saw her by the pool."

Lexi swallowed hard, goose bumps breaking out across her flesh as his thumb continued to caress her arm. She didn't know what to do. Vincent had basically confessed to watching her all day at Anna's. She was the one who held his attention. Her heart spasmed in her chest as if it was screaming for joy. It was now or never.

"Well, the brunette can feel his eyes on her, and she likes it. She loves the way he watches her, the secretive glances, and the playfulness between them. If she'd turned her head just a little farther to the side she would have caught him looking and would have been captivated by him, unable to look away. His admiration makes her bolder than she ever thought she could be. That confidence you see in her is because of him."

"Do you think she wants him?" he asked in a husky voice, moving closer to her.

Lexi shyly peeked up at him from under her eyelashes and took the chance of her lifetime. "I know she wants him. She has for a very long time." She held her breath and waited for his response.

A second passed... two. Just when Lexi was about to panic that she'd crossed the line with their little game, Vincent took a deep breath, and she waited.

"He wants her more than he has ever wanted anyone in his life."

Lexi turned away, the honesty in his eyes nearly stopping her heart. It was all too real now. Him sitting beside her, her face inches from his. The hardness of his body, the ease with which she could throw her arms around his shoulders and get lost in him completely. She immediately fixated on the picture and Jade's snarling face snapped her back into reality.

"An illusion. That's what the story of this photograph is, Vincent—something that will never be. Until there's no angry harpy looming in the background, these two can never be together. She won't allow it. He has to want her and only her, free and clear. Until then, they can see each other every day and pretend, pretend to be friends and colleagues, but nothing more."

Knowing she was right, Vincent leaned closer, his forehead coming to rest against hers. They stayed that way for a minute, maybe ten. Lexi lost track of time and just let herself be swept up in the moment, in Vincent. He held her gaze, his eyes full of longing and want, hers reflecting the same deep emotions.

Finally, she felt just the slightest of shifts and heard Vincent whisper, "I don't want to pretend any longer." The next thing she knew, Vincent's lips crashed into hers.

There was a possessive fire in his kiss that took Lexi's breath away. His tongue swept past her lips, penetrating her mouth and claiming it as his. Her heart exploded in her chest, and instinctively her arms wrapped tightly around his neck as she held him to her. Pouring her heart into it, all the years of longing and waiting, she kissed him back with just as much fervor, possibly even more. The growl of pleasure that came from deep in Vincent's chest made Lexi's entire body flush with heat. She kept kissing him, even if it meant depriving herself of oxygen. Nothing was more important at that moment than him.

Vincent's hands eagerly explored her body, seeking out her curves and gently ghosting his fingers over her flesh. When she started to pull away, he tried to hold on tighter, but she slipped through his fingers and jumped to her feet, breathless.

"Lexi, I—" He stood up and went to her, his chest heaving as he tried to calm his breathing and speak. Instead of being welcomed into her awaiting arms, he was met by a hard slap to the face.

Lexi picked up the picture that had fallen to their feet. Her eyes were on fire as she pointed at Jade's face in the photo. "Until she's out of the picture, *that* can never happen again."

Dumbfounded, Vincent watched her walk away.

· 28 ·

S how me what you got, girl," Hope called from the doorway of Lexi's bedroom. Lexi strode out and gave a slow spin to show all the detail of the elegant knee-length dress she wore. It was black with a white strap that wrapped over one shoulder. The beading detail and workmanship of the dress were impeccable.

"It's spectacular. You look stunning. Where did you get it?" Hope gushed.

"It's a present from Julian. An original Stone design." Lexi went to the mirror and gave her hair one final touchup, then she sat down beside Hope and slipped her heels on. "You look gorgeous too, by the way."

Hope checked her watch and smiled. "Thanks. Wait, Julian doesn't design women's clothing."

"Not in his line, but he does privately for Christina. This is one of those gowns."

"Good thing the two of you are the same size," Hope said as she ran her fingers over the black satin of Lexi's skirt. "I'm kinda nervous to be going to this event tonight. This party is a long way from the garage." Hope checked her makeup and hair again, suddenly frantic.

Her nerves caught Lexi completely off guard. Hope was always so together; nothing fazed her. She tried to put her friend's mind at ease. "It's just a fashion show. We sit, we look at the clothes, ooh and ahh, and then go to the after party where we make small talk with a bunch of people we'll never see again. What's the big deal? Sean won't be letting you out of his sight looking as gorgeous as you do tonight." Lexi turned off the light and went to get her purse off the kitchen table.

"This is Julian Stone's fashion show, Lexi. We're talking paparazzi and red carpets. I'm a grease monkey. I don't *do* red carpets." Hope tapped her foot nervously on the hardwood floor, the loud clicks echoing through the room.

A knowing grin crept onto Lexi's face. "You really like him, don't you? And I mean *really* like him ... don't you?"

Hope nodded her head and bit her lip nervously. "He's dated actresses, models, and heiresses, Lex. They know how to act at these things. I don't."

"So follow his lead. He'll never let you fall." Lexi made it all sound so simple when she was talking about someone else. Her life, however, was as complicated as the plans for the space shuttle.

"God, I'm turning into one of those whiny women I hate." Hope took a deep breath and gave her long hair a shake. After applying a fresh coat of lipstick, confident, sexy Hope was back. She glanced at the clock. "He better here and pick us up soon. And I swear, if one of those rags makes me a 'fashion don't' with a black bar across my eyes, I'm breaking someone's neck."

"There's my girl." Lexi laughed and opened the door when she heard loud banging. "Sean, look at you."

"Hey, Lexi," he said, shyly tugging at the lapels of his suit and glancing over her shoulder to take a peek at Hope.

"You clean up nice," Lexi whispered in his ear as she wrapped her arms around his neck and hugged him. "She's nervous about tonight. Go tell her how gorgeous she looks."

"Hope!" Sean boomed. "Holy hell, woman, you're smokin'." He let out a low whistle as his eyes raked down her body, taking in every detail of the black dress, which hugged her womanly curves.

She swatted his chest. "Laying it on a bit thick, don't you think?"

"Fine." Sean grinned. "How about 'You look so good all I can think about is dragging you across the hall and worshiping your magnificent body all night long'?" He nibbled down her neck and along her shoulder.

"Better." Hope gasped as his lips made their way up toward her ear lobe. "Much better."

"Um, excuse me? Hi, I'm standing right here. Can you not molest her in front of me?"

Sean grinned mischievously. "Sorry, Lexi. My bad. By the way, you look hot too. All eyes are going to be on you tonight … well, I know a pair of green peepers that will be glued to you, for sure."

Lexi shook her head and tucked a tube of lipstick in her purse. "You two gossip like old women."

"I hear you have a mean right hook too." Sean winked when Lexi's mouth fell open. "Come on, ladies. We gotta hustle so we can get there before the big rush." He propped the door open, then held out both arms to escort the two women down the hall.

"You know, I had a dream like this once or twice," Sean snickered as they waited for the elevator.

"Keep dreaming." Lexi let go of his arm and stepped inside the elevator, laughing. "And I definitely don't want to hear about any of your dreams with two women that take place in elevators."

"Those are some of my personal favorites." His eyes darkened as he whispered something in Hope's ear that made her giggle.

"Seriously, I'm right here!" Lexi pretended to be annoyed, but really she was happy for Hope. She was a wonderful woman who deserved every bit of the happiness she was finding with Sean. He was a good man, and he adored her. As Lexi watched them together, she knew they were the real thing. The passing glances, the little touches, the secretive smiles shared between them warmed her heart and gave her … hope. "You two are sickeningly cute."

The bell dinged, and the doors of the elevator opened at the ground floor. When Lexi saw the car that was waiting for them, she froze in place. "What the hell is that?"

"A limo? Technically it's called a super limo or something like that. Or are you talking about the guy? He's our driver. His name's Bernard. Nice guy, except he's a Raiders fan." When neither of the girls budged, he shrugged. "What's the big deal? Everyone's in there waiting for us. We better get moving."

Lexi's face paled. "Who's everyone?"

She and Vincent had spent the end of the week being all business after their incredibly intense kiss in his office and her subsequent slap to his face. Neither one of them had brought it up the next day, or any day for that matter, both acting as if it had never happened. Of course, every time Vincent walked past her, Lexi was reminded of the softness of his lips, his possessive kisses, and the strength of his body as it had wrapped around hers. The scent of his cologne now made her knees weak, taking her right back to that cool leather couch where all she could smell and feel was Vincent. That perfect moment in which they bared their hearts to one another. The moment that had so abruptly ended when Lexi reminded him that he still was with someone else.

The slap had been a reflex, the shock and surprise of being kissed mixed with Lexi's fury that he would still be with Jade when he felt this way about her. She had waited years to hear him say those things to her, dreamed of the moment even. But in her dreams he wasn't dating another woman, and a wretched one like Jade, at that. So for the next few days they did what they did best—pretended everything was fine, acted professional, and most importantly, ignored the big, giant, rabid, fire-breathing elephant in the room.

Sean saw Lexi tense up and gave her a sad smile. "It's all good, Lexi. He's not in there. Only the cool people get to ride in the limo. Anna, Erik, Elizabeth, and Mr. Dee." His little joke made her finally smile. "Come on, your chariot awaits."

"Good evening, ladies," Bernard greeted them, his dark sunglasses planted firmly over his eyes as he opened the door to the stretch limo.

"Hello," Lexi said. She stepped into the car and was warmly welcomed by the Drakes.

"Lexi, Hope, you both look lovely." Elizabeth beamed. "I hope you don't mind all of us riding together. This is a big night for Hunter. I wanted everyone to arrive together and make an entrance. Well, almost everyone." Elizabeth turned to face the window to try and hide her annoyance with the one member of the family who was clearly absent from the picture. Robert reached out and wrapped his arm around his wife's shoulder, pulling her against his chest.

"That dress is amazing, Lexi," Anna admired from beside her as she examined the exquisite detail on the crisp white strap that swept over Lexi's shoulder. "I'm totally jealous."

"You're wearing Chanel, Anna. It's not exactly a burlap sack." With a smile on her face, Lexi sat back in her seat and tried to prepare herself to see Vincent.

✦

The show was being held in a warehouse very close to Julian's studio, which was convenient since his studio was where the after party would be taking place. Everything was planned out, thanks to Christina, who had done a fabulous job on the prep work. Her work ethic impressed Elizabeth—no simple task.

Even amidst the laughter and jovial mood in the car, Lexi felt a twinge of sadness. There she sat, surrounded by three loving couples all in different stages of their lives together. Robert and Elizabeth were the perfect example of longevity in a relationship. They had been together for so long, they didn't know where one began and the other ended anymore. Anna and Erik were the picture of soul mates. So in tune with one another, words were often not necessary between them. They could convey more with a simple look or body language than words ever could. And then there were Hope and Sean. The newest couple, but the attraction between them was palpable. His eyes never left her, and she couldn't help but smile every time she looked at him. Whether or not they knew it, they were falling in love, and it was beautiful to see.

Jealous, Lexi wondered if she would ever get her chance to feel that. Would she ever know what it was like to have that one special person in her life who knew her better than she knew herself?

As the car turned the corner, she could see the people lining the streets, watching every car that passed, hoping to get a glimpse of who was inside. The limo slowed, trapped in a long line of traffic as the rich and famous stepped onto the red carpet. Lexi and Hope peeked out the windows, unable to curb their excitement at seeing some of the celebrities in attendance.

Lexi felt nervous for the first time when the limo stopped moving and Bernard whipped open the door, holding his hand out. "Have a wonderful evening."

"Thank you," Lexi said timidly. As soon as her foot hit the carpet, she felt all eyes turn to her.

Flashbulbs popped as the photographers reflexively started snapping. They weren't exactly sure who she was, but not wanting to miss the shot, they kept taking photographs in case she was here with someone important. Sean and Hope emerged to the same welcome Lexi had received, but when Erik and Anna stepped foot on the carpet, the flashbulbs exploded. Erik's name was called by every photographer in attendance, each wanting them to give a glance in their direction. He wrapped his arm around Anna and held her against his side as they smiled politely, trying to give the paparazzi a decent shot.

Sean guided Hope down the carpet, nodding and stopping to shake a few hands. Erik and Anna waved to the group of photographers near the entrance and began their slow journey through the crowd. Lexi was about to wander off behind the two couples when she felt a strong arm wrap around her.

"Where are you running off to?" Robert asked while Elizabeth posed for a few pictures alone.

Lexi smiled sheepishly. "I have no idea. Honestly? I was going to go hide behind Sean or Erik."

"There will be no hiding today, young lady." Elizabeth came over and took her hand, pulling her to her side as flashbulbs went off repeatedly in their faces.

"Who is that with you, Mrs. Drake?" one of the photographers asked.

"This is Alexandra White, one of Hunter Advertising's finest. We're so lucky to have her on board. Remember her name. She's going to do amazing things." Elizabeth waved a knowing finger at all of them and smiled as they scribbled notes on random pieces of paper. "She and my son, Vincent, designed the campaign for Julian Stone's clothing line. You'll get to preview some of their brilliant ideas tonight in the show. It's going to be a huge success." Elizabeth laced her fingers with Lexi's and gave her hand a squeeze.

"You work with Vincent Drake?" one of them shouted, and Lexi shyly nodded her head. "Are you two dating?" More flashbulbs went off. Even though her heart felt like it was going to burst from her chest at the questions, she pretended not to hear and simply continued smiling.

"Alexandra! Alexandra!" The photographers screamed her name, trying to get a picture. Lexi's mind raced as she smiled and turned from right to left, imitating Elizabeth's actions. She rolled her shoulders back, turned slightly to the side and prayed she looked good.

"Dr. Drake, get in one of the pictures," someone begged. Robert proudly strode over and sandwiched himself between the two beautiful women and grinned.

"Thank you, everyone." Elizabeth waved and heard a few groans as they started to walk away, allowing other people their face time with the paparazzi. When they were safely out of earshot, Elizabeth whispered, "Well done, Lexi. You handled that beautifully."

"Really?" Lexi asked, her voice shaky as the adrenaline surged through her body. "Because I think I might have had a small aneurism back there."

They continued down the carpet, Elizabeth stopping several more times to be photographed or greet colleagues. With each stop, she introduced Lexi and showcased her as much as possible. Lexi was completely overwhelmed by her kindness. In putting Lexi's name out there, it gave her instant credibility in the industry and made her known among the influential people in attendance.

When they finally caught up with everyone else, Anna was giggling with Hope. When they noticed Lexi staring at them, they both stopped and tried to look casual, but failed miserably.

"What's so funny? Do I even want to know?" Lexi watched them exchange a glance.

"Seems like you were the talk of the carpet." Anna winked at Lexi. "Everyone had questions."

"About me?" Lexi paled. "But th-they don't even know me."

Sean leaned over and whispered in her ear. "Walkie talkies, Lexi. The guys at your end buzzed the guys on our end, and they asked all kinds of questions."

Lexi held up her hand. "Don't tell me what they asked. Ignorance is bliss."

"Fine." Anna giggled as she walked away. "But keep your left hand hidden or there will be a Photoshopped ring on it by tomorrow, right next to your engagement announcement."

"Oh my God." Lexi grabbed onto Robert's arm for support.

"Lexi Drake, I like the sound of that." Robert grinned when her eyes tripled in size. "Rest assured, my son will eventually get his head out of his ass, and when he does, I hope you'll be the one to make an honest man of him." He nodded toward Elizabeth who was chatting with someone a few feet away. "Before I met her, I was a complete idiot. Now, she would probably argue that I still am, but I think I've come a long way with her guidance. She made me a better man. And you do that same thing for Vincent."

Not knowing what to say, Lexi was relieved when the surging crowd saved her from responding. There was an eruption of wild screams at the far end of the carpet, where people were exiting their limos. A number of photographers started rushing in that direction, light bulbs flashing. That's when Lexi finally heard what they were screaming.

"Jade! Jade! Vincent, Jade. Look here!" A swarm of people ran after the couple, trying to get the perfect picture.

"Have I mentioned lately how much I despise her?" Anna growled as she and Erik appeared beside Lexi.

Lexi followed her gaze, searching the crowd until she caught a glimpse of the man that made her blood race. The people milling around her cleared and gave Lexi a perfect view of Vincent. His black suit and dark tie were gorgeous together, his hair in its standard wavy-disarray, but somehow still appearing intentional and chic. The only "fashion don't" Lexi could find with his outfit was the demented woman dangling from his arm.

Jade was stuffed into a dress that was too short and too ugly for words. The sides of her black kimono-style dress had huge cutouts at the hips which drew the eye to her pasty, sun-starved flesh. As they were being photographed, her arms wrapped around Vincent so tightly that Lexi wondered if he was even able to breathe. From the uncomfortable look on his face, he wasn't enjoying himself nearly as much as the radiantly unstable woman beside him was.

Flash after flash went off in his face until he could hardly see through all the spots in his vision. When he couldn't stand the charade a second longer, Vincent stepped away from Jade and the cameras with a scowl, letting her continue to whore herself to the photographers alone. He crossed his arms over his chest and waited, his eyes scanning the crowd to pass the time. It only took him a second to find Lexi among the masses. He could have found her anywhere. The dress that Julian gave her fit like a glove, accentuating her curves in a simple but sexy way. Her hair with is brilliant caramel highlights spilled over her shoulders in big, loose curls. Nothing on her was overdone or screamed "look at me," yet she had his complete attention, as always.

"Smile, Vincent." Jade slithered back to his side and beamed her whitened teeth at the crowd. "I don't want you to look like you're having an enema in all the pictures."

An enema would probably be more fun.

In need of a distraction, Vincent peered into the sea of people and found Lexi again. When her eyes locked on his, he smiled. Even though things between them had been strained over the last week at work, the bottom line was she made him happy. He couldn't explain it and wasn't even going to try. All he could do was enjoy it and hope it would last.

"Much better." Jade kissed his cheek, not out of affection, but to give the paparazzi yet another picture. When the flashbulbs subsided, she hissed a warning in his ear. "And if you don't stop staring at your little pet, I'm going to cram her into a very small cage." Vincent opened his mouth to speak, but she interrupted him. "If you think I'm blind to the way you look at her you've got another thing coming, Vincent. I'm not stupid. We haven't had sex in weeks."

"You've been traveling." Vincent kept a blank look on his face, not wanting to give her any emotion to attack. "And you're exaggerating."

"Do I need to remind you that in the past when I would come home from a trip, we'd spend the next two days in bed? Now I'm lucky if you remember to send a car to pick me up at the airport." Jade kept her perfectly poised façade through the entire conversation, not allowing the volatile subject matter to change the expression of the fabricated bliss on her face. "As if all that wasn't enough, the most physical you get with me around *her* is a quick peck on the cheek as I leave." Her ice blue eyes were as frigid as an Arctic glacier. "You *need* me, Vincent. Don't ever forget that."

They caught up with his family, and he welcomed the distraction from Jade's ranting. This close, he could get a better look at Lexi too. She stayed off to the side with Hope, looking even more uncomfortable when Vincent smiled at her. He felt guilty for everything. For kissing her, for allowing his emotions to get the better of him, for wanting her beyond all reason while he was still ensnared in Jade's world, and most of all, for not protecting her from him and his baggage.

◆

"Vincent." Elizabeth grinned as she turned and saw her son for the first time. "There you are. Look how handsome you are tonight." She glanced over at Jade. "Good evening, Jade. My, is that a new tattoo? How...lovely." Elizabeth pointed at the black symbol that was peeking out of one of the cut outs in her dress.

"It's a Tahitian symbol." Jade proudly thrust her hip toward Robert so he could take a gander.

"Ten bucks says it's the Tahitian symbol for slut," Hope mumbled to Lexi and Anna.

Snickering, Lexi stepped away, needing to put some distance between herself and Jade before she said something she'd regret. She didn't get more than a few steps before she ran into someone. "Oh, I'm sor—" Her apologetic tone immediately turned snippy when she saw who it was. "Oh, Vincent. It's you. Please excuse me." She turned to walk away, but he took a hold of her elbow and refused to let her move from his side.

"Lexi, I—I just wanted to say—" He released her arm and raked his hand through his hair, struggling to find the words. "You look beautiful tonight."

"Thank you." Lexi instinctively smoothed out the front of her dress. "You look nice too."

"Thanks. Listen, Lexi, I wanted to talk to you abou—"

"Hey!" A voice suddenly called from the crowd. "Mr. Drake! Vincent, can we get a picture of the two of you?"

"Would you mind?" Vincent asked, tentatively reaching out for her hand.

Not wanting to make a scene, Lexi acquiesced and slipped her hand into his, relishing the warmth of his palm and the strength with which he held onto her. They took their spot before the crowd, and as the cameras were about to start snapping, Jade slithered over.

"Baby, there you are," she crooned and stepped into the picture, uninvited. Blubs flashed as Jade struck her latest outrageous pose on one side of Vincent, sandwiching him between herself and Lexi.

"Who are you wearing?" one of the people in the crowd shouted out.

"A new designer, Fredrique." Jade gave them a slow spin. Her arms were thrust up over her head to show off the fabric equivalent of Swiss cheese.

"Like Fredrick's of Hollywood?" someone yelled out, causing the crowd to erupt into laughter. The cameras flashed even more when Jade's face showed her fury. "Jade, step aside. We want a few of just Vincent and Alexandra." The photographers' hands frantically waved her away. "Alexandra, who are you wearing?"

"Julian Stone. His private collection." The shutters on the photographers' cameras clicked with insane speed, and each of them made sure to capture a shot of Lexi in one of Julian's rare pieces of women's clothing. All eyes were on Lexi as she stood there, the center of attention. Livid, Jade released Vincent from her grasp and sulked off into the background, seething as she watched her boyfriend wrap his arm around Lexi, who snuggled against his chest.

The crowd suddenly began screaming and pointing at the other end of the red carpet, excited into a near frenzy. As the crowd parted, two figures emerged—Julian Stone and Christina.

"Julian!" The crowd screamed and begged, photographers elbowing one another out of the way to get a picture of the man of the evening. "Julian, Christina, over here!"

Dressed in black jeans, a crisp white T-shirt, and a black leather jacket, Julian made his way over to Vincent and clapped him on the shoulder. Christina, dressed in a black gown with stunning fringe detail and fuchsia highlighting, came over and pulled Lexi into her arms, the two laughing, unaware of the media explosion going on around them.

"Julian! Julian!" the crowd screamed.

With a cheeky smile, he wrapped his arm around Christina and snuggled close to her. "Come on, you two, I need a picture with the brilliant design team that's going to help everyone in America know my name. Grab your girl, Vincent." Christina winked at Lexi, then turned a brilliant smile toward the blast of flashbulbs as they popped like endless fireworks in the night sky.

"Vincent, get closer to her," one of them shouted, so Vincent closed the small distance between himself and Lexi.

"Sorry," Lexi said through her smile as her hand accidentally slipped inside his suit jacket. When she tried to pull it away, Vincent held her arm in place and smiled.

"I don't mind at all." It was then that he felt her trembling. "Are you all right?"

"This is just slightly terrifying," Lexi said through her smile.

"I won't let anything happen to you. I promise." He caressed her back and pulled her more tightly against his side.

"Thanks, Vincent," she whispered, nuzzling against him.

"Lexi, Christina, give them a kiss," the photographers called out repeatedly. Christina shrugged, then planted her lips on Julian's cheek.

Lexi stared at Vincent for a long while, debating what she should do. Then she stood up on her toes. "Sorry again," she whispered just before she pressed her lips gently against his cheek. He wrapped his arm around her waist and lifted her feet off the ground. She gave a surprised squeak, then threw her head back and laughed. More flashbulbs popped.

The two men held the ladies in a variety of positions for the paparazzi, giving them the best shots they could. Christina whispered something in Julian's ear, and like that, the photo session was over. "Thank you, guys, but I need to get these two in their seats so I can start the show. See you when it's over." Julian waved and thanked the photographers quickly, then clapped Vincent on the shoulder and grinned. "Those should be all over the internet in ten minutes and on the cover of every magazine by morning."

With Jade nowhere to be found, Vincent caught up with Lexi and offered her his elbow. "May I?" he asked.

Her eyes peeked up at him from under her think, black eyelashes. "I'd love to." She slipped her arm through his, her fingers wrapping around his bicep and suddenly feeling an overwhelming sense of… home.

The two walked arm in arm into the building, the paparazzi still documenting their every step until the door closed behind them. Now, it was time for the show to begin.

◆

"That was brilliant!" Sean exclaimed as he ran into Vincent.

The show had been stunning, a huge success based on the chatter going on in the room around them. Reporters jotted notes and made frantic phone calls to meet their deadlines. A swarm of people surrounded Julian, trying to get a word with him and offer their congratulations. The crowd was growing by the second. Pouting because she wasn't the center of attention, Jade scurried off to talk with some of her modeling friends.

"I think that went very well. The music was the perfect complement to the designs. I'm so proud of the two of you!" Elizabeth beamed and pulled Vincent and Lexi into her arms. "What a huge success."

"Thank you so much for giving me the opportunity, Elizabeth. And Vincent, how do I even begin to thank you?" Lexi felt like her smile was going to be permanently welded to her face.

What a difference a few weeks made. Six months ago, she had moved to San Francisco with nothing but a few items jammed into random boxes and the clothes on her back. She was broken, devastated by Harry's death, and unsure of her decision to move, but she knew it was something she had to do or she'd never leave. And now, a few short months later, she had a life. A very full life with friends, a job, and a future. That was something she never thought she'd say again. She studied the smiling faces around her and saw people she was starting to think of as family.

While she had been lost in her own thoughts, the rest of the group had wandered away, leaving her alone with Vincent. "You don't need to thank me, Lexi. Every second with you has been my pleasure." He took her hand in his and raised it to his lips, never breaking eye contact with her. As his warm lips pressed against her hand and lingered, Lexi felt her body flush with a deep-heated desire only Vincent could cause. She knew her cheeks had turned pink when she saw his lips turn up into a sexy smirk. "You aren't going to slap me again, are you?"

Lexi raised an eyebrow, shocked he would bring up their last kiss like that. Her lips tingled as she thought back to the feel of his mouth possessing hers and the fire between them as his tongue caressed hers. "No, I'm not going to slap you. You can kiss my hand all you want." She tried to pull her hand back, but Vincent suddenly tightened his grasp.

"Really?"

She drew her bottom lip between her teeth when she saw his mischievous grin as his lips moved back toward her hand. "Vincent," she warned, but all rational thought was suddenly lost when his tongue darted out of his mouth and swept lazy circles around her hand, his lips gently sucking on her knuckles. Fire raced through her blood, and a delicious tickle settled in her stomach with each seductive stroke of his tongue. Her hand slipped from his grasp and hung limply at her side, every nerve ending tingling with excitement.

"Are you going to slap me now?" Vincent asked again as he surveyed her reaction.

She couldn't stop the devilish smile from creeping onto her face as she watched him panic. "I'm considering it."

"Listen, Lexi, I need to talk to you abo—"

"Hey, guys! This was incredible. I can't believe I was here for this. Who premiers their fashion line in San Francisco and gets this kind of industry turnout?" Hope asked, still checking out all the big names in attendance as they walked past.

"Only Julian Stone could pull this off. The guy doesn't do anything by the book, and people love him for it," Sean laughed.

"Did you see all those male models?" Hope smiled apologetically at Sean when his head snapped around. "Those were some mighty fine abs on that catwalk."

"You do realize that most of them are gay with absolutely no interest in you," Jade snarled as she strutted back to Vincent's side, hip checking Lexi out of the way.

"That doesn't surprise me at all. If they're stuck working all day with ball-devouring hags like you, I can see how that would turn them off to the entire female population," Hope remarked.

Sean's booming laughter made heads turn. "Leave a winner, Hope." He took her by the hand, and the two disappeared into the crowd.

"Did you hear that? She can take those saggy breasts and that Elvira hair of hers and shove it—"

Lexi stepped up to Jade and pointed a finger in her face. "Shut it, Jade. Or so help me God, I'll jam a Twinkie down your throat."

"I've had it with you, White."

"Lexi, baby! There you are." Peter strolled over but stopped short when he saw Lexi and Jade ready to scratch each other's eyes out. "Whoa! Am I interrupting something?"

"Yes." Lexi, Jade, and Vincent answered all at once.

"Looks like I'm just in the nick of time, then," he said with a cocky grin on his face as he wrapped his arm around Lexi's shoulders. "Can I walk you to the after party? It's just two doors down at Julian's studio."

"S-sure, I'd like that." Lexi gave Jade one last dirty look then smiled apologetically at Vincent.

"Vincent, always a pleasure." Peter held out his hand to Vincent and the two shook. Then he turned to Jade and gave her a perplexed look. "Oh, I'm sorry, and you are?"

"Jade," she informed him through clenched teeth

"Just Jade? Like Madonna or Cher, right? Nice meeting you. See you both at the after party?" Vincent gave a curt nod, and Peter smiled. "Excellent."

When she and Peter were out of earshot, Lexi asked, "Did you really not know who that was?"

Peter laughed. "Who, Jade? Everyone knows who she is. But you seemed a little pissed off at her so I figured I'd rattle her cage, maybe earn a few brownie points in the process so you'd save me a dance tonight."

Lexi threw back her head and laughed. "You'll be at the top of my dance card after that little display of brilliance. Let's go. I could really use a drink."

29

Julian's studio was the perfect place to host the party. Most of the furniture was moved off the first floor of the warehouse, leaving a huge open space for people to mingle and dance. Out back, off to one side was the basketball court and on the other was a gorgeous outdoor garden for guests to escape to if the noise inside became too much. Drinks flowed, and everyone celebrated Julian's success.

Jade kept Vincent trapped in the center of a swarm of her twig-like sorority sisters as they chain smoked just outside the veranda doors and pounded shots of tequila like they were water. Lexi felt Vincent's eyes on her when Peter whirled her around the dance floor, but she refused to make eye contact with him, knowing Jade would be at his side, staking her claim. Instead, she allowed herself to enjoy Peter's company, even if it was simply to put the screws to Vincent. He deserved it.

After her dance, she excused herself from Peter and searched the room for Hope. An unfortunately familiar face emerged.

"Alexandra White! It's my lucky day running into you." David Reid threw his arm around her shoulders, smelling of scotch and sweat.

"Mr. Reid," Lexi said curtly, stepping out from under his arm. "I wasn't expecting to see you here."

"Call me David." He reached into the crowd and tugged on someone's arm. A miserable-looking Erica popped into view. "My girl Erica here made it happen. Her brother knows a guy who works for Stone. Long story, but she got us in."

"Hey, Lexi," she said softly as she glared at the side of David's head. "How are you?" She forced a pleasant smile on her face.

"I'm fine." Lexi looked back and forth between the two of them. She was about to ask what was going on, wondering what could have possessed Erica to spend an evening with David under any circumstances, but before she could ask, Erica gave a slight shake of her head, stopping Lexi. "So, are you two enjoying yourselves?" she asked instead.

"Absolutely," David grinned. "Top notch booze, tons of targets in the room to work. My kinda party." He licked his lips. "You look gorgeous."

"Thank you." Lexi glanced at Erica and gave her a what-the-hell kind of look. Erica shrugged and pretended to gag.

"Erica, I need another drink. Can you go fetch it for me?"

At the word fetch, Lexi thought Erica's head was going to explode. Either that or she was going to stab David in the heart with the plastic stirrer that poked out of his empty glass of scotch.

"Sure, *Davey*." Erica didn't even try to hide her distaste, much to Lexi's surprise. "Lexi, we *really* must have a little chat later." The look in her eyes said it all. Whatever Erica had to tell her was important enough that she would put up with this ridiculous treatment from David.

"I can walk with you right now, Erica, and we can talk." Lexi took two steps, but David stepped in front of her.

"Actually, I need to talk to you about something. You girls can gossip later." He waved his hand, rudely dismissing Erica. "Now, where were we?" He shuffled them a few steps to the left and suddenly Lexi found herself in a quiet corner, alone with David. "Much better." He sighed, loosening his tie and smiling at her.

"What do you need to talk to me about, Mr. Reid?"

"Still with the formalities, Alexandra?" He leaned in and whispered, "Do you call Vincent, Mr. Drake?"

"What I do or do not call him is irrelevant to this conversation or any conversation we'll ever have. Again, what do you need to talk to me about?"

David's amused façade dropped, his tone turning serious. "Do you have any idea who I am? I'm a very powerful man, Lexi. I could make you a huge name in town. I have very deep pockets. Maybe if you were a little nicer to me," he ran a finger along her arm, "I could help. You know, you scratch my back, I scratch yours?"

"I'm not scratching anything of yours, Reid." Lexi was terrified and furious all that the same time. Fortunately her fury was winning out. She balled her hand into a fist, preparing to defend herself if necessary.

"I have connections. I can make things happen for you. I know you have the drive. I can see it in your eyes. And you're talented. You could be one of the biggest names in the industry with the right teacher. And the things I could teach you..." His voice trailed off suggestively, and Lexi had to fight down the bile that rose in her throat.

Lexi took a deep breath and controlled her raging temper. "Please listen to what I'm going to say so I don't *ever* have to speak to you again. I have no desire to ever work for you. As a matter of fact, if you so much as look sideways at me, I will be filing a sexual harassment lawsuit against you. I hear the guys in prison really like a man with a big mouth and deep... pockets." David reached out to take her hand, but Lexi stopped him. "Touch me again and you will lose a finger."

David pulled his hand back as if she had slapped it, but kept his twisted smile in place. "Bitch," he said smugly as he walked away, leaving her fuming in the corner.

Vincent watched David Reid stalk away from Lexi, looking like the pompous ass he was. They had spent quite a while huddled together in the corner—seven long, excruciating minutes to be exact. Vincent knew that because he had watched the entire encounter from start to finish. It began rather cozily, the two with their heads together. When David ran his finger down Lexi's arm, Vincent had an overwhelming urge to beat the life out of him. Vincent couldn't see Lexi's face very well from his angle, but from the shit-eating grin on David's face, Vincent assumed the conversation was going Reid's way.

He spent the first half of their conversation hoping Lexi would deck David. He then spent the last half of it wondering what the two of them could possibly have to talk about privately. His paranoia began to set in.

"What is she doing now?" Jade came out of nowhere, her eyes fixed on Lexi and David. "Is she throwing herself at *him* too?"

"I have no idea." Vincent turned away when he saw Reid finally leave Lexi's side.

"He looks awfully happy." Jade sneered.

"I need a drink." Vincent walked away, hoping to clear his head. He needed to get the picture of Lexi and David out of his mind before he did something stupid. Hitting him wouldn't fix anything, even though it would make Vincent feel a hell of a lot better.

As he tossed back his drink, Vincent caught a glimpse of Jade and her barely-there dress making a bee line for Lexi, who stood in the corner looking annoyed. He knew by the expression on Jade's face that this wasn't going to end well, so he made an attempt to intercept Jade. Unfortunately, before he reached his destination, Elizabeth caught his arm and introduced him to a number of the board members for Mello industries, one of the biggest pharmaceutical research companies in town. As he shook their hands, he lost sight of Jade. All he could do was hope for the best, but he truly expected to see security heading toward Lexi and Jade shortly.

Lexi's head throbbed as she pulled a bottle of aspirin out of her purse and took two, then paused and popped a third into her mouth. That's when she saw Jade. She debated chugging the entire bottle and just putting herself out of her misery, but then decided it was time to have it out with the high-priestess of evil once and for all. This conversation had been a long time coming.

"Jade," Lexi greeted the woman in a disinterested voice.

"I despise you."

"I assure you, the feeling is completely mutual. Nice talking to you. Are we done now?" Lexi glanced at her watch and shook her head.

"Not by a long shot, you whore."

Lexi threw back her head and laughed. "I'm a whore? That's rich. By definition, doesn't one actually need to be having sex to be a whore, Jade?"

"Enough!" People glanced in their direction when they heard Jade's high-pitched shriek.

"Quiet down, you fool. There are reporters everywhere," Lexi warned.

"Worried about a little bad press, are you? I would think you'd love it if the magazines printed stories about you and your beloved Vincent." Jade's voice took on a maniacal cackle as she spoke.

"If you have something to say, just say it so you can go away."

"He loves me, so back off."

"If you were so certain of that, you wouldn't even be worried about me, Jade. I'd be nothing more than a blip on your insecurity radar instead of a meteor plummeting toward the middle of your relationship."

"Admit you're in love with him."

Lexi debated denying it, but there was no point anymore. Everyone could see it. Hell, Erik even took pictures of it. "Yes, I'm in love with him."

Jade's jaw fell open in shock that Lexi had answered truthfully. As if trying to talk herself out of what she heard, she shook her head from side to side. "You don't love him, you can't. You don't even know him."

That comment made Lexi's blood boil. "I don't know him? Are you serious? Let's see how well you know him, Jade. What's his favorite color? Favorite food? His biggest fear? When he was little, what did he want to be when he grew up? Who is he named after?" Lexi stood toe-to-toe with Jade and didn't flinch, even when Jade seemed ready to gouge her eyes out. Jade's fury turned to stunned silence as she opened her mouth and closed it a few times, but never uttered a peep.

"He likes it when I wear red," she feebly offered as if bored by the questions.

Lexi stepped right in Jade's face and laid into her. "His favorite color is purple. His favorite food is a bacon cheeseburger, extra tomato. He hates your rabbit food. Biggest fear is drowning. Want to know why? When he was fourteen, he went cliff diving with his friends and nearly drowned. He wanted to be a pilot when he was little so he could 'fly like the birds,' and he was named after Elizabeth's favorite uncle."

"What does any of that matter? I'm the one in his bed."

Lexi sarcastically clapped her hands. "Congratulations for being able to spread your legs. You have a completely superficial relationship with him, Jade. Admit it. Physical, not emotional. You know where he lives, where he works, and how much money he makes. You know what designer clothes he looks best in and where he likes to eat. You know *about* Vincent, but you don't *know* him, you don't know the man inside. You have no idea what's in his heart."

That sent Jade into a tirade. "And you think you do? You're some poor, pitiful girl whose whole family up and died on her. He feels bad for you. It's pity, nothing more."

"So I was just some big charity case when he kissed me? Was that all part of his cheer-up-poor-pitiful-Lexi plan?"

"You kissed him?"

"Correction, he kissed me."

"Bullshit." Jade's whole body tensed.

"Twice."

"Miss Goodie Two Shoes, that whole I-won't-do-anything-while-he's-still-with-you speech was a big lie. You've been throwing yourself at him all along."

"No, I told you, *he* kissed *me*. I think all that hairspray is messing with your hearing. We would have done a hell of a lot more than kiss too, if I hadn't stopped it. Twice." Lexi mockingly held up two fingers to Jade's face.

"He doesn't love you." Her lip curled in disgust. "He couldn't."

"Maybe, maybe not. But based on the way he kissed me, I think he definitely feels a little something for me. It wasn't like kissing your grandmother; there was tongue, and lots of it. He's a really great kisser, by the way."

"I know he is," Jade screeched again, losing her temper. Lexi held back a smile. "Stay away from him." Jade shook her finger in Lexi's face.

"Not possible. We work together, *very* closely."

Fire burned in Jade's eyes. "For now." Suddenly her mood shifted, her anger oddly turning into amusement. "Enjoy it while it lasts, Lexi. I can't wait to watch you crash and burn, you insignificant little bug." She got right up into Lexi's face, her red lips turned up into a sneer. "I'm going to ruin your life."

"Do your worst. You don't scare me." Lexi watched a group of Jade's pals make their way to the bathroom. "Better go scurry off with your friends before all the coke is gone." Jade's eyes flashed black as she stopped dead in her tracks. "Lucky guess, but thanks for confirming it."

Jade stormed away as Lexi closed her eyes and began banging her head on the wall behind her. "Stupid, stupid, stupid." She repeated her mantra, unable to believe she had been so idiotic and told Jade, of all people, that she was in love with Vincent. "She's going to make your life a living hell. Nothing new there," Lexi said to no one in particular.

When Jade stormed off into the bathroom, Vincent breathed a sigh of relief. He even had to stop himself from smiling as he watched Lexi have an entire conversation with herself, throwing up her hands in the midst of her little rant.

"Vincent?" Elizabeth tapped her son on the shoulder. "Are you okay?" She followed his gaze to Lexi. "She's a lovely girl, Vincent."

"I know."

"She makes you happy."

"I know." Vincent smiled as he watched Lexi storm off toward the bar. "She is the most selfless person I have ever met."

"I know."

"You love her."

"I – I…" Vincent stammered, caught off guard. "I need to talk to her."

"Yes, you do. But first, I think you need to end things with Jade. Until that's cleared up, I don't think Lexi will be very receptive to any 'conversations' with you."

Vincent nodded his head in agreement, then turned to Elizabeth, who was beaming with excitement. "Don't get your hopes up, Mother. This all might not work out the way you hope it will."

She hugged her son. "Yes it will. Trust me."

Lexi downed two glasses of wine and was reaching for her third from the hunky bartender with the baby blue eyes when Erica swooped in and stole her away. "Hey, wait. He had a drink for me." Erica quickly walked Lexi to the back of the room and stopped. The look on her face was grave. Any buzz Lexi might have had was killed in that instant.

"What is it?"

Erica went in her purse and pulled out several folded pieces of paper and thrust the pile at Lexi. "You know how you left me that mysterious message about keeping my eyes open for anything strange? Well, I think you need to take a look at this."

Cautiously, Lexi opened the papers, and as soon as she glanced at the first one, all the color drained from her face. "Wh-where did you get these?"

"David was looking at them one day. I walked in the office, and he tried to hide them but accidentally stuck them in the folder I needed. When I saw your name on them, I knew it was bad. I made copies and stuck the originals back in the file. About five minutes later he came flying out of his office, demanding the file back from me. I played dumb."

"This is the Excalibur account. How did he get these? These look like," Lexi held the paper up close to her face, examining every detail, "pictures of the boards. Photographs of everything. Now that's odd—this one is different." She continued to flip through the pages, her stomach dropping. Excalibur had been her baby, Vincent trusted her with it, and she somehow let it slip through her fingers.

"What the hell is going on? How does David have your mock up? What does he care?"

"Someone at Hunter has been leaking our ideas to competitors. Vincent has no idea why, or who it is. This," she waved the papers at Erica, "is the account he gave me. The one he wanted protected above all others. Now I have to tell him David has the information, including private meeting notes, and our presentation date. This is bad."

"Oh my God," Erica gasped.

"Yeah."

The papers in her hand were all the proof they needed that someone was selling Hunter ideas, but as far as she could tell, nothing about them would be helpful in finding the culprit. "Can I keep these? I need to show them to Vincent."

"Absolutely. Now that I know what I'm looking for, I'll keep my eyes peeled for anything else fishy." Erica hugged Lexi and whispered, "I'm so sorry."

"Me too. I'm sorry you had to put up with David being awful just so you could give me this."

"Don't worry about it. I figure I'm just gonna get him liquored up and let him make a fool of himself. If I'm lucky, I can get my next Christmas card picture tonight." She earned a wry smile from Lexi.

After a reassuring squeeze to Lexi's arm, Erica disappeared back into the crowd. Lexi's mind reeled as she tried to figure out when the files could have been found and photographed. She had kept everything under lock and key, no matter where she was in the building. Maybe she thought she had locked the drawer one day, and it was actually left open. Vincent was going to be furious. He might even fire her. Everything she'd worked for would be taken away. A sudden wave of nausea hit Lexi, and she needed to get some air.

Out in the garden, everything was peaceful. Most of the crowd was still inside, while couples trickled through the garden looking to share some quiet time. It was the perfect escape. Lexi found a bench off to the side, sat down, and again scoured through the papers in her hand. In the dim moonlight, something caught her eye. She held the sheet up to one of the outdoor lights and froze. Scribbled on a Post-it note attached to one of the print ads was a name, underlined twice. *Jade* with an arrow pointing at the main female model in the shoot.

Staring at it, Lexi's stomach lurched. Who picks the model before the design campaign is even solidified? Why would he do that unless...

Just as she crammed the papers in her purse, she heard two very low voices coming from the shadows. "I'm going to take care of that little problem we have, once and for all. She's just getting in the way."

"Do you have anything else for me?" a deep voice Lexi immediately recognized as David Reid asked.

"Get me the Fitzgerald's modeling contract, and we'll talk. Until then, any other Hunter goodies I may have up my sleeve are available to the highest bidder."

"Jade, if you give another client to Parketti," David threatened.

"You'll what? I'm making you millions with the information I gave you. I have to spread this stuff around to keep everyone at Hunter guessing. I never give Adria anything good. Her ungrateful attitude really pisses me off. But she's gotten me the cover every time, so I'm not complaining. Vincent's completely wrapped up in his little Kewpie doll of an assistant. He has no idea what's going on."

Lexi's heart thundered in her chest, unable to believe what she was hearing. Jade had been selling out Vincent for months. She was the mole. It would devastate him when he learned the truth. There was a long silence and then a few sickening giggles from Jade.

"I love you," David said in the darkness.

Jade giggled again, and Lexi snapped. She shot up out of her seat and loudly cleared her throat, glaring into their hidden alcove. Jade and David peeked out from the shadows like two teenagers caught making out and froze.

"You make me sick." Lexi took great pleasure in watching the terror sweep across Jade's face. She mockingly gave a little finger wave. "See you in hell, Jade." Then Lexi turned on her heel and walked out of the garden, trying to scrub the image of David's hand threaded up through one of the holes in Jade's dress out of her head.

As she stepped back into the warehouse, she had one thing on her mind. Vincent. She needed to find him. Her eyes darted around the room, but the crowd seemed to have doubled in size while she was gone. Finally, off to the side of the dance floor, Lexi found Julian and Christina. Thinking they might have an idea where Vincent was, she hurried off in their direction.

"Lexi, love the dress on you. You having a good time?" Julian greeted her as he wrapped his arms around her and gave her a squeeze. When he saw the paled expression on her face he stopped. "What happened?"

"I was out in the garden. I just need to find Vincent—it's an emergency." Lexi's voice trembled with emotion.

"Are you all right?" Christina stepped forward in a panic. "Did someone hurt you?"

A very dazed Lexi answered. "What? N-no, nothing like that." She shook her head. "It's a work thing."

Julian eyed her cautiously. "Last time I saw him, he was near the bar, talking to his mother. Are you sure you're okay?"

"I will be. Thanks." Lexi hugged Christina and Julian and congratulated both of them on the evening's huge success.

After a few more minutes of pleasantries, Lexi's eyes continued scanning the room for Vincent. "Go find your man." Christina smiled.

"Thanks." Lexi waved and disappeared into the crowd. She caught a glimpse of Robert and headed in that direction as fast as she could. When she finally broke through the throngs of people, she found Robert and Elizabeth together, but no Vincent.

"Damn it," she muttered.

"Well, hello to you too, dear." Elizabeth laughed.

"Sorry, I'm looking for your son." Lexi smiled apologetically and then began scanning the room again.

"Oh, you know what? He's off doing something very important right now and really can't be interrupted." Elizabeth threaded her arm through Lexi's. "Why don't we go get something to eat? I see a lovely dessert table set up in that corner."

Lexi was running out of time and was becoming more desperate to talk to Vincent. "I'm not hungry. I don't mean to be rude, but I really have to talk to him about something." As she waved the papers at Elizabeth, she caught sight of Vincent and Jade heading upstairs. "Never mind, I see him. I'll be back."

"Lexi, wait!"

On the trip across the room, it seemed like Lexi ran into every person she knew, everyone wanting to stop her and chat about something. As politely as possible, she excused herself from each of them and continued toward Vincent. As she was about to go upstairs, a huge hand landed on her shoulder.

"Yo, Lexi. Where are you sneaking off to?"

"Sean, Hope, oh thank God! Listen, Jade's the mole. Someone from Reid gave me these papers. They're pictures of the Excalibur account—the boards and PowerPoint. Then I heard Jade and Reid out on the garden talking about it and ... making out. She's cheating on Vincent too." As she spilled all the sordid details, she became nauseated. She could only imagine what Vincent would feel like when he heard. Her heart broke for him.

"What?" Sean's smile evaporated from his face.

"That bitch," Hope snarled. "After all the shit she accused you of, here she is sleeping around on Vincent?"

"Yeah, I know. Listen, they just went upstairs. I have to go tell him. He needs to know. Screw Jade, I'll deal with her too."

Sean held out an arm to stop her. "Do you want me to go with you? Jade isn't going to take this well. I'd feel better if I was there."

She reached out her hand and laid it on Sean's cheek. "Thanks for the offer, but it's time someone showed Jade the door, and I'm thrilled to be the one to do it. But there is something you can do for me."

"Name it."

"Go find Anna. Vincent's going to need her when he finds out what Jade did." The two exchanged a sad look. Both understood this would hit Vincent like a ton of bricks, and his reaction would be explosive. It was the thing that he loathed the most: betrayal.

"Be careful," Hope whispered as Lexi started running up the stairs in search of Vincent.

The serenity of the warehouse loft was a definite contrast to the throngs of chattering people down below. Off in the distance, Lexi heard voices coming from one of the back rooms. She made her way down the hall, her stomach clenching with each step. She wanted Jade gone, but she'd never wanted to see Vincent hurt this way. With a trembling hand, she reached for the doorknob and turned it.

"V-Vincent, I'm sorry to interrupt." Lexi stepped inside Julian's office and waited for Vincent to acknowledge her. He was sitting in the large leather chair behind Julian's desk. Jade was perched on the edge of the desk, her back to the door. She slowly glanced over her shoulder, and the sinister curve of her lips sent a chill down Lexi's spine.

Jade's voice broke the eerie silence that had settled over the room. "Just the person he wanted to talk to." She stood up and stepped beside the desk, giving Lexi her first view of Vincent, who appeared to be devastated. His eyes were flat as he looked at her, devoid of all emotion. The tight line of his lips and furiously shaking knee scared Lexi more than anything.

"I need to talk to you," Lexi pleaded but his expression didn't change. It remained stone cold and dead.

"I don't think he wants to hear anything *you* have to say anymore," Jade snarled, her arms crossing over her chest.

"Back off, Jade. I'm in no mood for your bullshit right now." Lexi took a step toward the desk, and Vincent leapt to his feet as if he couldn't get far enough away from her. "Vincent, please?"

He wheeled around with fire in his eyes. "Please what, Lexi? What do you want me to do exactly? Listen to you? Put up with you overstepping your bounds in my office? With you worming your way into my family? Or should I just bend over and let you continue to screw me while you play footsies under the table with Reid? I just hope he paid you in cash for the information you gave him, because if he paid you with sex, you're a damn fool. The man doesn't know his dick from a rotten banana."

The malice and rage in his words floored Lexi. Jade grinned victoriously just out of his line of sight. Lexi tried to process what he was saying, but her head was spinning. "I—I'm not doing anything with Reid. He tried to come on to me tonight, and I told him to take a hike. Wh-where is all of this coming from?" Her eyes darted over to Jade. "What lies has she been filling your head with now?"

He laughed darkly as he leaned against the far wall, still glaring at her. "You want to know where it's coming from?" He pushed himself up and stalked toward her, scaring Lexi. "*This* is where it comes from." His phone was in his outstretched hand. "Go ahead, take it. Read the text I just got."

With a shaking hand, Lexi slipped the phone from his palm, careful not to touch him. The words on the screen stopped her heart.

Just heard from Reid's assistant looking for a meeting the day before you. Prelim ideas same. Excalibur is in play. There's your mole. - MJ

She read and reread the words a million times and still couldn't believe them. He was accusing her of being the mole. If there was one person who had been on Vincent's side, it was Lexi. Ever since she'd walked through the elevator doors of the twenty-third floor, she had put up with his crap, his yelling, his tirades, his satanic girlfriend with her fire and brimstone, all for him. Lexi's eyes locked on Jade, whose smile seemed ready to burst from her face.

"Do you have anything to say?" Vincent snarled.

Lexi's eyes flicked up to his and she held is gaze, her anger now growing to rival even his. She slammed the phone back into his palm. "I am not the mole. I haven't shared that information with anyone. It's been under lock and key since the second you gave it to me. I know where every copy is. They're all locked in my desk drawer and numbered."

Vincent rolled his eyes.

"I did not sell you out to Reid." Lexi bit out every word through her clenched jaw.

The two of them stood face to face, neither one breaking eye contact. Jade cleared her throat in the distance and spoke. "So then it's just a coincidence that the leaks started about the time you arrived? Is it just a coincidence that Reid sent you flowers and that you two were huddled together in the corner tonight? Then, soon after, Mr. Johnson gets a call about the Excalibur account? Vincent isn't stupid, Lexi."

"He is the stupidest man alive if he's listening to you and the load of shit you're feeding him."

"Why?" The strangled word came from Vincent's lips. His eyes were no longer angry; they were lost. The sadness seeped out of his pores, nearly smothering Lexi.

"I did *not* sell you out, Vincent. But I know who did." She cast a quick look in Jade's direction, long enough to see her pale, and then Lexi returned her gaze to Vincent. "So it all comes down to this—do you trust me?"

Vincent flinched at her words, breaking eye contact and fidgeting nervously with the change in his pocket. Time stood still as she waited for his answer. He turned away and began pacing the room, his hands raking through his hair and tugging on the tangled strands.

Sadly, Lexi had her answer. His silence spoke volumes. Overwhelmed with grief, Lexi turned toward the door and started to walk away. She reached out and touched the knob when she heard Vincent speak.

"Where are you going?"

"I'm leaving. I have my answer. If you had to think about it for even a second, you don't know me at all." She pushed open the door and turned back around. "Oh, and Vincent?" When he turned, she wiped the tear that was skimming down her cheek. "I swear on Harry's soul that I'm not the mole. Jade is."

And with that, she slammed the door shut and walked away from Vincent Drake.

30

Lexi! Wait." Anna spun around as her friend tore past her down the hall, tears and mascara staining her cheeks.

"Can't now, Anna." Lexi slowed her pace, falling against the wall and slowly sliding to the floor.

Panic hit Anna, hard. "Lexi, honey, what happened?"

"Vincent happened. He thinks I'm the mole," Lexi sobbed, her eyes wide and fearful. "I'm not, Anna. I swear."

Anna hugged her friend. "Of course you're not. You would never. Why would he say that? Is he drunk?" There was no way Lexi would sell out the family. She wasn't that kind of person; Anna was certain of that. It had to be a set up, and if it was, there was only one person hateful enough to do it, and that was Jade.

"No, he's not drunk, just stupid."

Loud voices came from the office, and Lexi scrambled to her feet. "I—I have to go. I can't stomach either one of them right now." She pulled the papers from her purse and tucked them into Anna's hand. "I swear, Jade's the mole. She's selling information to Reid and Parketti for sure. There might be others. Erica gave me these a couple minutes ago."

The wrinkled papers crackled as Anna unfolded them and began scouring the pages. "How the hell?"

"Jade. All roads lead back to her." Lexi took a few steps away, then turned and paused. "But that's not the worst part. She's also sleeping with Reid."

Anna's eyebrows shot up. "Does Vincent know?"

"That she's the mole? I told him before I left, but I don't know if he believed me. I didn't tell him about Reid and Jade. I couldn't."

Out of the darkness came more yelling. "Don't touch me!" Vincent's roar echoed down the hall.

Both women glanced toward the office and held their breath, expecting someone to come storming out. When things finally quieted, Anna exhaled. "Come with me. We'll talk to him. I'll beat some sense into him if I have to." She hooked her arm in Lexi's and tried to guide her toward the office.

Lexi shook her head emphatically. "No way. I'm done talking. I asked him to trust me and he paused. He paused, Anna." Her eyes filled with tears again. The sadness in her voice made Anna's chest ache. "It doesn't matter now. I'm leaving."

Lexi hurried down the hall, never once looking back. All Anna could do was stare at the silhouette of her broken friend as she vanished from view. It wasn't until she heard the voices again that she suddenly found herself enraged and went over and threw open the office door.

"Vincent Drake, what the hell have you done?"

"Not now, Anna." Anna had never seen him so pale and frenzied, pacing the room like a caged animal desperate for escape. "I have to go. I have to talk to Lexi."

"You aren't going anywhere until you calm down." Anna stopped him from making a break for the door.

"Move, Anna," he growled, looming over her, full of menace.

"Make me." Anna stood toe-to-toe with her brother, refusing to allow him to intimidate her. There was no way she was going to let him run off after Lexi half-crazed. She was already distraught, and the last thing she needed was to deal with an out of control Vincent. "Lexi just ran out of here on the verge of hysterics. She said you accused her of being the mole. Did you do something stupid? Did you hurt her?" Anna gave her brother a hard shove in the chest that had him staggering back a few steps. The stunned look on his face answered her question.

"I—I would never do that. You know me better than that," Vincent roared.

"I thought I did," Anna snipped. "But you're acting like a lunatic right now."

"Why don't you move so I can go talk to Lexi? *Then* I'll calm down." He took a deep breath. "Please, Anna. I need to see her."

"Get out, Anna!" Jade snarled from the corner of the room from where she had silently watched the family interaction play out. "Vincent, you aren't going anywhere near Lexi."

Anna pointed her perfectly manicured fingernail at Jade. "You need to shut your mouth now, or I'm gonna do it for you. I've had it with you." Her normally sweet, jovial voice was laced with venom and rage.

"Fuck you," Jade spat.

"No thanks, I don't take sloppy seconds from Reid. You're such a miserable tramp." Anna turned and faced her brother. "You and I need to have a conversation before you go anywhere. Either you get rid of her or I will. But if I do it, she'll need medical attention, I can promise you that."

Sensing things were slipping away, Jade began screeching. "She hates me, Vincent. She's going to fill your head with lies. Lexi's her friend. She wants you to dump me for her."

Anna snorted. "He could dump you for the potted plant in that corner or a prize winning dairy cow for all I care. As long as you're gone, it makes no difference to me who he ends up with. But if I get a vote, you bet I'd pick Lexi! She's ten times the woman you'll ever be."

"Will you both just shut up!" Vincent shouted, his hands laced tightly into his hair. "Anna, you need to move, now."

"No. You need to calm down. Lexi—"

"Lexi this, Lexi that. She makes me sick! She betrayed Vincent, you know." Jade's demented rant earned a savage glare from Anna.

"Enough!" Vincent's hands slammed down on the desk, his eyes black with fury. "She didn't betray me." He rubbed his hand across his face. "I betrayed her."

There was a long pause during which no one in the room spoke or even dared to breathe. The menace on Vincent's face made both women take pause. They stood frozen in silence, each wondering who would say something first.

"Leave, Jade," Vincent finally commanded.

With a glance in Anna's direction, she sashayed forward then reached out to run her hand down his chest, but Vincent swatted her wrist away before she could make contact.

"Don't ever touch me again. Don't ever talk to me again. If you see me, turn in the other direction and walk away. I am now, from this moment on, your worst enemy. Leave." When Jade's face paled and her mouth opened to protest, Vincent stepped closer to her until their noses were almost touching. His anger came off of him in waves. "I'd advise you to get a good attorney too. You're going to need one. I plan on suing you and your worthless partners in crime for every cent you've got and every cent you might potentially make in the future. When I get done with you, you'll owe me so much money, you'll spend the rest of your worthless modeling career working just to pay me. I'll also make sure that your name's on every blacklist in the industry by the time I'm through." Vincent's dead eyes never left Jade's face. "Get out!" His voice thundered as he fought a losing battle to remain in control.

In that moment, Anna saw her brother as the ruthless man she had always heard he could be, one devoid of emotion and full of rage. There wasn't a doubt in her mind that he would do exactly what he promised, not only to Jade, but to anyone else who deceived him. With great pleasure, he would ruin them all professionally and financially if he lost Lexi. He was livid, his temper barely held in control as he faced off with Jade. His expression was filled with wild, uncontrollable disgust for the woman standing before him.

"But I—I didn't..."

His expression turned deadly. "You have ten seconds to get out of this room or I'm calling security. The paparazzi would have a field day snapping pictures as they kick you to the curb. Or I could always do it myself." Vincent stepped toward the phone, and Anna moved quickly to his side. Shoulder to shoulder they stood, daring Jade to make a scene. "Ten, nine, eight..."

With a murderous glare, Jade slowly backed toward the door. "You're going to be sorry."

There was a long silence, and then Vincent responded as she turned her back, "I already am." With a loud crash, the door slammed shut, and Jade was finally gone.

Jade's exit should have been a time for rejoicing, but Anna felt more like throwing up. The moment Jade left the room, Vincent's body language changed. He was no longer rigid and furious. As he fell into the chair, his shoulders slumped forward, his chin dropping to his chest. He buried his face in his hands and was broken. Anna wanted to scream at him. She wanted to rub his stupidity in his face and scream "I told you so" about Jade, but she couldn't. Whatever had gone down with Lexi must have been awful. Anna's stomach dropped.

"What happened?"

She sat quietly and listened to him explain the last fifteen minutes to her. The words exploded from him with such deep sorrow and regret that it brought tears to her eyes. A few times she had to stop her jaw from falling open at his stupidity. When he finished the awful tale, he finally looked up at her, his eyes full of heartbreak.

"I'm so stupid. This should have been the greatest night of my life. I was going to break up with Jade, as I should have done weeks ago. Finding out the identity of the mole wasn't a good enough reason to keep Jade around. I couldn't stay away from Lexi another second. I had to be with her and prayed that she wanted to be with me. Anna, I love her." There was devotion in his eyes as he spoke of Lexi, but then a shadow washed over his face. "She's never going to speak to me again. I said such awful things."

"How could you accuse her? There isn't a more loyal person on the planet. She loves you, you big idiot. She's loved you since the moment she laid eyes on you back in high school." Anna threw her hands into the air.

"What? Lexi doesn't love me. I think, I hope, she's attracted to me, but there's no way..."

Anna snorted. "Men. You really are the dumbest creatures on the planet." Anna grabbed his shoulders and gave him a shake. "She wants to be with you. The girl takes care of everything for you, knows all your favorites, sneaks you burgers, stays at work all night to help you when something goes wrong. You two work seamlessly together, like you share a brain. You know what one another is thinking. It's like you can read each other's minds or something. Her eyes light up when you walk into a room, and when you compliment her, she blushes every time."

"Harmless flirting." Vincent downplayed their interactions, still not allowing himself to hope.

"Really?" Anna arched an eyebrow at him. "So you're saying Lexi goes around kissing random men she has no interest in? That doesn't sound like her to me."

Vincent exhaled. "That first kiss was supposed to just be a taste, a little something to answer all the confusion I had about my feelings when I was near her. I thought if I got it out of my system, I'd be able to get her out of my head and out of my dreams. But as soon has her lips brushed against mine, I was lost. The taste of her intoxicated me like a drug. The second kiss was something I needed from her. I craved her in ways I couldn't explain and was helpless to stop it from happening. I wanted that kiss to get under her skin, to brand her as mine in some way. Ever since, I can't think of anything but Lexi."

He looked at Anna, his face the picture of devastation. She'd never seen him so distraught.

"I have to find her and apologize." His voice came out as a shaky whisper as he rose to his feet. "If—if she doesn't forgive me, I don't know what I'm going to do. She's the best thing that's ever happened to me, Anna."

Anna held him and felt him shaking in her grasp. She patted him on the back and whispered reassurances in his ear, not entirely believing them herself, but she needed to give him something, some hope that he still might have a chance to make this right.

After providing her brother a few moments of comfort, she held him at arm's length and quickly wiped her tears. "You seem to be more in control." Vincent nodded his head. She took a deep breath, becoming very serious. "So, what do you plan on doing to fix this?"

"I have to find her and beg her to forgive me. I'll walk through the fires of hell if I have to."

There was a small grin on Anna's face as she patted his cheek. "Good man."

Vincent kissed her hand, then grabbed his jacket and took off for the door. "I have to go."

"How are you going to find her? She could be anywhere, even at the airport booking the next flight out of town."

Vincent thought about it, then suddenly seemed very sure of himself. "I know where she is." He cast one quick look back at his sister. "Can you explain everything to Mom? She needs to know."

"Sure, leave me to clean up your mess like always." Anna gave him a weak smile. "Go find her. Fix this."

"I love you. I know I'm a jerk and don't say it enough, but I do."

"I love you too, Vincent. Go!"

✦

Vincent made his way down the dimly illuminated street on the cool, dark night. The stars twinkled overhead, and the full moon hung low in the night sky. Couples strolled past, their fingers intertwined as they watched the water, whispering to one another. Their happiness made him long for Lexi even more. Would he ever get the chance to take her on a romantic walk, tuck her safely under his arm, and tell her how much he loved her and kiss her under the stars? Or was he destined for a life without love?

He passed in front of Ghirardelli Square and found Lexi's winding path through the riverside park. His steps became more tentative as he approached the shadowy figure sitting on the bench in the distance. There was no calming his thundering heart, his ragged breathing, or the pain in his chest. Every time she wiped a tear from her face, Vincent felt like his heart was being ripped out. He could tell the moment she heard his footsteps because her whole body tensed, but she didn't turn toward him.

"Go away."

The strangled plea knocked the breath out of Vincent. She sounded so lost, so hurt, that for a second he contemplated doing exactly as she asked. Leaving would be the easier thing to do. But that was the coward's way, and Vincent was done being a coward with his heart. He sensed that he had one chance to make this right with Lexi or he would lose her forever, and that was something he was not willing to risk. With painful slowness, he sat down beside her on the bench and prepared for the pitch of a lifetime.

He couldn't look at her. He couldn't stand to see the pain in her face or the anger in her eyes, so he sat silently beside her, breathing slowly as he looked out over the water and prayed for strength. The reflection of the moon shimmered in the gentle waves of the bay while car lights twinkled in the distance as they traveled over the Golden Gate Bridge. If he hadn't made such a mess of things, the setting would have been romantic, but under the current circumstances, it was eerie and fragile.

"I—I'm sorry." Such simple words, ones that couldn't possibly convey the depths of his sorrow or regret, fell from his lips. All he could do was hold his breath and wait for her reaction. Thousands of thoughts pulsed through his head—explanations, reasons, justifications—things he wanted to blurt out in an attempt to gain her forgiveness, but he realized they were all nothing more than excuses for his horrible behavior, excuses that didn't fix a damn thing between them. The one thing that could begin to repair this situation was absolute honesty. He owed her that at least, no matter how difficult it was going to be to tell her every detail of his mistakes.

The only sounds that came from Lexi were tiny sniffles. Occasionally she would raise her hand to wipe away a stray tear from her cheek, and the material on her dress would rustle. Other than that, she remained completely silent with her arms folded tightly over her chest, as if he wasn't even sitting beside her.

"I want to tell you what happened." The words tentatively slipped out. Vincent kept his head focused forward on the water, but he watched out of the corner of his eye to see if she was getting ready to bolt.

"I can't," she shook her head and jutted her chin into the air defiantly. "I can't talk to you right now. I won't."

Vincent braved a glance in her direction, and it nearly stopped his heart. Her eyes were dead, flat, and unrecognizable. Her cheeks glistened with the moisture from the thousands of tears she must have already shed. Her chin and lower lip quivered as she struggled to keep from sobbing. Keeping his movements smooth and slow to not spook her, he slipped his hand into his pocket and pulled out a handkerchief. When he offered it to her, his hand shook.

With her eyes fixed on her lap, Lexi unfolded one of her arms and tentatively reached for the handkerchief, taking great care to not touch Vincent in any way. She took the square and pressed it to her cheek, her head shaking gently from side to side in the darkness.

"I know you don't want to talk." Vincent chose his words carefully, not wanting to do anything to upset her further. "But would you agree to just listen for a little bit?"

Vincent counted seventeen chirps from the crickets around them before her shoulder raised and lowered in a shrug of indifference, seventeen long painful chirps before he finally allowed himself to exhale in relief. She had given him his chance, and now he had an unknown amount of time in which to explain his actions.

Proceeding with great caution, he began. "I can't tell you how sorry I am for doubting you. I believe you. I know you're not the mole and that you'd never do that to me."

Her only reaction was to wipe away a falling tear. Another trailed close behind it down the apple of her cheek, followed soon by another as her crying picked up again.

"I was wrong. I let my own issues cloud my judgment, and I reacted like an angry child in the middle of a tantrum. I saw you earlier tonight talking with Reid. He looked," Vincent paused, trying to think of the right word, "*pleased* with himself as he walked away. I didn't like seeing him, huddled in a private corner of the room with you, touching you. I'm not proud, but it made me incredibly jealous." He worked very hard to keep his voice calm, even though as he spoke he pictured Reid's fingers gliding down Lexi's arm, and he wanted to punch something.

"He propositioned me *again*." Lexi's voice was barely above a whisper, strangled by her sadness but still full of anger. "And for the record, I said no *again*."

Vincent's heart broke. "I know you did, sweetheart. I know. This was all me. I acted like a monster. I let my past screw up everything I have in the present and possibly my future. I was stupid and hurtful. There's no reason you should pay for my previous or current mistakes with women. With Jade—"

"I'm not *her*." Lexi wouldn't even allow Jade's name to come out of her mouth.

"You're right. You're nothing like her. You are kind and good, beautiful, intelligent, witty, and a light to everyone you're around. She's a parasite, a user, a manipulator, and a liar. You two are worlds apart and, frankly, I can't believe that someone as wonderful as you would even give a man like me the time of day. I'm a grumpy, suspicious, cold-hearted bastard, and if I were you I would have told me to take a hike a long time ago."

"Believe me, the thought has crossed my mind." Lexi's despondent eyes stayed fixed on the water in the distance. "I'm considering it right now, as a matter of fact."

A hair blew across her cheek, and Vincent instinctively reached out to tuck it behind her ear, but stopped short when Lexi flinched as his hand approached. She turned on him, and he saw the utter rage in her eyes. His hand froze mid air then limply fell back.

In the past when Vincent had hurt her feelings, she came at him with such vengeance, happily putting him in his place and telling him to go to hell. But now, her answers and comments were so brief, so clipped. It terrified him. It was as if she didn't care anymore, like she had already made up her mind that she was done with him. Forever.

Panic set in and he started rambling, hoping that something he said might make her stay or at least listen a little longer until he could form a coherent thought. "The truth is, my track record with women sucks. It has since high school. You know about Jennifer and how that ended. With Adria it was more of the same thing, times ten. Of course, she brought the business into it, playing me so she could get stature and success in the company before she left and took a ton of clients with her. She was conniving from the moment we met in college, and I should have known better. The signs were all there, but I didn't listen to my head.

"I thought I was in love, whatever that meant at the time, and refused to believe anything bad about her. I felt like such a fool when she walked out on me. I'll never forget the sight, her laughing as she ran down the laundry list of clients that were going to follow her to her new agency. She even implied she was sleeping with a few of them to ensure their business. To this day, I don't know if it was true or just to turn the knife a little deeper in my heart. Either way, she enjoyed telling me all about it, in graphic detail."

Lexi's tears finally stopped falling as she quietly listened to his depressing autobiography.

"I should have known better with Jade." Lexi's hands balled into fists in her lap at the mention of Jade's name. "In the beginning, she was kind and sweet. No. That's not true—she stroked my ego, and I liked it. She told me how brilliant I was and ... God, she was working me from day one." His shoulders slumped forward as his hands scrubbed over his face. "She was always interested in the business. Asked a ton of questions, who our clients were. She wanted to see all the campaigns I was working on, and she would sit there and tell me how great they were. She constantly visited the office and snuck into client meetings. I'm such a fool."

His entire relationship with Jade played back in his head in vivid color. Warning flags waved everywhere, but he had been so busy working and enjoying the emotional distance that he never noticed what was going on around him. He had completely underestimated her intelligence, allowing her to play the role of stereotypical airheaded model to his dashing young businessman. Every warning his family and Sean had given him, every lie she had told, every coincidence screamed at him until he thought he was going to be sick.

Half to himself, he continued. "She kept getting jobs on accounts we lost. That's been going on for months now. In the back of my head, I thought it was odd, but she's a well known model, and she fit the campaigns. I chalked it up as my loss being her gain. I think we even joked about it once. She's probably been laughing at me this entire time." He took long, deep breaths, trying to calm his now raging temper. He was glad he'd already ended things with Jade because if he ever saw her again, it would be difficult to not rip her to shreds.

"I'm glad you see what an evil bitch she is. Of course, you still believed her."

"Lexi, I'm sorry. God, you must be so sick of hearing me say that by now. I wish I could say something that would erase my abhorrent behavior, but I can't." The wind blew through the trees, the leaves rustling together as Vincent tipped his head back and stared up at the sky. "I can only tell you honestly what was going through my head and pray that when I'm done you'll consider what I've said."

She settled back on the bench and sighed, which Vincent took as an encouraging sign, so he cautiously continued. "Jade was the one who originally told me about the mole. Looking back, I think she did it because she sensed I was getting ready to end things with her. My feelings had changed, and my attention was directed … other places. She picked up on that and wanted a way to keep me in her good graces. She knew helping me with a crisis at Hunter was the way to do that."

Lexi sat like a statue and listened. She showed no reaction to Vincent's words. It seemed she was more interested in tracing the monogrammed letters on the handkerchief, which she had neatly folded into a square. But he kept talking. "She told me someone from Hunter was selling ideas and that she had found out some information from her friends during tone of their trips. A friend of hers was dating someone at Reid, and Jade was supposedly working her for details. At least that was the line of bull she fed me." He raked his hands down his face.

"She's sleeping with Reid." Lexi's voice sounded stronger, more annoyed than sad now.

"I know that now. Frankly, they deserve each other. They're both vile parasites who thrive by sucking the life out of others. I hope they're absolutely miserable together for many years to come."

Out of the corner of his eye, he watched Lexi nod her head in agreement. That, in his opinion, was progress. As a strong breeze flew in off the bay, he snuck a glance in her direction and saw that her arms were covered in goose bumps and she was shivering. He slipped out of his suit jacket. "You're cold."

Lexi gave no response. Her eyes stayed fixed forward, even as he laid the jacket over her bare shoulders. Her hands held onto the lapels of the coat, pulling the ends closer together to keep it in place. Vincent left his arm draped across the back of the bench, his hand lightly brushing against the fabric of his jacket. There was no way she could feel it through the thick material, but for him, it felt like he was doing some small thing to comfort her. He saw her turn her head to the side, her cheek nuzzling against the warmth of the jacket, and he smiled.

"I decided to try and flush out the mole by calling in key people on our design team and assigning them each a unique project to oversee. Some were real accounts, others were dummy accounts I made up with the contact phone numbers going places like Sean's cell phone or Erik's. If anyone from Reid or Parketti called to set up an appointment, then the person in charge of that specific account would most likely be the mole."

"All the meetings you had," Lexi mumbled as Vincent nodded his head.

"Yeah, the parade of people. I was assigning them something to watch over, with the assumption the mole would pass the juicy tidbit I gave them on to their contact at Reid or Parketti. That was my big plan to catch the mole."

Lexi turned and glared at him. "You set me up with Excalibur."

There was a pause and then his head began to bob up and down. "I did. I didn't want to, and I went back and forth about it." Lexi made a small sound of disbelief. "It's true. That's why I talked to you days after everyone else. You were the last person I assigned something to, but I had to do it, just to be sure."

Lexi turned away from him, but Vincent could see her thinking things over in her head, remembering the timeline of events and making sure he was telling the truth. He knew if he lied, or if she remotely thought he was lying, she would be gone, so he made sure every word was accurate.

"Martin Johnson is an old family friend and business associate. He's the one who sent the text about the mole. I'd asked him to be on the lookout for campaigns similar to the one I'd shown him for Excalibur. We are going to be working with him in the near future; that part's true. But the campaign itself—that was all a lie. The materials I gave you were from a presentation I worked on in college, one Adria never saw. It was an early version of my final senior project. I needed something fast, and I had saved copies of it, so I updated it at the last minute when I decided I should give you a project too."

"That explains it."

"Explains what?"

Another long silence stretched before Lexi answered. "The slight differences in the materials, the way she got the information to set me up. She saw the original version at your apartment, before you updated it. That's what was on the paper Erica gave me, a picture of the originals in your apartment. Jade knew what you were doing, and she set me up from the beginning."

Ruefully, Vincent nodded his head. "She would ask what accounts were in play and which ones she should be listening for information on, and I gave her everything. I basically handed her everything she needed to frame you. If I could go back in time, I would."

"It doesn't matter. What's done is done."

Lexi's words hung between them, the finality in them scaring Vincent. She was right. The past was unchangeable and had an effect on the future, no matter how hard either of them tried to ignore it. He knew his actions would have repercussions and change things between the two of them.

"I want you to know that I believed you. Before you swore on Harry's soul, I knew you were telling the truth, but I also know you well enough to realize that by considering you guilty for even a short time I've damaged our relationship. I only hope the damage isn't irrevocable." When he saw the tears had started again, he kept going, sensing his time was running out. "When Jade and I got upstairs, I sat her down and gave her the truth. I told her there was someone else I cared a great deal for and we needed to end things. She was in the middle of trying to talk me out of it when the text came from Mr. Johnson, and I admit, I was floored. My emotions were already a mess, and reading it just sent me over the edge. Jade saw it and went off, ranting about how you played me, pointed out that the time we started losing clients coincided with your arrival. She brought up you and Reid again, his interest in you, the flowers, the private discussion from earlier in the evening. She played on my jealousy and insecurities perfectly. She knew you were the woman I was leaving her for. She knew I wanted a relationship with you, and it drove her crazy. Jade lashed out and went straight for your jugular, and I stood by and watched."

Lexi's foot now tapped nervously, like she was desperately trying to stay in control of herself. Part of Vincent hoped she'd lose control and finally show some sort of emotion. A kicking, punching, screaming Lexi would be far less terrifying to Vincent than the totally apathetic woman sitting beside him.

"Right after I read the text, you walked through the door. There was no time for me to process it or reason things out. I was angry; I admit it. I was a hot-head, and I regret that more than I can ever say. My common sense was buried deep under my anger. I let my insecurities and pathetic history dictate my actions. In my head, I thought you had betrayed me, just like every other woman I had dated. Jade didn't convince me—I convinced myself that you were guilty."

A few moments passed during which Lexi's head simply shook from side to side as she digested everything Vincent had told her. Everything about her body language screamed "back off" but she said nothing and listened. He had held nothing back. Every ugly detail of his mistake was laid out for her to see. She needed to know all of it.

"The fact that when you asked me to trust you, I didn't do it immediately will haunt me forever. When you turned your back on me, I knew the truth. In the past when I had listened to my heart, I screwed myself. So this time, I followed my head. I ignored what I knew in my heart about you and let my paranoid head cloud my judgment. I'll regret that decision and hurting you until the day I die. The incredible thing is that I do trust you. I trust you with my life, my work, and my heart. I panicked. I've never wanted to give my heart to someone like I want to give it to you. Totally and completely."

The calm veneer that Lexi had put up finally exploded, and she scrambled to her feet, unable to sit there any longer. "Are you done?" she snipped, wiping her cheeks, straightening her dress and pulling herself together. "Because I'm done listening to you."

"Lexi—"

"Don't 'Lexi' me. This wasn't the first time you've been awful to me, Vincent. When I started working at Hunter, you were barely human. Then there was the incident where you suggested I be a whore for Hunter, or my personal favorite—all the times Jade spewed her hate at me or your family members and you stood beside her, suddenly struck mute and spineless." Vincent stayed silent while she continued, teeming with rage. "And if all that wasn't enough, you then have the nerve to accuse me of sleeping with that psychotic idiot Reid and saying I wormed my way into your life? Into the lives of your family? How dare you!"

Vincent was on his feet beside her in seconds. He was careful not to touch her, but he blocked her escape down the path and held his hands up in surrender. "Wait."

"I'm sorry, but I'm done waiting for you, Vincent Drake. I've already spent years of my life waiting." Lexi stormed past him, his jacket slipping off her shoulders and falling onto the sidewalk.

"Lexi, please!" the strangled cry came from deep in his chest. "Lexi!" he roared into the darkness as his heart began to rip apart in his chest.

Wheeling around, Lexi screamed back at him. "What do you want from me?"

"I want a life *with* you. I want what my parents have, what my sister has with Erik. God help me, I want to be able to come into work an hour late with a big goofy grin on my face like Sean does now that he found Hope." He slowly approached Lexi, who was sobbing, not even trying to hide her distress any longer behind a brave face. She was shattered, boldly allowing him to see just how deeply he had hurt her.

Without hesitation, he stepped over and wrapped his arms around her, crushing her against his chest. Her body stayed rigid, but after a few seconds he felt her emotionally exhausted body sag into his. They stood locked in an embrace for a long time, Vincent whispering apologies and begging her forgiveness as he pressed his lips to the top of her head. Carefully, he led her back to the bench and sat her down, taking great care to wrap his jacket back over her shoulders and make her as comfortable as possible. Instead of sitting beside her, he stayed on his knees at her feet, holding her trembling hands.

"I want you to know everything about me, Lexi, to see inside me, beyond my gruff arrogance, beyond the hurt and loneliness, to the man underneath it all. There are things about me that no one knows, but I want to share them with you. Believe it or not, I think you've gotten closer than anyone ever has to knowing the real me."

Taking the handkerchief from her hand, he wiped the new tears that had fallen. "You make me the man I want to be. You help me see the good in people. I have fun when I'm with you, even under the worst circumstances. Your smile makes me happy; your touch sets my body on fire. When you walk into a room, I feel like a teenager and can't help but look at you. I love the way you bite your nails when you're stressed, or stick pencils into your hair while you're working. You have five little freckles," he leaned forward and gently touched each one on the bridge of her nose and cheeks, "that I can only see when I'm this close to you. You're loyal and brave. The way you are with Madison is beautiful to watch. She adores you just like everyone else who comes in contact with you. My life felt like it was an endless night before you came along and showed me the sun again. I don't want to lose you."

Lexi's head dipped down, hiding her eyes from Vincent's view. When he hooked his finger under her chin and their eyes reconnected, he was overwhelmed by the emotions he felt. "You are the best thing that ever walked into my dreary life and rearranged my office without permission. I love your smartass replies to my angry text messages. I love the way you put me in my place when I act like an idiot. I love the way your nose wrinkles when you smile and the way you flick your hair over your shoulder when you walk into my office with that little yellow legal pad of yours." He paused, looking deeply into her eyes and knew it was now or never. "Lexi, I lo—"

At the speed of light, her hand found his mouth and firmly covered it. Her eyes were sad; the anger had dissipated and was replaced with misery. "Don't say it. I can't hear that from you right now. I don't want the memory of the first time you say that to me to be attached to this night. I dreamed about what it would be like to hear you say those words to me. If you care about me at all, wait. Let me keep my dream. Please don't take that away from me too."

As much as he wanted to tell her how much he loved her, he understood. This was not the time to do that. Earlier this evening, before he had made everything so damn complicated would have been better. He should have just grabbed her on that red carpet and kissed her in front of all the paparazzi and let that be it. Too little, too late.

His head bobbed up and down in agreement, and Lexi removed her hand. "What are we doing, here?" she whispered, her exhaustion finally showing.

"Talking, sweetheart, just talking."

She slipped her hand from his and reached out to touch his face, running her fingers lightly over his swollen eyebrow. Vincent winced at the contact. "You look terrible." Her fingers continued to trace over the swollen flesh around his eye that was starting to turn purple.

"It's nothing." His eyes closed, and he stayed perfectly still as she continued examining his injury.

When he opened his eyes the corner of her mouth was turned up in a little grin. "Sean?"

"Actually, Hope."

"That's my girl." A genuine smile crossed Lexi's lips for a second before it faded. "I have to go. I'm sorry."

This time when she got to her feet, Vincent didn't stop her. He too stood, and they took a few tentative steps down the path. He'd said his piece. He'd confessed his sins and begged for forgiveness even though he didn't deserve it. But most importantly, he told her how he felt. He let her see herself through his eyes and the beauty he saw within her. It was up to her now. Either she would forgive him or not, but she needed her space and time to think. With a heavy heart he decided to give that to her.

"How did you get down here?"

"Cab," she said as she slipped the strap of her purse around her wrist and started walking.

"May I walk with you then? Just let me get you a cab, then I'll leave you alone." Even if she said no, he was going to follow her. There was no way he would let her wander the streets of San Francisco alone at this hour.

"Whatever." She started walking, not waiting for him.

They walked side by side, in silence, each deep in their own thoughts. For Vincent, every step brought them closer to what could be their final goodbye. She could potentially step into the cab and that would be the last time he ever saw her. He planned to fight for her, but even that might not be enough.

Up ahead in the distance, a line of brightly colored cars sat waiting for customers.

His hand reached out and touched her shoulder, halting her in place. She slowly spun around, her eyes still puffy from all the tears. "I want you to know I'm going to give you some space. No matter what happens between us, please don't let it affect your relationship with Elizabeth or Anna. They love you and think of you as family. If you want to spend time with them, I'll respect that and stay away. I'll make sure I'm not there when you visit. I've done enough to hurt you. I won't get between your relationships with them." Lexi closed her eyes and nodded her head with a grateful smile.

Vincent tucked his hands deep into his pockets and watched her start walking to the cabs. The clicks of her heels on the concrete were the only sounds he heard. As she moved away from him, he felt a crushing pain in his chest, the fear of losing her overwhelming him, making it difficult to breathe. He screamed in his head for her to stop, begged her to stay with him, but she continued, her steps assured and strong as she separated herself from him. Then she paused and looked over her shoulder.

Every step she took back toward him made his heart soar. She was coming back to him. She wasn't leaving. The closer she got, the faster her steps came until she was on her toes in front of him, a polite smile on her lips.

"Here," she whispered as she slipped off her jacket and handed it to him. "I almost forgot to give this back to you."

His heart fell out of his chest. She didn't come back to him; she was returning his jacket. He quickly covered his sadness and smiled. "Thanks. Goodnight, Lexi."

With tears in her eyes she simply said, "Goodbye, Vincent."

31

Vincent and Elizabeth were splattered all over the paper for the next week with headlines like "Corporate Scandal at Hunter" quickly changing to ones of claimed innocence by the accused, namely Reid, Parketti, and Jade. The following day, the paper contained a lengthy interview with Adria in which she denied everything and accused Vincent of being a lover scorned. David Reid continued to publicly deny a relationship with Jade, and Jade did the same, making her way around the morning talk shows and playing the part of jilted girlfriend. Soon, everything became a case of he said/she said. Vincent's lawyers had advised him to not comment any further, so Vincent hid, and public opinion began to turn on him.

Lexi had been hounded by the press requesting interviews after Jade hinted that Vincent was having an affair with a co-worker. While Jade didn't accuse Lexi publicly, she put out enough sound bites and vague details that the news agencies had Lexi in their crosshairs within twenty-four hours.

Hope had been such a great friend to Lexi through the last week. When Lexi finally came home that horrible night, Hope was already waiting for her in the apartment, tending to her bruised knuckles in a small bowl of ice water. Lexi didn't even make it all the way to the couch and she collapsed into a heap on the floor, hysterically sobbing, overwhelmed with feelings of loss and despair.

That endless night turned into the following morning, and Lexi woke up in her bed, snuggled against her friend. The tears had finally ended, but the ache in Lexi's chest refused to dissipate. She had to concentrate on every breath and step she took, forcing herself to get up and out of bed to face the day. Sean came over, and he and Hope tried to talk Lexi into coming out to lunch with them, but she wouldn't leave the apartment. Hope made her a salad before she left, kissed Lexi on the head, and told her to call if she needed anything. Sean wrapped his giant arms around her and held her tight, as if to protect her from the crazy world that was spinning around her, even if only for a few seconds. She'd pressed her cheek against his broad chest, and bawled her eyes out, again.

"I'm sorry, Lex. I wish I could say something to help, but I suck at this." Sean felt her chuckle through the tears. He pulled her chin up and wiped her tears. "Don't know if it will make you feel any better, but I saw his sorry butt this morning and he looks a hell of a lot worse than you do. Except he doesn't have a snotty nose like yours. That's kinda gross." When the corner of her mouth turned up into a small smile, Sean hugged her. "Knew I could get a smile out of you." He kissed her head and let her slip from his grasp so she could grab some tissues. Then she ushered the two of them out the door and took some time to be alone with her thoughts.

On Sunday, Elizabeth and Anna had both called Lexi and left her messages, apologizing for Vincent's behavior and asking if there was anything they could do for her. Lexi appreciated the gesture, but she knew if she spoke to either one of them, she would be reduced to tears again, and she was trying to move on to a place where she could function despite her heartbreak.

Lexi remembered the shock on Hope's face when she came over to check on Lexi bright and early Monday morning and found her getting ready for work.

"Are you crazy?"

Lexi paused with the hairbrush in her hand. "For what? Going to work? Millions, actually billions, of people do it every day. No biggie."

"It is when your boss is Vincent Drake!"

The brush made a clanking noise as Lexi slammed it down on the counter. "The Marradesi presentation is Friday, and there's still a lot of work to do. I'm not walking away from that project. I've poured my heart into it. Professionally, it will be a huge accomplishment, one I'm not willing to sacrifice … for anyone."

Hope stepped out of the way as her irritated friend hurried past her, down the hall to the kitchen. She trailed behind Lexi, grabbing an apple out of the basket of fruit on the kitchen table. "Your dedication to your work is admirable, but what are you going to do about Vincent?"

Lexi tightened her grip on the refrigerator door and closed her eyes. "I'll cross that bridge when I come to it."

But she never had to cross that bridge on Monday or Tuesday or even Wednesday. Over the weekend, Vincent had apparently rearranged his schedule to be out of the office at meetings, including an overnight in Los Angeles. He sent Lexi E-mails, but only regarding their upcoming presentation. Every interaction was professional and necessary. Communicating with him this way was easy enough—the physical distance and the businesslike tone to his E-mails helped. There were no hidden meanings, no "I'm sorry" or "I miss you" messages, and every single one was signed V.D., his impersonal signature for business associates. He'd used that signature with Lexi when she'd first started working there, but he had long ago dropped it from his communications with her, and only her.

Even though he was out of the office, he wasn't out of her thoughts. All she had to do was glance up at any wall at Hunter and there were pictures of his past campaigns, reminders of him everywhere around her. She tried not to look at them and stay focused on her work, but it was impossible. He *was* Hunter Advertising for her whether or not she wanted to admit it. He was the thing she most looked forward to when she walked in the door each morning. Their interactions, their banter, their collaboration and friendship—those were the things that made work fun. Without him there, the office had a flat, lifeless quality for Lexi.

The one bright spot in her Monday had been the giant cup of coffee that had been left on the corner of her desk that morning, just how she liked it with two creams and extra sugar. As she trudged down the hall to her apartment that night, she'd smiled, thinking that maybe the next morning she'd feel brave enough to thank Leigh for the small act of kindness. Leigh knew how devastated she had been over the incident with Vincent and rather than question her, she gave Lexi her space, and some coffee to let her know that she was thinking of her. Lexi glanced down as she went to stick her key in the door and found her foot beside a beautifully wrapped package with a green ribbon on it. Puzzled, Lexi tucked the box carefully under her arm and hurried inside.

She casually tossed her mail onto the table and carried the mystery gift over to the couch. Her heart began pounding as she tugged on the silk ribbon, allowing it to pool onto her lap. With her hands shaking, she slipped her finger under the edge of the ornately decorated wrapping and gently pulled. She crumpled the paper and gasped as she read the print on top of the box. It was from the art gallery just down the street from Julian's studio, one of her favorite places to window shop because she knew the pieces inside were handmade and way beyond her price range. Lexi touched her fingers to the gold letters that spelled out "Capri," then took a deep breath and opened the box.

Inside was a crumpled pile of navy blue tissue paper, and on top sat a crisp, white note card with her name written on it. She closed her eyes and focused on her breathing as her blood raced through her veins. She knew that handwriting. She saw it every day at work, the perfectly scripted letters that made her name look more beautiful than she had ever been able to achieve with her own writing. Lexi picked up the card and dropped it three times before finally finding the courage to open it.

Lexi,
Just a little something to let you know I'm thinking about you.
Vincent

She reread the note, not knowing whether to hold it to her heart or rip it to shreds. It wasn't until the third read through that she noticed another line to the note, hidden under her thumb.

p.s. - Did I get the coffee right? Two creams, extra sugar?

He had dropped off the coffee. He had been at the office and left before she'd arrived. He was respecting her wishes, giving her space, but he also wanted to make sure she didn't forget about him. He wasn't running away. This time, he was waiting for her. She pulled the tissue paper from the box and peered inside. Nestled safely between the papers was a gorgeous glass vase. Her mouth hung open as she gingerly took it out of the box, and her breath caught in her throat as she examined it. It was tall and delicate with an intricate design along the bottom that reminded Lexi of the waves of the bay.

The topic of Capri had come up only once between them, the day of their presentation to Julian Stone. Even with all the stress they had both been under at the time, Vincent remembered. He had been paying attention to her likes and dislikes even way back then. That was what he wanted this gift to tell Lexi, the message he wanted to convey, and she heard it loud and clear. If only he had paid attention to other things about her, then they might not be in this position.

She set the vase on the coffee table, sat back on the couch, and admired it, enjoying the way the sun reflected off of it, spinning thousands of colorful rainbows onto the walls of her apartment. The box still felt unusually heavy in her lap. When her hand dipped between the pieces of paper, she found another small bundle tucked securely against the side of the box. She carefully unwrapped it, revealing two spectacular hand blown glass flowers. There was no way to stop the tears that fell the moment she saw them, because she knew immediately what the fragile purple hyacinth and the single red rose meant—*I'm sorry* and *I love you* respectively.

On both Tuesday and Wednesday morning, another cup of coffee was waiting for her at work when she arrived, and each evening there was another package sitting beside her door, containing a new flower with yet another meaning. Her vase was quickly filling up and growing into a gorgeous glass bouquet. Occasionally there would be another treat added in the box like licorice or another favorite candy of hers, making her smile. She suspected he must have even gone so far as to enlist Sean and Leigh to help with the deliveries while he was out of town so he wouldn't miss a day. That knowledge touched her more that she could say.

Late Wednesday night, Lexi stepped out of the shower and heard the phone ringing. She quickly wrapped a towel around her and snatched the phone off her bed.

"Hello?" There was a long silence so Lexi said it again with more force. "Hello?"

"L-Lexi?"

Vincent. The phone slipped out of her hand and smashed against the hardwood floor, skidding under the bed. "Shit, shit, shit," Lexi muttered, completely flustered as she stuck her arm under the bed looking for the receiver. He was the last person she expected to hear on the other end of the phone. Her heart crashed against her ribs as her fingers wrapped around the phone, and she pressed it to her ear. "Sorry," she whispered, readjusting her towel as she sat down on her bed and picked at the frayed edge of the cotton. "I dropped the phone. Hi, Vincent."

"H-hi." Vincent's reply was as tentative as hers. "If this is a bad time..."

"No, it's fine. What do you want?" The words came out harsher than she had intended, but she was on edge, wondering what could possibly be the reason for his call.

"Sorry for the late call, but I needed to talk to you."

"I don't have—"

"It's about work. I promise."

Lexi stared at her reflection in the mirror over her dresser, wondering if she should hang up on him. When her reflection shrugged, thinking "how bad it could be," she decided to hear him out and sighed. "What is it?"

"Well, I would have E-mailed, but I didn't know if you would check it before tomorrow or if you were in bed already, and I didn't know if you'd get a text, so…I called." He sounded downright uncomfortable, and Lexi gave her reflection a triumphant smile.

"Please spit it out, Vincent."

"Elizabeth wants us to have a breakfast meeting with her tomorrow morning."

Lexi's eyebrow shot up in suspicion. "I talked to her right before I left work. She didn't mention a thing about it." If she had to sit across the table from Vincent, she knew her stomach would do that awful squeeze and she'd never get a bite down. "I appreciate the offer, but no thanks."

"It wasn't an invitation. It's a requirement and non-negotiable."

"Everything's negotiable," Lexi quickly replied, spouting off one of the first things Vincent had taught her.

He chuckled. "I know I told you that, but when it comes to my mother, well, that rule doesn't exactly hold. I should have mentioned that earlier." Lexi could hear the smile in his voice, and when she looked in the mirror she caught sight of her own smile. She missed this kind of banter with him.

"Well, hell."

There was a noise that sounded like him shifting around in his bed, sheets rustling as he moved. "That's a lot of swearing from you tonight."

"I've had a lot to swear about lately." As the words escaped her lips, they brought reality crashing back down around her. Her tone immediately changed, all hints of playfulness gone. "Fine, I'll be there. When and where?"

"Um." He seemed taken aback by her sudden change in demeanor. "Tomorrow, nine o'clock at Rocco's Café. Do you know where it is? If not, I—I could pick you up."

"I'll Google it." An awful silence fell between them. Lexi began to panic, not wanting Vincent to change the topic to her or something even more uncomfortable, them. "Thanks for the call. See you tomorrow."

"Lexi?" Vincent's voice tentatively called out just as she began to pull the receiver away from her ear. She brought the phone back, her head falling back onto her pillow.

"Yeah?" she sighed and her eyes closed tightly as she waited.

"I just, I wanted to tell you," he stammered, and Lexi could almost imagine him lying on his bed, raking his hand through his hair. "Nevermind. Goodnight, Lexi."

"Goodnight to you too, Vincent." Even though she didn't want to, a smile flickered across her face when she heard him chuckling as she hung up the phone.

The conversation had been far from comfortable, but it also hadn't left her stomach in a burning, churning mess like she thought it might. The sound of his voice had made her heart race and her knees weak just like it always did. The only difference was the ache in her chest it now caused as well. Lexi crawled under her covers, knowing that in a few short hours she would be face to face with Vincent for the first time in days. Even though it terrified her, on some small level, it excited her too, though she wasn't ready to admit it.

✦

Thursday morning, Lexi overslept. Lexi never overslept. But on the morning of the meeting with Vincent and Elizabeth, she woke up a half hour late and ran around the apartment in her underwear looking for the skirt that went with the blouse and pumps she was currently wearing. She had laid it down somewhere in an undisclosed location that she had yet to discover. Just as she was about to scream, she found it neatly folded on the coffee table beside her vase of glass flowers from Vincent. She glared at the beautiful blooms she spent way too much time looking at and snatched the skirt. Sliding it up her thighs, she chastised herself. "Get your head out of the clouds, Lexi. He's a man, nothing more."

The words had felt good to say, empowering, but as she ran her fingers over the smooth, colorful glass blooms, she realized they were a complete lie. Vincent wasn't just some random guy. He was so much more than she wanted to admit.

With her head held high, and by some miracle, almost on time, Lexi walked through the doors of the restaurant and was greeted by a beautiful, golden-haired hostess. "Good morning, welcome to Rocco's. Are you dining alone or meeting someone?"

"I'm meeting two other people. They're probably here. I'm a minute or two late."

"A lady and a gentleman?" The hostess smiled knowingly.

"Yes, how—" Lexi watched her come out from behind the desk and grab a menu before she started leading her into the dining room.

"He had the same terrified look on his face that you have. Breathe. Whatever it is, it'll work itself out, one way or another." She nodded her head to a table in the corner. "This way."

Lexi could have spotted him in a crowd of a thousand. The second her eye caught a glimpse of his tousled hair, she was fixated on him. In his black pinstripe suit, he was more mouthwatering than the Belgian waffles Lexi had just walked past. The green tie he wore made the flecks in his eyes pop from thirty feet away. For Lexi, there was no one like Vincent Drake. Never was, never would be again. She raised her internal defenses and made her way to the table.

Vincent spotted her the moment she walked into the room. Her hair caught the morning light, the streaks of caramel becoming more visible than ever. Her eyes were like saucers, huge and afraid, as she scanned the tables, looking for them. She had on a fitted red blouse and a black pencil skirt that made it impossible for him to take his eyes off of her. As soon as she found his face in the crowd, she paused and then put on her best aloof, screw-you attitude and refused to break eye contact with him until she was standing right beside the table, her perfume swirling in the air all around him.

"Good morning, Elizabeth." Lexi's face softened as she bent over and hugged Elizabeth. Vincent jumped to his feet and held out her chair for her. When she stood back up she said a clipped, "Vincent," then took her seat beside him.

The hostess handed her the menu. "I hope you enjoy your meal."

"Thank you," Lexi said over her shoulder, allowing her badass façade to fall for a moment, making Vincent smile.

"I appreciate you joining us, dear," Elizabeth began hesitantly. "I know it was short notice." She glared at Vincent.

"That was my fault. I was supposed to call earlier, but I didn't want to bother you." The words fell out in an embarrassed rush. Vincent shook his head while Elizabeth simply grinned. Why, in the name of all that was holy, was he acting like an awkward teenager around Lexi now? Fortunately, he was saved from further humiliation by the server.

"Here you go. Three coffees." He set cups down for Vincent and Elizabeth, then turned to Lexi and smiled. "The gentleman said you'd like coffee as well. I hope that's all right." Lexi nodded her head appreciatively.

Without thinking, Vincent reached for the cream at the same time as Lexi, their hands crashing into one another, nearly spilling a water glass in the process.

"You can use it," Lexi pulled her hand back like it had been electrocuted.

Vincent let out a nervous laugh. "Actually, I was getting it for you." He wrapped his fingers around the tiny pitcher and offered it to her. "You know I don't touch the stuff."

Her fingers brushed against his as she took it from him, a tentative smile on her face. "Thank you."

"And how many sugars would you like today? Four or five?" The smile vanished from her face and she glared at him, but Vincent merely held the tiny packets in his hands, teasing her.

"Three," Lexi said indignantly, snatching the packets from his hand and pouring them into her cup one by one. By the time she got to the third packet, Vincent was already dangling a fourth out to her, knowing she had been lying when she said only three.

Lexi seemed to temporarily forget her annoyance with him and playfully grabbed the small white packet from his fingers and poured it into her cup. Vincent watched her swirl the spoon around, changing the dark black color into a muddy brown.

Elizabeth sat back and watched their interaction, smiling. They chatted briefly about nothing in particular and then placed their orders. Lexi chose the French toast with bananas and extra whipped cream as Vincent chuckled beside her, not surprised by her order. Elizabeth opted for the veggie frittata and mumbled something about skipping lunch today.

Lexi glanced at the menu, then said with a sneer to Vincent, "Egg whites for the gentleman? Perhaps a bran muffin too?"

Vincent's eyes flicked to the server who had his pen at the ready, then back at Lexi. "I'll have what she's having," he said, his eyes never leaving Lexi.

"Extra whipped cream too?" the server asked.

"Absolutely." Lexi arched one of her beautiful eyebrows at Vincent in surprise, but that was all the reaction he got until she shook her head.

"Living dangerously?" Lexi asked, smoothing her napkin over her lap, breaking their eye contact.

"Just making some changes. Trying new things." Again an awkward silence blanketed the table until Elizabeth cleared her throat.

"So, the reason I wanted to talk to both of you is, well, this." Elizabeth waved her hand back and forth at the two of them. "And this is Elizabeth Drake speaking, your boss, not your mother. If I was speaking as your mother, this would be a very different conversation." She looked back and forth between the pair and watched their heads slowly bob up and down in understanding. "I know there are some things of a personal nature that you both need to straighten out *together*." She stressed the last word, and Lexi's cheeks turn red. "The thing is, tomorrow is an extremely important day for Hunter. Marradesi cosmetics could easily be one of the most lucrative accounts we've ever secured, and I need to know that you two can put aside your personal issues and work together on this like adults."

"Absolutely," Vincent said quickly, shocked that she assumed he'd be anything but professional.

"Elizabeth, I'd never let anything interfere with the presentation tomorrow. I'll get Vincent everything he needs so he'll be ready."

"About that," Elizabeth paused and sipped her coffee while Lexi and Vincent both sat up straighter in their chairs, sensing she was about to drop a bomb of sorts. "I want you to give the presentation together."

Vincent nodded his head in agreement, but Lexi paled to the point that she looked like she might faint.

"Hear me out, dear." Elizabeth patted her hand reassuringly. "You two together are magical. I know you don't want to hear that right now, but it's true, and I'm not going to pretend it isn't. You're captivating, the way you interact with one another, the banter, the completing one another's thoughts. I won't even get into how much Francesca has asked about you in our phone conversations." Elizabeth sat back and let them both take in what she had implied.

"Elizabeth, you've seen the headlines. Hunter is still all over the front pages of the papers. How will it look if the woman originally accused of being the mole in the company is now making multi-million dollar pitches? The gossipmongers will have a field day."

"I don't care what people think, dear. I don't think you should either."

"But the press—" Lexi tried one last time, but Elizabeth shook her head and dug in her heels.

"I'll take care of the press." Confident and strong, Elizabeth raised her chin and laid down the law. "The bottom line is this: the client likes you together, and I like you together, so tomorrow you will be giving this presentation *together*. That means the rest of today, you two are going to be locked behind closed doors prepping for this. Understand?"

"Absolutely," Lexi and Vincent said at the same time, earning a big smile from Elizabeth.

"Excellent."

The food arrived and saved them from any further discussion on the matter. Vincent noticed that Lexi pushed her French toast around on her plate for a while and guessed that it had something to do with the news, but after a while, she seemed to find her appetite and polished off her meal. As soon as Elizabeth paid the bill, Lexi was on her feet and excusing herself, explaining that she had so much to work on that she didn't want to wait another second. She politely thanked Elizabeth for breakfast and told Vincent she'd see him in a few minutes in his office.

As soon as she disappeared from the restaurant, Vincent turned to his grinning mother. "That was low, even for you."

"I have no idea what you're talking about."

"You just manipulated her into spending the day with me. You know we have the Marradesi presentation nailed down."

Elizabeth shrugged unapologetically. "True, but she also wasn't speaking to you before my … what did you call it? Oh yes, manipulation. I didn't manipulate her, per say; I manipulated the situation so the two of you get to spend the day together working out the details of the presentation … or whatever else might come up."

Elizabeth tossed a few bills onto the table for the tip and took her son's arm as he led her from the restaurant. "Either way, you'll be talking. And together. So don't blow it." She took out her keys and unlocked her car door. "I was completely serious about the presentation. I expect you both to be professional and nail it. So you better find a way to make *both* work. Call me if you need me. I have to drop something off down at the Chronicle. Love you!"

· 32 ·

B ack at the office, Lexi pulled together the presentation packets and printed out the outline to make notes on when Vincent came back from his next appointment. When Elizabeth first announced that she wanted Lexi to be part of the presentation, part of her had wanted to run from the restaurant and crawl back into bed to cry the day away. But the other part of her, the one that was becoming stronger each day, wanted this. Lexi knew that she deserved to be a part of this presentation. She had worked her ass off and earned a place beside Vincent in front of the Marradesis. Elizabeth had given her a wonderful opportunity, and she was not about to let her down, even if it meant spending the day in close proximity with Vincent.

She rifled around her desk and noticed presentation boards were missing. In a panic, she rushed into Vincent's office, hoping to find them there, but they were gone. She was just about to call him when Tony turned the corner carrying a pile of boards.

"Hey," he said, sounding almost polite. "Were you looking for these?" He held up the boards, and Lexi fell back against her desk and sighed.

"Yes. What were you doing with them?" Lexi eyed him suspiciously.

"I—I made some changes to them."

Lexi's temper exploded. "You had no right to do that. We present tomorrow and—" She grabbed the boards and scanned them. Her eyes shot back to Tony, who rubbed the back of his neck and nervously shifted in place.

"Yeah, well, some things just needed to be erased. Before you freak out again, Elizabeth knew I was doing it. She gave me her blessing or I wouldn't have touched it."

Lexi hardly recognized the man in front of her. He was docile and apologetic and hadn't uttered a horrible word to her in the few minutes he'd been there, a personal record for him. The revised boards were spectacular, particularly the new background. "Why?" she asked.

Tony sat down in one of her desk chairs and sighed. "If you tell anyone this, I'll deny it, but Vincent and Elizabeth know and you may as well. Jade used me too. She flirted with me, came on to me all the time, did a few other things I won't go into detail about, but she was using me to find out information on other accounts. She fed me a bunch of lies, telling me that Vincent always talked about me and said what a loser I was. Those errors you guys always found in the boards, they were her idea as a way to get back at him."

"That bitch." Lexi set the boards down and folded her arms across her chest as Tony continued.

"Yeah, she was. She admitted the only reason she was with Vincent was to make contacts and further her career. I should have said something, but my stupid pride…" He tilted his head toward the pictures on the wall of Vincent and his campaigns. "He deserves every success. The guy's brilliant." He looked pointedly at Lexi and said, "I'll deny that was well, so don't go repeating that either."

A smile spread across her face. "Scout's honor."

He pointed to the boards. "So, do you approve of the changes?"

"You mean where you took Jade out and put Natasha in her place? Absolutely." Lexi laughed. Knowing how much Jade hated the other model only made it that much sweeter.

"She always talked shit about her, so I figured who better to replace her with." Tony stood up and stuffed his hands into his pockets. "Well, I guess I'll get going. If Vincent or you want any changes made, let me know."

"You know, when you're not being a complete jerk, you're a decent guy."

Tony snorted and started to walk away. "I have no idea what you're talking about, Girl Wonder. Try to not mess up my boards before tomorrow. They cost more than you earn in a month to produce."

"Bye, Tony."

Seconds later, Vincent walked past her, glancing back at Tony and stopping long enough to look at the boards. He laughed out loud when he saw the changes, mumbling something like "Maybe he isn't a total douche after all" before he went into his office and put his stuff down.

Usually the sight of Tony enraged Vincent, but this time he seemed amused. When the last of her papers printed out, Lexi walked into Vincent's office without even knocking on his door; they had work to do.

She found him sitting at his desk, the jacket of his suit draped over the back of his chair and his sleeves rolled up to his elbows. He was on the phone, but waved her in with a flick of his wrist and a smile. She came in, closed the door, and took her usual spot on the couch.

"Okay, that sounds good. Yeah, I'll call them back tomorrow. Sure. Hold my calls for the rest of the day, please. Leigh, hang on." He nodded at Lexi. "Do you want me to have Leigh hold your calls too?"

There was a long pause during which Lexi's brows furrowed together in confusion. Vincent watched her expectantly and waited for her answer.

"You're talking to me?"

"Is there anyone else in the room?"

"Um, sure hold my calls." Lexi looked around the office trying to make sure she was in the correct building and not trapped in some bizzarro alternate universe of her life. Everything looked the same, but nobody was acting the same. *First a polite Tony and now a considerate Vincent? What is the world coming to?*

"Hold Lexi's too. Thank you." He placed the receiver back into the cradle and jotted a few notes down, then leaned back in his chair. "Are you ready to start?"

"Sure."

Vincent heard the hesitation in her voice and mistook it for something else. He stood up and came over to sit on the couch beside her. "You don't sound too sure. Maybe we should talk."

"No. No talking." Lexi shook her head emphatically. "What we need to do is set some ground rules." She shifted her body away from him. "This is about work, not us. No talk about you and me or what happened, only Marradesi. Got it?"

"No talk about me being a complete idiot. Agreed. Anything else?"

Lexi watched the way he turned his body to face her and snaked his arm around the back of his couch. She thought she might have felt his fingertips graze the ends of her hair, but she couldn't be sure because she refused to look. Instead, she stupidly met his eye, hoping to scare him away, but instead finding herself wanting to crawl into his traitorous lap. She wasn't prepared to deal with those feelings right now. She needed to focus on the job.

"Yeah, one more thing." Lexi pointed her finger at Vincent's face. "You, work over there." She gestured toward his desk. "This," she gestured her hands around the couch and table, "is a Vincent-free zone."

He immediately tensed and sat back as if her words stung, but he didn't argue. He apologized, and returned to his seat at his desk.

"Stop that," Lexi snapped as she sorted the pile of papers in front of her, making a stack for herself and a stack for Vincent.

Vincent peeked over the top of his computer. "Stop what?"

"Being so damned agreeable. It's freaking me out. Just be your normal..." she struggled to find the right word.

"Dickheaded?" Vincent offered, trying not to smile.

"Yes... dickheaded works. Be your normal dickheaded self, please." She grabbed her flash drive and tossed it at him.

"Fine." Vincent caught the tiny projectile and folded his hands in front of him. "Give the Marradesi presentation."

"What?" Lexi stood up and began pacing back and forth across the office floor while Vincent sat back in his chair, grinning like a fool. He even went so far as to prop his feet up on the desk, thoroughly enjoying himself.

"You heard me, give the presentation as I would. I want to watch it, dissect it and see if there's anything we should change." He took a sip of his coffee. "Don't look at me like that. You know it as well as I do. You wrote half of the points yourself. And Elizabeth said she wanted you giving part of it, so let's see what part you're good at."

"Dickhead." Lexi ran her fingers through her long hair, shaking out the tangles and gathering the courage to present this monster to the master of presentations.

"That's Mr. Dickhead to you," Vincent quipped.

"No, it's not. Never has been, never will be. Let's get this done."

She stood in front of Vincent and retold every bullet point, every angle and opinion printed on the notes in front of him. Never once did she have to refer to the papers for information. She spoke from memory and from her heart. She even added a few things that popped into her head while she was talking, and Vincent made note of them. She transitioned from corporate history to current market trends and called attention to the pertinent details in the print ad.

She held her back straight, her posture confident, only giving away her nervousness by occasionally twirling a piece of hair around her finger. Vincent seemed mesmerized throughout her speech, and Lexi could feel his gaze on her lips as she spoke. At one point she stopped presenting to discuss a certain point with him, wanting to understand why he had included it. After talking about it for a few moments, she had a better grasp on his thinking, and jumped back into the presentation. When she finished, Vincent was speechless.

"Vincent?" Lexi asked, watching and waiting for some sort of reaction. Her stomach knotted, assuming he was just trying to figure out how to break it to her gently so she didn't fall apart. "Okay, just tell me what I did wrong on my parts so I can work on it before tomorrow. If I can't, then we can tell Elizabeth it didn't work out. I'll pretend to get sick or something, maybe laryngitis."

Vincent stood up and came around the front of the desk to where she was standing. Sitting on the edge, he tried to look like a hardass, but then the corner of his mouth twitched.

"You were superb."

Lexi's eyes rolled, her hands planting on her hips. "Just give it to me straight. Don't blow smoke up my ass. The truth, Vincent."

He folded his arms across his chest and paused. "The truth is you were fantastic. You twirled your hair when you were nervous, and you turned your back too much when you referred to the ads, so work on that. You also added things that weren't in the bullets, but they're included now because they were spot on. I couldn't take my eyes off you when you were up there. You were charming and engaging, and I think you'll have not only Paolo, but also Dante eating out of your hand. You were that good."

Lexi didn't even try to hide her shock. Her mouth gaped as his words ran in a continuous loop in her head. She had impressed him, Vincent Drake, the most captivating man in any board room, to the point that he felt comfortable standing beside her during one of the biggest pitches of his professional career. He was saying something. She could see his lips moving, but Lexi couldn't tell for the life of her what he said because millions of thoughts rushed around in her head at the speed of light. When his lips stopped moving, Lexi tried to speak.

"S-say that again? I'm hallucinating, or maybe this is an alternate dimension. I feel like I stepped into the Twilight Zone in this building today."

The tiny spark of excitement began to grow as Lexi considered what a huge opportunity it would be to have her name linked with this account if their presentation was accepted. But then she remembered what Elizabeth said earlier at breakfast about what a huge account this was for Hunter. Lexi couldn't risk her inexperience jeopardizing everything.

"Perfect. I'm so proud of you, and I meant every word I said. I think you'll be wonderful." He reached out and tucked a strand of hair behind her ear, his fingers sweeping over her cheek and lingering down the side of her neck.

Before she could stop herself, Lexi nuzzled the side of her face against his hand and allowed her body to lean against his. When she felt his arm wrap around her waist, she jumped, realizing the emotional turmoil she was causing herself as alarms started going off inside her head. She wasn't anywhere near ready to do this with him. It would be too easy to say the hell with it and fall into his waiting arms, as she had dreamed of so many nights alone in her room, but her wounds were still too raw. Every moment she spent around him helped heal the ache a little, but she didn't know if her heart could stand the unknown with him anymore.

"I can't do this with you, Vincent." Lexi stepped back, putting some distance between them.

"We belong together." There was no doubt, no question in his voice, as he said the words, only utter certainty.

"We're attracted to each other, but a future is another thing all together. A future requires faith and trust, two things that I'm afraid you've shattered." He winced at her harsh words, even though her tone was kind as she said them. "I know you're trying. I can see the effort you're making. I'm just not sure if it should be this much work. Maybe we just aren't meant to be long term."

"But Lexi—" She held up her hand and stopped him.

"I can't go there with you now. It took every ounce of my courage to walk into that restaurant and face you this morning, but I did it. The only reason I've made it through these last few hours, locked in this office with you, is because we've kept it all business, but talking about the future and my feelings, I can't do that. I know my limits." She grabbed his hand and held it over here heart so he could feel the wild thrashing in her chest and the sweat on her palms. "I can't do this right now. If I try, I'll end up in tears, and I am done crying over you. Done."

Lexi turned on her heel, letting Vincent's hand slide from her chest and slam lifelessly into the side of his leg as he watched her gather her things. "I'm not running away from you. Please know that. I'm just putting myself first for a change, and I hope you can respect my choices. Good luck with the presentation tomorrow, I know you'll do a fantastic job. I'll call Elizabeth and explain that I need a few days off. I need to clear my head and get away from here." She looked over her shoulder, needing to see him one more time so she could take every detail of his face with her wherever she ended up. "We'll talk when I get back. I promise."

◆

Lexi sat at her kitchen table, a bowl of Captain Crunch with extra milk in front of her as she started to unroll the Friday issue of the San Francisco Chronicle. She began scanning the headlines and stopped mid-crunch when she saw another picture of Vincent on the front page. All of the outside scrutiny on Lexi played a big part in her needing to take a few days off to get her head screwed on straight before she made any decisions about Vincent. She wanted to let the drama blow over so she could think and breathe again.

Despite Elizabeth's reassurances, she still worried about the Marradesis' reaction to this whole situation. Their public image meant everything to them, and they were very careful about business entanglements. If Lexi showed up, giving part of the presentation to such a high profile client with as little experiences as she had in the industry, it might look even worse for Hunter. For all of these reasons, Lexi had become more confident in her decision to bow out of the presentation. She would stay at home and wish Vincent well. He didn't need her help.

But seeing his face on the front page made her heart skip a beat. Quickly, she rolled the paper back up and tossed it into the trash, not wanting to read another slanderous thing about Hunter or Vincent Drake.

She was just fishing the last piece of cereal out of her bowl when Hope came barreling through the door. "Good morning, Hope. Come on in, make yourself at home."

Her friend stared at her in her flannel pajama bottoms and cami with her hair piled up on her head and asked, "What are you doing? You have a presentation in two hours and you're gorging yourself on sugared breakfast cereals?"

"Breakfast is the most important meal of the day," Lexi mocked as she stood up and tipped her empty bowl in Hope's direction. "Besides, I'm not going to the presentation. I told Vincent yesterday he could handle it without me."

"You did what?" Hope was flabbergasted. "You went to work every day this week because of how important this client was, how important it was for you professionally to be a part of this campaign, and now you're just stepping aside after all of the work you put in?"

"Pretty much." Lexi set her empty bowl in the sink and hopped up on her kitchen counter, her legs swinging beneath her.

"Interesting," Hope said a she leaned against the counter beside Lexi. "I never figured you for a quitter."

"What?"

"You're a quitter. You're giving up on your job, your future in advertising. Hell, you're giving up on Vincent too, hiding out in the apartment."

"I'm not avoiding anything. It's called self-preservation."

"No, it's called being a coward. Don't you enjoy your job? Isn't it everything you ever wanted?"

"Of course," Lexi snapped.

"Then why aren't you fighting for it? Because some losers are talking about you in the papers, or because you would have to be in the same room with Vincent for, what, an hour? You deserve this, Lexi. This is your chance to shine in the profession you love."

"There will be other presentations." Lexi shrugged and picked at the flannel of her pajamas.

"Let me ask you another question. What about Vincent?"

"What about him?"

"Well, are you going to give him a chance or have you decided what he broke can never be fixed?"

"I don't know."

"Are you any closer to a decision? Don't get me wrong, I really don't care which decision you make. I think he was a complete prick, and I support you either way. But ask yourself, what do you want? Vincent or a fresh start?"

Lexi chewed on her lip and thought about Vincent. She wanted to try. She wanted nothing more than to jump into his arms and forget the last week, but then, after a few minutes of happy thoughts, the darkness came back and she remembered the awful things he accused her of. Then she wanted to run far, far away. Her heart was in the middle of a massive game of tug of war, and no team was any closer to winning the battle. Instead her heart felt like it was closer to splitting in two.

"It's not that easy," Lexi said, wiping away the tears that always came if she thought about Vincent too long.

Hope rushed over to her friend and hugged her. "I know it's not easy, honey, but you can't stay in limbo forever. I won't let you. You already did that once. You have to pick a path and take a step forward, even if it's a tiny one. Like I said, I don't care which one you take, but you have to do something. Life won't stand still for you. It keeps moving, always changing, and time is the one thing you can never get back."

Now Lexi was the one wiping Hope's tears as her friend continued. "We both know that there comes a point when you run out of time. It happened to us with our parents. I just don't want you to wait too long and then realize what you missed out on if you do want to be with Vincent. Mistakes are part of life, Lexi. We all make them. God knows I've sure made some doozies. Should you forget about them? No. But learning from them helps us grow, makes us wiser, stronger, and better people in the end. Vincent knows he screwed up with you, and I have no doubt that he will move heaven and earth to make this up to you. The questions is, can you forgive him?"

"Forgiving him isn't the issue. I already have. Loving him is." Lexi buried her face in her hands and took a deep breath. "I don't know if I can love him without losing myself. Sometimes it actually hurts to love him. He can lash out and be a jerk one minute, then kind and loving the next. I feel like we are constantly taking one giant step forward and then two baby steps back, and I don't think I can take it anymore." Lexi's eyes were sad and full of heartbreak. "And then the stress of this whole fiasco at Hunter and the mole bullshit is just making everything worse. I feel like we're living our lives under a microscope."

"Do you still love him?" Hope's simple question cut to the chase and managed to make Lexi smile.

"So much that I can't breathe."

"Is he worth fighting for? Or would you rather cut ties now and start making a life without him in it?"

The thought of a life without Vincent made Lexi feel empty and incomplete. Before she could answer, her cell phone chirped. Hope glanced over at it on the counter and smiled. "Speak of the devil."

Lexi peeked at the phone, then looked away. A second later her eyes were back on it, her curiosity getting the better of her, even as she tried to play it off like she was wiping a spot off the counter.

"Go ahead, look at the message. You know you want to."

"No, it doesn't matter."

"Then why do you keep staring at it like it's the last piece of food on earth?"

"It might be important. It might be about the presentation."

"You mean the one you're not going to?" Hope made an indignant huff. "What do you care what he needs for that? It doesn't mean anything to you."

Lexi's eyes rolled. "I know what you're doing. I took Psych in college too."

Hope laughed. "Good, then pick up the damn phone and see what loverboy wants."

"He's not my loverboy." Lexi took the phone from Hope's hand.

Lexi
Traffic is bad on the bridge. Make sure you leave a few minutes early.

Her eyes narrowed as she read his words. He knew she wasn't going to the meeting. She had made that abundantly clear yesterday afternoon in the office. Her fingers began texting as fast as possible while Hope watched on.

Vincent
I don't need to leave early. I'm not coming to the presentation, remember? We had a whole conversation about it yesterday. Good luck.

"What did he want?" Hope asked innocently, even though Lexi knew she'd seen the message.

"He's acting like I'm still coming." Her phone beeped again. "Was he even listening when I was talking to him?" She read the new message and groaned. "You've got to be kidding me."

Alexandra
You're coming. I know you'll be there. Quit being stubborn and get dressed.

"How dare he!" Lexi snarled and pecked away at her tiny keyboard.

Dickhead
Cut the Alexandra crap. I'm not coming.

"Well, well," Hope said, grinning like a fool. "Someone finally has that twinkle back in her eye. Are your cheeks flushed too, my dear?"

"This man drives me crazy!" Lexi slammed her phone onto the counter.

"And you love it."

"I do," Lexi said, pathetically shaking her head. She wanted him in her life. It didn't mean she was ready to forget what happened, rather that she was ready to take a step toward fixing what was broken between them so they could see if they had a real chance together. "There's still a lot of stuff we need to work out."

"Have you seen today's paper, by chance?" When Lexi shook her head, Hope grabbed it out of the trash, unfolded it, and laid it across her lap. The headline read:

PROOF OF THE SUPERMODEL SUPERSCANDAL

The words jumped off the page, and Lexi's stomach rolled. She skimmed the blurb under the picture. It said that evidence from an unknown source had surfaced supporting Vincent's allegations against not only Jade, but David Reid. The full story could be found on page five. Lexi's fingers couldn't get her there fast enough, and when she finally spread the paper out in front of her, she gasped.

Three large pictures of Jade and David in various stages of physical contact stared Lexi in the face. All of the photos seemed to be taken while they had been tucked in the dark corner of the garden where Lexi had discovered them that night. One of the photos was grainy, like it had come from a security camera, but the other two were crystal clear. If you looked close enough, you could practically see his tongue snaking down her throat. The source of the photos asked to remain anonymous, but she was quoted as saying she "hoped they both are now seen for the scum they truly are."

Lexi couldn't believe what she was seeing. "How..."

"Everyone remembers that ugly dress."

"Now there's proof in black and white that I wasn't making everything up. Proof that Vincent was telling the truth."

"Yep, and the two of them are screwed because they've both publicly stated that they weren't having a relationship. I just saw on the internet that Jade's been dropped from three modeling contracts already this morning."

"Karma's a bitch."

"So, think about it. Now that Jade's out of the picture and everyone knows what a liar she is, don't you think that Marradesi would love to hear a presentation from the brilliant young woman who figured out who the mole was at Hunter Advertising and spoke the truth, even at great personal cost?"

"No, they deserve to hear it from a skilled presenter who oozes confidence and power and knows what the hell he's doing."

"Come on, Lexi. You know you want to do it."

"I have plenty of other accounts I'm working on. I can build my portfolio that way, even without Marradesi Cosmetics."

Hope smiled wickedly. "Don't ya even want to try, just to see if you can do it?" The wheels started turning in Lexi's head. "Can you imagine?"

The problem was that she could imagine it perfectly. She could see herself in that board room with Paolo, Francesca, and Dante, giving the presentation with Vincent at her side. Instead of scaring her, the idea made her genuinely excited about the possibilities.

For some strange reason, she flashed back to high school, to graduation day, and heard Michelle's voice in her head. *"And so my fellow classmates, I encourage you to leave this place and find yourselves. Become the person you are destined to be. Find that which truly makes you happy and have the courage to go after it, fight for it, and attain it. Let nothing stop you, because each one of us is special, and we have something unique to offer the world. Never forget to be true to yourself and go after your dreams, for dreams really do come true."*

This was her chance to go after her dreams and possibly get everything she ever wanted in life—an amazing job and a man she loved. The question was, did she have the courage to go for it?

Her head started to clear. The fog of uncertainty that had settled in since the confrontation with Vincent slowly faded, and she began to picture her future again. Hope was right. It was time to take a step. If it turned out to be in the wrong direction, that was fine. The great thing about life was that she could always change course. But for now, she was going to take a chance, and the first thing she was going after was Marradesi.

"Time to take a step toward my future. Come help me pick out something to wear."

· 33 ·

Lexi flew down the highway toward the local offices of Marradesi Cosmetics
with an excited smile. For the first time in days she felt alive again. Even if
things didn't work out and they lost the account or she looked like a bumbling
idiot, at least she was living the life she'd been blessed with and going after her
dreams, both of them. No regrets. Harry would be proud.

The receptionist greeted her as she stepped off the elevator and ushered her
into a conference room. Lexi stopped short when she found the room empty.

"Where's Mr. Drake?"

"He called and said he would be delayed, but that I should go ahead and get
you settled because you'd have materials that needed to be set up. Help yourself
to coffee, and if there is anything you need, feel free to ask."

"Wait," Lexi called to the receptionist started to leave. "Did Mr. Drake say
how late he was running?"

"He only said that you would know what needed to be done until he
arrived." The door closed with a click and Lexi whipped out her phone and
dialed Vincent.

"Where the hell are you? You left before I did. You should be here by now."

His deep chuckle on the other end of the phone made Lexi see red. "I had to
make a stop and was delayed. You know what you're doing. Just get things ready."

"How do you know I have anything to set up? You didn't tell me to bring
my copies." Lexi had opened her laptop so she could upload the PowerPoint.

"Because I know you. I'm sure you have everything, including a second copy of the PowerPoint on a flash drive just in case the copy on your computer is corrupted." Lexi smiled and patted the drive in her pocket. "You are the most organized person on the planet and do everything in triplicate."

With the phone propped between her ear and shoulder, she pulled a stack of papers from her laptop case and began to sort the materials into individual packets for Paolo, Francesca, and Dante, plus two extras in case anyone else arrived unexpectedly. "Yeah, well, you're lucky I decided to show up."

"I never doubted you. You're always there when I need you."

His kind words made her pause, but her smile was short lived. "I don't have the revised boards. You have the only physical copy."

"Don't worry about it. I'll get there before you're at that point in the presentation."

"You better be here before I start, pal."

"You can do this." His words held such certainty that Lexi was beginning to believe them. "I trust you."

Her eyes closed as she thought about the time she needed him to trust her and he hadn't, but then she reminded herself that she was moving forward. The past couldn't change, but people could. He was making an effort, and it was time she tried to as well.

"Well, I'd love to keep chatting, but you better be driving like a maniac to get your tail here in," she glanced at her watch, "twenty minutes. I have a presentation to set up because my boss is running late. Men!" His laughter and the revving of his engine were the last things she heard before she hung up the phone.

In record time, Lexi had packets of information, outlines, and projection numbers arranged. She quickly ran through the presentation outline from start to finish, paying extra attention to the areas Vincent had asked her to cover. The receptionist popped her head in to let her know the Marradesis had just arrived and would be down in a few minutes.

Lexi's stomach fluttered nervously as she paced the room, wondering how close Vincent was. She looked out the window onto the busy road below, hoping to catch a glimpse of his Matchbox car, but with every minute that passed, she accepted that she might have to do this alone. When the door to the board room flew open, Lexi thought she was saved.

"Vincent!" she sighed to herself, but when she turned around she found Paolo, Francesca, and Dante standing behind her.

"*Ciao*, Lexi! *Come va?*"

"*Va bene, grazie.*" Lexi swallowed. She was going to have to start this presentation and needed to focus. Francesca came over and kissed her on the cheeks and complimented her on her dress. Lexi shook hands with Dante and Paolo. Both men smiled but also glanced at the table, seeming anxious to get a look at the final presentation.

"Where's that man of yours?" Francesca asked with a twinkle in her eye.

Lexi knew she was blushing, but tried to play it off as no big deal. "He's on his way. There was an accident on the bridge, or so he said. I think he just wants to make a grand entrance for you."

While the men took their seats and examined the papers Lexi had set out, Francesca tipped her head toward Lexi and whispered, "I'm glad that horrible woman Jade was discredited in the paper today. She had the eyes of a liar." She lowered her voice even more as she spoke. "And please tell me you have something on that Adria Parketti too. She puts her hands on my husband again and she's going to get the *malocchio*." Lexi had to stifle her laughter, imagining Adria's demise at the hands of Francesca's Italian curse. When Lexi winked, Francesca clapped her hands together and happily joined her husband at the table.

"We don't need to wait for Vincent, do we?" Dante asked, impatiently glancing at his watch.

I trust you. Vincent's words drifted into Lexi's head, and she went with her gut. "Absolutely not. I know you're busy. Let's get started, and whenever he shows up, I'm sure he'll fill in any holes I missed." She hoped her voice sounded steady. Fortunately, she didn't need to use any notes, otherwise they'd be able to see how badly her hands were trembling.

Dante leaned back in his chair, watching Lexi's every move. His head occasionally nodded as she made a point, but other times he remained stone-faced and unreadable. Francesca was far more animated as Lexi presented, smiling and looking at her husband whenever Lexi said something she strongly agreed with. Paolo, like his brother, was reserved, but Lexi was encouraged by the smile that stayed on his face.

About five minutes into the presentation, Vincent slipped silently into the room. Lexi was so engrossed in the presentation that she didn't even notice him at first. When their eyes finally met and she paused, Vincent shook his head and waved his hand, telling her to continue. It was her moment, not his. He slipped into a chair beside Dante, shook hands with him, and then assumed a similar pose and watched Lexi. He never offered an opinion, never corrected anything she said. He simply watched and occasionally gave her an encouraging wink.

When she finished, she stood at the head of the table, grinning from ear to ear. She glanced at Vincent, and her heart soared when she saw the pride in his eyes and he mouthed "great job" to her. The fact that he had allowed her this moment meant the world to her. He could have jumped right in and taken command of the presentation, but he didn't. He stepped aside and let her show what she was capable of, not only to the Marradesis, but to herself.

While Paolo and Dante huddled in discussion, Vincent went over to Lexi and dipped his head to hers, whispering, "You took my breath away. You did it, Lexi. You did it."

Deep down, she knew she had nailed the presentation, but to hear him say it was overwhelming. She wanted him in her life. It wasn't the excitement of the moment telling her that, or the adrenaline that was coursing through her veins. It was her heart finally screaming to be heard after days of silence. He drove her crazy, he pushed her to her limits, and yes, he did hurt her. But because of him she also was stronger, more confident. He made her believe she could do anything. He was a man who was more than his mistakes, and Lexi decided to trust that he would keep his word and never hurt her like that again. More than that, she felt loved beyond reason, beyond explanation, whenever he looked at her. There was nothing she couldn't do with Vincent at her side, of that she was certain. Together they were better than they were apart.

She slipped her hand into his and felt like she had finally come home. "*We* did it, together."

Paolo cleared his throat and stood up from the table. "We would like to thank you for the presentation. It was superb, and the amount of work and preparation you put into it showed. Lexi, *cara*, you were wonderful." He walked around the table and kissed her on the cheeks, hugging her tightly before he held out a hand to Vincent. "Hang onto her, *capisce?*"

"*Si, grazie.*" Vincent gave a respectful nod to Paolo and wrapped an arm around Lexi. He turned to Francesca and Dante and said, "Thank you for giving us the chance to present our ideas to you. If you have any questions, feel free to contact us. We look forward to hearing from you."

Francesca nodded at her husband and brother-in-law. Both men smiled as she confidently placed her hands on the polished conference table and stood up with a twinkle in her eyes. "*Congratulazioni*, we'd love to work with you on this idea."

"Really?" Lexi gasped without thinking, earning a chorus of laughter from everyone in the room.

While congratulations were exchanged amongst the group, Dante excused himself to get back to work, leaving Paolo and Francesca with Lexi and Vincent. "What are you doing now?" Francesca asked. "I think we should celebrate. Are you both free for lunch?"

Vincent looked at Lexi, who nodded enthusiastically. "Absolutely."

Paolo and Francesca went to make arrangements for lunch, finally leaving Vincent and Lexi alone for a few minutes. Lexi gnawed on her bottom lip, lost in thought, and Vincent tugged on the hand he still held in his, trying to get her attention. "What's wrong?"

"I'm just wondering if all of this is real."

Vincent pulled her into his arms. "Of course it's real."

"It feels like a dream," she murmured into his chest.

He tipped her head back and stared deeply into her eyes. "You know, sometimes dreams do come true."

"I'm beginning to believe that."

His eyes closed as he pressed his forehead to hers. "I'm sorry."

She patted his cheek and waited until his eyes opened again and met hers. "I know. I forgive you. We need to talk."

"First, this."

Without warning, Vincent's lips met hers, tenderly at first, gently showing her how much he had missed her. He held her in his arms like she was the most fragile thing on Earth, cherishing her. But soon, his reverence for her changed into a sensual fire between them. Passionate wasn't a strong enough word to describe the kiss they shared. It was beyond that. It was...their forever. Her body melted against his as she deepened the kiss, pouring her heart into it. All the love, all the anger, and all her forgiveness was wrapped up into that one, unforgettable kiss.

Lexi's hands were woven deep into Vincent's hair, their mouths locked together as if their very lives depended on it, when the door to the board room opened and Francesca stuck her head in. "*Andiamo!*" she said. But then she saw the position Lexi and Vincent were in. "Ahh, *l'amore.*"

The two broke apart, grinning like fools. "We're ready, Francesca." Lexi laughed, giving Vincent's hand a reassuring squeeze and wiping her lipstick off his face. "Let's eat!"

✦

Lunch was an extraordinary celebration. They went back to Bravo where Angelo created the most extravagant meal Lexi had ever eaten. Course after course paraded out from the kitchen, each more decadent than the last. Dante and Paolo couldn't stop talking about the campaign and how excited and intrigued they were by the proposed twist on the Marradesi Cosmetics image.

While they discussed business, Vincent's arm wrapped around Lexi's chair, and she settled back into his embrace. It felt good to finally be herself with him, to enjoy being with him, without other things or people looming over their heads. Both of them felt free for the first time in ages, and it showed.

Vincent smiled at the conversation round him, but Lexi could tell that his mind was somewhere else. And it seemed he craved physical contact with her—his hand frequently brushed against her shoulder and touched her hair. Her body responded by curling towards his, desiring the contact as desperately as he did.

While Paolo and Dante discussed their latest real estate acquisition with Vincent, Francesca watched the new couple with great interest, and a knowing smile spread across her face. Lexi laughed as Francesca pulled her close and proceeded to ask probing questions about her and Vincent's relationship. She said she saw the chemistry between them and didn't let up until Lexi admitted she'd had a crush on Vincent since high school, which only spurred the woman's interest on more. "*Due dimezza.* Two halves." Francesca pointed between Lexi and Vincent, smiling. "He is the one. He's your soul mate."

"Shh," Lexi whispered, shaking her head and blushing.

"What?" Francesca said in her thick accent. "You love him. Don't deny it. I see it all over your face. I told you last time he had love in his eyes for you. So what are you waiting for? Life is short and meant to be lived."

"We have some things we have to work on." Lexi's eyes saddened.

"He hurt you," Francesca said, and Lexi nodded in confirmation. "But you still love him?"

Lexi's eyes met Vincent's, and he gave her a confused smile, as if dying to know what the women had been huddled together talking about. But he gave them their space, only occasionally winking to let Lexi know he was watching her.

"I love him with all my heart," Lexi whispered.

"Then tell him!" Francesca nearly shouted. She lowered her voice when people from the next table turned in their direction. "People spend their entire lives in search of what the two of you could have together. Men have killed for it, women died for it. Do not waste this chance. Even if it doesn't work out, at least you tried. I think the only mistakes we can make are ones where nothing is learned. You teach him, let him learn. Love him while he does."

Lexi found Vincent smiling adoringly at her, as if every breath she took was somehow fascinating to him. She also noticed the sexy way his eyes would darken as he gazed at her lips. His fingertips grazed the center of her back sending a shiver down her spine. Only Vincent could do that to her.

He leaned closer and whispered in her ear. "What are you two talking about?"

Lexi turned and kissed him on the cheek, just because she could. "Boys. Now leave us alone."

Vincent chuckled. "Talk about boys all you want, when you want to talk about men, I hope my name comes up in the conversation." He kissed the top of her head and slid back into his chair.

"*Marone*! He looks at you like he's hungry for you. Go, be with your man." Francesca turned to her husband and smiled. "You and Dante have a conference call within an hour. We need to get back to the office because if we're late, we'll never hear the end of it."

Everyone stood up and said their goodbyes. Dante graciously invited Lexi and Vincent to come to Italy in a few months to see their new villa once they finished the renovations. He promised them the trip of a lifetime. Paolo again thanked Vincent and Lexi for their work on the campaign and expressed his excitement about getting started. Francesca hugged Lexi, insisting she call her next week so they could go to the spa while she was in town. Lexi blushed and agreed. Vincent got a pat on the cheek and a few words of wisdom whispered in his ear before the trio left the restaurant and went about their day.

Vincent wrapped his arm around Lexi's shoulder and led her to his car. "Want to go for a drive with me?"

"Someplace quiet, so we can talk?" she suggested softly as he opened her door. "You read my mind."

✦

Once Lexi was tucked into the passenger seat, Vincent slipped into the car beside her and lowered the top on the Lotus, knowing how much she'd loved that on their last drive together. Her smile was all the encouragement he needed before he sped out onto the highway and drove them along the coast.

The ride was quiet. Lexi seeming to enjoy the sun, the wind, and the scenery as they sped for miles. Once they hit the open road, Vincent reached over and took her hand, his thumb feathering across her skin. He eventually pulled off the road and found a small supply shop where he purchased a large blanket and some cold drinks, then he jumped back in and drove a few more miles north until he found a secluded beach were they could stop and talk. He parked near a tiny footpath that meandered through the shrubbery before finally spilling onto the white, sandy beach. They both kicked off their shoes and walked hand in hand toward the water. When they found a good spot, near a large log, Vincent spread the blanket out and offered Lexi a bottle of water.

She sat down and patted the space beside her. "Sit with me?"

He took off his suit jacket, untucked his shirt, and rolled up his sleeves, getting comfortable before joining her on the blanket. The wind came off the water and blew her hair back. She leaned back against the log and watched as the waves rolled onto the sand a few feet in front of them. Taking his place beside her, he pulled Lexi against his chest. For the longest time they just sat there, quietly enjoying one another's company before they began what would certainly be a difficult discussion. Lexi was the first to ask a question.

"This has been driving me crazy. Where the hell were you today? You're never late to a meeting, let alone a presentation. You always arrive at these things at least a half hour early, and traffic wasn't that bad."

Vincent smiled sheepishly. "I had to make a stop on the way. There was something I had to get."

"You were shopping?" She didn't even try to hide her shock. "You left me, a complete nobody, to give the biggest presentation in Hunter history, so you could shop?"

"*Technically* no, I had already shopped for said item two days earlier. Today I was merely picking it up. And you are not a nobody. You're a very talented woman who just needed a chance to prove it, not only to some very influential clients, but to herself." She rolled her eyes. "Fine, I wasn't only shopping. I also might have stopped for a cup of coffee across the street. I figured that way *if* you needed me, which I knew you wouldn't because you're always so prepared, I could get there in time. If not, I could enjoy a nice cup of coffee and show up fashionably late."

"But the boards—I needed those." Lexi punched him in the shoulder.

"Please, you didn't need those until about fifteen minutes into the presentation. If you noticed, I showed up at exactly the five minute mark. I chatted with the receptionist for a while before I came into the room, so really, I was probably there from the moment you started. You just didn't know it."

"You were late on purpose?" He nodded his head. "So you basically gave me the Marradesi presentation?"

"I didn't give you anything. You worked on it just as much as I did. All I did was *trust* you with it." Lexi's brows furrowed together as she listened. "I'm sorry. I know when you needed me to trust you, I let you down in the worst way. Today I tried to prove to you that I did actually trust you by stepping out of the way and letting you run the show." He playfully poked her arm. "You did a hell of a job, you know." He held his breath when she didn't say anything. "I screwed up again, didn't I? I know I probably went about it all wrong, but I—"

Lexi's fingers covered his lips to silence his babbling. His whole body tensed until he saw her lips curl up into a smile. "That is probably the nicest, most underhanded, selflessly brave thing anyone has ever done for me. Don't ever do it again, but thank you."

"You're welcome," he forced out from behind her fingers, still unsure if she was going to get angry.

When she sensed his apprehension, Lexi quickly continued. "Your heart was in the right place. You were also right. If you would have asked me to do the entire presentation, I would have said no. You suggested it yesterday and I refused, because I didn't think I could do it. Honestly, it was the opportunity of the lifetime, and I thank you for it. I never thought I could pull something like that off in a million years." She sat up straight, nearly bouncing with excitement. "It was so exciting and terrifying. But more exciting than terrifying, I think. I had all this adrenaline in my system. I think I still do. Is it always like that?"

Vincent smiled as she rapidly relived every moment of the meeting. She asked his opinion on certain aspects of her performance and he gave her honest feedback, which she seemed to appreciate. He shared a few things Paolo and Dante had mentioned at lunch that they would need to tweak, but overall the presentation was a huge success, thanks in no small part to Lexi.

A quiet moment turned into an awkward silence that sent Vincent's pulse racing. Things were going too well. He had no idea what she was going to say next, and this whole day could be one last happy moment shared between them before she said her final goodbye. He braved a glance at her and found her deep in thought.

"I'm sorry," he blurted out in a total panic.

She simply smiled in return and whispered, "I love you." There was such tenderness as she said the words, and everything stopped in that moment for Vincent. No more waves crashed against the sandy beach, no wind blew, no birds squawked, and no cars whizzed down the highway behind them. There was only Lexi. She loved him.

"You do?" He didn't even try to hide how dumbfounded he felt or how amazed he was that someone as wonderful as Lexi would love someone as flawed as he was. She deserved the world, and he wanted the opportunity to give that to her.

"Of course I do. That crush in high school wasn't so small. It was actually pretty big, hence my ability to recall every single detail about you, your life, and food preferences. Truthfully, I've thought about you almost every day for ten years. I couldn't drive by Riverdale High without looking at the space where you used to park that ugly car you had."

He clutched his chest in horror. "You did not just mock my car seconds after telling me you loved me. That was a cool car."

"Only because you drove it." Lexi laughed, then became serious again. "I think I've always known it was you."

"I wish I could remember you from back then, but every time I try, I draw a blank."

Lexi chuckled. "I'm glad you don't remember me. I wasn't ready for you then. I had so much to learn about life, about myself, about the world around me before we were meant to cross paths. I wouldn't change a thing."

There was such love in her eyes as she poured her heart out. He had to touch her. His fingers locked with hers as she spoke, and his lips brushed against her forehead. He was desperate to feel close to her.

"I didn't know who I was or what I wanted back then." She squeezed his hand and smiled. "But I've grown up a lot, and I know what I want now." She was self-assured and calm as she spoke. There was no uncertainty or doubt in her decision, just determination. "I want you, Vincent. I want to try with you. I've thought a lot about this."

"Are you sure?"

"I've never been more sure of anything. But there are some things we need to talk about, and I want to be totally honest with you."

"You can tell me anything."

He felt her hands tremble as she took a steadying breath and allowed the words to come. "When you didn't believe me that night at the fashion show, it broke my heart. I've stood by you since day one and have never given you a reason to question me or my loyalty. But, out of nowhere, Jade plants her little poisonous seeds in your head, and the first time my commitment to you or Hunter is called into question, you believed the she-wolf in trashy clothing rather than me, Lexi, the one who was always at your side, looking out for you, helping you."

Lexi's foot began tapping nervously as her emotions continued to flare. "I can't even think about her, even now, or I see your face and remember the angry way you spoke to me that night, the things you said..." Vincent reached out and squeezed her hand, not saying a word, just offering her some reassurance and a silent apology. "It's going to take some time for me to get over that. I'm not trying to punish you for it. I even understand why you reacted that way. I know you better than you know yourself. You're a complex man, one with a gentle heart that you hide behind that pit bull exterior of yours. I love that part of you, the real Vincent. And I love the broken side of you, the man who has been so terribly damaged in the past that at times he can't function. I want to hold him in my arms and cry with him. But I think you need to do some work to fix that part of you so that old misery doesn't create new."

"I don't deserve you," Vincent whispered, his lips pressing against the top of her head as he peered out over the water, unable to look her in the eye.

She placed her tiny hands on his cheeks and pulled his face to hers, needing him to see her. "I won't lie to you. We aren't going to ride off into the sunset together and have everything fixed overnight. I know that, and I think you do too. But I'm willing to work at it, if you are. I do love you. I mean that with every cell in my body, every breath that I take. I think you're worth it; I think we're worth it. I think you could be the great love of my life, Vincent Drake."

It had been torturous to hear what his actions had done to her. He wished he could go back in time and relive that moment and change the past for the better. But mistakes were a part of life, especially for Vincent. He needed to learn his lesson and then move on so that Lexi's pain would not be in vain. She was right. He did let an old hurt ruin what they had, and if he didn't do something about it, there was a chance it could happen again. He needed to let go of the past and focus on his future... with Lexi.

"I love you, Alexandra White. You are the miracle that walked into my life not once but twice, and I'm not going to let you go. I can't. You're a part of me now." His thumb wiped the tears that began to fall from her eyes. "I will never forgive myself for hurting you, but I promise that I'll spend the rest of my life trying to make it up to you. We can take it slow. I can give you space and time as long as I know you love me. Wherever you are is home to me." Vincent shifted and knelt beside Lexi and pressed his lips gently to hers, tasting the salt of her tears. "We have been given this once in a lifetime opportunity, and if you let me, I will love you until my dying breath."

Lexi threw her arms around his neck and nuzzled her face against his shoulder and cried. Tears of joy mixed with tears of sorrow as every emotion she had kept bottled up her entire life came spilling out in a tidal wave. She cried for her mother, for Harry, she cried for the childhood she lost and the love she had gained with Vincent. Angry tears fell over Vincent's betrayal, and hopeful tears were shed to celebrate their new beginning.

When the tears stopped, she felt like a weight had been lifted from her shoulders. The burden of her sadness replaced with the lightness of hope. Her anger was released, and love filled her body as she watched the man beside her, the one who cradled her in his arms and whispered words of love and devotion to her through it all. The man who promised to love her, always.

They stayed on the blanket and watched the colors of the sunset shimmer on the ocean, the reds and oranges painting the sky above them. When the last ray of light was extinguished and the moon began to glow in the newly born night sky, they packed up their things and started their journey back home.

When they got back to Lexi's apartment, Vincent could tell from the way she had been gnawing at her bottom lip that something was still on her mind. He asked if he could walk her to her door, which she thankfully agreed to. He wanted to find out what was wrong, and he still had a gift to give her.

Once inside, she kicked off her shoes and laid her purse on the kitchen table. Vincent led her to the couch and pulled her down beside him. She stayed nestled in his arms, still clearly distracted as her knee bobbed up and down at a furious rate.

"Talk to me," Vincent whispered against her cheek.

She seemed scared and uncertain, so rather than push her into talking, he decided to give her the gift he had been carrying around all day, waiting for the perfect time to give it to her. He dug his hand deep into his pocket and pulled a small, wrapped box out and placed it on her leg.

"What is that?" Lexi's entire body stiffened as she looked at the box like it might explode if she even dared to breathe.

"A present. It was from my big shopping excursion today. Open it."

"You really didn't have to."

He took the box off her leg and ripped off the scrap of ribbon and paper, crushing the remains in the palm of his hand. This time, he put the unwrapped box into her hand. "Please, open it."

With shaky hands Lexi managed to pry it open and gasped. Inside the box was an exquisite gold necklace with two interlocked hearts hanging from it, diamonds sparkling along the outer edges of the pendants. Attached to it was a note that said, "My heart is yours."

"Oh, Vincent." Lexi's eyes filled with tears.

She held the case out to him, and Vincent quickly had the necklace out of the box and around her neck. The pendants dangled against her chest, the hearts forever linked.

"Thank you. It's amazing." Her hand kept reaching up and touching the hearts, her finger tracing their outline as she sat contentedly beside him. When he felt her take a deep breath and heard her sigh, he knew she had finally worked up the courage to tell him what was on her mind, what the last unsettled detail between them was.

Wanting to feel closer to him, Lexi crawled into his lap and faced him, her legs straddling him on the couch. The surprised look on Vincent's face at her bold action was just the tension breaker she needed. "Easy, Vincent. I just need to tell you something, and I want to see your face. Don't get any ideas."

He grinned unashamedly as his eyes raked over her body. "Too late."

She gave his chest a playful push then became very serious. "Remember what Francesca told you today?"

Vincent's head cocked to the side. "About women always being right? Sure."

"Good. Keep that in mind when you hear what I have to say." He gave her a weary nod and encouraged her to continue. "I love you. I want things to work between us, and I think we have a very good chance at having our fairy tale ending. But there are some things I need to do for myself in order to make that happen. I went from the limbo of caring for my dying father into the whirlwind of loving you again in the blink of an eye. Lexi got lost in there somewhere.

It's time for me to find out who she is before I can give myself to you. Can you understand that?"

"Of course. I won't rush you. Anything you want, I support you." Vincent pulled her hand to his lips and placed a gentle kiss on top of her knuckles, then tugged her down even more and captured her lips. His kiss ignited a fire throughout Lexi's body, his hands tracing paths over her skin that felt like they were electrically charged. Lexi's hands dropped and snaked under his shirt. She savored the defined muscles of his chest and abdomen as she began to explore him as well. Finally, when Lexi felt like she was going to go up in flames, she pulled away. Vincent grinned with deep male satisfaction when he saw her breathless in his lap.

"I love you," he said, his eyes reflecting the truth in his words.

"And I love you, forever." She gave him another chaste kiss, then whispered against his lips, "I quit."

· Epilogue ·

...18 months later

M iss White, I have Christina Stone holding on line one," a perky voice rang out over the phone.

Lexi rolled her eyes and closed the laptop on her desk. "Thanks, Erica. Can you do me a favor and cut the Miss White crap? You know it drives me crazy."

"I know, that's what makes it so amusing," Erica laughed. "Fine, go ahead. Suck the fun out of my day, boss lady. I'll be out here surfing for porn if you need me."

"Just put the call through and behave out there."

"I will be the perfect picture of Lexi White's advertising firm. Hell, I should be the poster child."

There was a pause, and then Christina's voice came over the line. "Lexi?"

"Hey, newlywed, how are you?"

Christina sighed. "Here in New York, blissfully happy, completely lame and nauseating to everyone around me. How are you? I know you talked to Julian the other day, but I haven't talked to you in a couple weeks."

"I'm good. Really busy." Lexi began organizing a few loose papers on her desk and tucked them in her drawer. "I'm so glad to hear from you, what brings you to New York?"

"Hi, Lexi!" Julian hollered in the background.

"Go do something," Christina told her new husband and then giggled. "No, not that. You're incorrigible."

"I like to call it animal magnetism," she heard Julian snicker.

"Sorry, my husband is a pain. We're in town because we just bought an apartment. Figured it was time to bite the bullet and at least have a place in New York, even though the stubborn mule refuses to move his base of operations here."

Lexi laughed when she heard Julian protesting in the background. "I'm really happy for you guys, and me, because now I'll get to see you more."

"Yep," Christina laughed. "Speaking of which, do you have any classes tonight?"

Over the last year and a half, Lexi had started taking night classes on everything from business management and advertising principles to graphic design. Running a company wasn't as easy as it looked, and she wanted to have a solid handle on all of the business aspects, which was what had initially prompted her to take classes.

"Nope, I just finished. I have to turn in a final project for one class, but it's done." Lexi laughed as she glanced over at the presentation boards beside her. "It looks eerily similar to the Midnight Corporation's upcoming summer campaign that I've been working my tail off on for the last three weeks. So long story short, yes, I'm free. What's up?"

"We wanted to take you to dinner, and then maybe show you the apartment?"

Lexi didn't even try to hide her excitement. "That would be fantastic. When and where?" She grabbed a pen and got ready to scribble the address down.

"How about Remote? Have you been there yet?" While Christina rattled off the intersection, Lexi heard a rustling noise on the other line and Julian picked up.

"Am I making the reservation for a party of three or four?"

Lexi pinched the bridge of her nose and closed her eyes. "Three, Julian. You know it's three."

"I know, sorry. Sore subject. What time do you want to meet us there? We're wide open."

They worked out the details so that Lexi could run home and change quickly before meeting up with them. Christina sounded so excited to show her the apartment, and Lexi was just happy to have something to do. The nights were the worst. She finished her work a little early, grabbed her bag, and headed out the door. She stopped at Erica's desk and peeked over her shoulder to see what she was doing.

"Are you leaving for the day?"

Lexi nodded. "I'm heading home to change and then meeting up with Christina and Julian."

"You doing all right?"

"I'm fine." That far away look in Lexi's eyes told Erica different, but she let it drop.

"Since you're leaving for the day, do you mind if I shut down our side of the office and sneak out too?"

"Absolutely." She linked her arm in Erica's, and they strode toward the elevator together. "Do you want a share a cab?" she asked as she dug into her bag for her keys.

"Nope, I have some shopping to do, but thanks." She gave Lexi a wink and a wave, then disappeared out the door.

Lexi collected her mail and walked into the big, empty apartment. She flitted around her room, changed her clothes, and freshened up her hair and makeup. As she regarded her reflection in the mirror, her mind wandered, thinking about how different her life was now than it had been two years ago. Life really did wait for no one. You either lived it, or you were left behind.

She gave her lips one last coat of lipstick, then turned off the light and grabbed her purse off the bed. Lexi walked out of her bedroom and ran her fingers over the smooth glass petals of the flowers in the vase on her dresser, as had become her custom every time she passed them and thought of him.

✦

Remote was just starting to get busy when Lexi arrived. A small group of people were gathered just inside the doors. The hostess saw Lexi and smiled. When Lexi mentioned the name Stone, the woman's eyes sparkled with excitement.

"Right this way."

At the table, Christina and Julian were so deeply engrossed in one another that they didn't even notice Lexi standing there. A small twinge of jealousy spread through Lexi as she watched at the happy couple, so obviously in love. She scolded herself for being selfish and instead smiled at her friends, clearing her throat to get their attention.

"Mr. Stone, your next guest has arrived."

"Lexi!" Christina released Julian's hand and jumped to her feet to hug her friend. "You look gorgeous."

Lexi blushed and slipped into the chair Julian held out for her. She wore a simple black dress and had spent a few extra minutes putting her hair in hot rollers, so huge curls draped over her shoulders giving it a sexy bounce. Julian kissed her cheek, then took his seat beside his wife.

"How you doing, Lexi?"

"I'm great. Busy, but great." They chatted for a while about the things going on with Lexi, and then Christina launched into the story of buying the apartment in the city. A sad smile fell across Lexi's face.

"What's wrong?" Christina asked, catching the faraway look in Lexi's eyes.

"Nothing. I'm fine," Lexi said a little too cheerfully. She reached out and picked up her water, taking a tiny sip to hide her face. As Lexi set the glass down, Christina's face broke out into a huge grin.

"Don't look so sad, beautiful lady," a smooth voice whispered in her ear. "Is this seat taken?"

Lexi froze, her entire body stiffening as his warm breath tickled her shoulder. When she felt his warm lips touch her neck, she closed her eyes and enjoyed the way her heart began to flutter like a hummingbird in her chest. She knew that voice. She heard it in her dreams, in her sleep, and in her heart.

"Vincent," she sighed, her smile so wide she worried that her cheeks might burst. She bolted out of her chair and wrapped her arms around his neck as he lifted her into his arms, her feet dangling below her. "Vincent!" Her lips immediately found his, hungry, needy for him.

"Hello, sweetheart," he whispered against her lips when they finally stopped their voracious kissing to take a breath.

"Why don't you welcome *me* home like that?" Julian grumbled, nodding his head toward Vincent and Lexi, who were still wrapped up tight in each other's arms. The entire restaurant had turned in their seats to watch the couple's very public reunion.

"We're old married people now; they're young and in love. Wife handbook page twelve: 'Husband comes home from trip, remind him to take out the garbage.'" Christina teased Julian.

"All right, all right. People are trying to eat here. Either sit down or get a room. What's it gonna be?"

"Mind if I sit on his lap?" Lexi asked with a sinful little smirk as Vincent kissed Christina on the cheek. Her whole face had changed since Vincent walked in the room. Gone was the polite smile. Now Lexi's face was vibrant and joyful, her voice playful and light. Eyes sparkling with excitement, she looked at the man she loved, her body in constant contact with his.

"I'll give you five hundred dollars to do it right now. The old guy at that table will have an absolute heart attack." Julian nodded his head toward a balding man in his late forties whose mouth dangled open.

"As much as I love to see you part with your money, Julian, I'm not going have her sit on my lap," Vincent leaned over to Lexi and whispered so only she could hear, "until later, when you have on far less clothing."

"I'm so glad you're home," Lexi whispered against his lips, curling her fingers into his hair. "You weren't supposed to be back for three more days."

"I missed you, so I made a few changes in my schedule so I could come surprise you." He twirled one of her curls around his fingers. "Are you surprised?"

"Best surprise ever." Lexi clapped her hands together. "Tell me about the baby!"

"Anna had the baby?" Christina asked, taking a bite of her salad.

"Hunter was two weeks early, but already he's my buddy. Went right to sleep when I held him, and he even smiled at me," Vincent bragged as he proudly pulled a picture of the baby from his pocket that made Lexi and Christina melt.

"It was probably gas, Vincent." Julian laughed as the girls continued to ohh and ahh over the baby.

"Details, details," Lexi begged.

Vincent recapped his visit to San Francisco, passing on his family's love to Lexi and letting her know they were getting impatient for her to visit. They knew Lexi had been busy starting the company and building up a clientele, but they missed her terribly.

As she sat at the table, she smiled. The day she told Vincent she loved him had also been the day she quit. He had shown great compassion as she listed her reasons for leaving Hunter. He accepted that she was stretching her wings, trying to fly, and he loved her enough to let her. Elizabeth, however, was not about to accept her resignation, and Elizabeth was a woman who was used to getting what she wanted.

His mother had taken Lexi out to lunch to discuss what she could do to help Lexi achieve her goals. Lexi wanted a fresh start to see what she could do in the industry without relying on the Hunter name and without Vincent over her shoulder. She had a sizable sum of money from Harry's life insurance that she had been saving. What she wanted was to open her own firm where she was her own boss, not under anyone's control.

After the meeting, they came up with a plan. Elizabeth had always wanted to open an east coast branch of Hunter Advertising. Lexi agreed to allow her company, which would be called White Advertising, to be a subsidiary of Hunter, but independently owned and run by Lexi. In doing that, she could still work on her current accounts as well as solicit new ones. A month later, she was packing her things and heading across the country, terrified, but exhilarated to begin this adventure.

Leaving her in New York was the most difficult thing Vincent had ever done. There were tears shed and plane tickets already purchased so he could come back again the following weekend. The only thing that allowed him to get on the plane was the fact that she wasn't alone. Erica had quit Reid Industries the night of Julian's fashion show, and she had been the first person Lexi hired. The two of them had big plans for the modest office that was White Advertising and were excited to get started.

"When are we going back to San Francisco?" Lexi tugged on his arm, pleading. "I have to see this baby and squeeze those little cheeks!"

"Julian and I are leaving on Friday," Christina bragged.

"I just want to hold him, kiss him, and smell him." Lexi sighed.

Vincent crowded Lexi with his large body, trying to seem intimidating. "Should I be jealous?"

Not to be outdone by Vincent's games, she crooked her finger and called him even closer. His eyes were captivated by her plump painted lips as she whispered "Don't worry. I have a whole different list of things I want to do to you."

Shocked at seeing Christina so over the moon with baby-induced joy, Julian panicked. "Oh great, you've unleashed the obsession. I can hear their ovaries screaming now."

Christina gave him a swat. "You know the baby obsession isn't all that bad. We should probably practice, a lot, before we actually try and do something big like that, don't ya think?" The purr of her voice made Julian grin and start bobbing his head in agreement.

"Yeah, that's true. Gotta practice for the big game. I like your thinking, wifey."

"Well, I'm bummed. I probably won't get to see baby Hunter for a month with my schedule," Lexi complained

With a low chuckle, Vincent reached into his pocket and pulled out a pair of plane tickets, waving them in front of her face. "How about going out there this week?"

"Get out!" Her face glowed. "But you just flew all the way across country."

"I told you, I missed you." He kissed her lips gently. "And I wanted to see you."

"But I have to work."

"Work can wait. Family is more important."

Lexi gazed at him in wonder. Sometimes she had to pinch herself to believe her life was real. The last eighteen months had been difficult, full of change and growth, but in many ways they'd been the best of her life. Vincent's hand reached out, his fingers interlacing with hers under the table, their own private moment to share. His touch still made her stomach flip, his intense gaze made her cheeks flush without fail, and no man could set her body on fire with one wicked grin like Vincent could.

The tiny voice in the back of her head had questioned her cross country decision daily, but she knew it was the right thing. It was her chance to see what she could do. She couldn't be Vincent's assistant forever, she had to be something more, and in San Francisco, that was what people knew her as. She needed time and space to become more than that in everyone's eyes.

Elizabeth and Vincent had been so supportive. Vincent answered every stupid question that popped into her brain no matter what time of day or night. Elizabeth made the transfer of her work seamless, and she made sure Lexi knew that if this didn't work out, she was always welcome to come back to Hunter.

Work was exciting from day one, meeting people, getting to know the area. The client contacts she had made in San Francisco began to pan out quickly, and her business was up and running. When she decided to take night classes it was a big decision, but she was never happier. The one thing that broke her heart was not being with Vincent.

Their long distance relationship lasted two months, and then late one night there was knock on her door.

Lexi had been up late, working on the Garaday Restaurant project when she heard the pounding on her door. At first she thought it was coming from across the hall, but the second time, it was unmistakable. She set her laptop on the coffee table and tiptoed over to the peep hole on her door to see who it could possibly be at this hour. Who she saw standing out there took her breath away.

She hastily fumbled with the locks and threw open the door. "Vincent!" she gasped, reaching out and touching him to make sure he was real. "What are you doing here?"

"I can't do this anymore." He seemed nervous as he came in and placed his suitcase on the floor before sitting down at the kitchen counter.

Lexi offered him a beer from the refrigerator and waited for him to continue.

He took a deep breath and started talking very softly while he anxiously picked at the label on the bottle. "I miss you. I know you wanted some time and space, but I don't think I can stay away from you anymore." His eyes peeked up at hers, trying to gauge her reaction to what he was saying.

The funny thing was that Lexi had been missing him too, terribly. Without a word, she reached over on the counter to a blue envelope that was addressed to Vincent.

In the letter Lexi confessed that she was miserable and how much she missed him. She told Vincent she needed him in her life and asked if he would consider moving to New York so they could be together. While he read the letter, Lexi held her breath.

He looked up and flashed Lexi a smile. "So..."

Lexi shrugged. "I was just thinking." She bit her lower lip as she paused and then said in a rush, "...that it would be nice if you were, you know...here...all the time." Vincent stood up and walked around the counter, backing Lexi up against the wall of the kitchen. In a sudden burst of insecurity, she began rambling. "But I know you can't leave San Francisco, you're too busy and your family is there. Just forget it. It was my pathet—"

She never had a chance to finish her sentence because the next thing she knew, Vincent's strong lips were pressed against hers, taking her breath away. His hands came up to cradle her face as he continued to ravage her with kisses, his tongue teasing and tantalizing hers until she couldn't think of anything but him. All her apprehension and nerves vanished. It was only her and Vincent.

"I talked to Elizabeth. She'll transfer my accounts out here. I can fly back for meetings when necessary, but I need you too. I love you, and if you really want to do this, I'm ready. I think we would be great business partners."

"White & Drake Advertising, I like the sound of that...Hunter's east coast expansion is complete. It would be my pleasure to work with you again, Mr. Drake." Her fingers played with the buttons on the front of his shirt, popping them open one by one. "Day or night."

With a sinful grin, Vincent began running his lips down the side of her neck. "You were saying something earlier about being sad that my side of the bed was empty. Why don't we go do something about that?"

Vincent had packed his things and returned to New York within the week. Their life together had finally begun.

The business exploded, their professional reputations bringing people to the doors of White & Drake Advertising by the dozens. When Lexi continued her business courses, Vincent picked up the slack at work and encouraged her to follow her dreams. They were true partners in every way.

Lexi felt like she was floating on a cloud for the rest of dinner. Her hand kept reaching out to Vincent, as if somehow checking to see if he was still there. He had been gone for two weeks in California on business, traveling from San Diego to San Francisco, tying up loose ends and then visiting with his family. He had invited Lexi to come with him, but she had deadlines that kept her in New York. It was the longest they had been apart since he moved in with her the year before.

As Vincent and Julian argued over the check, Lexi pulled Christina aside. "Would you be terribly upset if I bailed on the tour of the apartment?"

"Go. Get out of here now, before we both go up in flames." Christina peered over Lexi's shoulder. "Where's that sexy husband of mine?"

Julian and Vincent turned toward them, their less-than-innocent intentions written all over their faces. Their darkened eyes stalked the women, focused and intense, and their confident swaggers hypnotized Lexi and Christina as they came closer.

Vincent reached out and pressed his lips to Lexi's. "You're irresistible." He tickled her side and scooped her up in his arms, carrying her out the door.

Julian held open the door of his car for Christina, tucking her safely inside. "When you guys get back from your trip, we'll have you over to the new place." Christina's hand waved out the window as they peeled down the street.

The sun was setting, and the sky had a beautiful orange glow to it as the darkness crept closer and closer. Vincent held Lexi in his arms and he seemed to savor the feel of her. Her face nuzzled against his chest as she clung to the front of his shirt, like she was afraid he might disappear. Lexi knew by now he wasn't going anywhere. He couldn't. She was a part of him now; she was his heart.

"Come on, sweetheart. Let's go home."

There were times, like now, sitting in Vincent's car holding hands as they braved the crazy New York traffic, that everything seemed so normal, like they had been together forever. Yet those were the times when Lexi was most often convinced everything in her life was a spectacular dream she might one day wake up from. No one was this lucky, especially not her.

"Crap!" Lexi shouted out of nowhere, ruining their quiet moment. "I can't go to San Francisco this week. I have that three day seminar for the woman's leadership conference you made me sign up for. Damn it, I can't believe I forgot about that." Her head fell back against the seat in disappointment.

The car rolled into its parking space, and Vincent escorted his now gloomy girlfriend into the elevator and pushed the button for their floor. His silence was driving Lexi crazy.

"You don't seem very upset that I can't go to San Francisco."

"That's because you're going to San Francisco."

"But the meeting,"

"Has been rescheduled."

Her eyes narrowed. "You can't just reschedule a leadership conference. It's three days long, and we paid for it."

Vincent rolled his eyes. "I don't care about the money. So, consider it rescheduled." When Lexi shook her head in disbelief, Vincent nodded toward her purse. "Check your schedule."

With a very suspicious look, Lexi found her phone as the elevator doors opened. Vincent took her by the arm and led her down the hall to their apartment as she played with her BlackBerry and pulled up her calendar for the week.

"Great, something happened." She tapped the display screed with her nail. "I think it's broken or something. Look, it erased all my appointments for the next two ... no, two and a half weeks! Oh hell, now I have to get a whole new one." Lexi leaned against the wall in disappointment, still pecking away at the buttons, hoping to resurrect the missing document.

She only glanced up when a shadow fell over her keyboard. Vincent stood inches away, the heat from his body warming her in all the right places. He came closer, putting his hands on each side of Lexi's head, trapping her against the wall.

"Will you trust me?"

Words that once would have sent a knife through her heart, now made it sputter to life. Whenever he said those words, it meant he had something wonderful planned for her, something that she would most certainly love because he had kept his word. He spent every day reminding her how much he loved her and how special she was. Instead of reminding her of one dark day, those words now made her think of all the romantic and thoughtful things he had done since then. In a way, he had rewritten that part of their history.

"Always," Lexi whispered breathlessly as his lips met hers.

Awkwardly he ushered her through the door, his hand covering her eyes as he prepared to surprise her. When she was completely inside the door, he pulled his hand away and waited anxiously for her reaction.

"Why did you leave your luggage in the middle of the family room?" Lexi asked, slightly annoyed. "Just drag it into the laundry room like you always do. And why the hell did you take all of this luggage?" She looked at the pile of bags at her feet. "Wait, is that my suitcase?"

Vincent gave her that smile that told Lexi something big was coming. He was notorious for planning a great surprise and then giving her clues about what it could possibly be, but it was always up to Lexi to figure them out. Her stubborn streak kept her from asking for help, so instead, she would stand there, chewing on her bottom lip, occasionally even biting her fingernails as she tried to decipher the clues in front of her.

Vincent nodded his head in answer to her question. "I don't want to rush your mental exercises, but for this one we are kind of working with a time constraint."

She waved her hand in his face to quiet him as she continued pondering. Before long, she jumped up and down. "Let me see those tickets again."

"They're in my pants pocket. Why don't you get them yourself?" There were no words to describe the smug grin on his face as Lexi's hand slowly snaked around his hip before dipping into his pants pocket. She slipped the papers out and squealed.

"We're leaving tonight for San Francisco? Are you crazy?" With a single leap she was up in Vincent's arms, kissing his face. "Don't answer that. I know you're crazy, but I love you anyway."

They stayed locked together, kissing and touching one another, celebrating being together for the first time in weeks. Lexi glanced over her shoulder at the bags and tapped him on the chest so he'd let her go. She slithered down his body, loving the feel of his muscles along the way.

"You know," Lexi skipped through the pile of suitcases, counting as she went, "four suitcases for us to go to San Francisco is a lot of luggage."

Cocking an eyebrow, Vincent waited patiently for her to figure it out. She was getting closer, and the sneaky smile on her face was proof of her imminent victory. She peeked up at him through her lashes, then looked back at the tickets in her hand, not only inspecting the ones on top, but fingering through the pile until she screamed and began jumping in place.

"We're going where?"

Vincent laughed out loud at her reaction. "You tell me. Where are we going, Nancy Drew?"

Her entire face lit up. "We're going to Italy!" Her eyes sparkled with excitement. "How did this happen?" Her mouth hung open as she gaped at the tickets in her hands.

"Paolo called. The renovations were finally completed on the villa and Francesca insisted we visit. You know it's impossible to say no to her."

Lexi laughed and tossed her BlackBerry at Vincent. "And my malfunctioning calendar?"

Vincent sat down on the couch and pulled her into his lap. Instinctively, his fingers reached out and began playing with the ends of her hair. "So I might have had a little help on this one."

"Erica!" Lexi groaned, suddenly mad at herself for not thinking of it sooner. "That little sneak."

"She's quite crafty. The women's leadership conference, it was all Erica."

She stole another peek at the tickets, still trying to process all the information he'd just dumped in her lap. "So we really have…"

"Two and a half weeks with absolutely nothing to do." He picked her up off the couch, her legs wrapping tightly around his waist. "First, we're going to go to see baby Hunter, and then," he pressed her back against the cold wall and kissed her neck, his tongue running leisurely over her skin, "you're mine. All mine."

"I like the sound of that."

When his lips finally were within reach, Lexi took control and kissed him. Her hands shot into his hair, her fingers holding him as close as she could get. The only thoughts in her head were of Vincent. He consumed her mind, and his hands devoured her body.

"What time is the flight tonight?" Lexi asked, tugging anxiously at his belt buckle.

"We need to be at the airport in an hour." Vincent panted, his pants dropping to the floor as he pulled Lexi's sweater over her head. "As much as I want to do this, I think we should maybe…"

"Do you trust me?" Lexi gasped as his mouth ran over her skin, and then giggled and squirmed away. She squealed when she took off running down the hall, knowing Vincent would follow.

As she leaped into the air and landed on the bed with a whoosh, Lexi turned to see Vincent right behind her. They had found one another. They had overcome all of their demons and were happy together. It was in that one perfect moment that Lexi realized that dreams really do come true.

He crawled onto the bed, looking down at her with complete love and devotion in his eyes. "Of course I trust you, with my life."

· THE END ·

WANT TO READ MORE FROM VICTORIA MICHAELS? TURN THE PAGE FOR A PREVIEW FROM HER FIRST NOVEL...

Boycotts
& Barflies

a novel by
Victoria Michaels

Boycotts & Barflies

*G*race smelled the popcorn as soon as she stepped off of the elevator.

Meg and Bianca must be close to starting the movie, she thought as she rushed down the hall, not wanting to be late.

"Hi, honeys! I'm home." Grace came through the door and gently tossed her keys into the wicker basket on the counter.

Meg and Bianca were perched on the couch, remote control and popcorn in hand. "Grace," they squealed in delight, "you escaped!"

Bianca, Meg, and Grace had been best friends for nearly four years. They met during their sophomore year of college, and after a horrible time living with insane roommates in the dorms, they decided to get an apartment together their junior year and had been living together ever since.

Bianca and Meg graduated with undergraduate degrees in interior design and currently worked at Baker Design House in downtown Portland. They had been there for the last year and a half, and even though they were only twenty-four years old, they had started to make quite a name for themselves. They were becoming two of the most highly sought after young designers in town.

Grace was the same age as her friends, but she was still in school and would be graduating in June with her Master's in Literature. In the meantime, she was teaching English Lit classes at the local community college. The classes she taught didn't make her a ton of money to live on, but her parents were very supportive of her education and were helping her financially until she finished her degree and could get a full-time job at the university.

Even with successful jobs and graduate level educations, the girls still found themselves failing with men. These days, they were in the midst of a "dating drought" as they liked to call it. It seemed none of them could find a decent guy for any sort of long term relationship. They had been going on a series of random dates that ranged from bad to disgusting on the date scale. Lately, their Friday nights involved one or two of them ending a bad date early, a big bowl of popcorn, and a "chick flick" to take their minds off of their misery.

Grace glanced over at the couch and saw the leggy redhead stretched out there, flipping through a magazine. "Bianca, what are you doing home already? You had a date, too. How'd you get home before me?" Bianca had left for her date at the same time as Grace, but she had already been home and screaming in the background when Meg called Grace at the restaurant.

Bianca blushed furiously at the question. She had very high standards when it came to guys. To Bianca, chemistry with a guy was everything, and if she didn't feel it immediately, she wasn't going to wait around for it to blossom. That was Bianca. She was a strong, beautiful woman, and she needed a man that was her equal; that was just how she was wired. If it was a blind date, she always had the guy wear a red rose on his lapel so she could check him out before she actually went so far as to introduce herself to him, giving her the option to walk away if she wasn't attracted to him. Of course, even the good looks and chemistry would only get a guy so far. He'd better have a brain and a personality to back it up, or she would leave him the first chance she got.

Meg wasn't nearly as bad as Bianca, but she was a hopeless romantic, looking for her one true love, convinced she would know him on sight. Her personality was quirky and wonderful. She too went on many first dates, but very few second dates for just that reason. Sometimes Grace envied Meg's faith in true love and happy endings more than she cared to admit.

Bianca laughed darkly, and then launched into the story of her disastrous date as the previews played on the TV. "You know I hate blind dates. I did it as a favor to this girl at work, and after seeing this guy, I'm not sure I'm going to ever speak to Cindy again! He was this scrawny blond guy with a cheesy mustache! I mean really, when have I ever liked a guy with facial hair? Ugh! I gave the hostess twenty dollars to tell him I threw up in the parking lot," she said, completely unashamed of her actions.

Bianca was not one to waste her time with being nice; she always cut to the chase. Grace was glad Bianca liked her, because she wouldn't want to be on her bad side.

The girls joined Grace in the kitchen and plopped down onto the bar stools across the counter. Grace smiled as she looked at them, so opposite in looks but similarly dazzling.

Bianca's long, red hair hung down past the middle of her back, thick and straight. Her blue eyes were mesmerizing and framed with thick, lush eyelashes. Blessed with a wonderful metabolism, she had a curvy, womanly body to die for without ever going to the gym. Women were jealous of her; men were enamored instantly. Throw in a pair of killer legs that went on for miles, she was gorgeous.

Meg was average in height, but next to Bianca's long legs, everyone looked tiny. Her small frame and currently chocolate brown hair made her a much more exotic beauty. Always a work in progress, she changed her hair color as often as some women changed their nail color. Last month it had been platinum blond with pink highlights. No matter what, her deep blue eyes shone under the veil of her thick hair, twinkling with life, just like Meg herself. While average in stature, Meg had one of the biggest personalities you would ever come across. Everyone she ever met remembered her. Her smile lit up a room, and people just naturally gravitated to her warmth and happiness.

Grace placed the foil swan with her leftovers in front of Meg. "Thank you for saving me from Tony the Dull," she said with a bow as she stood across the counter.

"No problem, but next time, please listen to us when we tell you someone isn't right for you. We're designers, for goodness sake; we can tell when things go together and when they don't. It's what we do." Meg rolled her eyes and dramatically snapped the neck of the swan, digging into the leftovers. It was her silliness that Grace loved most about her.

"So I guess we're the big losers this weekend, Bianca. At least I got a decent appetizer out of it and Meg got a foil swan of lasagna." Grace laughed, trying her best to be a "glass half full" girl.

Bianca shrugged her shoulders. "True, but that's also an hour of your life you'll never get back, an hour wasted—on a dork. I, however, spent my hour productively shopping! Look at these fabulous shoes I found." She squealed as she threw her foot into the air revealing a sleek black stiletto.

After an extensive discussion about the versatility of black patent leather heels in one's fall wardrobe, Grace let out a loud sigh. "Girls, what are we going to do about all these losers we've been going on dates with? Where are all the good guys hiding?"

Meg laughed. "If we just keep going, eventually we will have dated every loser in the greater Portland area, and then, by process of elimination, we'll finally come across the nice guys."

"Yes, but we might be eighty years old by then, in a nursing home, eating pudding, and making Popsicle stick sculptures," Grace teased.

"Oh, can we be roomies in the nursing home?" Meg asked excitedly. "Then we can wear our Juicy sweat suits and make all the other old people jealous of our fabulous style."

"Enough about getting old and wrinkly, please. Let's focus on the here and now, where we're twenty-four and looking fit and fantastic. I'm with Grace; I'm tired of kissing frogs. I really want to make out with a handsome prince," Bianca whined. "Is that really so much to ask? One sexy, gorgeous, mentally stable, gainfully employed guy with an amazing personality, that doesn't smell like mothballs or live with his mother?" Her eyes glazed over as she began to daydream about her perfect man.

Grace glanced over at Meg and found her deep in her own fantasy as she gracefully swayed with an invisible dance partner, probably named Mr. Right. Struck with an idea, Grace went to the refrigerator, took out three beers, and opened them, placing one in front of each of the girls. "I propose we go on a boy-boycott until the new year," Grace said as she happily waved her beer in the air. "Who's with me?"

Both of her friends considered the idea for a few seconds before smiles crept onto their faces. Meg, of course, had questions. "What are the rules of a boy-boycott? No dates, I assume, but what else? Can we kiss random boys? What if they kiss us? It doesn't happen to me much, but Bianca gets that a lot, so I figured I'd ask…"

"Hold on a minute, Meg. Let's make a list!" Grace dug in the drawer for a pen.

Bianca snatched a notebook off the nearby desk as Grace tossed her the pen she found. "OK, Boy-Boycott Official Rules," she wrote across the top of the page.

Rule number one: No dates.

Rule number two: No tongue kissing with boys. Closed lip kissing is fine. If a guy crams his tongue down your throat unexpectedly, it doesn't count, unless you kiss him back. (AKA Bianca's rule)

Rule number three: No sex… of any kind. If you wouldn't want to see your parents do it, that counts as sex and it's off limits.

Rule number four: Each of us puts $200 into the pot. If you break the rules of the boycott, you lose the money. The last person(s) standing gets the money to spend on a hot new pair of shoes to be worn on her first date of the new year and gets eternal bragging rights about her superior will power.

Bianca flipped the paper around so Meg and Grace could read it and check to see if they agreed with all of the rules. They quickly scanned the list; Grace was the first to sign the paper, followed by Meg, and finally Bianca. Grace ran into her room, her wavy black hair flowing behind her as she grabbed her wad of emergency cash. She slammed $200 onto the counter. Meg and Bianca disappeared for a few minutes, and then did the same. They hid the winnings in the cookie jar and tucked it into the back corner of the counter.

"To the boycott!" Grace cheered as she raised her beer high into the air.

"To the boycott!" Bianca and Meg toasted in unison.

· ACKNOWLEDGMENTS ·

Thanks to all the amazing people at Omnific who helped make this book possible.

My editor Beverly Nickelson, who managed to keep my wordy writing in check—you were truly a Godsend and a pleasure to work with. The rest of editing and marketing team including Cindy Campbell, Micha Stone, and Kathy Teel—thank you for your expertise and all your hard work.

To Elizabeth Harper, the woman behind it all—thank you for another amazing opportunity to share my stories and for your friendship.

Emma Taylor and Barbara Hallworth—you know what you two mean to me and how much I value you. Throughout everything, you have given me guidance, support, and encouragement when I needed it most. Thank you from the bottom of my heart.

To everyone who made my Thursday nights so much fun – you ladies always make me smile. Thank you for the fun and laughs.

To my family—maybe I'll tell you about this one. *wink*

And last, but not least, thanks to the most important people in my life, my husband and kids.

I love you more than I can ever say.

· ABOUT THE AUTHOR ·

Victoria Michaels is a wife and mother of four who lives her life in what seems like a constant state of motion. Kids' sports, meetings, homework and general family fun take up twenty-seven hours of her day. In her thirty seconds of free time, Victoria likes to read, write, and travel the country with her husband.

She enjoys writing about love and laughter, two things that are central to her everyday life. If you would like to know more about what's coming next from Victoria, please check her out at

victoriamichaels.net for updates, news and sneak peeks at future releases.

CPSIA information can be obtained at www.ICGtesting.com
Printed in the USA
LVOW13s1745090214

372970LV00001B/392/P